The Stone Circle Queen
The Stone Circle Series
Book Two

Ophelia Wells Langley

The Stone Circle Queen, Book Two of The Stone Circle Series by Ophelia Wells Langley

Published by O.W.L. Publications, LLC

www.opheliawlangley.com

Copyright © 2023 Ophelia Wells Langley

All rights reserved.

No portion of this book may be reproduced in any form without permission from the publisher, except as permitted by U.S. copyright law. No part of this book may be reproduced in any form or by any electronic or mechanical means, including information storage and retrieval systems, without written permission from the author, except for the use of brief quotations in a book review.

All characters are a work of fiction, any names, places, or references therein are merely coincidental.

For licensing permissions, contact: opheliawlangley@gmail.com

Dev. Editing by Jo Thompson

Cover by Nora Adamszki & O.W.L. Publications, LLC.

Formatting by OWL Publications, LLC

This is the Author's Preferred Text, updated April 2024.

ISBN: 979-8-9862973-7-8

For my sons,
May your roots grow deep and your leaves reach toward a sky full of dreams.
I love you,
Mommy

Being deeply loved by someone gives you strength while loving someone deeply gives you courage.

— Lao Tzu

Pronunciations & Content Advisement

Pronunciations:
    Sorcha - Sor-ka
    Conall - Con-uhl
    Achill - Ak-ull
    Geannie - Jeen-ee
    Gealaich - Gee-lach
    Maolchluiche/Maol - Maul
    Cloddiwr - Clod-oo
    Feothan - Fee-o-han
    Aodhfin - Eh-fin
    Aine - On-ya

TRIGGER/CONTENT WARNINGS:
In an effort to be transparent, this is an adult fantasy romance intended for audiences eighteen years and older. Please read the trigger warnings carefully. To avoid spoilers, you can find the content warnings located here.

One
Sorcha

"*Sorcha, get up. We have to go. Now.*" Conall's voice echoes in my head. His wolf form looms above me on the stone. He nudges me with his nose again as he hovers above me. His green eyes pierce straight to my core as he watches me figure out where I am and what happened.

Rubble from the stone sarcophagus covers me, and I shake my arms out, coughing as the dust settles. Tiny rocks fall off the edge, cascading down to the floor as I stretch the stiffness from my limbs. I wipe the dust from my face and struggle for air. My lungs are tight, my throat is dry, and I cough a few times to clear the stagnant feeling in my chest.

Finally, I sit up. Conall sits back on his haunches, on top of my feet. We are still nose-to-nose when a tiny, wingless pixie pops her head over the black wolf's ears, scrambling over his face and nose. She grabs my face in her tiny hands. "Hi, Princess," Hazel squeaks out. She stares into my eyes and whispers, "The King is coming!"

Overgrown and wild, the conservatory windows are broken from the plants taking over while I slept.

"*We have to go,*" Conall snuffs. His wolf stalks around the rubble, enormous paws leaving prints as big as my hands. Uneasiness pours off of him in waves, though he is still a wolf. His tail swishes impatiently as it brushes up against my legs.

I look at Conall's wolf and then at Hazel, a thousand questions burning in my mind. Barely able to swing my legs over the side of the stone platform, I am still too weak from being asleep for so long. Chills creep along my arms when my bare feet touch the cold stone floor. "I'm not going anywhere, Conall, until you can tell me what happened."

Hazel tugs at my shirtsleeve, but her eyes are locked on the conservatory doors. "But, they're coming..."

"Not if I can help it," I say, flexing my hands.

Nothing happens. Though my fingers shimmer with green, and I envision vines crawling across the floor, no magic comes forth. I stare down at my fingers, confused.

"You haven't finished your Rites."

"But didn't I?" I shake my head.

He's right. I never reached my ancestral lands to finish my Rites in the stone circle.

"We have to go, Sorcha," Conall adds a growl to the end of his sentence. Hazel scurries behind the stone sarcophagus and under the shadowy boughs of ferns. How she blends so seamlessly into her surroundings baffles me.

"Conall, what's happened?" I ask.

"You've been asleep, Sorcha. For a year. A lot has changed since your magic woke within you."

Just a year? Spots dance in my vision, and I rub my face to clear the sensation. It seems as if only days have passed instead.

"Why are you a wolf? Where were you this past year?" I stare him down, raising an eyebrow, and though I want to go to him, I don't trust that my legs will hold my weight.

Shouts sound from outside, and Hazel runs back to me, shaking. I scoop her up into my arms. She scurries atop my shoulders and tugs on my hair urgently.

"I want to tell you more, Sorcha, I do. But not right now. We need to move." Conall glances toward the doors, his hackles rising. A low growl rumbles in his throat at the sounds of the guards in their armor clanking down the steps outside. He positions himself between me and the door.

2

"Why didn't you come sooner?" I ask, holding back tears of anger at being left in the hands of such an evil fae.

Conall stretches, and he shakes his head. *"I wanted to, Sorcha. I tried."*

"He wasn't able to," Hazel whispers, her eyes filling with tears. Her tiny hands touch my cheek. "He was kept from you."

"You were... kept from me?" Memories flood back, hazy at first, and then all at once, my dreams come to life—the screaming from that mysterious hallway and the king's disappearance each night. Horrified, my eyes lock with Conall's, and my stomach swirls.

"The phantom pains. The screams in the hallway. It wasn't all just a dream. Everything happened?"

Hazel is quiet. Conall's ears twitch, but he refuses to look at me.

"He tortured you, didn't he? That's why you couldn't come..."

Conall dips his head and nudges me with his nose, and I thread my fingers in his fur. He closes his eyes as I grip his scruff. He doesn't have to tell me. I can feel his answer in my bones.

"I'll kill him." I pull him closer to me. "Why aren't you shifting back?"

"I—"

The doors to the conservatory rattle loudly as more guards push against them. Conall bares his teeth and growls at the door. His paws shimmer with green, and vines twirl around the handles, wrapping the entire building in a network of roots. He pants with effort as if even that bit of magic was too much for him.

Hazel clings to my neck, and my fingers tingle with green light, but no magic vines sprout from the earth. The trees don't bend and shake. Again, nothing happens.

Conall leaves my side and paces impatiently at the back of the conservatory structure. He lopes behind several dry fountains, their cement bases cracked and covered in moss. My eyes snap to Conall's as the doors shake again. Glass shatters as they shove their swords through the windows to hack the overgrown foliage.

"This is where you get down and you leave. Now," Conall growls, flashing his teeth. Hazel tugs me toward the fountains, and she jumps down as I squeeze into a small tunnel at the back of the

conservatory. Ferns grow from the bases of two cracked fountains, obfuscating the entrance to the small underground passage.

"Conall?" I ask, looking over my shoulder when he doesn't follow.

More glass shatters in the doors, and the fae guards shove their swords through to clear the shards—a hand snakes through the opening, searching for the handle.

Someone shouts, "Keep her alive!"

The guards shout, "Aye!"

Vetiver, lemon, and the acrid smell of smoke fill the air. My stomach drops, and the world tilts. Panic claws at my throat.

"Conall!" I scream, turning to reach for him. "I can't leave you with him again!"

"*Yes, you can. Go, Sorcha.*" He jumps on the stone sarcophagus, planting his paws, and lets out a long, low howl. Several more howls resound from outside the conservatory. Faint green shimmers around his paws as he shifts his stance into a lunge. He paws at the ground a few times, his claws scraping against the stone. The ground shakes beneath my hands, and dirt crumbles on top of my head as the edges of the tunnel fall in.

The last moments I see are of flames leaping into the conservatory. Conall's hackles raise as he braces for impact.

The tunnel falls around me, and I can barely make out Conall's desperate command in my head over the din, "*Please. Go.*"

Two
Sorcha

I scramble backward out of rocks and dirt that tumble down before me. Conall disappears behind the cascading earth, shutting Hazel and me in complete darkness. The rumbling in my ears subsides as the ground stills. Dust swarms my lungs, and I cough a few times. Pushing off my elbows, I shuffle my hands around, grappling my way back to the entrance.

"Conall!" The earth swallows my words as the pull of the heart-call grows faint. I lean against the wall of earth, trying desperately to hear any sounds on the other side. My fingernails scrape at the rock, digging and digging as tears stream down my face.

"You can't!" I choke out, clawing at the wall of stone and dirt. "You can't do this! I won't let you!"

"*You have to,*" Conall says, his voice punctuated by growls and snarls. Is he fighting off the guards?

I dig, ignoring my fingernails that break into the earth and bleed. But I keep digging, trying to carve my way around the large boulders.

That bastard!

He doesn't get to sacrifice himself just like that, not when we were finally together. Pebble by pebble, I *will* claw my way through this wall.

"Your Highness?" Hazel's tiny voice calls from behind me.

"Not now, Hazel," I snap, picking away at the rocks. Several large boulders block my way through, and I lean my shoulder against them, trying to push back into the conservatory.

"Sorcha," Hazel says again, louder.

"I can't leave him, Hazel. Achill will kill him; I know he will." I dig harder, push harder, and scream harder at the wall of rock, beating my fists against the barrier that keeps me from my mate.

My mate. I scream again, furious that my earth magic won't work.

My mate in the hands of that evil bastard? Again? No. Not if I can help it. I bang my fists against the stone. "Conall!"

Images of him fighting off the soldiers in his wolf form flood my vision, howls echoing and screams of the guards as his jaw clamps down on their throats. The conservatory fills with smoke, and Conall's fear is palpable as it washes over me.

"Please, Sorcha, go..." I can hear the exhaustion filling his bones, and it weighs me down through the heart-call. He isn't fighting anymore, which can only mean one thing.

"I didn't save you when I should have. Now, I will. Find Murdock. Finish your Rites. I'll see you soon."

"No." I collapse into despair, sliding down onto the tunnel floor. My fingers are raw, and my face turns into a muddy river of tears as I heave with sobs.

"Oh, Sorcha." Hazel stands next to my shoulder and brushes away some of my hair, patting my head as I cry.

"I just don't know why he thought this was the answer." My voice hitches, and my throat is tight and raw like someone has a vice grip on my neck.

"He didn't leave you."

"Then why am I here and he's there, Hazel? You know Achill and what he's capable of. He was supposed to come with me."

"I don't think that was ever the plan." Hazel continues to pat my head.

Her words hit their mark, stinging my ears. Heartache washes over me, but Hazel's gentle hands find some of my hair, and she twists it back into a braid. I brush her off, shrugging my shoulder, ashamed of my stubbornness earlier. Stubbornness that got him back into the hands of an evil creature. I wipe my eyes on my shirt, quiet resolve surrounding me like a blanket.

"Fine. What am I supposed to do, then?"

She hems briefly and then says quietly, "I don't really know."

"Great—" And then I double over as a phantom pain crawls up from the center of my stomach to my throat.

"Your Highness?"

Another pain lands in my ribs, and the air leaves my lungs. I groan as if someone has rammed me through with an iron fist.

"We should leave." Hazel's hands pull me to sit up.

The pain subsides to a light throbbing, and I sit back on my heels. I send a silent plea down the heart-call, trying to soothe his pain and my anger by tugging on the only connection we have.

"Okay," I say, defeated. I scoop her up and place her on my shoulder, crawling down the tunnel and away from Conall. The further I go, the more it feels like I'm leaving a limb behind.

WE DIP down and up and crawl for what seems like hours. The darkness is so thick, and the sounds so muffled that it feels like down is up, and we are circling back to the castle instead of moving forward. It feels as if the walls are caving in, pressing into me, and I try to calm myself down, but I choke on the musty scent that smells so similar to the dust and rocks from the stone I just emerged from. What if this is all a dream? A twisted delusion the king set up for me.

A warm sensation fills my body as the heart-call pulses in my chest, slowing my heart rate down. Hazel's tiny hands stroke my hair, and she hums a little lullaby as I squeeze my eyes shut a few times. Eventually, the dizziness stops, my breathing returns to normal, and I can keep crawling.

"Hazel?" I ask to the tiny form lying between my shoulder blades.

"Yes, princess?" She doesn't stop petting my hair, and I almost nuzzle into her comforting touch.

"Why did you come?" My mind swirls, trying to piece together the last year I was asleep. What happened in the days of freedom I had before whatever spell Achill put me under?

"What's left for me at the castle?" Her tiny voice sounds even quieter than I would have thought possible.

"The other pixies...?"

"No, I can't fly with them. I can't run as fast as the brownies, either. I'm in the in-between." Her voice is withdrawn, and she adds, "Like you."

How right she is. I am neither human nor full-fae blood but a mix of something in between since my father was half-fae and my mother was human. So, a half-halfling.

"Like me," I whisper. "Well, I'm glad I have you with me, Hazel."

"Me, too." Hazel turns over, lying down on my back. "It was an awful year, you know. Watching over your stone bed."

"You watched over me?"

"Of course," she says, matter-of-factly, "How else was I supposed to tell Murry know you were ok? The plants wouldn't let anyone inside. They have a mind of their own, you know, when you're near."

"When I'm near?"

"Yes, it's your earth magic. They hear it and wake up, almost like the old days. Before the plants went to sleep," Hazel says, a wistfulness to her tone that could easily be mistaken for sadness.

I smile into the darkness, fingers curling into the earth, and silently thank the Goddess. The blood magic may have worked, after all. I have to figure out why whatever magic I still have doesn't seem to work anymore. My knees and hands are sore from constant contact with the packed earth, so I lie down on my forearms to give them a break. The smell of musty dirt, salty sea air, and fresh greenery fills my nose.

"I smell a change in the air. Unless being underground for so long is meddling with my logic."

"No." Hazel sniffs at the air. "I smell it, too. Your fae side is getting stronger."

With a renewed sense of purpose, I push back onto my hands, groaning at the pain in my wrists, and keep crawling until we reach a fork in the path. Faint light shines from the tunnel on the left, and the tunnel to the right dips down, swallowed in pitch-black darkness.

"Do you have any idea where we're supposed to go?"

She leans over my shoulder and whispers, "I've never seen the sea..."

"Left it is," I say, eager to be out of the tunnel and into the light.

The tunnel inclines slightly the lighter it gets. Roots poke through the ceiling, and sunlight dapples the ground. Sea air and pine compete with the scent of damp earth, but I slow, none too eager to emerge into a potential trap.

"Conall? That you, chum?" A familiar voice sounds from the end of the tunnel.

Murdock.

I practically fly through the rest of the tunnel as I shout, "Not Conall! Sorcha!"

Scrambling over the rocks and loose dirt, I clamber into the sunlight. I blink my eyes against the brightness, emerging into a small glade of yew and alder trees. They form a tight circle, encasing us in a dappling of shadows near the sea. Salty, humid sea air coats my skin, and I welcome the freshness into my lungs.

"Conall isn't with you?" Murdock looks over my shoulder, peering into the tunnel behind me. Worry flashes across his face, and then he frowns, "That stupid son of a—"

"I... He..." I choke out, at a loss for words. Shame washes over me when I realize I may have condemned Conall to death. I stifle tears.

He steps forward, and his eyes rake over me, taking in the dirt that's caked to my skin and my bloodied fingernails. His mouth forms a tight line, and he bites out, "He left you?"

Hazel speaks up, "He stayed behind."

"That wasn't part of the plan," Murdock says, frowning. He steps closer and grabs my forearms.

I look away from the pity in his eyes. I swallow thickly, but my voice still cracks. "It was my fault."

"No," Hazel shakes her head. "He had plenty of time."

"What happened, Princess?" Murdock gives my forearms a reassuring squeeze.

My throat tightens as I struggle to tell him about my last few moments with Conall. Murdock stands there, watching me closely and listening.

He nods a few times as I finish and then asks, "When did he shift? Was he a wolf when you woke?"

"Yes," I say, recalling that cold nose touching mine. "But he could talk to me in my head."

"Ah, yes, so still there, then." He hems and haws a few more times, blue eyes glazing with thought.

Hazel climbs to my other shoulder and says, "We heard other wolves, too."

Murdock kicks a rock. "That'll explain the cave-in, then. He was too weak to have shifted on his own, let alone cause the tunnel to cave in. His damn brothers, always sneaking about." His lips quirk into a smile at my confusion, and he turns to the sea air. "Come, I'll fill you in."

My shoulders sag at the thought of more walking when Murdock waves his hand before him, and water swirls from his fingertips. Murdock holds his hand out to me, waiting, one foot stepping into a portal where, on the other side, an ancient forest looms in front of us. The trees are so tall that the entire belly of the woods looks black. Tentatively, I take his hand, gripping it tight to keep the shaking at bay and step through the portal into the wild forest beyond.

Three
Achill

The king stares out the window, watching the conservatory plants take over the building as his guards fight to rush in. They keep hacking away at the branches and roots that swallow the building. He exhales in frustration and storms down the balcony stairs into the garden below. These incompetent guards are nothing like his soldiers used to be—hardened fae warriors, bloodthirsty and cunning.

With a wave of his hand, the shrubs of the labyrinth alight with flame. A multitude of tiny screams erupt from the will-o'-the-wisps as the fire traps them in their homes. They sound the warning for the other creatures who have called this royal garden their home for centuries.

Achill stalks through the burning fauna, hands held at his sides, flames and smoke pouring from his fingertips—wildling fae scurry ahead of him, running to safer ground.

"Move!" he shouts to the guards, who are still struggling to hack at the overgrown fauna. The conservatory windows shatter as trees burst through the top of the structure. Vines wrap around the glinting metal, climbing into the air beyond, swallowing the silver structure under their leaves.

The guards slash at the conservatory doors when flames and smoke swirl at their feet. They clamber to get out of the way, toppling over each other, clumsy in their haste. One guard goes down, trampled on by his compatriots, and the king's flames consume him, swallowing him whole as he screams. Neither of the guards reaches down to help him nor tries to combat the king's flames as their friend writhes.

Figures. Weaklings will always sacrifice one of their own to save their hides. A breath of hesitation from Achill before his flames reach the conservatory doors, and then his magic swallows the trees. He needs to get inside and see if Sorcha is still lying there. Did she wake? Or has someone gotten through his wards to her?

All of his careful planning will be for naught. He furrows his brow, focusing on the weakest part of the door, and watches as the metal melts under his flame.

The leaves flare orange as the fire swallows the building.

"Your Highness!" a guard named Rhys shouts, running from the far side of the garden. He calls out again, trying vainly to get his king's attention.

"Move," Achill says, his voice dangerously low.

Flames race higher, swallowing up the canopy of trees. The ornate silver metal liquifies, dripping into shining pools on the stone below. A brief pang of regret snags on Achill's memories and how he used to catch Aerona in here, tending to the garden like his mother used to. Her laughter as she sprayed him with water and her screams of pleasure as he knelt before her, her sweet essence coating his tongue.

And then it's gone.

He clears his throat, shifting focus to the human princess inside.

That persistent guard is calling his name again. He exhales and lowers his hands, just a hair.

"Sir, the treaty," Rhys tries again. "You kill the princess and..."

The fire dies as the king's hands fall limp at his sides. He turns to Rhys and waves dismissively, "Fine, do what you must. Try to keep her *alive* if you can."

Achill stalks away from the conservatory, smoke billowing about in the wind. He can almost faintly hear Aerona's belly-deep laughter echoing behind him.

Something has changed with the princess. The trees shouldn't have taken over unless someone with Earth magic was near. Howls echo in the forest, and the ground rumbles. Recognition flashes across his face, and he spins on his heel.

That pesky wolf shifter.

The wolves howl again; this time, their chorus sounds further away. Achill runs back. He knew Conall would come back for her. Fated mates are so predictable. Achill twists the ring on his finger, shaking his head at how pathetic that bond makes people.

Achill should know.

The guards toss aside the doors to the conservatory; the hinges long since melted beyond repair. Inside, the wolf snarls, and a guard screams as an arm flies through a window. The glass shatters in the sun, spraying glittering shards everywhere—blood pools under the dismembered limb, rivulets flowing in between the stones.

The wolf growls, rumbling the earth beneath Achill's feet. His eyes snap up to see the giant black wolf standing atop the rubble. It tears into another guard, ripping him in half quickly. The others circle him with their swords drawn, hesitating to attack. Easily the size of three large fae, the wolf circles the stone sarcophagus that lies shattered on the floor.

Achill's smoke dances along the floor. Conall's green eyes glint with anger as the king walks through the trees. The wolf snaps the guard's neck in his maw, and a low snarl builds in the wolf's chest. The guards stand down, speechless, as they watch the smoke crawl up their legs.

The smoke curls toward Conall's paws, and the wolf fights against it. He leaps onto the top of the cracked stone, but Achill's smoke is faster. It pulls the shifter down, wrapping him in a heavy cloak, and crawls down his throat. The wolf shudders and yawns, lying down among the rubble. Achill pushes the magic further, filling the smoke with his intent, and soon, the wolf's fur ripples, revealing a naked, sleeping Conall.

Achill stares at the guards. The guards stare at him.

He waves his hand dismissively and says, "Take him below."

They file out, carrying Conall between them, and leave Achill alone.

He walks around the stone coffin, fragments of rock littering the floor.

A year ago, Achill carried her through the portal, which was strenuous for his aging body, so he left her on the table. Her pulse was so faint and so weak. He knew beyond any doubt that his smoke magic had gone too far.

He had planned to keep her there until she woke, but the conservatory was quiet when he returned the next day. The wards pulled at his body, relaxing as soon as his magic was recognized. But the conservatory was unrecognizable; the plants had grown overnight. Ferns that had once been brown turned a vibrant, lush green. Exotic trees that hadn't flowered since Aerona was alive had fruit hanging from their branches.

Then he saw the stone coffin.

An effigy of her likeness was carved into the top, and it looked so familiar that Achill thought someone had moved Aerona's tomb into the conservatory. He was furious. But as he drew closer, he realized it was Sorcha. He figured some fae had come in overnight and encased her in magic, so he tightened the wards.

But now he wasn't so sure.

The lush interior sends his memory whirling, and he wonders if perhaps it could have been something with his waning magic that caused this change because something about the human princess changed.

And he will be damned if he can't find out what it is.

Four
Sorcha

"Are we in the right place?" I ask, staring into the depths of darkness—the trees now tower over us, giants against the sky that swallow the sun.

"A lot has changed while you were under the sleeping spell," Murdock says. His mouth quirks into a half-smile as he shrugs. He pushes his way through the undergrowth, and the ferns are taller than his head. I follow, staring up at the mammoth evergreens that guard this place.

"These are..." I cannot describe what I see without sounding like I am losing my mind.

There is no way that they grew this large in such a short time. Giant redwoods loom over us; their trunks are at least three people wide. Only a few trees remain the same size, and I immediately pick out the one that spoke to me when I first entered these woods.

"They've awoken." Murdock turns around and touches the bark of the nearest tree. "Your blood vow, your return to this place, has greatly changed your homelands."

My hands shake, and I lean against a tree for support before I head back into the forest where Achill took me. The last time I was here, an entire entourage of King Achill's guards chased me. They pressed me further into the forest as my blistered feet bled into the floor of the ancient woods.

Beneath my hand, the bark glows a bright green, shimmering with power, and its leaves rustle above my head.

A face forms in the wood above me.

"Welcome home, Deoir-born," its scratchy voice whispers.

I dip my head in reverence, my ears trilling with my grandmother's name. I feel pulled toward this place and yearn to see the stone circle. But the woods feel tainted with memories of the past. I have missed so much in the past year. Anger and shame fight inside my chest like hungry wolves feeding off my worries. I curse as I misstep, my foot rolling on a loose rock.

Murdock turns, concern etched on his face, but I shake it off and smile. I don't want him to know I am filled with countless worries. After all, who would want a Queen who isn't at least a little self-assured? If I can finish my Rites and become the rightful heir, then perhaps I can fix everything I fucked up last year and get Conall back for good.

***

THE WOODS ARE full of birds singing, and the wind slips through the uppermost canopy, rustling in the canopy above. I am quiet, awash with so many conflicting feelings, as I follow our path toward the river that travels to my ancestral home. The roaring water in the chasm below beckons me to see if Opal is there.

After she helped me run from Achill, I never got to thank her for using her magic to help me get away.

I never got to say goodbye.

The river churns below at the bottom of several hundred feet of sheer cliffs. I pause, unable to wrap my head around how fast the water has carved a path into the rock.

"Many things have changed," Murdock reminds me again, his voice low in my ear.

He stands at my elbow, and his fingers graze my shirt as if he fears me tumbling over the edge. Hazel perches attentively on his shoulder, looking from me to the water and back again. She flashes me a smile, but her eyes are full of pity. When we reach the Deoir lands and settle, I know this river will be the first place I will return to.

"Yes, I see that now," I say, shaking my head at all that happened in a year. "When I woke, it felt like only days had passed. But here? It feels as if it has been centuries."

"Come," Murdock says and tugs on my sleeve.

"What else do I need to know?" I ask, carefully dodging fallen logs.

Murdock mumbles and finally speaks up, "Achill has... he's started the war again. Err, he's tried to."

"What do you mean, he's tried to?" I hurry to catch up, the sounds of the rushing water fading behind us.

Hazel's tiny voice pipes up on Murdock's shoulder, "He's tried, but we have met him with more resistance than before."

"Is my father ok? Does he know what happened to me?"

"We couldn't tell him anything," Murdock says.

"You couldn't?" My head swims, and my chest tightens with anger. "Wait...What does my father think happened to me? What do my people think happened to me?"

"The resistance wouldn't tell me. But I can tell you that your father grew restless waiting for news that never came, and after a while, with no word from you, things took a turn." Murdock walks toward the standing stones.

"Took a turn. Did my kingdom pick up arms? Start fighting?" I ask, puzzling things together. If I have to assemble an army of Earth Fae, so be it. I reach out to Conall through the heart-call again, wishing he was here to tell me precisely what we need for war.

"When the king took you back to the castle and placed you in the conservatory, no one could get in or out of that building without him knowing. Except one." Murdock jerks his chin to the side.

"Hazel," I exhale.

"She was the only one who could loosen the wards undetected and slip out to give us any information. But even then, his smoke magic rendered her weak and her memory fuzzy, so what she could tell us was met with much skepticism. No one believed you were encased in a stone sarcophagus... of magic. Magic that wasn't even supposed to be yours because you're human." Murdock's voice is calm and almost reverent.

His fingers reach up and pat Hazel on the head. She grunts and continues to unravel her trademark braids. Her hair floats around her shoulders, and the pink marks of her scars peek out of her mismatched clothing. Wingless, nearly magic-less after Achill tore the wings from her, she was the only source of hope hundreds of people and fae had.

Does she know how brave she was?

Murdock continues, forging the path ahead. "Conall's brothers and I had to get together and scheme. With Conall captive—"

"And now back in the King's hands." Impatience builds in my chest, and my skin prickles with anger. "How much longer until we're at the stones, Murdock?"

Thoughts of what the king is doing to my mate make me turn around.

Murdock looks back at me, frowning at my sudden change in demeanor. He stumbles over a fallen log and curses. "Are you well, Your Highness?"

"Fine," I snap back.

Murdock frowns. "We'll be there soon, but you must go first."

Before I can ask why, the trees in the distance groan; their roots pick themselves out of the ground and slide out of the way. An unobstructed view of the stones looms before us. They rest atop a mound of lush green grass, clear blue skies beyond, and their stones glisten in the sun. One tree dips down, a branch brushing the path clear to the stones as if gesturing *welcome home.*

THE DEOIR BORDER LOOMS. With each step I take towards the stones, I feel lighter than I have since I woke up. This is farther than I got before Achill took me, and the tension in my shoulders instantly releases. Murdock hangs back with Hazel clinging to his shoulder as I near the border to my fae homelands.

The stones hum and shimmer with green. The trees bend out of the way. I glance down at my hands, which shimmer with the same green and pulse in time with the light emanating from the stones. Swirls shift and move on the face of the monolith, sliding on the stones like snakes.

Wards.

"We cannot enter unless we're with Deoir blood," Murdock says, noting my hesitation.

The rising moon and the setting sun fight to highlight the shapes of the stones from underneath their mossy coverings. Though my fingers shimmer, no magic comes forth, and I look to Murdock, deflated. He gestures toward the stones again. I step tentatively through the outer edges, and the air bends and shifts as it pulls the breath from my lungs.

Murdock and Hazel step from behind me as we leave the cover of the ancient forest. Through the warded stones, a vast landscape opens up before us. Grassy knolls gracefully roll into the foothills of the mountains; a lush forest covers the land like a downy blanket and cascades into valleys. The river rushes under an ancient stone bridge covered in cobwebs, moss, bracken, and mud until it heads to the sea.

"The sea?" I ask, turning to Murdock. "I didn't realize that we were this close..." Salty air wraps itself around my skin.

"Aye, the sea," he sighs, peace in his words. Murdock inhales a few more times, and the worry lines disappear from his face.

We cross the stone bridge and hold our breath, carefully testing whether it will withstand our weight despite decades—or perhaps centuries—of neglect.

The forest is eerily quiet on the other side of the river, and each step we take in the undergrowth echoes throughout the woods. Our footfalls echo despite the lushness around us, making me cringe, worried about waking the wrong creatures.

"I have never seen this forest so quiet before," Murdock whispers, as if he is worried we'll wake something.

"What happened here?" I place my bare feet on the water-sodden moss and sweep away over-hanging branches as we enter the darkened depths.

"I haven't been here since the High King's coronation, but it looks like all the rumors were true," Murdock says, picking his way carefully through the understory, twigs snapping underneath his boots.

Two large conifers overlook an expansive pastoral estate with a crumbling castle and overgrown gardens.

"Och, it would almost look foreboding if it didn't look so damn magical," Murdock says, the corner of his mouth lifting into a smile.

He looks down at me, but all I can see is a ruin, the earth reclaiming the stone buildings before us. Rose bushes tangle and weave around the outer rock wall covered in moss and lichen. A metal gate hangs off rusty hinges, its ornate details almost entirely hidden by vines. Towers that once reached the sky lean haphazardly against each other, leaving gaping holes where roofs collided. Birds fly in and out of the eaves, and a solitary fox with a mouse in its jaw darts from underneath a collapsed piece of the wall and into the woods to the east. Besides the chirping of the birds, no sounds come from the castle ruins, almost as if the castle itself has been put to sleep for centuries.

An old oak tree grows near the forest's edge to my right. As I pass, a face shimmers in my peripheral, and the weathered bark forms a sleeping silhouette. Its branches shiver as if breathing deep in slumber. I rest my hand on the bark, and a familiar feeling pulls me forward as if the entire place was waiting to be woken up again.

Five
Achill

King Achill paces in the study, flames flickering on one hand, smoke swirling around his figure. But his other hand holds a delicate necklace with an opalescent pendant, his thumb and forefinger twisting the gem between them. He had it cleaned since that human wore it last. Her neck didn't deserve to wear such a fine piece of dwarven jewelry. However, when the princess wore it, it made him feel closer to Aerona, and he considered bedding Sorcha to win her over.

A shudder passes through his body at the thought.

No, he would never sully Aerona's memory in such a way. His hand squeezes the necklace, the metal digging into his palm, and he sighs.

Aerona last wore this jewelry on their wedding night. She looked radiant in a blue and green silk dress, the silver glinting on her skin. The necklace didn't have the Aphroselene pendant.

Instead, it was a simple freshwater pearl. One of the largest in the Deoir collection. She beamed when he complimented it.

Goddess, it was perfect. The night was perfect. *Aerona* was perfect.

How sweeter would it be if he remembered the perfume she wore that night?

"Milord?" Rhys asks, his voice coming from a crack in the door.

"Hmm," Achill murmurs, lost in the memories of the last time he was intimate with Aerona. The ice cuffed his hands, and her magic flowed around them as she rocked her hips on top of him and refused to relinquish control.

Now, all he has left is just empty moments, flashes of what used to be.

"Sir?" Rhys asks again.

The door creaks open further, forcing the recollections deep into Achill's mind. He swallows back tears - a king cannot be seen as weak. With a wave of his hand, his smoke creates a screen between the door and the king's unglamoured form.

"Yes?" He sighs, sounding tired even to himself.

"We think we know where they are headed," Rhys starts. His sword clangs against the doorjamb as he tries to slide his body through the door crack.

Achill snaps, "Then why are you not following them?"

"The entire forest is magicked against us." Rhys shuffles his feet and clears his throat.

"A likely excuse," Achill grunts. "Leave. If you are incapable, I suppose I shall do it myself."

The door clicks behind Rhys, and Achill drops the smoke magic. He returns to pacing until he ends up in front of the map above the fireplace.

It stares back at him, the border to Aerona's homelands making a mockery of his title as High King. There, north and west of his castle, are the smudged markings to the Deoir lands: a vast forest and the entrance to the land beyond the northern mountains. The Deoirs had promised the lands would be Achill's once he had mated with Aerona and produced a legitimate heir. That day never came to pass, and now he knows it's because Aerona never intended for him to have her inheritance. She never intended to mate with him, and she never intended him to become the true High King of the Fae. He clenches his fist around the necklace and throws it into the flames of his magicked fireplace.

The pendant shatters and melts in the fire.

"You stupid fool," he hisses and dives toward the fire, scrambling to gather up whatever is left of the gemstone as it liquefies. A solitary piece remains on the edges of the fire, and he picks it up. There is a brief flicker of vitality, a shock of power, as his skin touches it. But then it hisses and vaporizes between his fingertips. Achill swears he can feel her pulse, and he is so hungry to feel any part of her again like he used to when she was alive.

What wickedness is this that makes him crave her so much, even a century after her death?

He shakes his head against the intrusive thoughts, trying to keep his other side at bay. How he'd love to forget the pains he went through to keep her soul frozen eternally—the things he did to keep her with him forever. Every day, he regrets releasing her soul with fire. He should have found someone to encase Aerona's lifeless body in glass so he could look upon her flawless form forever. Instead, he was overcome with shame and built an effigy of her likeness out of stone and burned the remains of her body.

A flicker in the corner of the room catches his eye, and he watches as a brownie scurries underneath the bookshelves. It rushes to clean up the fragments of the necklace. He leans down, pointing to a piece of jewelry the brownie missed. The creature cowers in the shadows, and Achill scoffs, trying to stand upright again. His ancient bones creak, and his curved spine forces his shoulders forward as he licks the metallic sheen from his fingertips.

"My love," he breathes, a solitary tear running down his weathered cheek. Smoke unfurls from his fingers, and he covers himself in the usual glamour again. Thick white hair cascades down his back; his spine straightens, and his fingers become less claw-like.

"Rhys!" he shouts, flinging open the door. His voice echoes into the hallway, but the soldier at the end turns around. "Get my horse ready. I will go after her myself."

Six
Sorcha

"Your ancestral home, Princess," Murdock says, gesturing to the gardens beyond the rubble.

"Everything feels so familiar," I sigh. An invisible reverberation through the ground settles into my psyche. It is the calmest I have felt since leaving Conall. Though the ruins are extensive and the amount of work it will take to restore them overwhelms me, the castle has a comforting atmosphere. I know I could easily make this place a home.

My *home*. Tears well in my eyes at finally being able to call someplace home. For the first time, it feels right. I am *meant* to be here.

"Och, that would be your Deoir blood," Murdock says offhandedly.

A breeze pushes through the woods to our right, carrying the scent of pine and cedar. My heart yearns for my fae shifter to be here with me, too, witnessing my return to my ancestral home. I feel a shimmer of comfort through the heart-call and press my hand to my chest, fighting against the desire to turn back and free Conall right now.

And when I do see him again, he will get an earful from me.

Rose bushes, full of late-blooming flowers, are thinner by the fallen wall, unable to fully grow amongst the rubble. I reach out to move some brambles out of the way and prick my finger on a thorn. A tiny drop of blood forms, and I put my finger into my mouth.

Murdock clambers over the lower part of the wall and reaches his hand out to help me through. He hauls me up, balancing precipitously on loose rock. Still gripping my hand, he helps me balance over the unstable rocks down the other side. Like Conall, his hands are strong and callused, but I feel strange accepting his help.

"When you were there that night," I ask, hesitant to even bring up the night the king attacked me. I run my tongue along my teeth, the metallic taste of blood still so fresh in my mind.

Murdock releases my hand, balancing on the rubble. "Aye?"

"How did you plan to get me out?"

He straightens and places his hand on the sword's hilt at his hip. "I was working with Thorne. They were supposed to wait in the forest by the old entrance that had been blocked off centuries ago. When I saw their bird land on your balcony, I knew trouble was brewing."

Realization dawns. "So you were a part of the king's guard this entire time?"

"Aye," he says, still refusing to look in my eyes.

"And you were watching me the entire time?"

"Aye," he nods. He swallows slowly, and the muscles in his neck strain.

Confusion swarms my memories, and the bitter taste of betrayal coats my tongue. If Murdock was watching out for me, why didn't he stop the king from attacking me? How did I not notice him before?

I nod back and give him a pacifying smile despite the questions that form.

Murdock guides us through an overgrown courtyard, brushing away the vines with his hands as he stoops beneath a broken archway and more rose vines. Thorns snag at my hair, taking strands with them as we pass underneath.

Through the arch, an overgrown garden is full of broken benches and dried-up fountains. Greenery grows in the bases and around the statues of fauns that spout air. Shrubs that once lined the pathways crawl and clamber over the stone, obstructing any clear movement forward.

Murdock hacks away at the shrubs with his sword, clearing a small path forward. "This castle was once bustling with life, full of Earth Fae, Water Fae, Air Fae, and, sometimes, even Fire Fae."

He stops and leans on the tip of his sword. His eyes are unfocused as if he is watching memories of the past unfold before his very eyes.

"What happened?" My hand grazes the soft rose petals to my right. I keep waiting for my magic to come out to play, but there aren't any green shimmers on my fingertips. Murdock watches my hand, so I tuck it behind my back.

"Something that happens so often when places get forgotten..." He moves forward, seamlessly stepping over a broken bench.

"Forgotten?" I ask. Underneath all the shrubs and overgrown greenery, there are stone figures. I reach out slowly to touch one, a faun whose stone face is relaxed in eternal slumber.

Murdock turns to me, glancing over his shoulder, and says, "Yes, Princess. These were all once creatures of this court. But now..."

Some of the stone figures lay as if in sleep, others as if they're in the middle of taking a step. But they are all covered in dirt and plants from centuries of unkemptness.

Shouldn't they have woken up since I have returned home as the heir?

Murdock stops at the base of crumbled stone steps leading up to the castle's front door. I stand beside him, our shoulders almost touching, and take in the ancient oak doors. Carved with beautiful scenes of flowering plants and dryads dancing in the middle of the woods, they stand off-kilter from their joints. Vines crawl around the doors, obfuscating entry, but I step forward, my hands tingling with energy.

"I wonder..." Curious to see if my magic calls to the Deoir castle, I hold my hand up to the door and hover my fingers over some plants. The curtain of greenery parts and a gorgeous front entry with a grand hallway and wooden columns stretching three stories high lie beyond. I mutter, "Looks like some of my magic still works."

Stepping into the room beyond, a large yew tree grows several stories high at the far end. Its branches weave around the columns supporting the castle's upper-level balconies. The tree roots weave into the worn wooden floorboards and surround a stone throne at its base. Was it placed here on purpose, or did they build the room to fit around it?

"This is the throne room, Princess," Murdock sighs. He grazes my shoulder as he squeezes past me and enters the large hallway.

Overgrown with vines that climb around the columns, smaller trees have tried to find their home between the floorboards in the center of the room. Fresh mint and mossy, damp earth emanates from the room. Part of the roof is missing, but the branches of the yew tree cover the missing pieces of the ceiling, providing a decent amount of shade and cover from the elements outside.

"Is that the scene of The Hunt?" I point down at the inlaid floor and the carvings depicted at my feet.

Four High Fae ride four-legged animals - the Water Fae on a kelpie, the Air Fae on a Pegasus, the Earth Fae on a unicorn, and the Fire Fae on a multicolored dragon. In the distance, a stone circle sits atop a hill they have just left.

"Yes," Murdock says, pointing to the border made of interconnected lines knotted together that surround the picture of the fae. "All High Fae seats have a depiction of The Hunt to remind us we're all a part of a larger, interconnected system."

"But, isn't The Hunt..." I falter, hesitant to show him how naïve my upbringing was. Though I was raised knowing I would marry the High King of the Fae, my education was severely rife with prejudice from old tales to scare children at night. "Isn't that the night when the fae roam the human lands to steal children away?"

Murdock barks out a laugh that echoes around the hallway. Through his laughter, he says, "Nay, Princess. That is not what The Hunt means."

My cheeks flush a bright red, and he stops laughing.

"Our Hunt is about the changing of the seasons. The Winter

Solstice and the shift of light coming back. We used to ride at sunrise, starting in the East as if we were pulling the sun from its great sleep, and it was upon us to bring light back into our lives once more."

"Oh, that's beautiful," I muse, walking along the gorgeous inlay, noting the difference in expressions between the fae depicted here and the Fire Fae castle tapestry.

"Aye, it really is." Murdock follows me. He points to the picture of the Air Fae ruler on a pegasus. "In our lore, the Air Fae King blows away the wintery snowy days, making way for the warmth of spring thaw."

Murdock then points to the Fire Fae on a dragon. "The pegasus takes the Air Fae toward the Fire Fae kingdom, whose dragon helps bring the early morning sun to thaw the rest of the land. The Earth Fae Kingdom carries the sun toward the west on their unicorn; tiny snowdrop plants grow in their wake to signal the spring. Finally, the Water Fae Queen carries the sun in her arms as the kelpie dips below the horizon, tucking the sun to sleep."

Each High Fae ruler, made of different variations of wood, wears a jubilant look on their face. They rejoice in their hunt for more daylight and longer days. Atop each High Fae rests a crown, and distinctly colored jewels rest in the center.

I look up to find him staring at me. "Why did the fae stop celebrating The Hunt?"

Murdock crosses his arms and rocks back on his heels. "I'd say for the same reason we stopped celebrating the seasons. After you've lived long enough, keeping track of time becomes tedious and reminds you of your immortality."

I walk toward the throne, reminiscing on the seasonal celebrations back home. The dances, the bonfires, and the music filtered through the royal gardens while I sat there with Geannie, wishing to be a part of the revelry. One year, I ran into my father on the night of the autumn bonfires, and I asked him if the fae celebrated the shift in the seasons like us. He looked at me with a sadness I had never seen before. Perhaps his sadness was a longing for something he had always missed but had never known.

"Immortality means a great deal to those who can mate," he continues, walking toward the throne with me. "For those who haven't found their mate, immortality is drudgery. Who can we share our time with? Every morning becomes dull, and you forget that the changing seasons mean anything more than just another passing in your life of everlasting eternity."

I want to ask him how old he is and who he wants to share his time with. But I don't. A faraway look on his face holds me back, and his mood has turned sour. How long has he been waiting for his fated mate?

The castle is eerily quiet, and our soft steps are the only sounds that echo in this room. Leaving Murdock by the steps, I walk around the base of the yew tree. The hagstone warms against my skin, but I do not bring it to my eye. I want to see if the fae in me can spot any of the glamour on my own.

The tree is ancient, and it pulses with magic. My hand weaves around the tree trunk, dragging behind me. My fingertips shimmer, but the green light fades quickly when I knick my finger on a splinter of wood. I stifle a cry, unsure if any strange fae are watching me. I use my teeth to dig the shard out as I return to the throne.

I step carefully over the gnarled roots that grow from the floorboards and when I look up, the ruined castle is gone. A brilliant throne shines in the sun, and the hallway no longer looks as if it is abandoned. The columns all bear unique bark patterns of a specific tree, and the tops form branches that support the ceiling.

Murdock watches my reaction closely, laughing when he sees my jaw drop open. "You see it now, don't you?"

"Yes," I breathe.

The entire room comes to life before me as if a sheet is being pulled away slowly. Vines and cobwebs disappear, and vibrant, rich colors fill a once-dull and dusty hall. The inlaid floors shine, and the scene from earlier is painted in bright hues. The entire hallway becomes a living forest within stone walls. "Was it like this the entire time?"

"No," Murdock says, looking at me in awe. "It's like this because of you, Princess."

"Welcome home," a voice from the upper balcony calls out.

A merlin falcon with bright purple eyes flies down and shifts mid-air. Thorne stands before me, robes billowing.

"Oh, Goddess, how I've missed you." Relief fills my bones, and I sag into their embrace.

"And I, you, Princess." Thorne takes me under their arm and walks me back toward the dais. They gesture to the throne and sigh, "It is a good day when we have Deoir blood back in the Earth Fae castle."

"This entire place is..." I struggle to find the words. It *feels* like home, but I have never been here before. Is it possible to be homesick for a place I have never been? Will I be happy here? I can't see how without Conall by my side. A light tug echoes down the heartcall, and my hand goes immediately to my chest. "It's home, I suppose?"

"You are the Earth Fae heir, Princess. As soon as you stepped through the wards, the land and the castle knew. This is your home." Thorne's gentle, soothing voice immediately puts me at ease. Ah! I almost forgot."

Thorne waves their robes with a flourish and withdraws two books, one about stone circles and the other the warded journal my father gave me. I take both of them gingerly from Thorne's hands. I had forgotten I had given them to Thorne for safekeeping when I ran from the king. I flip through the pages of the journal, and the light catches the slight indentations where the wards keep the text hidden from sight.

"I took excellent care of them, I assure you." Their eyes are a vibrant amethyst, catching the light in the room and twinkling.

"Thank you," I whisper, clutching them to my chest.

With their free hand, Thorne gestures to the room. A few feathers fall from their robes, floating gracefully down. "It is nice to be back here once more. Even the air is shifting."

Stroking the soft cover of the journal, I watch in awe as the rough-hewn floors turn smooth. Very detailed, colorful inlay decorates the floors - a seamless blend of wood and stone. The doors, too, have straightened themselves, pulled up by an invisible string, and set back in the jambs before my eyes.

Thorne watches me take in all the changes. A slight crease forms in their brow as they look into the shadows beyond. "Soon, I imagine, every creature will wake, too."

But what if they don't?

I flex my hands at my side, eager to feel my earth magic. I may only be a half-halfling, but I easily called out to the vines and the earth before Achill's smoke put me under. Something changed. Otherwise, I would have saved Conall.

Thorne squeezes me again, shaking me from my thoughts.

I look into their vibrant purple eyes.

"I daresay I have missed you something fierce," I sigh and lean on their shoulder.

"Och," Murdock scoffs behind me. "Where exactly have you been, Thorne?"

"Keeping tabs on me, Murry?" Thorne drops their arm and turns to face Murdock, raising an eyebrow.

I open my mouth to brush off the comment, but Murdock speaks up, an edge to his voice. "Aye. Someone has to keep an eye out for Sorcha while Conall's impris—"

Thorne's smile drops, and their head snaps over to me. Their purple eyes turn stormy, and fear flashes across their face. "Achill has Conall?"

My tongue is thick as I stammer, "He's... he... I tried, but... I couldn't."

I want to say I was too stubborn and concerned about trivial things when Conall was trying to get us into the tunnel and out of harm's way. That it is my fault, Achill has him. My stomach churns at the thought of Conall imprisoned at the High King's castle. But the words fade, shame keeping me from saying more.

Thorne takes my chin in their hand, tilting my face up.

"Stop that," they say, shaking their head. "You think those thoughts, and they'll become true."

"But it *was* my fault, Thorne."

"Och, Princess, he stayed by choice," Murdock chimes in. he, too, steps closer as if his presence alone could push away my doubt. "He also, might I point out, shifted into a wolf against the advisement of his brothers and myself."

"What do you mean?" I turn to Murdock, fighting away tears.

"If a shifter shifts in a weakened state, their ability to return to their fae form is impossible."

"Not impossible," Thorne shakes their head.

"Aye, not impossible. It just makes everything else harder. And if he shifted into his wolf form, he exhausted himself too much to use any more of his magic. He couldn't have kept you safe beyond staying behind and causing the cave-in," Murdock leans in and touches my arm. Iridescent purple scales on his wrists flash briefly before he snatches his hand away as if my skin is on fire.

"How did you finally break out of the spell, Sorcha?" Thorne asks, changing the subject.

I close my eyes, thinking back to the last few moments of my dream before I woke. "I was in the Deoir forest and close to the stones."

My eyes snap open, and I find Thorne's amethyst ones staring back at me. "You had handed me a purple bottle. It was the last thing you gave me back at the river before you flew off."

Thorne tilts their head. "Yes, and you took it?"

"When I was awake, I did. But not in the dream." I rub my face, concentrating on what happened before falling asleep. "But I ran into the forest, herded by wolves. That terrible fog felt like it was pulling me down. And then Achill showed up, and I took the draught. But since I didn't drink it in the dream, perhaps that was why I woke. Because Conall was finally able to get through?"

Thorne nods, a sly smile gracing their lips.

"What was in that bottle? After I took it, everything went black. I was too tired to do anything more."

"Merely a fainting concoction." Thorne turns and walks behind me toward one of the many doors in the hallway as if they own the place. "To make it as hard for Achill to get you back to the castle as possible and to buy us some time."

My head whips around. "Wait, so *you* put me under the sleeping spell?"

Thorne stops, looking like I had just struck them across the face. "I—Sorcha. I would never."

Their face softens as their eyes find Murdock's, and realization crosses their features. "I wonder, however, if my tincture enhanced the effects of the king's magic. Perhaps that is why Sorcha slumbered instead of merely fainting."

"Aye," Murdock mulls this over, crossing and uncrossing his arms. "That would make sense. Explains why it took so long for Conall to get through to Sorcha. Conall had mentioned that something was keeping her blocked."

"Blocked? Yes. Yes, I could see how the sleeping concoction mixed with Achill's smoke magic - which, who knows what kinds of ill-conceived intent he had behind it - could put her into a deep trance until the effects of either weakened."

"Can we stop talking about me like I'm not here?" I say, stepping between them. A spark of anger flares in my chest, and the thought of Achill keeping me asleep forever turns my stomach. "I was asleep for a *year*, and you're all just now figuring out what happened?"

"Well, I was the only one able to get around the wards on the conservatory." Hazel's tiny voice comes from a branch on a tree next to my shoulder. Her ability to sneak around unnoticed is a gift I wish I had.

Thorne holds their hand out, and she gingerly steps into the outstretched palm. Thorne says, "And you were mighty brave, Hazel."

Hazel shimmers with pride at Thorne's words, an ear-splitting smile gracing her face. If she had wings, they'd be fluttering at top speed. She turns to me apologetically, "The wards made me so tired. It wasn't until the plants started growing faster that his magic weakened."

I meet Thorne's gaze, their purple eyes missing nothing.

"The vines kept getting thicker; the wards got weaker." She twists her hands in front of her, hesitating.

"It's okay, Hazel. You were brilliant," I say. "What happened?"

"I would get so tired from fighting against the wards that I would need to sleep. And sometimes, when I slept, I'd forget things. But the first time I passed through and didn't get so tired, I knew it was time to try."

Murdock nods, "Hazel used a network of fae to get messages through, clever pixie." Hazel flushes at the compliment. "When we heard the wards weakened, we attacked some border fae guards. Drew Achill's attention from the castle."

"And then once Conall was free, the closer he got to you, the faster everything grew." She shrugs as if this information is something we should all know.

"Well, that certainly is interesting," Thorne tilts their head at me. "Did the plants keep growing, Hazel?"

She nods her head. "They were fast, at first, like they were getting ready. But then Sorcha woke up, and they slowed down."

"I haven't been able to call on my magic since I woke." I hold up my hands for Thorne to look. "No vines, nothing."

"Och, but you could walk through the wards, see through the glamour here, and return this castle to its former splendor." Murdock holds his arms wide and turns in a slow circle for emphasis.

"But these fae remain frozen in time." Thorne points to statues in the corner of the throne room that I hadn't seen before.

"I — I think I need to sit down." I rub the center of my chest to ease the tight grip around my lungs.

Murdock's hands are on my elbows, and he helps me sit, concern etched across his face.

"I think it's time for you to rest, Princess," Thorne says, setting Hazel down so she can scurry away.

My head falls back against the headrest, and I breathe in the earthy scent of the yew bark. The sound of my heart beating rapidly fills my ears, and the crushing weight of despondency presses me into the stone.

"I don't want to go back to sleep." My voice sounds far away and small. Invisible hands clamp down on my chest and squeeze, not wanting to fall asleep should all of this still be a dream. The world warbles in my vision, and I feel utterly helpless.

"Right. Up we go," Murdock says, his hands scooping me up in his arms. But I only want one pair of strong arms to hold me. Murdock shifts me closer to him, and a subtle scent fills my nose. It's soothing in a strange way but does nothing to ground me.

"But I need to get Conall out of there," I whisper, shame, anger, fear, and worry taking turns roiling in my gut.

"Let's just get you somewhere you can lie down for a while," he says, grunting as he kicks a side door that opens to a spiral stone stairwell. "This should take us to the royal wing. We'll find you a bed that's *not* made of stone, Princess."

His scent of salty sea air and jasmine smells fresh, like the linens back at home. He carries me up the curving stairs, and I close my eyes, pretending the arms around me is Conall instead.

The heart-call pulses in time to a slow heartbeat, and Conall's voice is a whisper that matches the tempo.

I'm here. I'm here. I'm here.

Seven
Achill

The horse is out of breath, puffs of air filling the dead of night. Achill circles his steed around enormous trees that he swears weren't there moments ago. Out of the corner of his eye, he sees another tree shift slightly, its roots obstructing the dirt path.

"Blasted Dryads!" His fury echoes into the woods, and flames lick at his fingers.

"That won't work here, Smoke-blood," an ancient voice says from the treetops.

"You don't scare me, Dryad," Achill says, his voice a little too loud for the stillness of the forest.

His fire flares brighter, challenging the old forest spirits in this wood. A branch swoops down and douses it, the leaves shaking in soft laughter. Goddess, how he hates it when he's the butt-end of a joke he doesn't understand.

Achill holds up his hands in surrender. "Fine. No more fire. Let me pass."

The trees shake their leaves at him, and their admonishment slithers over his skin as they angle their branches toward him. Finally, the forest grows quiet again.

"If you can make it to the stones..." That same voice whispers close to Achill's ear, and he whips around. Nothing is behind him anymore, but the trees have shifted again.

He kicks his horse, but it doesn't move. Achill kicks his horse again and smacks it on the rear. The horse whinnies but doesn't move, and Achill looks down to see vines holding each hoof in place.

"So be it," Achill grumbles. He slides off his horse and stomps through the woods. He pushes his smoke through the forest. It crawls along the forest floor as he infuses his desire to make the forest sleep. The stones glow in the distance, their warded colors dancing along the surface of the rocks. He takes a few more steps and is proud that he could get to her this easily.

He takes another step, lifting his leg high over a fallen log, and then his feet touch down in his study.

Achill roars furiously, and flames shoot from his fingertips, catching the rug on fire at his feet. Smoke unfurls from his fingers and smothers the fire.

The dryads are stronger. They couldn't create a portal when he went after Sorcha. His smoke magic worked to keep them all asleep.

But not this time. He is right; something changed.

It was as if her presence in those woods was enough to wake the dryads. And if the land is waking, then there is something more to her than he thought.

Achill flings the doors open to his study and stalks down the hallway to the dungeons. He'll get his answers from the only fae who knows her better than herself.

Eight
Sorcha

Conall stands in the center of the stone circle. The mist swirls, dancing around the edges of the stones. His fae form is even more handsome in the low light, silvery moonbeams dancing off his dark hair.

I rush towards him, and he catches me effortlessly, crushing my body to his as if we could absorb each other by how tightly we cling to one another. His scent envelops me, and I breathe him in, wanting to imprint the way he smells into the tiniest corners of my mind. I press up against him, every part of me thrumming with want.

"I've missed you." Conall nuzzles into my neck, lightly nipping at the curve of my shoulder. His fingers weave into my hair, and he shakes my braid free.

"I've missed you, too," I sigh, aching for him and his touch in real life. But if this is all I get, being with him in this heart-call space, I plan to make the most of it.

We pull apart, and I stare into his green eyes. "Please tell me you're all right..."

"I don't want to talk about that right now," he smiles wanly and then peppers my face with kisses. He pauses long enough to say, "I just want to be here with you for however long we have."

He tugs on the hair at my nape, exposing my neck to his hungry mouth, and trails his lips down the sensitive skin, only stopping to hover over the curve of my shoulder. When his tongue flicks at my pulse, I moan.

His lips find mine, and I am lost to the sensation of his tongue inside my mouth. He coaxes me open, and I shiver at the thought of his mouth elsewhere. Of his tongue, his fingers, his hands touching the more intimate parts of me. One of his hands travels down and grabs my backside, pushing me closer to him. His length is hard between us.

"I want you, My Queen," he murmurs through kissing. "I need to be inside of you."

"Yes, please," I beg, fighting with clothing that is suddenly too restrictive and tight.

He scrambles at my laces. My fingers grapple at his shirt. He tugs at the ties around my waist, and after a few agonizing moments, my pants fall to my ankles. His calloused hands scratch my skin as he lifts my shirt over my head. I have to suppress a giggle as I grab at his shirt and struggle with him as he takes off his pants. It's a mess, but I am so eager to see him, all of him, that I don't care.

Time stops as we stand there, taking each other in. Desperate to be with him, I admire the small silvery scars that pepper the cut lines of his body. I want to commit every part of him to memory, scared that His eyes travel over my soft curves and we finally come crashing back together.

Skin on skin, chest to chest. I run my hands down his back, his corded muscles flexing beneath my touch. His hands find my backside and lift me so I can wrap my legs around his waist, and he carries us over to the altar stone in the center of the circle.

He dips his head and trails a tongue down my neck. "If we mate in the real world, I will bite you here."

"Please," I breathe, threading my fingers through his hair.

"And then I am going to bite you here," he says, trailing his mouth down to my breast. Liquid heat pools in my center as he teases one of my nipples with his teeth. His head moves lower to my waist as he kisses his way down my stomach.

"And here." He nips at the sensitive skin at the top of my leg. My knees fall open for him, and his fingers slide through my folds. I arch my back, giving him better access.

"And I will bite you here," he says, dipping his head to flick my bundle of nerves with his tongue.

"Oh, Conall." I grip his hair, pulling him closer. "Bite me, now."

"As you wish, Your Highness," he says between my thighs. His mouth clamps over me, and he flicks his tongue as he slides a finger inside. I buck against his hand and cry out; his movements increase as he slides another finger inside.

"Conall," I pant. "I need you."

"Mmm," he murmurs, continuing to work my clit with his teeth. He goes slowly, agonizing in the way he draws out my orgasm. My legs shake, and he pulls back just as I am about to peak. His fingers slow, and he says, "You are so delicious. I have craved you for too long."

His words reverberate through me, piercing me through. I know that as soon as I wake up, all of this will be over and that he isn't here with me. If only this had been what my year-long sleep had been like instead of reliving every single horrible thing that happened with Achill. If my dreaming moments had been full of a naked Conall, I could have easily slept for a hundred years.

"Conall..." Words stall on my lips, and he must know that my mind has drifted because he dips his head and nibbles on my clit again. Instinctively, my knees want to close, the sensation overwhelming, but he holds my legs with his other hand. It is only when my walls tighten around his deft movements, threatening my release again, that he withdraws his fingers. I whimper at the sudden emptiness. My head falls back, hitting the altar stone. My head swims with want.

"Yes, My Queen?" His lilt is low and sultry. "What do you need?"

"I need you," I breathe. My chest heaves with each breath.

Conall stands, and I can see the tip of his hardened length glistening in the moonlight. Scraping my eyes up his chiseled body, I meet his devilish grin with one of my own. He slides up between my legs, settling against my entrance. I wrap my legs around his waist. He drags his tip over my entrance, and I shudder.

"Conall, please," I beg. He slowly slides in, inch by agonizing inch, until he is seated against me. He flexes inside me, and I moan, "Oh, Goddess Above."

"No, My Queen," Conall whispers in my ear. "Just us."

He withdraws, easing himself back in, taking his time. It is as if time has slowed, waiting for the two of us to take in every breath, pulse, touch, and thrust until we are entirely sated. If I could stay here forever, our bodies entwined in the moonlight pressed as close together as possible, I would.

Conall emits a groan so deep it drives me wild, and I wrap my legs around his waist. His eyes are glassy, and he hangs his head as he rolls his hips forward. His tip throbs with each thrust, and I lose all sense of space and time.

"Oh, Go—"

He growls, and his lips smash into mine, his tongue driving into my mouth as he thrusts harder. I never want to stop being so full of him. He bites the side of my neck playfully, and I want to tell him to bite me, to claim me, but before I can get the words out, he lifts me and pulls me from the altar stone.

Clinging to his shoulders, I wrap my legs around his waist tighter and thread my fingers in his hair. I gasp as his movements impale me on his shaft.

"I will not have you calling out the Goddess' name," *he growls into my ear.* "Not when it is me giving you such pleasure."

He gingerly sets us down in the middle of the stone circle. His shoulder muscles go taut as he braces himself, ready to finish what he started.

But I reach up to cup his face, and before he can object, I roll us over and straddle him. Conall's eyes widen with intrigue, but he doesn't fight me. Instead, his green eyes take in everything. I shake my head, letting my hair fall over my breasts. Suddenly self-conscious, I try to hide my soft stomach with my hands.

"Please," *Conall says, brushing my hair from my breasts.* "Never hide your body from me."

"What?" *I ask, not hearing the words that he said. His cock flexes inside me, and a purr escapes from somewhere deep in my throat.*

"Sorcha, please don't cover yourself from me." *Conall takes my hands and holds them out to the side.* "You are the most beautiful creature I have ever seen, and I will not stand for you thinking of yourself other than that."

"Oh," I say softly, wishing I didn't have such a human body; the stretch marks, the sagging stomach, and the crow's feet in the corner of my eyes. I am only thirty-one years old and already feel like an old maid compared to his godlike body.

Conall runs his hands up my waist, cupping my breasts, flicking the nipples with his thumbs. "I love these."

I smile crookedly and try to protest, but he continues talking while slowly driving into me.

"I love this." His hands slide down my waist and hips, trailing on the stretch marks there that glisten in the moonlight.

"I love this," he says as he cups my backside, pushing me forward so I have to brace myself on his chest. He growls, and I dig my fingernails into his skin lightly. His hands stop on my stomach and I try to keep from flinching. "And I love this, too."

I wish I could lean into his adoration of my body. "This aging human body?"

"Whether you live an immortal or mortal life, I will love every part of you forever."

"Love?" I exhale. His hands travel over my body, worshipping every inch. Gooseflesh erupts under his fingertips, and I shiver, unused to this unadulterated adoration.

"Yes. Love. I knew it the moment I laid eyes on you. Bloodied and at the mercy of that awful fae in the forest, the chunk missing from his neck, your mouth covered in his dried blood. I thought to myself, what a beautiful, ferocious creature. She must have fire in her soul." He chuckles, and his eyes are far away. I shift on top of him, bringing him back to awareness. His eyes roam over my body and then stop at the scar on my forehead. He sits up and slides a hand along my back. His other hand trails up my neck and finally cups my cheek. I lean into his touch, nuzzling his palm.

"Watching you sleep at the Inn, I knew I had gotten myself into trouble."

"You watched me sleep?" Tears line my eyes.

He nods. His fingers graze my temple, and he traces the faint scar.

I drive myself down, rolling my hips as he thrusts upward. We groan in tandem, panting together as our rhythm intensifies. He takes *one of my breasts in his mouth, and I tighten around him, craving his thickness bottoming out inside me. Our release builds, and one of his hands trails down my backside, his finger playing intimately with my puckered entrance. I throw my head back, my body buzzing with desire. His teeth take my nipple between them, and I moan, threading my fingers in his hair. His hands find my waist, and he holds me down and roars with his release. He finishes thrusting, and a second wave of ecstasy floods my body.*

We collapse back down to the earth, and his arms encircle me, caging me against his chest. I nuzzle into the crook below his shoulder, sighing contentedly as he pushes the hair from my face.

"You are divine," he whispers. "Never in my life did I think I would find someone like you."

"You said 'love' earlier," I whisper back, butterflies swarming in my stomach at those words.

Conall hums, the noise low in his chest. "I did. Did that scare you?"

My hands stroke his sweat-covered skin, caressing the tiny scars that pepper his arms. "No, because I love you, too. My mate."

He squeezes me tight enough for the air to leave my lungs.

"My mate," he repeats.

I want to stay here forever, still full of him as his seed slowly spills out of me, wrapped in his arms, our bodies covered in sweat. This bliss is almost enough for me to forget that outside of this place, Conall is with Achill - again. I push up, humming with delight when his still-hard cock moves with me. His lips curve into a smile, and he growls, pulling down to consume my mouth again.

But instead of a kiss, he sucks in a breath and winces.

"What's wrong?" I search his face, trying to get him to look at me. "Conall?"

He cups my cheek, recoiling against something that I can't see. "He's coming."

NINE
SORCHA

"Something has changed in the castle this morning," Hazel's tiny voice sounds in my ear.

I stand on the balcony of my private room, leaning against the cool stone and looking out at the forest below. Unable to sleep after Conall left our heart-call, I left the warmth of the furs and blankets of my swinging bed to watch the Earth Fae lands below come to life in the morning light.

The early morning sun climbs ever higher in the sky, its soft rays touching the tips of the trees as I worry my lip so much it bleeds. The birds are quiet at first, but as the periwinkle hues of daybreak fade into bright blue, their melodious songs fill the air. It is enough, for a few moments, to help me clear my head.

My hand reaches up to touch the hagstone. Worry consumes me, knowing that something terrible is happening to Conall. I tug on the heart-call, desperate to hear his voice, but only feel a faint shimmer.

Hazel tugs on my braid, trying to get my attention. She's perched on a little ledge above my shoulder, covered head-to-toe in dust. I give her a tight smile, "What have you been up to? You're covered in dirt!"

"Trying to make myself useful." She smiles, coyly adding, "I've already made friends with some boggarts."

"Boggarts?" I recall Conall's words about neglected brownies. I peer down at the floor, wondering if I can see them in the shadows.

"I'll get through to them soon." Hazel jumps down from the ledge. A cloud of dirt puffs, and she shakes her head. She tugs on the hem of my dress, pulling me inside. "We have a lot of cleaning left to do, still. But your wing of the castle is so pretty."

A solitary heavy oak door, carved intricately with flower blossoms and vines, leads to what I assume must be the stairs Murdock climbed last night. Above me, a large tree creates another ceilinged canopy with its branches. Roots weave up through the smooth stone floor seamlessly, just like the yew tree near the throne.

With the walls open to the elements on the east and the north, the bed has an almost entirely unobstructed view of the sea to the west and the mountains to the north and east. I sit down on the edge of the bed, wary of the slow swinging motion.

"Isn't it *lovely*?" Hazel squeals and dives into the plush blankets. She pops her head out, wiping her face on the edge of a blanket. "It's a swing. A swing for you to *sleep* in."

I smile, but my mind is elsewhere. A tangle of vine stalks weave around the boughs of another, smaller yew tree that grows along the south wall. The vines are like ropes that hold the bed up. I rock my body back and forth, staring at Hazel, who grins wildly and then dives to the foot of the bed to snuggle into the furs. It feels like something is missing, and my hand wanders to the empty side of the bed, wishing it had Conall in it. I feel so incomplete without him next to me, wanting that part of me that I never knew was missing.

Anger scratches underneath the surface of my skin, tainting even this experience. I should feel relief that I made it home and am in the Earth Fae castle to fulfill my birthright. And yet, the one person I want to share that with isn't here. Instead, they are locked away, enduring Goddess-only-knows-what kind of torture until I can get him out. But how will I get to him if my magic is gone?

Hazel clears her throat. I flash her a quick smile. "It's lovely, Hazel. Never in my wildest dreams did I ever think that trees would grow out of the middle of a building. And now I had a bed that swings."

"Eek!" she squeals again. "Let me show you the sitting room!" Hazel's eyes twinkle with joy. Her face is clean from rolling around in the furs, but her hair is a static mess that frizzes around her head like a halo. She shakes herself free and jumps off the swinging bed.

Her joy wraps around me as I climb out of bed. A shawl rests on a chair, and I take it, pulling it tight around my shoulders to keep the chill of the open castle away. She darts through the crack and into the shadows, fast as a brownie. The freedom with which she moves here, away from Achill, in the safety of this castle, gives me pause.

How many other creatures are trapped in his castle and unable to leave? A sense of hopelessness builds inside me, an ever-growing weight that settles on my back as I head downstairs to the sitting room. If I planned things well, I could free more helpless creatures from his control.

Another large, carved oak door sits ajar at the bottom of the stairs. I lean my shoulder against it and shove. It creaks open, revealing even more trees that grow from the ground. Several plush swings hang from the branches. A small waterfall cascades over moss-covered rocks. Floor-to-ceiling windows line the walls, and sunlight streams through the panes, warming the room to an almost tropical atmosphere. Large oak doors line the walls on the far side, elaborate carvings in a triptych - each door part of a larger picture.

Hazel chirps from up above, "Your Highness!"

Her tiny body slides down a vine and lands on the ground; she scurries over to me. I scoop her up and place her on my shoulder. "Well, you've certainly made yourself at home."

"Magnificent rooms, aren't they?" Thorne says, stepping through the balcony's glass doors. Feathers fall from Thorne's robes, floating gracefully to the floor. "Aerona and Cariad did well when they magicked these rooms centuries ago."

"Oh. Hello, Thorne." I keep my face neutral, but I am elated they choose to share a tidbit of their life with me. "They must have been so powerful."

"They were," Thorne whispers, reaching out a hand to touch

the nearest tree. "It was so rough on Cariad - watching her sister walk toward a fate she had no control over."

"Were you close to either of them?"

"To Cariad, yes. Not so much Aerona. She cut most of us off after her mating bond snapped into place with Achill," Thorne says wistfully.

"That must have been difficult," I say. I refuse to look directly at Thorne for fear of scaring them away since they are in such a sharing mood today. Their notoriously avoidant demeanor slips even more.

"It was, but my friendship with Cariad bloomed with her sister's absence. And I will forever be grateful for those years." They flash me a muted smile, the corner of their mouth quirking. They step away. "Let's see what the rest of your home looks like now, shall we? I seem to recall these walls once held one of the most magnificent libraries in all of Fae."

Thorne explains what they know of the castle's history as we navigate the curving corridors and topsy-turvy towers. Vines and flowers climb through the open windows, and butterflies flit between the flowers.

I am lulled into imagining what this place might have been like in its heyday as Thorne weaves a story of how this castle was host to various fae. Some came here for knowledge, others for magic, and most for a place to call home. The Earth Fae kingdom was once the epicenter for the Fae lands. The Water Fae castle, inaccessible to those without water magic, lay to the west. Air Fae to the north, Fire Fae to the east, and the Earth Fae kingdom was the apex of the land. The castle was full of bustling creatures from all the elements.

Thorne stops and flashes me a smile. "I wanted to wait to show it to you. The Royal Library was my favorite place in the castle."

We make a full circle of the grounds, my arms full of flower blossoms and shiny stones as gifts to leave for the boggarts. The building breathes easier each time I place a flower on a windowsill. Each room has tiny hints here and there of the boggarts causing trouble, their small footprints, and messes everywhere. The gardens are still a mystery, with the stone figures locked in a timeless sleep and the vines overgrown. Now and again, I look down at my hands, wondering if the green shimmers will show, but I still see nothing.

Thorne leads me down a well-lit hallway, large windows open to the elements. The scent of drying pine needles, lilac blossoms, and bark wafts through the air. We pass a balcony leading to a part of the gardens I haven't seen before, and I crane my neck as we walk past. A bird swoops down in front of me and then loops up in the air through the archways of the hallway. It trills its song and finds a resting place among the eaves outside.

At the furthest end of the hallway, wide double doors greet us, framed by live birch trees.

Thorne stops suddenly, turns to me with their hands on the doorknobs, and whispers conspiratorially, "The Library."

They jiggle the handles, but the doors are locked tight. Frowning, Thorne turns to me. "These never used to be locked when Cariad was here. Wait here, Princess, maybe Murdock will know..."

A puff of air and Thorne shifts into their merlin falcon, flying off to find Murdock and leaving me alone.

An archway frames the door to the library, the birches bending and twisting together at the top, beckoning those who wander by to enter the room beyond. A gentle breeze dances among the vines that cling around the columns of stone in the hallway, shaking their leaves and pulling my skirt around my legs. Lilac blossom and pine weave together, and I am comforted by the delicateness of the blooming flowers. I turn and head back to the doorway we had walked by, curious if I can find some flowers for some of the boggarts in that garden.

The balcony overlooks an interior oasis surrounded by the towers of the castle. Pockmarked with light, a carefully manicured sitting area sits underneath a grouping of large conifers. Their vanilla-scented bark warms in the sun and the pleasant aroma of the wind. As I descend the stone stairs, the space is much bigger than the view from the balcony.

Lilacs in full bloom catch my nose again, and I follow it to the furthest wall, a patch of overgrown shrubs tucked behind the trunks of the enormous pines. Lilacs and roses used to be some of my favorite summer scents back home.

A small stone bench sits surrounded by unkempt bushes, a tangle of branches overrun with lavender-colored flowers. I thank the bushes first, apologetic that I don't have my earth magic at my fingertips to replace any of the flowers I take. The soft petals coat my fingers in their aroma as I pluck them from their stems, placing them on the seat at my knees. A solitary cluster of flowers climbs the stone wall, an intense purple blossom, unlike the rest of the bush. I reach my arm through the tangle of foliage, ready to pluck the panicle from its branch, when carefully carved images appear.

"Well, isn't that interesting?"

Sweeping the limbs out of the way, the carvings form a collection of writing I have only seen once before, in a book in the High King's castle. I push away more of the branches, and the bottom image of a stone circle appears, with markings etched into the sides.

I trace a finger along the edges, following the shapes and swirls. "What're these?"

"Ward markings and runes," Thorne says behind me.

I yelp and turn. Thorne stands behind me with Murdock, both of them wearing snarky smiles.

"*Waterboy* over here thought we wouldn't be able to surprise you," Thorne says, purple eyes glinting with mischief. "I told him I had a few tricks up my sleeve."

Murdock's cheeks flush pink and his mouth opens and closes. "I... I..."

"You look like a fish when you do that," Thorne chuckles, gently pushing Murdock. Murdock's face flames red, and he huffs out a haughty breath.

Thorne squints at the wall over my shoulder.

"Ancient," they breathe, their eyes widening the more they see. "I haven't seen writing like this since..." Their voice drifts off, and they step forward. Air magic swirls at their fingertips, brushing the plants away and keeping the shrubs from clinging to the surface.

"Oh!" I gasp.

An entire scene unfolds before our eyes, covering the length of the far wall.

Before us is an entire map of stone circles within the northernmost land of Fae, complete with ward markings and runes for each monolith.

"This... is this the monolith we crossed through earlier?" I ask Murdock, pointing to a small cluster of stones near my head beside a castle.

Murdock hums, "Aye, seems so."

He reaches up and points at another cluster of stones, his body close enough to warm my back. The scent of ocean air and jasmine follows his movements, and tiny, iridescent scales flash in the sunlight along his wrists. He adds, "These stones are in the bay near my cave."

"You're a mershifter?" I ask, turning my head to look up at him. My eyebrow lifts in question as my eyes flick down to his chest. It, too, shines with purple scales.

The tips of his ears flush. He clears his throat and steps back. "Aye, Princess."

"And you have a cave?" I ask, turning back to the wall. My eyes follow the path of the stones, but my finger trails the river near the Earth Fae monolith. I end up at a convergence of seven rivers joining the center of the mountains. A lake sits high among the ridges and peaks, forming the headwaters.

"Aye, Your Highness, I have a cave. I'm not a vagrant. There are stones like these on the coast. They've stood there for centuries, but the whorls have worn down between the winds and the wild winter weather. I doubt I could even tell you which stone has which symbol anymore." He steps backward, putting more space between us. "It's a shame. The Water Fae should have taken better care of these monuments."

Murdock sounds almost forlorn, his eyes growing distant.

"This looks like major headwaters," I say, pointing to the lake.

"Yes, I spent much of my youth in those waters," Thorne says. Their eyes flick to me, and they get all misty-eyed. "That lake was home to seven sisters of the water. I have forgotten the rest of their story, in any case. After Achill visited the lake, they were never heard from again. It's such a shame."

"Here," Murdock says, shifting at Thorne's somber tone. "Look at these markings." He points to some indentations that resemble the symbols on the stone circles.

I point to a few more Ancient Fae marks. "The writing looks similar to a book I found in Achill's library. It was about Fae ancestral lines. But this... is interesting. Aren't these the lyrics to the shifter lullaby Conall was singing?"

Thorne cranes their head and reads out loud the first verse:

"The stones overflow,
 With the magic in our souls.
 When the flowers bud,
 Bestow your blood,
 Underneath the moonlight,
 Beneath the Goddess' sight,
 The forest sings in our bones...
 Can you hear the magic stones?"

Both Thorne and Murdock give me puzzled looks.
"What?" I ask.
"You were humming along." Murdock nods his chin toward my hands, but his eyes never leave my face, and his eyebrows knit together subtly.

"Oh," I breathe. "It was the song my ladies' maid used to sing. It wasn't until I was with Conall that I knew it had lyrics."

Thorne tilts their head, purple eyes alight and curious. "Geannie?"

I nod, and a memory resurfaces, clawing at the edges of my mind.

Geannie was sitting on my bed, the edge of the mattress dipping down while she settled. I am a young child, perhaps only seven or eight, and she reads to me from a collection of fairy lore and folk tales. Stories of brownies, both loved and forgotten. Myths about kelpies and banshees, harbingers of death and grief. Delightful stories of unicorns and magical swords that only the hero could wield. And then her gentle hands lovingly tucked me into bed, kissing my forehead before she, too, turned in for sleep in the adjacent room.

"Do you see this?" Murdock asks, breaking my reverie. He moves to a faded section, tapping the wall. "It seems like the verses keep going."

I nod, excitement building in my chest, and continue, "It says something I can't quite make out, and then..."

> "...But be with all and not just one,
> Be ye low or highborn,
> Remove the sword from whence it stands,
> And with it, ye shall join the lands.
> Underneath the moonlight,
> Beneath the Goddess' sight,
> The elements sing in our bones.
> Can you see the magic stones?"

Murdock hums, closing his eyes. "I vaguely remember that song, but the words were different. We were told it was about mershifter. I have never heard *these* lyrics before."

I step on top of the stone bench and point to where a faded image rests among the largest of the stone circle carvings. But it is less apparent than the other carvings and looks more worn down by time and weather. Shaped like a cross, wedged into the land, it rests at a crossroads. I point to the picture and lean in, tracing my fingers along the smoothed edges. "Does this look like another cross to you?"

Murdock murmurs a harrumph. He steps back, and his eyes scan the entire image before us. Thorne's purple eyes watch me; though I could be mistaken, they twinkle with interest. I hop down and take a few steps back, marveling at the image as it unfolds before me.

Thorne releases their magic. Then, the wind dies, and the bushes return to their original place against the wall. Only pieces of the engravings poke out from behind the hedge, hidden in plain sight unless you were looking closely.

Thorne turns to me and says, "Not a cross, I don't think. I saw a sword during my rites, but it was just an apparition. Everyone who did their rites back then saw it. That *was* several centuries ago," Thorne muses.

"Several centuries?" Murdock jabs his finger at Thorne. "You're well over eight hundred years old, Thorne. We'd all be chuffed if you could remember anything from your rites."

Thorne rolls their eyes and shoves Murdock back with a puff of air. "Aye, real mature, *Birdy*."

"Watch it." Air swirls around Thorne's fingertips.

"Cut it out, you two. I didn't agree to babysitting today." I say, stepping between them with my hands outstretched. My fingertips glow a subtle green, but the green disappears as soon as I wiggle them to call forth my magic. My hands drop, and with them, my head.

"Princess," Thorne says, cutting into my thoughts. My eyes snap to theirs. "Your magic...?"

"Still nothing." I hesitate but show them my hands. The green shimmers flicker and fade. I flex my hands, trying to call to the land, and nothing happens.

"But you can read Ancient Fae..." They drift off, their purple eyes doing that far-away stare when they concentrate.

"Yes, can't you? I could read several texts from the king's library."

"I can, but I have taken centuries of Ancient Fae studies," Thorne says. "It was a part of my training as a medical worker. The Ancient Fae had many tinctures they had to write down. For some fae, reading the ancient texts comes easily, as if it's a part of their blood."

"So I can read those words because of my fae blood?"

"Possibly." Thorne's amethyst eyes sear into my soul, twinkling with something I can't make out.

"That or you're lucky," Murdock chuckles. "Ow!"

I slap his forearm.

"Thanks for that. I'm curious if there is something in the library about finishing one's rites?" I turn and head back towards the stairs and the balcony, itching to figure out why my magic hasn't been working and if I can speed up rescuing Conall. My foot reaches the bottom step, but I stumble and cry, "Is there — Ahhh!"

The tender flesh of my feet sear like they have been lit on fire, and a feeling of anguish washes through me. My body shakes immediately, and I break out into a cold sweat. The floor wobbles beneath me, and my vision turns spotty.

"Princess!" Murdock lunges for me as I go down on all fours, knees crashing to the stone stairs. I grimace at the impact. Concern flashes across Murdock's face, and he goes down on one knee beside me. He leans down, unsure where to put his hands, and asks, "Princess?"

Thorne is standing and then shifting, their bird circling the gardens from above.

Another surge of intense pain crawls up my legs, and I shiver. Through the pain that resonates up my entire body, I squeak out, "I...?"

"Are you okay?" Murdock wraps his arms underneath me and pulls me up.

I lean on him, clutching his forearms, afraid to put much weight on my feet.

The phantom pains. I would know this feeling anywhere. My body shakes, and bile fills my mouth.

Achill is hurting Conall.

"I-I think... yes, I think I'm okay. I've felt something like this before, though." Terror cascades through me in waves, and I feel like I am back at the castle, in that hallway, fainting from the pain that I didn't know was coming from Achill torturing Conall.

Murdock wraps an arm around my chest and helps me up the stairs. His body is stiff, battle-ready, and I can sense that he is ready to leap into action any second.

Thorne flies overhead, dipping low, and lets out a short call. Immediately, the tension leaves Murdock's body, and he visibly relaxes. We start up the stairs, tentatively at first, and Murdock follows closely behind and off-center as if he is bracing for me to fall again.

Murdock's eyes search my face, concern etching itself as a frown on his forehead. He asks, "You have?"

"Yes, phantom-like pains when Conall..." I swallow down more bile. The words barely leave my lips. I'm too ashamed to say it because I'm the reason he's there.

We round the corner into the hallway, and Murdock stares at the garden below, searching the shadows. Thorne is already at the library doors, a few feathers still floating down to their feet.

"What is it, Sorcha?" Thorne asks. Their hand reaches for mine, and they squeeze it gently. Something about their touch fills me with calm. "You're safe here. No one else has gotten through the wards."

My mouth goes dry. "He's being tortured again."

Thorne squeezes my hand tightly. "Tortured? Again? How do you know?"

"It's the heart-call, isn't it?" Murdock shifts uneasily on his feet, looking at a spot over my shoulder.

"I think so, yes." I nod, still trying to figure out how I can connect to Conall despite never having mated and my magic refusing to work. Frustration grows, and my throat tightens. Every day away from him, a piece of my soul sloughs off. And though I will be the Earth Fae queen, a tremendous honor and title that I'm sure my ancestors wore with pride, I never thought life could seem so unfair. I tuck my fingers into my skirts, embarrassed at my petulant thoughts and lack of magic.

"You can still feel Conall, even from this distance?" Murdock asks, jarring my thoughts.

"Yes," I answer, hoping they don't hear the hesitancy in my voice. But I can't stop the onslaught of questions that spin in my head. Is it just me who feels the heart-call waning?

Murdock frowns, the timbre of his voice lower than usual. "Well, then we need to get some answers."

Thorne procures a large key, slots it into the lock, and the doors swing open. The scent of old leather and dust fills the hall. I wish I could take in the beauty of the old Royal Library, but my vision tunnels from the leftover tremors of pain that pulse in my feet. What happens if I can't get to him in time - if Achill kills Conall before I figure out how to get him back?

Thorne curses and then mumbles something as the shuffling of parchment sounds from somewhere in the bowels of the library.

"I swear there has to be something useful in all these old tomes." I can hear them stacking books on the floor, one after the other, after the other. Thorne comes from around a large shelf, arms stacked high and more stacks flying behind them on a current of air magic. Gingerly, they set down their load and start rifling through the book on top. They flip through its pages and put it down. Dissatisfied, they reach for another.

Tension fills the room as Murdock, and I wait with bated breath to see if Thorne will find or remember something.

Panic squeezes around my throat, threatening to shut off my voice and my breath. I do the only thing I can think of that will calm me down - I tug on the heart-call. A faint humming echoes in my head, a pulse lands in my stomach, and I immediately breathe a little easier. It comes through once more in a slow wave, a comforting bass note that fills my bones.

So long as I can still have that, everything should be okay. Conall is still alive, and there is *some* magic within my half-fae body. I touch the hagstone, smoothing it between my fingers, and blurt out, "I need to finish my rites."

Both of them turn to me. Thorne's mouth drops open, and Murdock's frown is so deep that it casts shadows across his brow.

They speak over each other, "No, princess."

"Absolutely not."

"I cannot allow such reckless behavior from the future Queen."

"Conall will have my scales."

"There is a time and place for such things, Princess."

I lift my chin, "It's the only option."

Thorne shakes their head and stands. "The equinox is less than two days away, and I can feel the stones' pull. You should wait until the Goddess' power is more potent."

I raise my eyebrows.

"Don't look at me like that, Princess. I know that look of yours." Thorne raises a finger at me.

"I'm not giving you a look." I cross my arms over my chest.

"Yes, you are. You gave me that look the night you ran from Achill. You gave me that look after you killed the ogres." Thorne shakes their head. "Stop looking at me like that. It's not a good idea."

"So it's the difference of a few days," I say, standing my ground. I turn to Murdock, knowing he'll be more likely to convince Thorne if I can convince him first. I hold my hands up and shake them in his face. With more force than I mean, I say, "My magic isn't... magic-ing, Murdock. I don't know what else to do. How else do I get to my mate?"

Murdock groans.

His head falls back, looking up at the ceiling. "You know, Conall is going to have my scales if *anything* happens to you."

I flash him a smile. "Thank you, Murry."

When I say his nickname, shock registers on his face, and the tips of his fae ears turn pink. Murdock clears his throat and grimaces at Thorne. "She's right, Thorne."

"I know she's right," Thorne snaps. "I just thought perhaps we had a little more time to prepare. But it would seem that the Goddess has other plans as well. Which reminds me, it has been several centuries since I went through my rites, but Baby Murdock, here—"

"Hey!" he interrupts. "I'm only a few centuries younger than you."

"A few?" They scoff. "You're still young, *Fishboy*, so you remember the rest of the Rites better. You can take the princess to the stones in two days."

Thorne's face is impassive, but their purple eyes twinkle with mischief. Maybe this was a lousy idea...

"This is because I said she was right, right?" Murdock grumbles and shuffles their feet.

The heart-call pulses, but it's faint. Maybe it's my imagination, but it grows weaker each time I feel it. I can't lose him.

"Tonight." I look at both of them.

"Tonight?" Murdock balks, and his eyes flash to Thorne to see what they say.

Thorne fluffs their robes, a few feathers cascading from the folds. They squint their eyes at me, and I stand taller, just waiting for them to protest. They succumb with a simple head tilt. "I just have to get all the offerings together. Ideally, we would have done this during the equinox when the energy is the strongest. Either way, we can still try to manifest and call in the Goddess' magic for your rites. It may not go entirely too smoothly, though."

"Not entirely?" I ask, worrying my bottom lip between my teeth.

Thorne shrugs, avoiding my eyes. "The Goddess is everything in this world and the next. She is a force to be reckoned with. I've never done the Rites earlier. Or later. Only precisely when they are supposed to happen; it's how it's always been done."

"You think this is a bad idea," I hedge, wishing they would tell me more.

"I will find all the offerings, but the rest of what happens inside the circle is up to you, Princess." Thorne rolls up a few more parchments, refusing to meet my eyes.

I swallow thickly, but whether this goes well or poorly, I have to know if there is something else I can do other than wait here and hope my magic returns.

Murdock turns to me and says, "If it makes you feel any better, Sorcha, I will be there the whole time."

My brow quirks when he uses my name. The informality sounds strange coming from him. He looks away quickly.

"Ideally, everything should fall into place here, too." Thorne gestures to the castle grounds. "When your magic came during your altercation with the ogres, it came from a time of need. Now that I look back on it, I foolishly thought it was enough of a test for your rites. It must not have been since you have little fae blood. As much as I hate to admit it, it seems this is the only way to regain your magic."

A tangle of emotions weave around inside me.

Worry sits on my chest like an old friend, even though I have trained to become a queen my whole life. But now that it is staring me in my face, I am apprehensive about it coming true. Dread fills my bones at the thought of not getting to Conall in time and at him dying at the hands of Achill since we never mated and my soul isn't tied to his. And anger simmers deep below the surface—at myself, the king, everything. How naive I was to think I could refute a centuries-old obligation without repercussions. I acted like a foolish child running away from her nightmares. Nightmares that just grew in size and scale the further I ran.

A soft, familiar tug near my heart lingers, much fainter than before. It pulls me back to the library, where Thorne and Murdock look at me with concern.

Thorne touches my arm and says softly, "It is up to you, Princess."

As if on cue, my arms throb with intense pain, and I grimace, folding in on myself, clutching my hands to my chest. A solitary image flashes in my mind of Conall in a dungeon, chained up in a damp, windowless room. A shadowy figure appears in the peripheral, and I can hear it cackling at my mate lying broken on the floor.

I cradle my arms, the throbbing lessening as my voice sounds distant when I demand, "Conall doesn't have much time. It has to be tonight."

Ten
Sorcha

Murdock leads the way to the stone circle in the moonlight, a basket in one hand and his sword strapped to his back. I had insisted he leave his weapons behind, but he refused to part with everything, so we compromised. I roll my eyes at the glinting metal. The last thing I wanted to do tonight was to insult any fae we might encounter with Murdock armed to the teeth. I still think it is overkill, but I wonder if Conall would have done the same thing.

As we draw nearer, Murdock slows. He waits for me to catch up and then says, "The Rites have to take place in a stone circle for the magic to work. Usually, we'd have several other High Fae here to oversee the ritual, but..." He shrugs.

The stones loom above me in the soft moonlit dark, pressing down on me with unspoken judgment as if they know I am not a full-blooded fae. Am I a traitor in this sacred space? Have any halflings done what I am about to do?

I wish Conall were here to coach me through this instead of Murdock.

The grass is cool under my feet as we pass through the outer stones. An altar stone is in the center of the circle, and the moon, though not quite full, illuminates small carvings on top. Worn down through time, the face of the rock is smooth and feels different than the one I dreamed of with Conall. I run my hands over the carvings, tracing them with my index finger. Cariad had figured out that the stones could help amplify magic, but she also thought they could be used for something else.

Murdock's voice cuts into my thoughts, and I realize I've missed some vital instruction. "The strongest element with which you resonate will come to you during your rites. I've never heard of a *rushed* Rite with a halfling before, so I don't know what to tell you to expect. If you were fae, I'd tell you that usually the element will be represented somehow, that you'd feel it before you saw it."

"The element presents itself," I repeat back. Will my magic even be amplified with such weak fae blood? I swallow thickly. "And you'll be here the whole time?"

"Yes," Murdock says, his eyes finding mine in the dark. He sets the basket down at the base of the altar stone. "I'll be here the whole time. You needn't fret, Princess."

I pull out four jars; one with dirt, another with water, another with Thorne's feather, and the other with some ash and put them in the center of the altar stone. On top of the altar stone is a carving of a collection of swirls and knots, all connecting. Along the outside are four words in Ancient Fae, and I place the corresponding jars atop each carved rune corresponding to their element.

"That's done. Then, what?"

"I'll be over there," Murdock says. He points to a stone resting against a tree outside the stone circle.

When Murdock turns, I draw my dagger blade stealthily from the holster at my hip. Before he turns around, I draw it across my forefinger. Blood wells from the cut, and a few drops land in the center of the altar stone. I pinch my fingers together to stop the bleeding, then slide my dagger back into the holster.

Nothing happens.

I look at Murdock, who is leaning back against a tree. I shrug. He tilts his head and shrugs, and the world around me disappears before I can open my mouth to ask what else I need to do. I lurch forward, my hands landing roughly against the altar stone.

A starry night sky mingles with a bright midday sun.

I do not know how it's possible, but the sky swirls with the colors of twilight and dawn. The stones loom like giant sentinels, their shadows dancing across the ground. No castle lies in the distance. Nothing lies outside of the stone circle. It is just myself, fused to the altar stone and the giant monoliths that tower over me, complete in their structure.

Fog rolls in, and at first, I startle, worried that somehow this is a trick from Achill, but then I hear singing in a lilting tune that sounds vaguely familiar. It surrounds the stones, growing in their resonance, filling in the voids, reverberating through them and into my bones. My cheeks grow wet with tears, and I try to lift my hands from the altar stone, but they are leaden as if they are now a part of the rock itself.

"Hello, child." A warm voice surrounds me. "It has been ages since I was called up here."

My mouth drops open, words refusing to form on my tongue. Unable to see her, unable to speak, I am infinitesimally smaller than I have ever felt before, my confidence shrinking by the second.

"Out of words?" She laughs, sweet and thick.

The sound trickles over my skin like honey on a warm piece of bread. Gooseflesh spreads from my head down to my toes. I run my tongue along the roof of my mouth, trying to work up the courage to speak. In their preparation, Thorne never mentioned meeting with the Goddess.

When I don't respond, she asks, "Did you not mean to call on me?"

An edge of irritation fades with the end of her question, echoing among the stones.

"Yes, I did. Don't go," I scramble, blushing and afraid she thinks I'm wasting her time. I yank my hands off the stone and stumble backward into the center of the circle. "I need your help."

The stones are quiet.

"Please," I add.

Fog swirls around my legs. I fight against my instinct to pull away and to run as memories of the forest and the king surface. Bile rises in my throat.

"My child," her voice soothes.

I fall to the grassy knoll on my knees. The light shifts as the sun sinks low on the horizon, slipping behind the lodestone. At the same time, a figure appears from the fog.

Vines climb her legs, and her skirt blows in an invisible wind. Her hair floats around her shoulders, framing her face in a bright red curtain like the flames of a fire, and her eyes are a solid blue, like the darkest depths of the ocean.

She leans down to cup my chin. I rehearse what Thorne told me repeatedly in my head, worried that the entire truth will come out if I open my mouth. "What do you need help with, Princess?"

"I need to finish my rites," I say with as much confidence as possible.

"Is that all?" she tilts her head, stroking my chin with her thumb.

I nod slowly, worried the truth will come out if I open my mouth.

"Don't lie to me, child. I can sense you holding back," she whispers. Her fingers flex a little tighter on my jaw.

Anxiety grips my stomach as I try to explain the predicament I have somehow found myself in again. "I need to finish my rites to take the Earth Fae throne. Become the rightful heir, defeat the evil that pretends to be High King."

She smiles slowly, but her lips do not part. Her eyes swirl a darker blue, almost black, and I can see myself in their reflection.

"Mmm," she says, "you are keeping something close to your heart, child."

I say nothing, willing my pulse to slow with a few breaths.

"Very well," she stands, walking around me. "Have they told you about who I am?"

"A little," I say.

"Go on, tell me. What do you know?" she asks, weaving between the stones.

Has the monolith grown, or is it getting darker and the shadows thicker? Thorne's words about the Goddess echo in my head. *She is a force to be reckoned with.*

I choose my words carefully. "You are both life and death. You are light and dark. You embody all things of this world and the next."

She steps behind a stone, disappearing from my view. Her voice echoes through the monolith, "I am also a giver and a taker. I am both Mother and Father. If you need my help, there must be a balance. This is not simply just a Rite. You made it much more when you offered your life force, your blood. You need something more. And for that, I need something from you."

Though I carefully wait for her to emerge from behind the stone, her voice whispers close to my ear. Her hands rest on my shoulders, and I jump at the contact.

"Why did you come here, child? Answer me truthfully and set right the balance of your sacrifice."

"My... sacrifice?" I swallow.

"What are you willing to give me so that you can be everything you need to be?" She lifts her hands from my shoulders, pulling away. "What do you need, Sorcha?"

"I — " My eyes search the stones, waiting for her figure to emerge—a pulse of desperation tugs at me through the heart-call. I close my eyes, trying to connect with him again.

Conall.

"Ah," she says, walking toward me. "You want your mate."

I nod, worried I'll make a promise I can't keep if I say anything. Genuine fear reverberates down my spine. Is it fear from Conall? Or is it mine? A sudden searing pain lashes against my back, and I cry out, bending forward against the invisible pain. The Goddess stands there, frowning. I peer up at her through the curtain of my hair and watch as realization washes over her features.

She bends down in front of me, sadness filling her eyes.

"It was never supposed to be this way," she says, her voice soothing. She tucks some hair behind my ear. "But I cannot control the will of others as much as I would like."

The pain happens again, and I cry out once more.

"What do you need, Sorcha?" she asks firmly.

"I need to get him away from there. I... I need my magic to do it, and it's not — ahh!" My back lights up in pain once more, and I cry out, clawing my fingers into the ground. I know it isn't real, at least for me. What's happening to Conall, however...

She nods, a silvery tear slipping down her cheek. She holds my hand, palm up, and kisses it. "What will you give me if I give you your power back?"

Tears slip down my face, another invisible lashing licking at my skin. Conall is probably bleeding profusely and unconscious now because I can't feel him through the heart-call anymore.

"No, no, Conall!" I whisper, clutching at my chest, tears flowing freely.

The Goddess pulls me to my feet; concern etched across her face. "What will you give me, Sorcha? For my help?"

"Anything," I sob, my back still on fire from the invisible whipping. She rubs my back slowly, and the pain stops. I can only hope that Conall can get some relief as I send him a sense of ease.

"Very well," The Goddess' fingernail elongates, and she draws it across my palm, opening it up so it wells with blood. "With this offering of your blood, I give you magic. But that is all." She squeezes my hand, and blood pours forth onto the ground at my feet. "In exchange, I will take your fae blood. You will be fully human and live a human life."

Fog swirls around her feet, the cool air licking at the tears drying my face. I meet her eyes once more, tiny flames dancing around her eyes that are now hazel. She flashes me a brief smile and closes my hand in on itself. Something sharp tears itself from my chest, and I heave as if someone punched me in the gut. I look up at her, and she regards me sorrowfully. My palm drips with blood, flowing freely to the ground. Where my drops fall, tiny white snowdrops bloom. Wrapping the hem of my shirt around my palm, I clutch my hand to my chest, wincing against the throbbing ache.

"Sometimes, my child," her voice washes over me. The throbbing in my palm eases. "When we feel like the world is caving in, we want to crumble with it. I do not think this is the lowest you have been. Nor do I think it is the last time you will feel so lost."

She straightens, gently pulling me up and guiding me back to the altar stone. "When all of my creatures once walked this land together, magic was in the air you breathed, the water you drank, the food you ate, the fire you cooked with. Everything everywhere was magic. Magic flowed through the veins of each creature as readily as blood until creatures started seeing the difference in each other. Until the humans and the fae realized they had different ears, different teeth, and differences everywhere. Creatures who once lived in harmony soon started warring, living separately, eating different foods, and calling those differences *less than*. But we all have the same blood, bones, and magic in our hearts. We all have the same elements present within us. We can all choose to make magic out of our lives."

As she talks, her hands spin a tale in the sky, figures made from mist and fog, creatures dance across the canvas, painting the history of her creatures. I am awed by the images of fae and pixies and humans living harmoniously together, tilling the land, and working with all elements of magic. The land, too, looks different. Vibrant greens, luscious forests, ample harvests, gardens overflowing with abundance.

"It took only one," the goddess says, sorrow lacing the rest of her tale. "Only one to sow the seeds of doubt, to find the differences, to find the problems within each creature, to create rifts. Negativity spreads like a wildfire. Doubt digs its claws in and festers within the host. By this time, I was just a memory, long forgotten, only partially revered when the creatures wanted their magic."

I look down at my hand and then back up into her eyes. "So the blood offerings were how we could feel you again, if only fleetingly."

She nods. "Because the connection between me and my children weakened, blood is the strongest way to get to your deeper soul magic. But you do not need to use it to have your magic, to access it," she says.

I look at her, confused, and flex my hand. "Are you saying I didn't need to?"

"No, I needed your blood to know your promises are not empty. I once made a bargain, and they did not strike the balance." She laughs. This fae was sly. They played upon my sympathy for lost love and tricked me." She spits out that last word and clenches her fists together. "Consider this blood vow your commitment to helping balance return to the world."

"And how do I know that your end of the bargain is fulfilled?" I ask, skepticism hanging off my words. "I just gave up the only thing that would let me lay claim to the Earth Fae kingdom."

The Goddess steps forward. She takes her hand, cupping it over my bleeding one, and places both of our hands over my chest. "You do not need to be fae to be the heir. You have magic. You have your heart. But, you will also have this." She gestures behind her toward the altar stone, where a sword stands straight up out of the rock.

"A sword?" I step closer. It glimmers in the moonlight like a mirage, wavering before me.

"Yes. I think you are familiar with the tale. *Remove the sword whence it stands, and with it, you shall join the lands.*" The Goddess smiles when the recognition flashes across my face. "A sacred symbol can do just as much to unite the land as a confident ruler."

She releases my hand and says, "Take a few breaths, child. Do you feel the warmth from my hand? Imagine that warmth wrapping you up inside a ball of light. Then imagine the light everywhere, in the water you drink, the air you breathe, the fire you make, the earth you walk on."

I tilt my head, but the white light evades me. "I... don't feel anything."

"Try again," she whispers. The scent of fresh lilacs cascades from her auburn hair.

As she speaks, I imagine a wave of white light growing from my head to my toes and back up again. My arms float with an invisible wind, my hair whipping about my face. The sensation of water rushes over my toes, and I wiggle them in the grass. Velvety leaves caress my cheeks, and fire lights within my soul.

Her voice echoes in the air, "Remember your bargain. You will need your strength in the days to come."

When I open my eyes again, the Goddess is gone, and I stand in the middle of the stone circle. Alone. On top of the altar stone, the sword glows, starlight woven through its handle. It shimmers in the low light, radiating with reverence.

My hagstone warms against my chest, and I draw it from underneath my top. I place the hagstone to my eye, and the sword vanishes through the hole in my necklace.

Baffled, I drop the hagstone.

If the sword isn't in the stone, then where would it be?

I spin slowly in a circle until a yew tree comes into view just beyond the stones. Its shape looks oddly familiar. The roots grow from the ground, and the branches reach skyward as if supporting something invisible. I walk toward the tree, whose leaves shake the closer I get, and stretch my arm toward the trunk.

A gentle breeze pushes me forward, and the tree beckons me to come closer with its branches as they caress my shoulders and pull me forward.

I have seen this tree before.

I look down at my feet, almost expecting the inlaid wood floors and the columns of trees to line the hallway. There is no stone throne; instead, the sword's hilt is nestled within the trunk.

The hagstone warms, and I pull it to my eye, half expecting to see the sword disappear again. However, it remains embedded in the tree trunk. The hagstone flares again, almost burning my skin as I wrap my hands around the handle and yank. I tug upward, trying to free it. As the cut on my palm reopens, I hiss through my teeth. The sword doesn't budge. It is wedged tight.

I drop my hand and step back, frustrated at my human weakness. Once again, I am a human in a powerful, magical world.

The top of the handle holds a shiny black stone that glints in the moonlight, and starbursts flare to life. It is an almost perfect match to my hagstone, and as I lean in closer, there is a notch in the handle where a second stone is supposed to fit. Oddly shaped, I look from the hagstone to the hilt and back to the hagstone again.

Could it be?

Slowly, I unhook my necklace and slide the hagstone off.

The stone is hot as I manipulate the angle, matching the holes to the formation in the hilt until it locks into place. Starbursts flair to life, shining from the seams where the sword and the hagstone join. The air around me shimmers, the standing stones dissipating around me.

A shadowy figure in my peripheral screams my name, but I'm too focused on the magic pouring out of the sword. My hand reaches out, still dripping with blood, and I grasp the handle. The sword slides effortlessly from the tree trunk, and I squeeze my eyes against the bright light as the blade comes free.

I am standing in the throne room when I open my eyes again.

"Welcome home, Queen of Fae." A face in the yew tree appears in the bark.

A dryad in the ancient yew?

Speechless, all I can do is gape at the gentle smile the dryad gives me before the face disappears into the bark again.

"Princess!" Murdock's voice bellows outside, and the doors to the throne room burst open. He shouts into the hall, his voice bouncing off the walls, "By the Goddess! First, you disappeared right in front of me. And I only stayed put because Feathers-for-Brains said I needed to wait. Do you know how worried I was when it was almost daylight, and you *still* hadn't reappeared? And just when I thought I needed to look for you, you reappeared on the other side of the stones. And then a tree-portal-something-or-other opened up, and you were gone again and—"

Murdock stops short when he sees I am holding the sword. Time must have moved slowly in the stone circle because the hallway is filled with morning sunlight that streams through the roof. I really must have been there for hours. Now, in the throne room, with Murdock mere feet from me, the entire world comes rushing back into focus.

"I—I have the sword," I say and try to lift it. I hiss as the hilt digs into the wound on my hand, getting it slick with my blood. Without my fae strength, the weight of the sword is deceptive. I can only move it a few inches before dropping it again. "I passed my Rites."

"Aye, Your Highness," Murdock says, breathless with relief. He strides forward, eyes searching my face, but I become a steel trap. No one can know what I've sacrificed, the bargain I just struck. His eyes dip down to my hand, noting the blood around my hand and on the sword. He reaches out, but I pull it back. Murdock frowns but doesn't press on; he dips his head and says, "Let's go make you a Queen."

Eleven
Achill

The whip cracks against the wolf shifter's back again, and he goes down, finally broken. Conall's scream echoes in the room, and Achill smiles. Maybe this time, he'll get some answers out of the pup.

Achill strolls around the hunched-over figure in the middle of the dungeon, wondering if Sorcha can also feel the shifter's pain. He vaguely recalls the shared emotions that traveled through the heart-call with Aerona. But after a century without his mate, it seems as if his memory continues to fail him. Did they ever share thoughts like fated mates do? No, because she never let him mate. He never got to bite her, mark her, claim her. The only claiming that ever happened was in the bedroom, and though those moments were magical, they never resulted in the sealing of the mating bond.

He has been alive far longer than he thought he would be. His bones ache, and his mind wavers, but nothing is worse than the gaping hole left in his chest after Aerona died. When the heart-call sheared from his soul, the agony was unlike anything he had ever experienced. If he hadn't learned about soul magic from his uncle, he would have never gone to the Goddess and made his bargain. He was so desperate, so delirious, so distraught that he promised anything to bring her back. But it was already too late. Aerona had already left for the Forever Night, and even the Goddess couldn't bring her back. He could only keep a part of her with him forever, her soul in the petrified scales of the dragon that looked like the moon.

Blood coats the back of his hand, marring the perfect white face of the Aphroselene ring on his finger. He wipes it on his coat, rubbing harder than he should to ensure the stone is clean.

"Well, pup?" Achill asks, pulling the bloodied whip into a tight circle and passing it off to a nearby guard. "Have you figured out whether you will tell me what is happening with your mate?"

Conall sighs, his weight supported by his hands and knees on the stone floor of the cell. Achill rolls his eyes when Conall shakes his head. What an insolent, love-struck fool. Disgust roils in Achill's stomach. To think, he used to act this foolish, too. All bravado and hopeless romantic, wishing for things that would never come to pass - a family of his own, a mate proud to be with him, a legacy of Fire Fae for the crown to pass to.

"Have you mated?" Achill asks.

Conall doesn't move.

"Did you wake her?"

Again, Conall doesn't move. His head hangs down; his breathing is ragged, and his back seeps blood with wounds that are slow to heal.

"Find a healer," Achill tells one of the guards. "I want him well by tomorrow."

The guard dips his chin and turns, running down the hall, through puddles, and up the stairs. The heavy door slams shut.

Impatience claws at Achill's throat, and he is tempted to end Conall's life. But he doesn't. Instead, he walks around Conall slowly, hands clasped behind his back.

"You should know better than to think you can avoid this. Or that you could lie to me. Every crack of the whip, every broken bone, every lick of fire that touches your skin - your mate can feel it. End her suffering, end yours, and tell me what you know."

Conall doesn't move. The wounds on his back have stopped bleeding.

"Get up!" Achill yells.

But the wolf shifter is still as stone. But then, Conall mumbles something so quiet that Achill has to lean down to hear.

"Say that again, dog," he barks out.

Conall winces and sits back on his heels. "You've got blood on your shoes."

Achill stops pacing, his eyes briefly flickering down to his blood-covered shoes. His eye twitches slightly, and he curls his lips into a sneer as he whispers, "Wrong answer."

Smoke billows from his Achill's fingertips, wrapping around Conall's throat, and the wolf shifter sinks to the floor, struggling against the smoke magic. Achill watches as fear and torment mix on Conall's face when the waking nightmares come for his sanity. Achill pushes the smoke a little farther, hoping that Conall will break and that he will finally confess something. The fae is strong, but he won't be for much longer, especially if Achill can keep his smoke magic flooding Conall's thoughts, especially when the fated mate's tether starts to wear thin.

Sooner or later, Conall will be like putty in his hands, spilling secrets about everything. Achill watches dismissively as Conall twitches in his sleep, fighting against the nightmares that plague his dreams.

"I will make sure she comes." Achill bends down and whispers into Conall's ear. "Hide her from me all you want. She will come. And when she does, she won't get away."

He spins on his heel, storming out of the dungeon. He snuffs the fire out from the torches, leaving the wolf shifter to fight off the dream demons in the dark.

Twelve
Sorcha

"A Queen," I exhale, gripping the sword.

I glance at Murdock, and he still frowns at my injured hand. He crosses his arms, nostrils flaring as he breathes. It looks as if he might say something, and instead of waiting to find out what it is, I pivot to the stone throne. There is no portal in the yew tree, only the rough bark and a slight indentation that looks like the hilt of a sword. Had it been there all along?

A rainforest has taken over the dusty hall. Overgrown with vines, birds flit amongst the branches. A lush carpet of moss travels from the large double doors up to the throne's base. Dappled light caresses the stone throne, the quartz in the rock glinting in the soft light like a thousand stars in a cloudy sky.

"You passed your Rites," Thorne's voice echoes from the far end of the hall, and my head swivels back to find feathers floating around them as they shift. Thorne sidles up to Murdock's left and nudges him with their arm. "And it looks as though there was a sword."

"Aye," Murdock says gruffly. His eyes have not left the hilt of the sword the entire time. Finally, he peels his gaze away and meets mine, frowning softly.

I swallow thickly and say nothing, unsure if I want to share anything with them. Do I share about meeting the Goddess? Or even the hagstone and how it fits into the handle. Instead, I'm afraid I'll tell them entirely too much if I tell them anything, and my legitimacy to the throne will be questioned. And then, I will lose everything—and I will lose Conall.

"Are you ready to take the throne?" Thorne's gentle voice cuts through my thoughts. They've stepped closer to me, their fingers grazing my elbow, and give it a quick squeeze.

I nod, and my hands shake, wondering if I can convince the Earth Fae that I am the rightful heir. My fingers glow green, and vines curl from around my fingers, over the hilt of the sword, down its blade, helping lift it with minimal effort. My eyes fill with tears of relief as I watch my earth magic flow through me again. The bargain I made hangs heavy over my head, knowing what I had to give up to have this magic at my fingertips.

"Come, sit," Thorne gestures toward the throne, guiding me up the steps. Tiny flowers and moss unfurl before each step I take.

As I walk across the mossy carpet, I hear the rumblings of stone cracking and the quiet murmuring of voices from the recesses of the shadows. The castle appears as if it has finally woken from its slumber.

Though the castle feels lighter, each step toward the throne is like walking through mud. A pit of uncertainty grows in my stomach, and I'm worried that my subjects will see straight through my deception. At least before all of this, I could have said I was part fae, but now? I am merely a human, again. Yes, with magic, but that is another abomination in its own right. Will my subjects stay loyal to me, a human Queen? Or do I even tell them I am no longer a fae?

A lump forms in my throat. Guilt gnaws on my conscience as I rest the sword against the arm of the throne, my hand resting on top of the sword covered in vines. The yew tree branches reach down to caress my head.

"*Queen,*" a voice whispers, and I startle, looking over my right shoulder. A small, withered face appears in the tree's bark, so subtle that even I almost miss it before it fades back into the trunk of the yew.

The roots groan, and the tree sighs as my body settles into the chair. Did it whisper those exact words when my grandmother sat here? Or her sister, Aerona?

Murdock dips into a low bow. Thorne dips their chin, and Hazel, who has materialized over Thorne's shoulder, sits there beaming at me.

"All Hail, Sorcha, Queen of the Earth Fae!" Murdock chants to the hall.

As his voice resonates through the archways, that quiet murmuring grows soft at first and then an uproar. Doors at the side of the hallway swing open wide, and crowds of fae, both high and wildling, rush through, filling the throne room with cacophonous conversations. Their bodies swarm forward, collecting into the nooks and crannies of the room, pushing forward. All eyes turn to me, the fake halfling sitting on the throne.

I can make out only snippets of conversation, "She looks just like—," and "The prophecy!", "Do you think they know?", "I never thought I'd see the day!"

My hands shake uncontrollably. I clench them into fists and hold them in my lap, seeking Murdock's ocean blue eyes and Thorne's amethyst ones in the sea of fae faces.

Thorne mouths, "*Queen.*"

I clear my throat, pushing down the guilt of claiming a fae throne as a human. The crowd starts murmuring, waiting for me to say something. Everyone is still covered in light dust. They continue to shake their clothing free, but their eyes are glued to me.

I swallow, worried they see right through me; they must know I am not worthy of this throne. Bile rises in my throat, and the last thing I want to do is to lose the contents of my stomach in front of hundreds of fae who just woke up. My free hand flies my mouth as I fight to keep the acid in my stomach, and I stand abruptly. The sword, still wrapped in vines around my fist, I rush through the side doors that lead to my rooms without a glance backward.

The spiral stairs are tight and dizzying; the walls push in on me, and I break out into a cold sweat. I can't stop spinning when I reach my room, so I drop the sword on the floor with a clatter and rush to the balcony edge. I grip the baluster, worried I'll topple over the edge since the world is spinning so tortuously fast, and take lungfuls of air.

I lean down, pressing my forehead to the cool rock, when I hear a rustle of the wind above me. A gentle hand rubs calming circles on my back. The scent of lavender immediately brings my pulse down, and I open my eyes. I turn my head to the side and give Thorne a sad smile.

"I'm sorry," I whisper.

"It's okay, Your Highness." Thorne's soothing voice sends relief cascading over me. I almost cry, but my stomach swirls once more, and I force my breathing to slow again.

"I can't... I can't do it," I stutter. "I can't be their queen."

Thorne continues to rub circles on my back. They say nothing; they stand beside me and look at the land below.

"When I was in the circle, Thorne, I—"

"You don't have to tell me anything," Thorne says, cutting me off. "I can only imagine how you must feel right now."

Slowly, I right myself and face in the same direction as Thorne. The fae lands shimmer with vitality. Hues of vibrant shades of green radiate from below, and the flowers in the gardens below are more colorful, their petals reaching out toward the sun. Even the air feels crisper as it billows around the treetops, pushing them all to wave in tandem at me.

The wind caresses my skin, and a shockwave of power travels up my arms, gooseflesh climbing up my neck. Thorne glances at me, the wind playing in their robes, and they raise their hands.

"It is interesting, isn't it?" Thorne asks.

I can't stop watching the air twist around their fingers. "What?"

"That magic is everywhere; all we have to do is look for it." Thorne looks at my hands, and I hold them up. Many colors swirl at my fingertips: white, blue, green, and red. They quirk a smile, "That's interesting, too."

Is this what trading my fae blood meant?

Thirteen
Sorcha

The coronation.

I want to stand confidently before the fae, but I can't. Despite Murdock announcing that I was ill when I left the throne room, I know the fae aren't entirely convinced I am their rightful heir. How could they be when I ran away from them? When I look nothing like them? When I know that I am no longer fae?

It seems nowhere is safe from prying eyes, and I catch curious stares whenever I wander the halls—several pixies flit by, their arms full of linens and drapery. I sidestep out of their way, anxious to be alone for a few minutes, and slip down a darkened, unused corridor. Cobwebs hang from the ceiling, grabbing at my shoulders and hair. I brush them away as I walk through, carried further down the hallway by the smell of cinnamon and baking bread.

Messing with my hair, making sure the braid covers my ears, my mind wanders to thoughts of Geannie. What would she think about me in my birthright castle? I know that she would not have approved of me running from my commitments, to begin with, but if she had known Achill was a ruthless dictator, a king only in name? I daresay she would have been proud of how I handled everything.

Clanging pots and shouts from someone who must be the cook

echo down the hallway. The sound pulls me even further into the chaos of the castle's enormous kitchens. I round a corner, orange light flickering from the ovens, and the scent of cinnamon and freshly baked bread pulls me closer.

The shouts from the cook increase, and shadows of pixies flying every which way cast shadows along the hallway walls. I keep to the shadows in the doorway and watch the chaos of the kitchens unfold before me. Flour flies everywhere; all manner of fae are elbow-deep in bowls, kneading and mixing and folding bread. Several fire sprites flit back and forth and carry stacks of wood to the large kitchen ovens built into the stone. A few of them make eye contact with me and bow their heads, glancing away as they bustle about their business of keeping the fires going. I make a mental note to ensure they always have dry wood nearby.

The cook's back faces me. Their arms roll out the dough to paper-thin sheets, spreading a mixture of cinnamon, sugar, and butter onto the interior. Bright red hair is pulled tight into a bun and swept out of her face. They work with a fury. A pixie places a bowl of cinnamon-sugar mixture down before them.

"Thank you, dearie," Fern says.

My stomach drops to the floor, and fear claws up my throat as I back away into the shadows before she can see me. I bump into a grain sack near my feet, and it tumbles over, spilling onto the floor in a rush. The seeds cascade over the stones, and the entire kitchen goes silent.

All eyes but Fern's turn on me. Her shoulders sink, and she stops spreading the cinnamon mix onto the dough. Slowly, she wipes her hands on her apron and turns to face me. At first, her eyes shine with hope, then sadness creeps in when she takes in my shocked face.

"Your Highness." She dips into a curtsy.

"I'm sorry," I say, gesturing to the grain. Then I turn and flee back through the hallway. I dart up a stairwell to my right and take the stairs two at a time.

My lungs heave as I pass several landings, but I keep going until I reach the end of the stairs. I push through a heavy oak door at the top. It sticks. Cursing the loss of my fae strength, I shove my shoulder against the wood until it catapults me through. I exit at the top of a tower, cool air licking against my flushed face. The door slams closed behind me. I sink to the floor, winded, and cradle my face.

Fern.

Fern is here in my castle. I should be relieved, and I should be happy to see her. I should have asked her how she escaped Achill's clutches... but then, *did* she escape his clutches?

And if she did, how did she make it here? To the castle? When I find out who let her in, I am going to have—

"Your Highness." Murdock's blue eyes scan my face. "Is everything ok?"

"I'm fine," I say, waving it off. I can't keep running from all of my problems, anyway. "I'll be fine."

"What happened?" He steps closer, crouching down in front of me.

I don't answer, but I close my eyes. The sadness in her eyes was so visceral that it felt like I had let her down and betrayed her to the king instead of the other way around. What in the Goddess does she have to be sad about?

"I saw Fern." I shiver as the chill of the stone wall at my back seeps through my clothes. Did she know what the king had planned for me? Did she know that he wanted to marry me only to honor his blood vow and keep me trapped in the tower for the rest of my life? Did she know that he was going to kill the humans after the Border came down?

Murdock frowns, rubbing his hands together. His purple scales shimmer in the light. "Yes, she offered to take over the kitchens since—"

"She was the one who betrayed me to Achill."

"What?" Murdock sits back on his feet, a frown on his face. "But — "

"She gave the letter meant for my father to *him*. She must have alerted him to my movements and everything. I *watched* Achill burn it in his fingers, Murdock. Fern was working with him this whole time. She had to have known what he had planned for me." The words spill out of my mouth as I frantically try to piece everything together from the night when Achill attacked me.

His blue eyes look off into the distance like he's trying to piece everything together. "If what you say is true, then we have to ask her."

"What if she's a spy? A traitor? Working with Achill?" My heart rate ratchets up once more and I immediately yearn for the heart-call connection with Conall, his calmness, his stoicism. I lean into what I imagine his presence would give me: calm and steady direction. What if Fern is here to uncover all my secrets, just like she did in Achill's castle?

"We don't know, Your Highness. We should ask for her side of the story. She has done good work for the resistance."

My stomach swirls with nerves. "I don't know if I can speak to her. I don't know if I can even look at her without..."

"Och. I have had centuries of practice dealing within the courts," Murdock says. His hand reaches out for mine, and I take it. He squeezes it gently and pulls me up to stand. "I will be there the whole time should things go awry. But, ultimately, these things are better dealt with sooner should there be any issues," Murdock says, grimacing.

"I understand," I say, my voice calm despite my rapid heartbeat. I stand up, walk to the notch in the turret, and look down in the gardens below. From up here, I can almost feel separate from the world I am to rule, from the lies I have to tell to take my throne in Fae. Vines begin to crawl up the sides of the stone, inching their way closer to me. The wind wraps its cool caress around me, pulling me closer to the edge. A few ivy leaves reach my fingers. I stroke their waxy surface, and they lean into my touch like a cat needing affection. The thought of confronting Fern makes me want to run away again. But I know that this time, I can't. It won't do anyone any good to have a traitor amongst us.

"What would you like to do, Your Highness?" Murdock asks. I turn to face him.

I rub my face with my hands and push my hair from my face.

Feeling like a queen for the first time since I chose this path, I say, "Clear out the throne room and bring her before me. I want you there, though."

"Understood, Your Highness." Murdock dips his head and leaves.

I stand there, looking out across the vast landscape before me, long enough for the ivy to take over the turret. The wind ushers in an early autumnal evening, shaking the leaves. It whips at my braid, pulling a few strands from around my face, and I close my eyes. Leaning into the breeze, flashes of Fern replay in my mind. How careful she was when she covered my broken ribs in healing cream, eating with her and the other pixies in my rooms, and then the last few moments I took to speak to her before I ran from the King.

Shaking my head, I steady myself for a confrontation I do not want to have and open the door to the stairwell.

I ENTER THE THRONE ROOM, which is vastly empty compared to the bustle of bodies earlier. Thorne hovers behind me a few paces and then disappears into the shadows, Hazel still content hanging out on their shoulder.

As I near the throne, the yew tree shakes its branches and touches my shoulders, ushering me to sit. I reach out a hand and touch the bark reverently. A low thrumming fills my ears. The tree straightens its branches and settles to watch over the proceedings.

Murdock stands to my right, his hand on the pommel of his sword, and his voice drops an octave. He says, "If it comes out that she betrayed you, I will ensure your word is final."

Power ripples through him, and I can see why he and Conall are brothers. Though Murdock is the light, carefree one to Conall's dark, broody side, he holds secrets of his own that I am just starting to see.

"Thank you, Murdock." I swallow thickly, trepidation closing up my throat. "Let's hope it doesn't come to that."

A pixie escorts Fern to the doors at the end of the throne room.

The scent of cinnamon and bread wafts in with her. It has been twenty years since Geannie's death, and I have to try harder to separate Geannie and Fern, the two people in my life I had the closest contact with, so I don't warp my judgment. I wait until the pixie leaves the room, close the doors behind her, and then find Fern's eyes.

"Your Highness," Fern says, dipping into a low curtsy.

She stays there, waiting for my command, and as tempting as it would be to keep her in that prone position, I wave my hand. "Rise, Fern. Do you know why you've been summoned here?"

"I can imagine, Your Highness," Fern says, eyes downcast.

"Speak freely, then." My voice carries through the hallway, even though I tremble from nerves.

"My hands were tied." Her lips are already trembling. "He left me no choice, Your Highness."

"No choice?" I look at Murdock, who shrugs slightly. He gives me a look that I can only describe as let-her-talk-and-see-if-she-tells-the-truth.

I feel a soft tug on my braid, and Hazel climbs my arm. She sits comfortably on my shoulder, keeping my nerves calm. If anyone can help me decipher if Fern is telling the truth, it's her. I sit a little straighter and wait for Fern to answer.

"He has my sister." She raises her chin, looking me square in the eye. "You know what he is capable of. You all do." Her eyes dart from me to Hazel to Murdock, then back to me again.

"Your sister?" I ask, but then it hits me— the cinnamon, the bread, and the ease with which Fern commanded the kitchens below. "Beatrice is your sister. Oh, Fern. What did he have you do?"

The floodgates open, and she breaks down. Her tears fall freely from her cheeks as she relays the tragic story of how Achill stole her sister's voice with his smoke. He keeps her down in the kitchens, cooking away, and she hasn't seen her family in centuries. There was a time when Fern could sneak Beatrice's family to her after Aerona's death when Achill went into seclusion for several decades. But then Fern was caught, and to pay for her insolence, Achill charred one of Beatrice's hands with his fire magic in front of Fern. Fern was able to restore part of Beatrice's hand, but she lost two fingers, and the skin never fully healed.

As Fern talks, my heart shatters for everything she has witnessed and the games she has had to play.

The hall is deathly quiet as Fern stops talking. She dabs at her eyes with her apron. Her breathing is shaky, but she is calm enough to reveal the events of the night I tried to escape.

"I left through the servant's corridor. It's the only one with a key to your rooms. Before I left, I tucked Lord Conall's sweater in a hole in the wall so the King wouldn't take it."

"How did the sweater get to Conall?" Murdock asks. He then turns to me and whispers, "Conall was wearing it before he left our camp, the night before he left to go get you."

Realization washes over me.

"I knew something was between you when I found his sweater under your pillow. I brought the king the letter you wrote to your father, knowing that if I gave him just enough information, he'd think he'd have the upper hand. While he was distracted, reading the letter to your father, I sent several messages out to the few pixies I could trust. Cherry, Lily, and—"

"Hazel," I say, putting the last pieces together. Fern was a part of the resistance, after all. Hazel snuggles into my side.

Fern nods.

"This explains why Murdock was there when I was semiconscious after the king attacked me and why Hazel was there upon my waking from the stone tomb. But Fern, you betrayed me to the King..."

"Your Majesty, for that, I will eternally regret my choices. I had no knowledge that he would attack you. We all thought you were too valuable for him to do what he did. I am so sorry," she says, pleading in her eyes. "I understand if you no longer trust me."

"Were I to cast you out? Where would you go?"

"I would find my way once again. I wouldn't return to Beatrice's family for fear of the King searching there. I may go back into the mountains and offer my services to the workers in the mines."

"And if I were to find you a place here? Knowing that you could betray my trust once more?"

"Whatever you decide, Your Highness, I will understand."

I look at Murdock and nod. He strides to the door at the far end of the room.

"I need to speak with my counsel and will let you know shortly." I walk down the dais, reaching for Fern's hands. I grasp her weathered hands in mine and look her in the eyes. "Either way, I am sorry for the trials you and your family have gone through with that farce of a king. As your queen, if I decide you can stay, I promise you may always speak freely here and never be held against your will."

Fern's eyes are red-rimmed and bloodshot. Standing close, I can see how much she has weathered in the past year. Deeper lines paint her face, and a few grey streaks are woven in her braids and beard.

"Thank you, Your Majesty." Fern squeezes my hands back, then curtsies and follows Murdock out the door. The scent of cinnamon and yeast hover in the air where she stood, and my heart twists, full of sadness for her and Beatrice.

"Well," I say, turning to the shadows, sensing Thorne lingering behind a tree.

"Well," Thorne echoes and steps from the shadows beneath a bough. Their face is impassive as they regard me.

"Hazel?" I ask, looking at the pixie on my shoulder.

She nods.

"She stays," I say firmly. I cross my arms, half expecting protestations from Thorne. Instead, I am greeted by a soft smile and a nod of approval. I nod back, but inside, I am beaming, feeling triumphant at making the first of many tough decisions as Queen.

Fourteen
Sorcha

Conall lies there in the middle of the stone circle.

Is he sleeping? Or is he just resting?

I take tentative steps toward him lest I wake him when he needs rest.

His bare chest rises and falls with the pattern of a deep sleep.

Moving around the cracked altar stone, I sit quietly beside him and watch him sleep. I brush away some of the hair on his forehead, a tear slipping down my cheek.

His face is scrunched in pain, but he mumbles something.

I lean down to see if I can hear him, and his eyes pop open. He looks straight through me as he screams.

I shoot up, my heart pounding in my chest. A distant rumbling echoes through my room. Sweat covers my body, and the smell of rain and lightning hovers in the air as it flashes across the sky. Shortly after, a resounding boom echoes, shaking the floor of my tower and pulling me from the comfort of my bed. The bed swings with my movement, and I sit there momentarily, wishing to be lulled back to sleep.

But Conall's scream still echoes in my mind. I walk to the open balcony, my skin itching from the electricity hanging in the air.

A light rain falls, and the drops begin their gentle descent onto the stone as if they have purposefully slowed their fall from the sky for my enjoyment. The canopy of the tree in the middle of my room stretches, reaching to cover the expanse of the roofline and shelter my room as the onslaught of the storm begins. Gooseflesh pricks my skin, and lightning streaks across the sky.

I hold my hand out, catching drops in my palm, and they collect in the center. Still cupping my hand, I dip my fingers toward the ground, and the water rolls down my fingertips. I tip my hand back to my chest, and the water coalesces again in my palm, coating my skin with a smooth surface. Never have I seen water move this way before, and I stay there for a few beats, playing with the water on my hands, mesmerized.

Lightning cracks directly overhead, and I jump out of my trance, shaken to the core. My skin erupts in chills, my hair standing on end, and I dart back inside. My clothes are soaked, but when my hands go up to wring out my braid, my hair is dry.

I head to the door, knowing exactly where I must go to figure out why the water is acting differently. At the last minute, I snatch a woolen shawl and wrap it around my shoulders as I open the door and take the stairs at a run, excited to see my old friend.

As the heavy wooden door opens, the rush of cool autumn air pushes the shawl from my shoulders. The storm has abated, floating over the land on the back of a cool breeze. Stepping out into the side garden, the scent of rain-soaked earth and the quiet lull of animals after a storm greets me.

And then I hear a wolf howling.

My pulse thrums in rapid succession, a glimmer of hope that it could be Conall, so I tug on the heart-call; nothing answers back—a sensation I am becoming familiar with.

The muddy earth squelches beneath my bare feet, and I move through the castle grounds to the stone circle. The monoliths stand like quiet giants guarding the path into the forest. I head into the woods, aiming for the last place I saw her before our paths separated. If I could see Opal and know she is okay, I feel all would be right in the world. That there is justice for the good, that everything works out in the end, that she is living a free life, and that her helping me wasn't some horrible mistake.

Crickets chirp occasionally as the wind knocks the canopies together. Cold air wraps around me, and I tug the woolen shawl closer, pulling part of it over my head to stay warm. Despite nothing coming back, I keep sending Conall my thoughts as I tiptoe through the ancient trees.

Dryads peer at me from the shadows, their pinecone eyes watching their Earth Queen closely. Do they know I am no longer a fae?

Will-o'-the-wisps flit in and around the bushes in the distance. I am so tempted to follow their magical flickering through the parts of the forest I have yet unearthed. But my pull to the river is stronger. Soft steps pad behind me, and out of the corner of my eye, a grey wolf lopes through the giant ferns. Could this be one of Conall's brothers?

I take a small game trail down the hill, descending toward the rushing water. Slipping a few times in the mud, I finally reach the river bank. Moonlight reflects off the water in a variegated dance of silver and white. Down in the river valley, sheltered from the wind, the sound of the water cascades over the boulders and fills my ears. It's a welcome distraction from the constant noise inside my head. I dig my toes into the soft sand at the water's edge and sit on a cold rock, aware that the wolf watches me from the ridge.

My mouth opens to call out to the animal, but I stop. If the wolf is one of Conall's brothers, can he sense the fated mate bond and if it is broken?

I hang my head, utter defeat climbing up my throat.

I turn to the water and the reason I came here.

"Opal," I speak to the water, hoping she can hear me. I roll a smooth stone in my left hand, turning it over between my fingers. "I noticed something odd today when the rain fell. It played in my hands. I've never seen water move before. And it made me think of you in the river moments before we separated and how I never got to say goodbye. I never even thanked you. And we may not have spent much time together, but I hope you're well."

And so I talk to her in a calm voice, knowing how shy she is but hoping that this is the river she called home. I share with her what happened after waking up and how I left Conall behind. How angry I am that I can't go after him right now, and everyone keeps holding me back. I tell her how lost I feel and how only a few of my actions feel queenly. And finally, I tell her how much I miss her. My right hand burns from the icy water, so I remove it, tucking it between my legs to warm up.

The grey wolf has taken up his seat across from me, watching me with his head cocked to one side. I swear it knows that Conall being taken captive was my fault. Guilt and anger pulse through me.

"I will fix this," I say to it. I *have* to fix this. "You have my word."

I turn back to the water as the sound shifts, foam rising at the river's edge, and then she appears. This time, she doesn't wear a glamour—her dark green, luminous skin shimmers under the moonlight.

"Nymph," I say, standing. This time, I am not afraid of her. I raise my chin and refuse to dip into a bow. Instead, I meet her pitch-black gaze directly. A queen, on my ancestral land, I greet her as an equal.

"Queen," she whispers from the middle of the rushing river. The water carries her voice into my ear, and I straighten, crossing my arms over my chest. She cannot intimidate me anymore.

The wolf lopes off into the shadows and up the ridge. With each delicate step she takes toward me, the river gurgles at the edge of the banks. Her toes float just above the moss, and the river rushes forward, lifting her higher until her face parallels mine.

"I am calling in my debt," she says.

"Debt?" I ask, and then clarity hits me—the debt I agreed upon when I first looked at her through the hagstone. My shoulders slump slightly, and her eyes mark the movement. I release my arms and hold them stiffly at my sides. "My promise."

She nods and hands me a blade.

"The dagger?" I turn the sharp blade over in my hands; its weight is a familiar feeling in my hand—comforting. I look up, meeting the nymph's black eyes. She regards me impassively. Finally, I say, "But this isn't your river. The other nymph..."

"No, this river belongs to one of my sisters. You have not met her. You met our cousin who lives in the Air Fae lands. My sister hasn't seen these waters in centuries." She takes a tentative step on land. The nymph navigates her way around the rocks, tiny streams from the river trailing in her wake. "This river, and several others, belong to me and my seven sisters."

I turn to follow her pattern, uneasy with her being at my back, and try not to interrupt.

"They've been held against their will at the Smoke King's castle since his coronation." Her eyes flick to mine, watching me for a reaction. She sits on a rock facing me, leans in, and continues, "I want them freed."

Tilting my head, I narrow my eyes. "And?"

"And to do that, you need to kill Achill."

"I'm sorry?"

She smiles a lethal smile, her sharp teeth glinting in the moonlight, "You have to kill Achill. For what he's done to the people of this land, your family, you, and your mate."

"I—" Is Conall even my mate anymore? "But how?"

She raises her hand, gesturing like she's slicing with a blade. "The sword."

"I can barely lift it. Ever since—" I snap my mouth shut before telling her I am human now and that I gave up my fae blood. "Ever since I pulled it from the stone, its weight has been significant."

"It is a symbol," the nymph says, nodding. "An ancient legend foretold of a bearer of a powerful magic, one who can stand at the crossroads of the creatures."

I close my eyes, remembering what the Goddess said. Surely, I am not the one. There has to be something more, someone else? A shiver crawls up my spine and settles over my shoulders. I pull the shawl tighter around my shoulders and ask, "A crossroads?"

"If you take up this mantle, you will need help," the nymph says, refusing to elaborate. She stands on top of the rocks, leaping from one to the other on her tiptoes.

"Killing Achill? Or freeing your sisters?"

"Both." She turns her head toward me and smiles.

"And how do you suggest I do this?"

"You have something that used to belong to us," she says, her eyes flashing with mischief. She leaps, darting across several large rocks on her tiptoes. She reaches down and pulls a rock from the water. In the moonlight, it almost glows from the sheen left by the water. But it is covered in tiny holes carved by the currents of the water over time. She turns it over a few times, playing with the weight. The nymph brings it up to her face, peering through the holes, and then flicks it across the river. It skips seven times and lands on the other side of the bank. "I know where you can find allies who do not challenge the legitimacy of your throne and heritage."

"Challenge my legitimacy?" I find the ends of my hair and twirl them in my fingers. Does she know I am no longer a fae?

"Consider my help as part of your bargain to free my sisters. You need allies to get you into the castle, rescue your mate, and free my sisters. Under the mountain in the land of the dwarves are those who can help you. You must cross into ogre country—but you're familiar with them."

I scoff. "Yes, unfortunately, I am. But, I came here for Opal..."

"She is fine." The nymph waves her hand dismissively. I open my mouth to get more information about Opal, but she cuts me off before I can. "Opal has found her place, happily. Her power is great despite her darker past. With our support, she is embracing her magic. The strongest we have seen in some time."

Relieved, I ask, "And what is your name, Nymph?"

"What makes you think I will eagerly divulge that information to you, Queen?" She tilts her head.

"You know mine; it seems only fair if I am to kill someone that I know whose favor I have earned," I say and pick at my nails nonchalantly.

"Dubessa of the Low Lands." She regards me through slitted eyes and then says, "You know, Queen, that this is the only way."

"To bring about the balance," I say, wishing it wasn't true. But then images of Conall being hurt flare in my mind, and I am full of rage and fire again.

She leans in closer. "You have seen him, haven't you?"

I nod. "I used my hagstone to see through his glamour when he turned his back."

"You know he shouldn't be here. To live for a century after your fated mate has already passed is some dark magic, indeed." She clicks her tongue and shakes her head. The edge of the water foams when she dips her toes into the water, wading into the rapids.

"Wait," I call out. She turns slowly. "Why me?"

"Because," she smiles and looks to the sky. "You are the one who is at the crossroads."

Fifteen
Sorcha

The sword glints in the sunlight, its edges sharp, and its metal shining to perfection despite being stuck in a tree for, Goddess knows, how many centuries. I grunt and try lifting it again. The sweat on my palm makes the hilt slick. I can barely lift the longsword high enough to swing with my one good hand. The cut on my other palm heals slowly despite Thorne's magical tinctures, and I can't help but wonder what their purple eyes saw when they first slathered the cut in balm.

Murdock laughs, twirling his sword effortlessly. "I keep forgetting that you're still half-human."

"Is that how you talk to your Queen?" I ask, skirting around the secret I keep from him. The sun beats down on us, filling the garden with the late summer heat of a sun soon retreating to shorter days. My hair has come undone and sits plastered on my damp skin. I stab the sword into the ground to plait my hair carefully over my now-human ears. "As much as I would love to be able to master this sword, I would much rather learn about magic."

"Aye, a longsword is a different beast in combat," Murdock says, switching his sword to the opposite hand. He twirls it in his right hand and makes an arch in the air before sliding it into his scabbard. Then he flashes me a cheeky smile and bows. "The Queen wishes to battle with magic? I am merely a humble servant."

"I do." I flash a mischievous smile as vines crawl silently behind him from underneath the foliage. I gesture to the sword, hoping to distract him from the vines that almost touch his feet. "After all, if this sword is for unity, then why on earth am I learning to fight with it?"

"The real question is, why, after centuries upon centuries of rites, are you the one who could see the sword and pull it free from the stone?" Murdock's hands spin orbs of water in midair.

That question stumps me. After all of this time, why me? I exhale and focus on the vines wrapping around Murdock's ankles. He grunts in surprise when the vines snap him up and hang him upside down. At the same time, he throws his orb of water at me, drenching me in the face.

I would be lying if the cool water wasn't welcome at that moment.

"I don't know, Murdock. Why me, indeed."

He readies another orb of water, and I flick my wrist. The vines drop him with a thump, and his orb of water collapses on top of him.

"You're going easy on me," I laugh. "I thought you were a seasoned warrior like Conall?"

Murdock sits up, wiping his face. He shrugs and says, "Och, I grew up quite differently than Conall. Peace was always the aim of my people. I learned to fight after my Rites, much to the detriment of my family."

"Who is your family?" I ask and place my hands on my hips.

But Murdock doesn't answer; he is already on his feet and readying his magic again. This time, two water orbs materialize above his palms in a swirling liquid mass. I back away slowly, my magic calling the vines to gather behind me.

A vine whips out and tries to grab Murdock's foot, but he side-steps. His eyes laser focus on my hands, watching the green shimmer with a bit of blue. He squints and asks, "When you think about your magic, what do you feel?"

"I feel alive. I feel strong." I flick my fingers, and he dodges the next vine. He throws an orb at me in the blink of an eye, but I throw my hand up and block it with water that pours from my hand.

I drop my arms, stunned. Was this why the water danced on my skin last night?

Murdock's jaw drops, but he closes it quickly. His orb dissolves.

"Och, that was interesting," he says, lifting his chin toward my hands.

I lift my hands to my face, awestruck, as blue and green swirl around my fingertips. And then I get an idea. I flick the fingers on my right hand, vines hover over my shoulder, and then I flick the fingers on my left hand. But nothing happens. I flick them again— still, nothing.

"Now that is interesting," Thorne says, feathers flying as they step from underneath a tree limb. "Water and earth."

"Water..." Murdock mumbles.

"And earth," I finish, still staring at my left hand, trying to get water to materialize from my hand. "But the water isn't working now?"

I shake my hand a few times. The blue disappears, leaving only the green shimmers.

Murdock flexes his fingers. "Let's try something. Do you trust me?"

"Yes," I say, still distracted.

"Good. Look up, Sorcha."

A wall of water heads toward me, and I throw my hands up to block but get drenched from the side. Shocked, I shake my head and look to my right, where the water came from. Another Murdock regards me casually.

"There are two of you?" I look straight ahead to the first Murdock and then back to the Murdock at my right. Another blast of water heads straight for me, and I shoot my hands up, a wall of vines blocking the water from landing.

"Good!" Thorne shouts from the sidelines. They poke their head around the large trunk of a tree.

"Chicken," both Murdocks laugh. They throw a stream of water at Thorne and then turn to me, and another blast of water pours in my direction. Thorne squawks and dives behind the tree as a fountain of water explodes against the trunk. I dodge Murdock's magic and run at the Murdock in front of me, throwing my hands forward. If I can contain one Murdock, I can deal with the other. Vines cascade around me, and the Murdock I was running toward dissipates as soon as the vines begin to weave a cage around him.

I stop short and look back at the real Murdock, who is cackling so hard he's bent over, bracing himself on his knees. When he sees me looking, he straightens up and clears his throat. Though his face is beet-red from laughing, he is calm as he pointedly says, "You use too much logic."

"And how do you know that?" I turn toward him and cross my arms.

Murdock holds up his hands in surrender and opens his mouth.

Thorne timidly looks around the tree, cutting him off before he can speak. "There's nothing wrong with logic, Your Highness, but magic is more about the feel than anything else."

"But I had the vines," I say, almost wanting to protest that I was doing everything right. If I was, though, why didn't the water return?

Thorne joins me as I sit in the shade of a large tree. I am soaked through and wring out my braid, tossing it back over my shoulder. I squeeze out the excess water by gathering up the hem of my shirt. It drips toward the grass. Maybe I'm too tired, but I swear the drops hover briefly before landing by my feet.

"You hesitated," Murdock says. "Your vines were too slow, exposing your back to the real me. The illusion Murdock was just there to show you what certain water fae can do to fend off natural predators. For mershifters, we use it underwater when sharks or human ships are nearby."

"Like a magical defense mechanism. That's genius." I look back at where the illusion of Murdock once was. A giant puddle of water seeps into the grass.

Thorne shakes the water from their robes, swirling a small gust of air around their sleeves to dry themselves off. The breeze brushes up against my skin, drying some of my shirt. "Yes, but someone could have easily taken advantage of your weakness. You cannot heal quickly like a full-fae."

I nod, wondering if Thorne knows I am no longer a half-halfing. I glance at them out of the corner of my eyes, but nothing in their face gives them away. "So I should keep my back protected at all times."

"Hopefully, you won't have to because either Thorne or I will be there," Murdock says firmly. Then he adds quietly, "That is if Conall can't be."

The words slam into my chest.

If Conall can't be.

Certainly, Murdock doesn't think I am incapable of getting Conall back. Does he? A wave of guilt washes over me as if these past few moments have meant I completely forgot about Conall and that he's still captive. I tug on where the heart-call used to sit, feeling nothing in return. What does it mean for a fae to lose a mate before sealing the bond? In what world is it fair that the Goddess forces these choices on her creations? Your fate is tied up with whether or not you have a partner.

I close my eyes and rest my forehead on my knees. How am I supposed to return the balance to Fae when I can't even bring the balance back into my life? I ran away from becoming a queen. And now Murdock thinks I'll never get Conall back?

At this point, the possibility of failure feels inevitable, and a part of me wishes I had never run from the king, to begin with. I should have gone along with everything like the good little girl my father tried to raise.

"What is it, Your Highness?" Thorne nudges my shoulder.

The fear sits in the center of my chest, and I rub at it absently.

I shake my head and stare into the distance, silently refusing to back down to the tiny voice of doubt that keeps creeping in.

I may have made these choices out of fear, but I will not let that fear win.

And I'll be damned if anyone keeps me from Conall.

"I'm just remembering the conversation I had with a water nymph," I say, trying to sound nonchalant.

Murdock crosses his arms and regards me thoughtfully. Along the curve of his neck, purple scales glint in the sunlight. "Crafty creatures, those nymphs."

"Yes, they are. What do you know about them, mershifter?" I flash Murdock a bright smile in return and hope that my charm gets some answers from him.

He flushes, and his face and neck turn bright red. Murdock clears his throat, holding up his fingers to count as he says, "Well, ahem, for one, their magic is potent, Your Highness. Second, their wit is as sharp as a blade. If you ever encounter one, tread lightly. Third, they choose to wear a glamour with everyone unless you've earned their respect or your offering appeased them. "

I laugh at his last words. "Oh, so I suppose Conall never told you?"

"Told me what?" he asks, tilting his head.

"I have encountered a nymph before," I say. Murdock winces, but I press on, "And I may have promised her something I shouldn't have." What I don't tell him is that I promised her a debt owed after looking through my hagstone that Conall expressly forbade me to do, especially since I hadn't done anything to earn the trust of the local fae.

"Och," Murdock groans, rubbing his face, "You didn't."

"I did." I cringe. "All will be well once I free her sisters."

"Pardon?" Thorne and Murdock say together.

"Yes, but to do *that*, I must go to the dwarf country. There, I will find my allies, who will hopefully help me sneak into Achill's castle, free the Sisters, and get Conall back. It is too easy." I try to keep a smile on my lips, knowing I chose not to tell Murdock the most essential part of the bargain with the nymph. Out of the corner of my eye, the sword glints in the sun, almost twinkling at me as if it knows what's in store.

"Is that all?" Thorne snickers. "Just a light jaunt up to the dwarf country, eh?"

"Don't get any ideas, Thorne. The last time *you* went to Dwarf country, it took a good century for him to forget about you." Murdock grumbles and jabs a finger at Thorne. "I did my time there, cleaning up your mess. No thanks to you. I hate being under the mountain."

My eyes dart from Murdock back to Thorne. I snicker a bit.

"And I thanked you a thousand times for helping me with that." Thorne smiles wide at Murdock and turns their purple eyes to me. I raise my eyebrows. They shrug, adding, "I may have left too good of an impression on a certain dwarf royal a few hundred years ago. Thankfully, it was a long time ago, and I will stay here while you two go."

Murdock guffaws and throws his hands up in the air. "Me? What did I do?"

"You're better equipped to handle their testy behavior, Merman. As if I would go back there and risk upsetting them." Thorne scoffs and turns to me, their eyes smiling. They wink before turning back to Murdock and giving him a leveling stare. "You think me being there would go over well? Especially if you're supposed to be gathering allies?"

Murdock looks up at the sky and groans, then rubs a hand down his face. "Aye. As always, you're right. Your Highness, allow me to be your official escort into Dwarf country."

"You say that like it's a bad thing. Grindel, the purveyor of the Land's End Inn, seemed jovial enough. Fern was... well, Fern was kind enough. Surely, heading into their lands shouldn't be too treacherous?"

"I'm not worried about the dwarves but the ogres who have moved into the areas surrounding their lands."

I wave my hand dismissively. "Ah, yes, ogres. I'm familiar."

"Och! What else has no one told me?" Murdock looks from Thorne to me and back to Thorne, who is smiling again. "When did you encounter ogres?"

"Twice," I add, stifling a laugh as Murdock's face goes from shock to horror. Now that I have my earth magic back, my fear of the ogres has abated. I remember clearly the vines under my control, dismembering each of them around the campfire after I escaped from Achill. Remembering each moment is like reliving a fever dream. How could I, a tiny halfling, kill three ogres with the power of my earth magic? "Once on the way to Achill's castle and again as I fled that same castle."

"She handled herself remarkably—"

I cut Thorne off before they try to inflate my ego even more. "Thorne is neglecting to tell you that I called forth some earth magic that killed the ogres the second time I encountered them. The first time, well…"

"Conall." Murdock nods. "Yes, he's a history with them."

"He does?" I ask.

Did he ever mention that? It would explain why he was so upset when I took off on Gealaich and headed straight into Ogre territory. He fought against our interaction; every touch and word between us was carefully constructed. Conall fought with his baser nature until the moment we parted.

That entire time, he was afraid of losing me.

Happiness blooms in my chest to know that he felt the same way. And my tiny flame of hope flares up again despite being unable to feel the heart-call, that he still might feel the same way—that he will choose to be with me despite me no longer being fae. Maybe, just maybe, he can hold on a little longer since we're no longer fae mates.

Thorne's voice cuts into my thoughts. "When do you leave for the dwarf country?"

"As soon as possible," I lift my chin, calm settling in my bones.

It's time for me to choose to be a queen.

Thorne nods. "As you wish, Your Highness. Oh, and try to keep him from losing his temper under there."

I look at Murdock's receding figure. "Him?"

Thorne laughs. "Just do not let him drink the whisky."

"I'll make sure he behaves." I flash Thorne a distracted smile, my thoughts still spinning. All I have to do is get Conall back, rescue the nymph's sisters, and kill the king. Easy.

Murdock grumbles something as he walks away.

"What?" I shout at his back.

"I said, *fucking dwarves*," he yells back at us over his shoulder.

Thorne leans down to whisper conspiratorially into my ear, "I think you'll finally get to travel by portal."

Sixteen
Achill

Achill walks the halls of his castle, throwing his smoke magic around like a ball and watching it smash into the walls, disintegrating into the air as he passes. He mulls over Conall's refusal to speak - the stubbornness, the quiet resolve, and how he refuses to betray his fated mate. The loneliness wears him down. And it rankles him to no end like he's been missing a limb for a century. But which limb? He wouldn't be able to tell you now. Some days, it feels like he's missing his arm - annoying but manageable. On other days, it feels like his entire heart collapses inside his chest, like he can't take another step without crumbling to the floor because of how much he misses Aerona.

But it's been slightly more tolerable since the wolf shifter is in the dungeon because if anyone can share how Achill has felt for the past century, it's Conall.

The castle is quiet since his servants started fleeing once Sorcha woke. He still does not know *how* she woke. If he had his way, she should have slept for a hundred years, and right now, he would be the sole ruler of Fae.

And yet somehow she woke, and when she woke, not only did it threaten his rule as king, but she took his servants, too. Feet slapping on stone breaks Achill out of his thoughts, and he sees Rhys, his ever-loyal Fae guard, headed his way.

"Your Highness," Rhys heaves, out of breath and frantic.

"Out with it, you ran all this way," Achill says. He waves his hand dismissively, assuming it's some trivial castle business about more fae leaving or another pixie spreading information to the resistance fighters.

"She is Queen of the Earth Fae," Rhys stammers and closes his eyes, bracing himself against the onslaught of fire magic.

But nothing happens.

Achill is too stunned to speak.

How could she be Queen of the Earth Fae? For any fae to earn their title to rule, they must pass their rites. You can't pass your rites unless you have fae blood.

The color drains from his face.

Unless you have fae blood.

When she wore her hair down like he liked it, was it pure coincidence that it reminded him so strongly of Aerona? Memories swirl and details are fuzzy, but he supposes there is a bit of resemblance.

Aerona didn't have any children he knew of, so… who? It wasn't long after Cariad disappeared that the Deoir royals passed, so Aerona and Cariad couldn't have any siblings.

Which leaves Cariad. But how? She was long gone before Aerona and Achill married. He can barely remember what she looked like, having never met her. He waves his hand, dismissing Rhys, who leaves him in the hallway. Once out of sight, Achill pivots on his heel and runs toward the Royal Library.

There is one book that can tell him everything he needs to know, and it has been in the library for generations. He opens the doors, rushes up the spiral staircase, and runs to the shelves where the book rests. His eyes scan book after book, looking for *Fae Ancestral Lines.*

But it's gone.

He roars and shoves the shelves as flames shoot from his hands. Fire licks at the wood and parchment as the bookcases topple over, knocking into each other and cascading down toward the far wall. Books tumble, pages go flying, and catch the flames as they descend to the main floor. The entire upper level of the library roars with flames, and Achill stands there, watching the fire burn away his history.

Seventeen
Sorcha

The edge of another burned forest comes into view, rippling at the edges like waves lapping on the banks. Murdock takes my hand, and he steps through quickly. I lift my leg, and the air rushes out of my lungs, squeezing my muscles like I'm being pulled underwater. Murdock tugs, and I lurch forward, finally reaching the other side.

It's eerily quiet, and I jump when a few dead trees creak and knock together. The portal snaps closed behind us, pulling a few strands of my hair from its plaiting.

I lean over and retch all the contents of my stomach out. My head throbs violently, and I know that my body would not react so strongly if I still had fae blood. Murdock watches me closely, concern on his face. He takes a step closer, but I hold out a hand, worried he will ask a question I don't want to answer. I keep my arm outstretched, keeping him at bay until I am finished throwing up.

Finally, my stomach calms. I quickly adjust my hair to cover up my ears. The world still spins tortuously, but at least the throbbing in my head eases the more fresh air I breathe.

I turn to Murdock, but he holds a finger up to his lips and scans the standing deadwood. He waits a few moments, then glances back at me, gesturing to his left. I give him a slight nod and follow in his wake. We skirt down along the edge of the burn scar, keeping to the green grass so we don't leave footprints.

The mountains loom above us; their peaks are craggy and sharp, covered in year-round snow. The wind whips at the tips, washing the sky with wisps of white. A cool breeze cascades down and blows the hair from my ears, pulling strands free from my braid. I know we're being watched, the entire landscape full of eyes that miss nothing as we make our way further north into the foothills of the mountains. The forested terrain blends into shale that sloughs off after every step. A barely noticeable footpath leads us to the mouth of a slot canyon.

Murdock stops. I draw up close to him, not wanting to be this exposed on the side of a mountain in Ogre territory.

He leans toward me, his strawberry blonde braids brushing my shoulder, and whispers, "Ogres are too large to fit through this slot canyon. This should take us to the entrance to the dwarf kingdom. This doesn't mean this canyon is safe. We're lucky it's a dry day, and no rain is on the horizon. You will need to stay close. Good thing you're still fae because you'll need the agility." He winks at me and turns to climb down to the canyon's floor. He lands with a grunt and then asks, "Ready?"

My pulse thunders in my ears, and I swallow thickly. His blonde head is no longer visible below the cliff face.

"Ready," I whisper to myself.

Surely, this would be much easier if I were fae and not terrified of falling. My fingertips vibrate with green, and I sit down at the lip of the rock, ready to use my earth magic to help me down. My feet dangle over the ledge, and Murdock grabs them to help ease me down. We inch through the canyon like this, climbing down and through stone walls woven together so tightly that we must turn sideways to fit. Other times, we're scrambling up over slick rock. A few times, I slip, and Murdock's hand snaps out and grabs my forearm to keep me from falling. His reflexes are much faster than my magic.

Now and then, I swear his eyes are on me. Does he wonder why I am so slow or clumsy? With each silent moment between us,

I worry he has already figured out that I am no longer of fae blood.

We finally make it through, cresting over a few large boulders to stand at the edge of a clearing. The large rocks lie haphazardly in front of an enormous stone slab with elaborate carvings of axes and picks crisscrossing the surface. It looks like a door, but there are no handles or windows.

I step forward, but Murdock's hand is on my forearm, halting me in my tracks.

"Before we go further, Your Majesty, you should know a few things about Dwarven politics."

Sweat drips from my forehead and cheek, and I wipe my face off on my shirt. Exhaustion pulls me down, and as much as I want to collapse on the dirt and pout, I refuse to give in. Instead, my tiredness churns into irritation, and my skin crawls. I squeeze my shoulders up to my ears and release, but the agitation stays like a sticky substance at the back of my head. Though I know I won't get a response, I tug on the heart-call again.

Nothing.

I scoff, knowing that my irritation and exhaustion are now centered on Murdock. "You think *now* is the time to do this, Murdock?"

His eyes flash to mine, and then he looks down at his feet.

I add, a little too snippy, "I would've thought there would have been a lesson or two while we were clambering up rocks."

He opens his mouth and then shuts it, face flushing.

"Fine. What do I need to know?" I snap, exhaustion curling itself around my muscles. Ancient Fae carvings line the outer edge, looking similar to the etchings on the castle walls in the garden. Try as I might, though, I can't read them. My entire body is coiled tight after the multiple reminders that I chose this and that I bargained away my fae.

Murdock steps closer to me.

I step away, but he grabs my wrist and keeps me in place. He leans down slowly and whispers into my ear, "They are watching, so everything you do from here on out is on display."

"Noted," I say through gritted teeth. I try to tug my hand away, not wanting to be consoled by anyone but Conall. "Continue."

"They are quick to temper with those they are unfamiliar with."

The earth rumbles beneath our feet, and despite my annoyance at him, I grab Murdock's hand, gripping so hard I turn his fingertips white.

"And, third," he says into my ear, the rumbling of the earth shakes the rocks from the mountain high above us. "If we get lost in these tunnels, and we piss off the wrong dwarf, we will never get out of here alive."

We slide backward as rocks tumble from the mountainside on our left. There is a scraping sound, and the stone doors push outward as a low hum echoes inside the mountain.

I can only watch in awe as two tiny dwarves open the gigantic stones.

"I think you also forgot to mention how strong they are," I whisper, holding Murdock's hand tightly.

He leans into my shoulder, whispering, "Sorry, Your Majesty. They are mighty strong."

I glance at him, and his mouth curves into a cheeky smile. Something about the look on his face makes me chuckle, and my irritability lessens. He squeezes my hand and subtly dips his chin.

The stone doors stop halfway open, and the singing drones behind the two dwarves as if they carry the notes on their backs like a cloak of mystery. From the darkened depths, another dwarf emerges. He wears a belt adorned with tools of all kinds, and atop his flaming red head of hair, he wears a simple golden crown.

"Your Majesty," the dwarf booms. "We've been waiting for you."

The dwarf stops a few yards away, eyes flicking to my hand in Murdock's. I immediately let go. Murdock steps in front of me, dipping his chin to the dwarf.

Murdock steps aside, sweeping his arm wide toward me. "May I present Sorcha Salonen, Queen of the Earth Fae."

"Your Highness," I say and step forward, reaching to shake the Dwarf King's hand.

He takes mine in his rough, callused grip. And though he is shorter than me, his hand still engulfs mine. The Dwarf King shakes my hand vigorously my arm feels like jelly when he finally releases me. "I know who she is, mershifter. It's a pleasure to meet you, Your Majesty, and I would love to stay for more pleasantries in these ogre-infested lands, but I hear we are on a tight schedule. Now, if you will, please follow me."

Without so much as a look backward, the dwarf spins on his heel and heads inside. Murdock closes on my left side, and the stone doors close behind us.

Pitch black envelops my senses; darkness presses in around me. The air, though chilly, is suffocating. No sounds echo now, not the song from earlier, nor even the shuffling of feet. Only the thrumming of my heart fills my ears.

I close my eyes against the press of invisible walls, but despite my best efforts, my chest tightens, and my pulse races. Earth magic tingles in my fingertips, the only indication of light. I take a half-step backward and bump into Murdock's broad chest.

"Easy, Your Highness," Murdock whispers. "I'm right here with you."

But it doesn't calm me.

The dwarf sounds from somewhere in front of us. "Let's get some light in this place, eh, laddies?"

Grunts of agreement and a whoosh of warm air push forward in the black as torches flare to life. Within seconds, the tunnel lights up with flame, and the chill is replaced with warmth—the last traces of my breath mist the air in front of me. I step away from Murdock and find myself pulled down a side tunnel by the shimmering veins of gold and silver. Glittering pathways mesmerize me further into the darkened cavern.

Murdock grabs my arm, and the Dwarf King's voice cuts the air. "Careful, Your Majesty."

I jump, the trance broken.

Several dwarves look back at me as Murdock pulls me back into the torchlight.

"I wouldn't go down any of these tunnels without us," the dwarf says, jutting his chin to where I once stood.

"Thank you," I say and withdraw my hand, keeping it at my side. "But how do I know to trust any of you without a name to your face?"

The dwarf looks me up and down, a smile splitting his face. "Well, Your Majesty, some on the outside call me Your Highness or Maolchluiche, but down here, you can call me Maol."

Being under several thousand tonnes of solid rock makes me antsy, and my skin crawls with the agitation. It takes everything I have to keep the memories of crawling away from Achill and leaving Conall behind at bay. I know I need to be down here, but my body wants to turn around and run.

The king's voice is soothing, and he steps close to me. He must sense my apprehension as he says, "I have several fae eager to meet you. I need you to put one foot before the other because we have a long walk until we get where we need to be."

Maol takes a long look at me, and he breathes deeply, gesturing for me to do the same. I mirror his breathing, inhaling deeply like Geannie had taught me to keep my anxiety manageable all those years ago. My hands shake, a warning of an impending panic creeping in, so I clench them at my sides instead.

Maol walks in front, followed by another dwarf—two others who stay close behind Murdock and myself.

"Come," Maol says lightly. "We won't eat you."

"Not yet," a dwarf says behind me, earning a few chuckles from his comrades.

Murdock glances at me out of the corner of his eye, and we follow the dwarves into the belly of the mountain.

MORE LIGHT FILTERS through the end of the tunnel up ahead. Varying songs lilt through the tunnels, harmonizing together in their resonating echoes. The clanging of metal hitting rock and the occasional drop of water seeping through the ceiling of the passage adds to the chorus of voices.

Murdock, walking close behind my right shoulder, leans in. "Have you ever heard of the legend of the Tommyknockers?"

"The who?" I ask, still entranced by the gold and silver veins that dance along the slate-grey walls. But I don't touch them; I keep my hands stiffly at my sides.

"Tommyknockers beckon the dwarves into the darkest regions of the mountains to find the richest veins of gold and silver. If not treated well, they can be mischievous, hiding your things throughout the thousands of mazes that are now abandoned."

"They sound like house brownies," I muse, curious if the shadows that dance along the walls house these little creatures. Without my hagstone around my neck, I cannot see through glamours.

"Aye, the Knockers are some of the most helpful creatures we have here in the mountain," says Maol. He glances back at us. "Just leave some food for them and keep your valuables close."

"They are definitely brownies," I smile at Maol's back, happy that these little creatures are also taken care of here.

My hands instinctively slide to the sword on my hips and the dagger on my thigh. I am relieved that no Tommyknockers have taken them.

The chanting grows louder, and we come to an enormous cavern with branches of tunnels traveling in six different directions. Some of the gold travels down a few tunnels to the left; silver veins creep along the walls to the tunnels on the right. The tunnel in the middle is pitch black, and this is where Maol leads us. I hesitate, the yawning entrance of the tunnel swallowing his form as he leaves me standing in the center of the cave.

"Come on, Queen!" His voice echoes in his wake.

I run to keep up, Murdock close at my heels. The other dwarves have left, descending into other tunnels, leaving us alone with their leader.

We walk for a few feet until an enormous quarry opens before us. Large chunks of the rock have been chipped away through the centuries, and elaborate staircases and bridges crisscross in the bowels of the mine, some bridges suspended thousands of feet in the air.

Maol stops at the lip of a cliff. A set of stairs clings to the side of the wall, traveling up to a labyrinth of more stairs at the top of the quarry. Another set of stairs carves its way down to the bottom of the quarry, clinging to the edge of the rock.

"No handrail," I whisper to Murdock. His face is ashen, and he nods back, his throat bobbing as he swallows slowly.

Singing rings out in a gorgeous call-and-response rhythm. Dwarves are busy hacking away at the stone. Their bodies look like ants besides the gigantic blocks they've carved out. Metal clanging against stone rings out in time to the echoed songs they sing. Tears well in my eyes as I have never heard such a melodic cacophony of voices before.

Maol heads down the stairs, and I sigh, grateful we don't have to travel up to get where we're going.

Murdock gives me a tight smile and places his hand along the curve of the wall. I carefully place my feet on the small steps that will take us to the base of the mountain, and my knees almost give out. My thighs shake, and I lean my shoulder against the solid earth as I slide my body in tandem with my wobbly legs.

Down, down, down, we walk toward a collection of small buildings at the bottom. The slate grey stone fades to white marble and back to light grey quartz, and I trail my fingers along the cool surface. We walk in silence, listening to the dwarves singing as they work.

Soon, we reach the bottom.

"Aye, it's a sight, isn't it, Your Majesty?" Maol says, a weight to his voice. His face has changed, eyes going wide, and the corners of his mouth creased into a smile. He takes in the spirals and the bridges, and I realize it is a look of admiration. "My people have always been amazing crafters, but nothing amazes me like that."

I tilt my head back, staring up at the empty stomach of this enormous mountain. The carved bridges and stairs make a constellation of patterns that dance across the open air like delicate spirals. Awe fills my body with every detail before me. "It is pure wonderment."

"Is that water, I hear?" Murdock's strained voice comes from behind me. His face is still stone-grey ash, and his usually bright blue eyes are dim.

A sheen of sweat covers his skin, and I silently mouth, *"Are you okay?"*

He gives me the slightest head nod, but I can tell his hands are trembling.

"It is, mershifter," Maol says, a twinkle in his eye. "We added a few features since your last visit. This way."

Murdock gives the king a tight smile.

Maol takes us through the lower buildings, waving at a few dwarves who whittle away at chunks of rocks, freeing precious gemstones in their raw form. Amethyst, emerald, and sapphire line the worktables strewn with the tools used to shape and hewn.

The dwarves don't look up from their practice as we pass, either unaware that we are in their presence or so involved in their work that they can't be bothered, and for that, I am relieved.

Maol opens a wooden door behind one stall and takes off his boots. He stacks them on a rack near the door, then looks pointedly at us.

We hurry to unlace our boots and stack them by Maol's before he opens another door that leads into a well-lit hallway. Thick wooden doors line each side, and a lush rug travels across the entire expanse.

Maol holds the door open, pointing at one door. "Your rooms are here, merman." Maol points to the one next to Murdock's. "And, Your Highness, this one is yours. Should you need anything, ring the bell-pull inside your room."

Murdock and I step onto the plush rug, the heavy door to the mine closing quietly behind us. I wiggle my toes in the fibers, reveling in the carpet's plushness.

"Your people are waiting for you," Maol says, pointing to the door at the end of the hallway.

"Thank you." I smile down at him and nod to the door. "Will you be joining us?"

"No. But should you need anything, ask for me, and someone will find me." Maol dips his head and quickly returns to the mines.

Murdock and I take lock gazes. With a subtle nod of my head, he reaches for the handle. My heart beats like a war drum at my first test as Queen of the Earth Fae—meeting unknown allies who want to bring down a king.

Murdock turns the handle and pushes the door open. Warm air surrounds us, and an extravagant room lies beyond.

If we hadn't descended several stories into a quarry, I would not know we are underneath hundreds of tons of earth. Quartz columns carved several stories high support an arched ceiling. Torches burn along the outer walls, warming the space to a pleasant temperature and casting shadows along the carvings. Even more light filters through open windows carved high into the walls on one side of the room. Thick vines weave down from the ledges, crawling from outside and wrapping their tendrils down to the base of each column. Birds fly about, perching on nests built into tiny holes in the rock high above us. Along the far wall, a large fountain cascades into a pool that leads to an underground river, and carved water nymphs and merfolk hold shells that catch the crystal-clear water, splashing onto stones covered in moss at the pool's edge.

A stone table carved from the earth is in the center of the room, situated perfectly between the rows of columns. Several fae sit around the table, but they have stopped mid-conversation, and their eyes are fixated on Murdock and me.

Only one set of eyes bores into me amongst the rest of the creatures.

The words squeak out from between my lips, "Father?"

Eighteen
Sorcha

"Sorcha." My father's voice resonates against the stone, and suddenly, I am the small child curled up on his floor reading late at night. He stands up, eyes locked on me, and a smile spreads. The corners of his eyes crinkle, and his smile grows wider. "It is nice to know that the rumors are true."

Stiff from shock, I step forward as he comes from around the table. Though he opens his arms up for an embrace, I have to force myself to meet him as regally as I can despite my craving to collapse into his comforting embrace.

I stammer, breathless, "H-h-how are you here?"

"The wards have weakened?" He shrugs, and I let him pull me into an embrace. I am surrounded by his powerful arms and the scent of old leather.

Suddenly, I am eight years old again, building a fort within the hedges of the royal gardens. I ran away from Geannie and my maths tutor and ended up in the library. Geannie would have a fit if I tore another hole in my fancy dress, so I discarded my outer garments quickly and fled to the gardens. I wandered around in the labyrinthine bushes, plucking flowers along my way, weaving a crown with their blossoms until I found my hideaway hole. Inside the hedges were my favorite things - a hairbrush I pretended was a dagger, colorful stones I used as coins, a feather wand, and a snail's shell that was a fairy's teacup. All pieces of the world that I imagined existed beyond the Border. I sat there for hours, covered in mud, my undergarments snagging on the branches, as I pretended I was part of the mysterious fae creatures. But I wasn't their queen; I was some wild thing instead.

I didn't realize I was hungry or that the sky had turned from a light blue to a burnt orange until my father called for me. Crawling back out of the hedge, I took one last look behind at my secret home, not knowing that would be the last time I would ever see that place. I rounded a corner, and my father stopped in his tracks. When he saw me, worry, fear, and anger flashed across his face. He scooped me up in his arms and squeezed me so hard that I couldn't breathe, then whispered into my hair, "Oh, I am *so* relieved to see you."

He wouldn't put me down until we were well inside the castle. That night, I got to dine with him in his study, staying up too late to take a bath, and I fell asleep on his lap as we read on the sheepskin rug. Father then scooped me up and carried me to my room. In my half-asleep haze, I thought this was the safest I would ever be. I felt so guilty about hiding away and causing him to worry that I vowed silently never to return to my hideaway.

A part of me still yearns to close my eyes and be back in his study, hiding and running from my responsibilities and countless expectations. He pulls me into another hug, rubbing my back like he used to when I was a child. My entire body relaxes, and I have to fight the urge to break down in front of all these strangers. How welcome his comfort is to the small child inside me.

As if he knows my thoughts, he whispers into my hair, "I am *so* relieved to see you."

I turn my head to look up at him, eyes laced with tears. I can see the tips of his slightly pointed ears through the gaps in his braids. I reach up, pull his hair away, and frown. "How did I never notice this before?"

Father clears his throat and glances around the room before he says softly, "I had to hide it my entire life. Even from you, my child."

The firelight catches in his blond hair, and the glint is so subtle I almost miss it, but grey strands weave through his braids, and he suddenly looks so much older than I remember. Fine lines at the corner of his eyes and mouth have etched deeper into his skin. And, though he still towers over me, his shoulders have rounded slightly. There is a slight hunch to his posture as if the secrets he had to keep for decades were worn on his shoulders.

He clasps my hands in his, and they are covered in sunspots and blue veins that map out the grief and worry that plague him. Could he have foreseen that all his work toward everlasting peace would slip through his fingers when I chose to run from my responsibilities?

Finally, he pulls away and gives me a tight smile. A pained look dances in his eyes, but then his diplomatic mask falls back into place.

Father says loud enough for everyone to hear, "I am here because I need reinforcements."

He gives me another quick squeeze before letting go, the space between us coated in bittersweetness as I finally see my father again, but in front of people I have never met.

"What kinds of reinforcements do you need? Forgive me; I am just now catching up on what I've missed this past year." I try my best to regain my composure, glancing around the room. Several figures shift in their seats to get a better look at me, drawing my attention away from my father.

And then I meet the eyes of a half-ogre, half-water nymph.

Opal flashes me a toothy grin, and I return her smile with earnestness, thrilled to see her.

"I knew..." Father begins, his voice wavering. I wonder how much more worry I caused him when I shirked the peace treaty. "I knew that something happened to you as soon as I could get messages across. There was no announcement of marriage, and there was no correspondence from you for months. The king communicated frequently, detailing all the time you spent together. But then, the wards never dropped. And then the attacks increased."

"Attacks?" I ask, noting there have been more.

He nods. "At first, we thought they were just rebel fae, wanting to stir up discontent between our lands. But the kingdom wasn't entirely unprepared. I had been stockpiling certain weapons in case things went awry during the wedding or the Fae King tried to outmaneuver us."

"What about the first attack on the border village?" I ask, hopeful the news isn't all bad.

Father flinches. "That took us by surprise. If it weren't for Thorne sounding the alarm..." He looks around, finally realizing that Thorne isn't with me.

"They stayed behind to oversee the castle," I say.

Recognition flashes in Father's eyes, and he beams down at me proudly. "Yes, that's right. Queen of the Earth Fae."

"Looks that way." I flash my father a smile, then turn back to Murdock. "Father, this is Murdock."

"Your Highness," Murdock says and dips his head.

"Come." Father gestures to the table behind him. "There are more people here you need to meet."

Stone chairs surround the table, each carved from a different color of stone. My father points to one with a green stone embedded into a carving of a vine crown.

"This, Queen Sorcha, is yours," Father says, standing behind me as I sit.

He gestures to the rest of the fae at the table. "This is Aodhfin, a salamander-shifter with several fire sprites you might recognize."

The salamander shifter nods. The fire sprites shift under my gaze, and their bright flames dim with attention. One fire sprite folds so tightly within itself that it almost snuffs out its flame.

"The sprites? From the kitchens in the castle?" I ask. They titter. The less-shy one briefly meets my eyes but then looks away.

"We're here as representatives of the Fire Fae who feel wronged by the past Fire Kings," Aodhfin explains, but he doesn't introduce the two fire sprites. Aodhfin sits in a stone chair with a bright red ruby nestled into a carving of a simple crown surrounded by flames. The jewel glints behind his head, and I swear I've seen that crown before but with a moonstone instead of a ruby.

All eyes fall on me. Opal sits next to a throne with a blue sapphire embedded into a crown carved to look like waves. Another water nymph sits beside her, but not in the jeweled chair.

"You look familiar." I tilt my head, trying to place her face.

Her smile is a gentle tug on her lips. "I am Dallis—Sister to Dubessa of the Low Lands. My river is farther north, beyond the Dwarf territories. And you," she shifts her gaze to Murdock and gestures toward the empty seat, "will sit here, Your Highness."

I turn to Murdock and try to hide my shock, but my eyes widen.

Murdock glances at me, and he winces. He steps forward, elegantly addressing Dallis, "You know I have no place at this table, Dallis of the Winter Water."

She gives him a devious look and holds her hand out beside her. "But you do, heir to the Water Fae throne. This is your seat since your Father refused to come on land."

Murdock clears his throat, tugging at his braid. "Aye, well, when you put it that way."

He skulks to the throne and sits down stiffly. Dallas looks pleased as she shifts in her seat, scooting closer to Murdock.

My father continues with the introductions. "The Air Fae here - a few pixies whom you may also know, Cherry and Lily, and an eagle shifter, Feothan."

Feothan sits on a throne with an opal nestled within a crown of feathers. He looks mildly perturbed but perks up when my father calls his name. I imagine his feathers would have fluffed if he had been in his eagle form.

Cherry and Lily rise, beating their wings profusely, and dip into a reverent bow. They intone together, "Your Highness."

"Happy to see you both." I smile, curious if they were part of Fern's spy network inside the castle. With their wings intact, they fled of their own accord or must still be working within the castle walls. I make a mental note not to say too much before them until I am sure.

Murdock must sense my suspicion, for he says, "Feothan, a pleasure to see you again. I thought the air shifters wanted nothing to do with pixies and politics."

Murdock tilts his head toward the Air Fae present.

"I owe it to Thorne and others who have been neutral in their positions. I speak for all the Air Fae when I say we do not support the illegitimate High King." Feothan picks at their fingernails. His eyes flick to Murdock's, and a flash of scrutiny crosses his face before a mask of impassivity replaces it.

Father turns to the last remaining seats at the table. I meet the eyes of Grindel, the dwarf who runs the Land's End Inn, and I smile, remembering fondly meeting him for the first time. Another Earth Fae sits next to him, one who looks remarkably similar to Conall. I meet their rich brown eyes, trying to hide my shock. Though the shape of his face and eyes resembles Conall's, the similarities end there. His hair is a silvery blonde and braided in a solitary braid down their back. He has luminous, rich amber skin, shades darker than Conall's. Where Conall's jaw is angular and scruffy, this Fae has a softer, clean-shaven jawline. They meet my gaze and give me a knowing glare that has me blanching from the intensity. I straighten, remembering that I am their Queen and, as far as they know, I am still Conall's fated mate.

My father says, "Grindel, purveyor of the Land's End Inn, representing the dwarf fae, and Maccon, second in command of the MacSealgair clan."

"Grindel, I'm glad to have you here," I say, hoping calmness resonates from my posture. I'm elated that he's seated next to me since I know he was part of the resistance from my time before the sleep. Knowing I can trust Grindel, Maccon, and Murdock, my nerves ease a little.

The others, however...

One of the fire sprites hovers above their chair, seemingly unsure whether she is welcome to sit with the other fae. A tiny orb of flame hovers between her palms, and she twirls it around nervously.

I lean toward Grindel and whisper, "What are the fire sprites' names?"

He strokes his long beard and whispers gruffly into my ear, "Fia is the fidgety one, playing with the orb in her hands. The other is still too shy to speak up, Your Majesty. I don't know her name."

I straighten in my chair. "Fia, would you be a dear and sit by me?"

Fia's eyes shoot straight up and find mine, dark black pools against flaming orange skin. She puts her hands down, and the gyrating flames disintegrate into the air as she makes her way around the table. She performs a small curtsy and waits patiently for me to speak.

"Thank you, Fia. Please be at ease here. I wanted to ask you why you felt you needed to be present. Are you comfortable sharing in front of the others?"

"Aye, Your Majesty." Her voice sounds like the whisper of water as it touches fire and turns to steam. Her coal-black eyes flit around the room, staring at all the fae, and finally settle back on me. "I followed Fern to the Earth Fae kingdom, Your Highness. We all started leaving when we heard of Lord MacSealgair's plans to get you out from underneath the King's clutches. Slowly, at first, and then in droves as soon as the King left to go to the Border."

Fia looks up at me, concern etched into the tiny embers of her face. I gesture for her to continue, giving her a smile that appears warm and not condescending.

"We came to the edges of the Earth Fae kingdom, waiting, hoping for your return and a safe place to be. Lord MacSealgair's lands were available, but some wards were weakening, and we didn't know how long it would be until they overtook his lands—"

At that sentiment, Maccon shifts in his seat, bristling. He doesn't speak, however, and I note broodiness must be rampant in the MacSealgair family tree. My eyes flash to his, and I raise an eyebrow.

"Go on, Fia," I say to her, but keep my eyes on the fidgeting wolf shifter. I bite my cheek to keep from laughing at how much he reminds me of his older brother. Instinctively, I tug on the heart-call again.

Again, it goes unanswered. I rub absently at the place in my chest where I would have felt it.

"Well, we fled. Most of us lived as close to the Deoir Forest as possible, and others fled to the dwarven outposts to wait... To wait until... Well, until you returned."

Their wait must have been strenuous. They did not know when or even if I would return to the Earth Fae lands as they fled from a dictator, heading toward what they hoped was a safe harbor. "Do you know how many wildlings are left in his castle?"

Fia shakes her head. "I do not, Your Majesty. My apologies."

"You've been through quite an ordeal, Fia. If she allows it, can you tell me your companion's name?" I ask, hoping that I haven't pushed away the shier sprite.

Fia looks to the other sprite, who curls in on herself, tucking away her flames. I almost miss it, but the sprite nods and then scurries over to Aodhfin, who holds his hand out so she can climb up.

"Her name is Aine," Fia says.

"Aine. What a beautiful name." A tiny spark flickers around Aine's head, but she refuses to meet my eyes, so I focus back on Fia. "I welcome you both to sit with me. When this is done, please know that my lands are yours." Fia visibly relaxes, and a genuine smile graces her face. She returns to her seat, and all eyes at the table find mine. My hand reflexively touches the hilt of the sword at my hip. The time to run from my duties is over; I can no longer expect loyalty from the fae if I do not choose to lead.

I wait until Fia settles, and then I clear my throat. "Thank you, all, for being here. I came here with the impression that you are the resistance, meeting here to overtake King Achill."

I meet the eyes of everyone at the table but then hold Dallis' eyes when I say, "But first, I need to get the water nymph sisters and my fated mate back."

Nineteen
Sorcha

The stone chair does little to ease the numbing in my legs, and I shift as subtly as I can. My father drones on, and I have become so accustomed to tuning him out that I am only slightly aware that the energy shifts around the table.

Father's stance is wide as he smooths out a rolled parchment, revealing a detailed map of Fae. His tone is brisk, "As I was saying earlier, The MacSealgair Borderlands are the main holdout, preventing us from getting our weapons to the resistance. If we take out a few of the standing stones..."

"Yes, we *could*, but it is also preventing the king from fully attacking the lower lands," Grindel says. His throat bobs as he swallows nervously, and his eyes flick to me.

"Speak freely, Grindel," I interject, inserting as much command in my voice as possible. "I would like to know your objections."

"My mate is at the Inn, and I've been receiving word that the fae army *can* make it through the weakened Border. But they are less... powerful. They can't access their magic like they can on this side."

My thoughts immediately flash to Geannie and how she was killed. No magic was used, just sheer brute force and a sharp blade. I nod, encouraging him to continue. Grindel flashes me a brief smile and presses, "We weaken the Border, and it'd be full-on war again. Which, I assume, we all want to avoid."

The Air and Water Fae nod, but the Fire Fae frowns at the map.

"What Grindel is leaving out is if we take out the stones, it opens up the Borderlands to everyone. The fae there are all former subjects of Achill's. They are *refugees*," Maccon says, a low growl in the back of his throat. His eyes flash to mine, and I can see his resemblance to Conall clearly in his anger at injustice.

My father straightens, pointing at a spot on the map. It is too far to see, but I strain my neck anyway.

"I don't see another way around this," my father says, shrugging. "The Border weakened as soon Sorcha crossed, but without the marriage and the rest of the agreement being fulfilled..."

I open my mouth to ask what else was included in the rest of the treaty, but Maccon cuts me off.

"You'd open our lands up to an onslaught!" Maccon growls, his forearms braced on the table as he leans forward in my father's face. "You can't do that to the innocents."

My father stares nonchalantly at him, a practiced look from decades of diplomacy. "If we sacrifice a few for the majority, do you not feel like it is a worthy cause?"

I blanch at my father's words. I have never heard my father talk of war like this before. It was always trade and supply routes and other alliances with human kingdoms from far away. Maccon seethes, and his eyes flash to mine, briefly, to see if I react. But all I do is stare at my father and wonder if I truly know him.

Maccon grunts and pushes off the table, storming through the door. The rest of the table is silent. My father opens his mouth to speak, and I cut him off.

"Please, Father," I say, holding my hand up. "I think you've said enough. Surely, we can't destroy harmless fae lives to gain the upper hand."

Some of the fae nod in agreement. I look down the table at Murdock, but he averts his gaze. I eye the space Maccon vacates, and my soul calls out to Conall before I realize I am seeking his comfort. I run my hand over the smooth top of the stone table. What would an Earth Queen do?

"Have we thought about confronting Achill privately?" I flush as all eyes turn to me.

Dallis' voice is solemn when she says, "Decades ago, we tried this."

"It didn't go so well," Aodhfin adds darkly.

Dallis nods. Her eyes dart to the Feothan before looking at Murdock. "We tried getting advocates from all four fae elements, but we came up shorthanded."

"But why would you need fae from all the elements?" I ask. Growing up on the other side of the Border, I've missed an entire history course on the intricacies of court politics in Fae.

Dallis leans forward, her skin glistening silver and blue under a skylight. She brings her hands out in front of her, water gathering between her fingertips. Droplets play along her slender fingers, and she weaves a tapestry made from water in the air. As she speaks, a watery image forms above us, not unlike what the Goddess did. Gooseflesh erupts along my arms.

"Achill is fire and air. His magic manifests in smoke. He has lived an unnatural amount of time after his fated mate died, and some of us speculate he has been dabbling in far darker magic than we have seen before. It has been my theory that we will need to find a fae creature that carries two elements within them. Because when we showed up in defiance, he casually ended the lives of several of the strongest and oldest fae. But," —she adds, her voice low and conspiratorial — "they were fae that came from a long line of singular elemental magic."

The water dissipates above our heads, and the scene ends with watery figures perishing above us on the mirror-like surface. I watch Dallis' hands play with the water, collecting it back towards herself. Dubessa knew more than she let on. I slide my hands from the table and hold them in my lap, looking down to see blue and green colors shimmering along my fingertips.

Murdock sits forward and adds, "In the decades that followed, we created a thorough network to find any fae gifted with these powers. We haven't found a single one. In fact—"

"Och, here he goes," Grindel groans and leans backward. I frown. He waves his hands at Murdock, explaining, "He has so many theories."

Murdock glares at Grindel but clears his throat and presses on. "I think that our powers are lessening. All younger Earth Fae can't hear the plants, and the Air Fae can't tell when the storms are coming. Some fire sprites only steam, and the Fire Fae can't keep the fires lit. And the Water Fae..."

"Water Fae are losing their ability to heal, to have visions we remember," Dallis says. Her large black eyes look to Opal and then to me.

Opal, who sits directly to my right today, shrugs and flashes me her sharp teeth in a goofy grin. She says, "I still strong."

"So we have less powerful fae, a Border that's weakened but still preventing magic from coming through." I stand up and pace, tucking my hands behind my back to hide the shimmering colors. Disconcertedness pulses through my limbs, making me restless. I daren't mention what else runs through my mind—a king living an unnatural life in a weakened, grotesque body and the Goddess' words about restoring balance.

The earth and water elements I now possess.

It's all connected.

"Your Highness, if we focus back on the problem at hand," my father says, casually redirecting the conversation. I exhale and nod, urging him to continue. "The most likely scenario is for us to figure out how to distract Achill, break down his defenses, and get more human weapons into the fae hands. Since their magic has weakened, our swords may be the only thing to give us the upper hand."

Maccon stealthily slides back into their chair, watchful eyes on me. I swallow a few times, not liking how naive I look in front of him.

"Have the fae always found their powers weaker on the human side before they created the Border?" I ask, knowing I am showing my naivety with this question. But if my father could never have powers on the human side, despite his longer life span...

"Weaker, but not non-existent. If you were a younger fae or newly immortal, your powers would struggle to manifest fully lower down the continent," Feothan says. He straightens in his chair, and I can't get the image out of my head of a bird pruning their feathers. "I never had a problem shifting and using simple air magic on the human side. But I am centuries older and come from a distinguished Air Fae line."

"Of course," Grindel says, a smirk hiding beneath his toothy smile and bearded chin.

"You question my lineage?" Feothan's voice raises to almost a shriek.

Grindel shrugs, "Och, no. I think Thorne would have something to say about it, is all."

"Don't you bring my brother into this," Feothan spits.

My head swivels to the bird shifter. "Your brother?"

"We look nothing alike. It's because *he's* illegitimate but still the golden child," Feothan sneers. "I'm the one with Air from both parents."

"And yet you still hold a grudge," Grindel says. "Sounds like you have a lot of hot air up yer arse."

The table erupts in soft chuckles as Feothan squawks, "I beg your pardon!"

"That's enough, Grindel," I sigh, rubbing my face. I bite my cheek a few times to keep myself from laughing. I continue, "If you can't be civil, then you can leave."

I gesture to the door.

"I—" Grindel turns beet red. "Yes, Your Majesty. Apologies."

I turn to Feothan, my voice firm. "I would kindly ask that you refer to Thorne how *they* would choose to be represented. If that is a problem, then you can answer to me."

Feothan blanches, color creeping up his face. "I—Apologies. It won't happen again."

"Good," I clip, my eyes meeting Feothan's one last time before moving on. "Now, weakening the Border would put harmless and helpless fae at risk of being slaughtered — by either side," I say, looking pointedly at my father. "I disapprove of this plan. The fae that come to the human side have found their powers even more strained. If they've been getting weaker since the Border was closed, perhaps it wasn't the Border, but something else has left the land unbalanced?"

"What are you suggesting then, Sorcha?" my father asks. The entire energy in the room shifts toward me, listening intently to what I am about to say next. My eyes flash to Maccon and then to Murdock, almost pleading for their support. I can't help but yearn for Conall's calm presence to be with me, but I know I am alone in making this decision. And I finally have to accept the fate I chose.

I stop pacing and lift my chin as I say, "I will be the one to kill Achill."

A heavy silence fills the room.

Then, Aodhfin bursts out laughing. "And how do you propose we do that?"

Everyone talks all at once.

"No," my father says. "I won't allow that to happen."

"But you're our queen!" Grindel yells.

"You're not even full fae!" Feothan snaps.

"Do you even have any power?" Maccon asks.

"Conall's going to kill me," Murdock groans into his hands.

Opal claps her hands and douses everyone in the water. They gasp, finally settling down. She beams at me with her toothy smile, and I nod.

"Thank you, Opal. Now, as to the question of my legitimacy and magic..."

I pull the sword from the scabbard on my hip and place it on the table before me. Everyone goes quiet, watching me closely. My skin tingles with all eyes on me.

Maccon asks, "Is that... what I think it is?"

"It can't be. No one has seen the sword in hundreds of years," Feothan adds, and his eyes find mine. A mix of perplexity and awe wash over his face.

"If this is true," Aodhfin muses, pointing to the sword and then back up at me, "then *you* are the one to unite all of fae. Not the false king." The words "false king" leave Aodhfin's mouth with a hiss, and he meets my eyes with a flash of anger that is soon replaced with hope. "He has lied this whole time."

Murdock frowns and leans forward. "Och, Your Majesty, is that... your hagstone?" He points at the hilt, frowning.

"Yes, Murdock," I say, toying with the empty chain around my neck. "It was a perfect fit that let me pull the sword from the stone."

Dallis is quiet, and her eyes travel from the tip of the blade to the hilt of the sword. "The whispers on the water were true, then. A powerful talisman indeed."

The fae murmur amongst themselves, staring at the sword and then back at me, looking around the table at each other. I look at the two water nymphs and Murdock, the representatives of the Water Fae, and Maccon and Grindel, the two Earth Fae. And then Cherry, Feothan, and Lily, all the representatives of the Air Fae. Last, I meet the eyes of Aodhfin, Fia, and Aine. My father is the only one who looks at me with an expression full of pride.

Memories of my father meeting with his advisors wash over me, and I am once again a small child hiding in the curtains and eavesdropping. My tongue sits thick in my mouth as I struggle to form inspirational words. Their eyes bore into me, and I swear they know I am no longer part-fae. I fold my hands together to keep them from flying up to my ears to ensure my hair is still covering them.

I rest my hands on the sword before me, grateful I have it with me despite its weight and the burdens it signifies. I close my eyes briefly and recall what the Goddess told me in the stone circle.

With as much brevity as I can muster, I say, "Our meeting here is about setting the balance in Fae and the human lands to rights. With your support, we can undo the damage that King Achill has done."

Everyone murmurs their approval, so I say, "He has lied to us all, hurt us all. He killed our family and friends over the centuries, and I will make sure he pays his dues. But, there are several High Fae who need our help first. The water nymph sisters are powerful allies that could help us turn the tides into an eventual war. And my mate,

Conall. Time is running out for both of us and our mating bond. Conall sacrificed his freedom for mine, taking on the King's Guard as I fled through a tunnel. I wouldn't be here without him, and it's high time I got him back. I have a plan, but I need to know if you're with me."

Twenty
Sorcha

The last of the Resistance filters out, and the doors close seconds before I launch into Murdock.

"When were you going to tell me you're the heir to the Water Fae throne?" I ask.

It's just me and him in the stone table room. The near silence is weighty, save for the sound of the water in the fountain. I glare daggers at him from across the table.

Murdock shirks, slouching even further down his throne. He whines, "Och, Your Majesty…"

"Murdock! As your Queen, I have a right to know why you kept something like this from me. How do you think it looks when I don't know that my right hand is an heir to the Water Fae kingdom?"

He stands and makes his way behind a column toward the pond. Carefully, he rolls his pants legs up and sits on one of the stones. He dips his toes in and sighs, his purple scales flaring as he shifts.

I follow him and say, so quietly it's almost a whisper, "I hate to think you're keeping something from me to undermine my legitimacy to the Earth Fae kingdom."

Murdock turns his head, shocked, "It wasn't… I'm not…"

"Then, out with it." I step closer.

Murdock kicks his feet in the water, contemplating something. I stare him down as he stands, straightening his pants. I tilt my head, waiting for him to answer, when he shrugs and says, as if he is ashamed to say loud, "I haven't decided if I'm going to take up the throne or not... yet."

"And why is that?"

"Because—" Murdock steps closer. His blue eyes bore into my soul, and the tips of his pointed ears burn red. He studies my lips, and then his eyes trail over my cheekbones and ears and back to my eyes again.

He clears his throat nervously.

"Because?" I repeat, realization dawning on me.

"I know you're fated to him, Sorcha." His voice is barely a whisper as he pushes me back into the column. His lithe body sidles up to mine. "But I am in love with you."

"W-what?" My mind whirrs. All this time, I was worried he would call me out about not being fae, and he's... been in love with me? Relief floods my body, and I sag against the stone.

He reaches forward and grabs my hands, which go clammy, and I kick myself for thinking that this is the better outcome. I look down, and his hands dwarf mine, faint purple scales shimmering near his wrists.

I open my mouth to object to whatever he is about to say, but he silences me with a look of desperation.

"I could never forget you. Your strength at the hands of Achill. It killed me, leaving you severely injured on the ground while I had to find help. Watching the light leave your eyes and the pain you were in. It killed me knowing that you were in his castle. If you were my fated mate, I would have never given you over to the King. I never would have left you in his care. I know what he is capable of." Those last few words leave his mouth, and I have never seen his face look so earnest.

I'm too stunned to move or to speak, so he continues.

"I would go to the ends of the earth to protect you, Sorcha. Something about you calls to me. It sings in my blood. And I haven't been able to let it go. I can't stop thinking about you - wondering if you're eating or sleeping enough. Wishing that I could be the one to wash your hair and bathe you after a long day." He pushes into me, one of his hands resting on the column above my head. Our chests almost touch. "Sorcha, have you thought about what happens if we can't get Conall back?"

"I — " The words die on my tongue, unable to let my mind go there.

"If we can't get him or if he can't shift back, you can always choose to mate with another. It won't be fated but still holds a strong bond." His hand cups my face, and I close my eyes.

The water in the pond laps at the banks, and my body wants to move with the sound. I can feel the swaying of the water pulsing through my veins. Murdock's jasmine and ocean scent wraps itself around me, and I can imagine, if only for a moment, that I am near the beach, surrounded by softness and calm.

His skin is soft and warm, and I have craved a comforting touch for days. Murdock's thumb strokes my bottom lip, and I part them instinctively.

He leans his head down, hovering just above my lips. I close my eyes.

What would it be like to kiss him? This kind, jovial soul?

He whispers, "What I would *do* to taste you..."

I inhale sharply, and my eyes fly open.

Murdock steps away at the last minute, dropping his hands and steps backward. My breath goes with him, pulled from my lungs at the sudden lack of contact. "I cannot. I will not. Until you've chosen."

Murdock heads toward the door.

I stand there, stunned, as I watch the mershifter walk away. But then I call after him, "Murry! Wait!"

He stops short and turns. "This is the second time you've called me Murry."

"Well, a bit of formality between us is gone. What with your heartfelt confession and everything." I smile so he knows I'm teasing.

"Sorcha, I meant what I said." He shifts from foot to foot, his face serious, his body still leaning toward mine.

"I know you did." I nod, adding some brevity to my words. "I know, and I appreciate your honesty, Murry. I do."

"But..."

I sigh. "No, but. I just wanted you to know that I appreciated your honesty. I also feel a pull toward you, but I don't know what it means. I don't know if it's because we've been spending so much time together lately or because you've always been kind to me, or..." I shrug, and my words fade, fearful that they will come true if I say them out loud. I clench my hands into fists, hiding the colors I think are coming through.

What happens if I really can't get Conall back?

I tug on that heart-call with all my might. An echo of nothing fills my chest.

Murdock nods, his eyes assessing every part of my face, and once again, I am pulled toward him. But I steel myself and step backward, wishing I would back into Conall's muscular chest. My soul aches, yearning for Conall to fill the space he occupies. And I know no one else can ever fill it.

I say, "I just need to see this through with Conall. I owe it to him; I owe it to myself."

He flashes me a momentary smile that doesn't reach his eyes and walks through the door. The handle clicks behind him, and I'm left alone with the sound of the fountain and the slow beat of my heart.

Twenty-One
Sorcha

As the day wears on, Murdock continues to avoid me, even during the planning stages of the attempted coup. I can feel his eyes on me as we plan and plot, looking at the maps on the table. But every time I look up, he quickly looks away. If his eyes could start a fire, the entire mountainside would burn with how often I can sense his gaze boring into the side of my face. Each time I turn to ask for his input, he sits back, and I'm blocked from his view. He makes his answers as quick as possible. However, his confession of love opened up the floodgates, and now I can't stop thinking about what he had asked.

What happens if we can't get Conall back?

The words crawl across my skin, itching to be answered. Though ever-present in my mind, I had refused to entertain the possibility at first. But now, a newfound sense of urgency presses down on me from all sides.

As much as I want to follow in my father's footsteps, more innocent creatures might die. I don't want to go along with my father's plans, but he has come up with the only solution to get into the castle undetected.

Do I let others die to get my mate back and free the water nymphs? Yes, we need the sisters' help, but at what cost?

And rescuing the sisters will be a feat since the powerful water nymphs have been held for so long. It must require immense magic to keep them there, and I can't shake this feeling in my stomach—a warning bell—that keeps telling me things could go wrong.

What if I fail?

It cannot be an option.

The water in the fountain calls to me, lulling my tired mind toward its refreshing cool. Sitting on the edge, I close my eyes, and images of the castle blueprints play out in the darkness of my mind. My feet dangle in the pond, and I sway back and forth as I drag them around.

A warm hand lands on my shoulder, and I'm jolted from my trance.

Opal sits down, scooting close to me. Her feet slide into the water next to me.

"You sad," she says, looking at me sideways. It's more of a statement than a question and the earnestness in her face tears away all the walls I have tried to put up.

My shoulders sag, and I lean into Opal's side, resting my head on her shoulder.

"Sad, confused, angry, unsure." I dip my hand into the pond, staring at my rippling reflection. The water in the pond dances around my hand, pulling and playing against my skin just like the raindrops did in my palms on my balcony.

"You are water," Opal says, watching the way the water reacts to my body. "I show you."

I sit up straight, almost relieved that she sees it and that I don't have to say the words out loud. Her eyes shine with delight, and she holds out a hand. I twine my fingers with hers. With her free hand, she touches the tip of her finger to my heart. "Feel here. Breathe. Water comes."

The water laps at my feet, and I close my eyes. I squeeze her hand and breathe out. Cool, liquid silk slides up my legs, and my body rocks backward as if my body were part of the water. It vibrates with a heartbeat all on its own, and in my head, hues of dappled sunlight swarm my vision—purple, blue, and soft sea green.

"I can feel it! I *see* it," I whisper, swaying with the current. I open my eyes and am astonished to find a fully formed orb of water floating above my open hand. "Oh, my Goddess."

Opal flashes me a smile. "See? Easy. Water magic in you."

She has a matching sphere floating above her other hand. Her fingers dance with it in the air, similar to how Murdock played with his during our sparring. Copying Opal's movements, I turn my hand around, flicking my fingers, and the ball jumps into the air, settling back down in my palm.

"I cannot believe it," I say, awestruck. "I have water *and* earth."

Opal tilts her head, gives me that same toothy smile, and then splashes me with her magic. It cascades over my shoulders, drenching me. She laughs, and mischief twinkles in her eyes as she reaches her hand over the water. She waggles her eyebrows before drenching me in another huge wave.

"Not fair!" I shriek and struggle to launch water back at her. Sweat breaks on my brow, but a few small water marbles finally form in the air. They land on Opal's cheek with an unsatisfying pop.

"No, this," Opal says and grabs my hands. "Feel."

She points at the water dripping from my clothes and onto the floor. Amorphous silver flows through the stone, carving its path back to the pond. The water drips into the pool, melting together as it returns to its origins.

"Flow," she says.

I swish my legs in the pool, watching the once-separated elements flow together, pushing away from my movements, bending and folding, shifting and falling together. I am merely a vessel within which the water lives. I am no more its master than it is mine.

Opal swirls her hands in the air, and globes of water gather together. They circulate each other, and she tosses me one. Without thinking, I hold my hands out to catch it like a ball, and, to my amazement, it doesn't pop. My jaw drops, and I meet Opal's stare over the sphere. She nods emphatically, and I toss it back to her. For the next few minutes, she and I play with the water magic, controlling the ripples in the water and creating more orbs of water, both large and small. She cackles when they pop over our heads.

Had I ever been allowed to play with other children when I was younger, would it have felt like this? Though I long to have known what it would have been like to grow up with friends or siblings, these questions are best left unanswered. Opal is like a long-lost sibling; the camaraderie I feel around her is immeasurable. I could stay here longer, feeling connected to the water and a friend I had missed terribly. But time is not on my side, and the bittersweetness of ending her lesson soon swallows me.

A gust of air swirls around me and shakes the vines around the columns before dying completely. I wring my hair around my fingers, squeezing the rest of the water out.

OPAL LEANS OVER and squeezes me, her part-ogre arms swallowing me up in a tight embrace. "I miss you."

I lean into the comfort. Her softheartedness is a welcome reprieve from the anger and fear competing for my attention.

"Thank you, Opal." My hands tingle, and the tips that used to be just green from earth magic now swirl together with blue and green.

Suddenly, her eyes glaze over, and her hand grabs my shoulder. Her other hand lifts and the water from the pond floats up in droplets, swirling into the air before us. It collects into one large oval. It shimmers, mirror-like in its suspension, and I can see someone huddling in a dark, dingy, water-filled dungeon.

I gasp, wanting to launch myself forward into the image before me, but Opal's hand grips my shoulder and keeps me pinned to where I sit. She closes her eyes, tears trailing down her cheeks.

And then I see him. Though I can't see his face, I know immediately who it is.

His body lies crumpled on the ground, covered in dried blood and gaping wounds that aren't healing. He huddles in the cell's corner, whip markings across his back.

"Conall!" I cry out. My heart tears from my chest and shatters before my eyes.

Opal starts humming, but her grip never loosens.

"Can he hear me? Can I talk to him?" The more the image comes to life in front of me, the more frenzied I become.

She shakes her head slowly, her eyes still closed. Thank the Goddess because she shouldn't have to see this.

The picture in front of me changes slightly. A light cascades into the cell from a door opening, and Conall shirks his body away, clamoring for the cover of darkness.

A figure appears in the foreground. Shorter, curvy, with a braid... *like mine.*

My hands fly to my mouth as the vision unfolds before me.

I'm running to him, kneeling on the wet floor, my hands reaching out to him. Tears streak my face, and I say something but can't hear it. I want to scream at Sorcha in the vision and help her pull him out.

Before I realize it, I reach out to touch Conall, and the water comes crashing down in the pool, splashing us as the vision ends.

"I didn't know you were such a powerful seer, Opal."

Opal opens her eyes, finally releasing my shoulder. My fingers hover at the blank space the vision once occupied.

Her hands reach out and grab mine. She gives me a toothy grin that doesn't reach her eyes. Instead, a flash of something else passes across her features, and her eyes look through me, filled with something akin to sadness. "You save him. You save us."

"If your vision is true, I will." I smile at her, infusing it with an emotion I dare to call hope. Even though "I swear to everything the Goddess touches, I am going to kill that king."

Twenty-Two
Achill

The library reeks of charred leather and wood, but he rifles through the stacks on the lower levels anyway. Though he knows his magic is waning, he can still smother the flames before they consume the entire room. Unlike when he was a young fae, his fire magic was uncontrollable, causing a whole wing of the castle to burn down.

A book falls in the distance, and Achill flinches, afraid his father will tear through the room to backhand him at his carelessness.

He scoffs.

What kind of king is afraid of ghosts?

He spies a book in the rubble, somehow unscathed, and picks it up.

Royal Fae Family Lines of the Last 500 Years.

The cover is deep green with gold embossing, and he vaguely remembers one of his old tutors talking about this text. He thumbs through until he reaches the Earth Fae section, skimming his eyes until he lands on the Deoir line.

The last entry is Aerona and Cariad. Achill reads on, intent on learning what little he can of his fated mate's family and throne. There has to be an answer here about the ascension to the throne. Perhaps the Earth Fae have a different way of gaining power and ruling their people.

...The eventual rise of some of the most powerful Earth and Water Fae to have graced the lands. The twin sisters were born under the full moon, in the center of the stone circle...

The entry stops at the end of the page. He flips to the next, but the text carries on mid-sentence about the different types of magic used to create the castle. His fingers travel down the center of the book, trailing the path where a blade has precisely and carefully shorn two pages from the chapter.

Achill slams the book shut and throws it into the burned stacks. Ash plumes float in front of his vision, and he swipes at the air like a madman.

"Where are those goddess-forsaken brownies, and why haven't they cleaned this mess up?" He roars into the room, smoke billowing about his figure.

Achill stalks out of the library, heading to Aerona's old rooms. The door looms in front of him, and he swallows. The last time he was here, his fingers twined in the hair of another. Sorcha's mahogany-colored hair was so similar in hue to Aerona's that if he squinted, he could almost pretend she was still alive.

Almost.

He turns the knob, and the pungent scent of lavender and rose assaults his nose first. It covers up what little he had been trying to preserve of Aerona and her lilac and ocean scent. Achill opens the door a little wider, covering his nose against the offending aroma. He hesitates on the threshold against the flood of memories that flash before him. He can so plainly see his lover twirling in the center of the room, reading in the sunlight of the window. Then, as the years wore on, her demeanor changed. It was subtle at first, and easy to overlook the changes. But back then, it felt like Aerona had woken up one morning and was different. Her smiles took longer to reach her eyes; she stopped sharing his bed and took up more time in these rooms.

If only he had known how his life would be without her, there would be so many things he would have done differently. He swears he could have given her everything she asked for.

With a sigh, he puts his head down and takes his first steps into the place that used to belong to his mate.

The room is earthier. And spotless, even after a year without anyone living in it. His hand trails the furniture until he stops before the books on the far wall. Several titles line the shelves, noticeably lacking dust, and he pulls out a tome about magicked flour. He flips through several pages, but he startles when he sees movement from the corner of his eye. His stomach flutters, and he spins around.

"Aerona?" Even he could hear the heartbreak in his voice that time.

No, it is only the sunlight coming through the trees, shadows playing against the wall. His shoulders sink with disappointment. He strides across the room, dropping the book on the table by the fireplace, and makes his way to the stairs. With each step, his mood lifts, wondering if he can find a trace of his lover here.

Alas, it isn't so.

He scrunches his nose. It smells even more like lavender, rose, and *human*.

The furs and blankets on Aerona's old bed are different. Someone, possibly Fern (*that traitorous dwarf*), moved it to a different wall. Soft, feminine curtains now hang from the four-poster bed. Plants grow with wild abandon all over the bathroom. Some vines even creep along the floor and wrap their tendrils around the canopy. Is there any place in this castle that the human princess-turned-fake-queen hasn't tainted?

Achill spins on his heel, flying down the stairs and slamming the doors behind him. His heart pounds against his chest, and he weaves through the castle halls until he is outside in the gardens, standing on the banks of the lake.

Here. His body almost sags into the mud with relief.

Here, it still feels like Aerona.

Gentle water laps at the grassy shore, the reeds swaying with the waves. The magicked boat knocks into the small dock, and he steps in, eager to head to the small temple. But something stops him from making it to the other side.

"Nymph," he growls at the blue-black hair that peeks over the edge of the boat. "Let me pass."

Only her head is visible as she kicks in the water, spinning the boat around in a dizzying pattern.

The nymph moves so effortlessly and pulls herself up on the bow, casually crossing her arms on the lip of the boat.

"Or what?" she asks, kicking her legs out behind her, spinning the boat around and around.

Achill rubs his forehead, fighting against the swirling in his brain. His hands swirl with smoke, and he smiles when she slides back down into the water a fraction.

The boat slows.

He pushes his magic into the bottom of the boat. It crawls slowly to where she rests.

"Fine," she says, shirking away from his magic. A cruel smile crosses his face. "But we should warn you…"

His smoke stops, hovering at an invisible edge, and a shiver crawls down his spine. The nymphs and their warnings are always right. Tilting his head, he regards her impatiently.

She flashes him a pointed-tooth smile. "No, this time, I don't think we will. It will be fun to watch."

Before his smoke can reach her, she pushes off the bow of the boat and dives underwater. He careens backward, and his head slams against the edge with a walloping thud as the bottom of the boat hits the banks.

Shaken, he straightens his coat and looks out at the water beyond. He knows they're watching him, mocking him, and laughing behind his back—they always do. All his loyal subjects, once eager to align themselves with him, are turning their backs on his ways. Fury, or perhaps desperation, builds in his chest. He refuses to let the water nymphs have the upper hand, so when the fire licks at his fingertips, he shoves his hands under his arms and leaves the lake behind.

Smoke trails from where he steps, seeping into the ground. His irritation leaves his body, replaced by something more sinister as he heads to the dungeons.

Twenty-Three
Sorcha

A tranquil breeze pulls a few strands of hair from my braid, and I sway with currents at the edge of a precipitous overhang. The lowlands of Fae stretch before me in the dying light of day. I relish the crispness of the fresh air filling my lungs. Though the dwarf caverns are beautiful, a testament to their incredible craftsmanship, and I have earth magic, my soul was itching for the open sky and greenery. Maol sent me to an old lookout of the dwarves that had been used centuries ago when ancient creatures took to the air.

Footsteps crunch on the gravel behind me, but the familiar scent of leather and wood smoke tells me it's my father. I don't turn to greet him, choosing instead to finish watching the setting sun paint the cloudy sky with a lavender haze.

"Sorcha," Father says gently. He wraps an arm around my shoulders.

I lean a little into the crook of his arm and squeeze him back. "Good evening, Father."

"You're a hard one to find," he says, kissing my head.

"I needed some fresh air," I say, releasing my hold.

We stand shoulder to shoulder, looking out at the world beyond. His lands are so far south that I can barely make anything beyond the fields and forests near the high king's castle.

"It's beautiful up here," he says, but his cadence is stilted, and I finally look up to see him fighting back tears.

"Is everything all right?" I ask. Turning to face him, I take his hands in mine.

"I wish I could see another way," he croaks. "I don't like putting any lives at risk. Decisions like today are hard, Sorcha. I never want anyone to die."

What isn't he telling me? "As you said, sometimes we must sacrifice a few to save the majority."

He shakes his head and continues, "I wish I could see another way out of it. Taking those stones out is the only way."

"Well, now we both know that's not entirely true," I scoff. "But we certainly can't attack the King right now—not when I don't have unanimous support."

"Mm," Father mumbles. The breeze tugs on his hair, and the tips of his ears show through the top of his braids.

"When were you going to tell me you're part-fae?"

I want to add that I was also part-fae, but I don't because I don't want to explain to him that I'm not anymore. He says nothing, just squints at the lands below. "Ah, I see. So, what, it was something you hoped I would discover?"

I cross my arms, looking at him in the dying light. The tips of his ears are more pointed than mine ever would be. Even his age is deceptive. When he should be closer to eighty, he only looks like he's fifty years of age. His hair, the same strawberry blond color as Murdock's, looks more luscious, too. He shifts under my scrutiny, tucking his ears back under his hair.

Suddenly, I'm angry all over again. "Why do you do that with your hair here? Because you can't let go of decades of deception? Even though you're surrounded by fae?"

"Don't be mad, Sorcha," he says. "It's not queenly."

"I can be angry if I damn well please, Papa!" I snap. He blanches at my childhood name for him. "Why wouldn't I be angry?"

"There was much I wanted to tell you," Father starts, but I cut him off.

"But what you *chose* to tell me was that I was promised to a Fae

King. Maybe a little about human and fae politics." I throw my hands out to my sides in frustration. "I grew up knowing nothing about the people I was to rule! I had to find stories in the library and beg Geannie to tell me what she knew."

And then I balk at my stupidity. Geannie was the one who gave me the hagstone, and she was the one who made me take a few classes with our weapons master. She brought me books on lore and fairy stories - even if the stories were all bedtime fables to scare children into behaving. Geannie knew about brownies and how powerful the fae are, and she knew how unprepared my father wanted me to be. Had she been setting me up for a life in Fae all this time, still looking out for me far beyond the grave?

"Did you know, too?" My voice cracks, and I fight back angry tears.

Father asks, "Know what?"

"The hagstone. The Fae. Was she hired because of what she knew?"

Father blanches, but his face softens when he realizes what I'm asking. "Yes."

"Incredible," I scoff. "Did she know she would one day have to sacrifice herself?"

Father shakes his head slowly. "I never meant for her to die. She knew what she was taking on when she accepted her position."

He says it so coldly that it makes all his admissions even more hurtful. Everything I've known feels like someone scooped it up, shook it, and then dumped everything back out. I feel scrambled and realize then that he has lied to me my entire life.

"Is the whole world just black and white to you? Constant strategizing and playing with people?" I ask. "How could you not even tell me about who I am? Why would you have me go in blind to this?" I gesture out behind me to the quieting lands beyond.

Father steps forward, his mouth open to speak, but I hold my hands out. "I can't believe that my father would deceive me. Whether you did it intentionally or not, I do not care. I cannot fathom having a child and keeping this from them."

I pull back, eager to have space between us again, but a part of my heart slices away with him, leaving a hollow place I know will never fill back in. I open the door that leads back down to the chambers. The handle clicks closed behind me, and I bump right into Murdock.

"Oof! Sorcha, is everything okay?" He asks, stepping toward me. The torches flare to life, and he frowns when he sees me.

I give him a tight smile, but my voice is thick with unshed tears as I command, "We leave now. Conall's been there long enough."

"If we rush this —" he starts.

"If you do not wish to come, I will go alone." I straighten, lifting my chin, and look up at him.

Murdock's lips quirk into a sardonic smile, and I glare at him until he stops. "Och, you will not go it alone, Your Highness."

"Fine, then you and I will go." I walk back to the room to grab my things, not caring if he is behind me.

His hand reaches out and grabs my forearm. I turn around and meet his piercing blue gaze. "Give me thirty minutes to get everyone together, and then we will go."

WE SET out for the Borderlands while the dying light of the stars gives way to a periwinkle dawn sky.

Everyone is quiet.

Most of the High Fae have agreed to help my father with his plan to remove the warding stones as a diversion, much to my chagrin. I know destroying the warding stones won't work, but most High Fae feel it was the only sensible option. Once they weaken them, it would buy us enough time for a diversion. Then, my small group can rescue Conall and set the nymph sisters free. Their ancient water magic would be tantamount to overthrowing Achill.

Now, standing on the edges of the dwarf border and the burnt ogre forest facing south, the Air and Fire Fae portal over to Conall's lands. Maccon, the only one able to open up the wards into the MacSealgair lands, holds the portal steady, and I meet his eyes again.

He steps toward me as if to say something, but he hesitates. Instead, he shakes his head before slipping away. The portal shuts behind him with a snap.

Opal opens a portal, and the Grotto appears on the other side. My father watches everyone else leave. He will stay with the dwarves in case anything happens to me. As the only other Earth Fae heir with Deoir blood still living, I need one of us alive to take the throne. He steps toward me, his voice grave as he says, "Whatever you do, my girl, remember you deserve to wear your crown. You are from *two* royal bloodlines. Every action you take is the action of a Queen."

I lift my chin like he taught me as a girl, giving him a tight smile. "Understood."

Father reaches out and folds me into his arms. Despite being angry with him, I soften into his embrace.

He whispers something into my hair, but I can't hear what he says.

I want to ask him what he said, but the words die on my tongue. My faith in this plan last night wavers in the early morning light. I can't bring myself to say what I want to say. My eyes water, and it's as if I am saying goodbye to him all over again. Growing up, I idolized the memories of him. Now, as an adult, I have judged the actions of him. But, as a Queen, who would I be not to *forgive* him? I murmur into his chest, wishing I was the little girl back home again. Carefree. Blissfully ignorant of what my future was. "I'll see you soon."

Murdock nods to my father. "She'll be in expert hands, Your Highness. This I swear to you."

With one last squeeze, my father let go, and I stepped awkwardly toward the portal. Murdock steps through first, sword drawn. At the last second, I snatch his free hand. He looks down at the contact with a frown, but his face softens as he grips me back and pulls me through the portal.

I lurch through; my back leg stuck back in the dwarf lands. Murdock has to tug me the rest of the way until both of my feet land on the other side. Thankfully, my stomach doesn't rebel like last time, but I am dizzy and disoriented as I come through. The portal snaps shut behind Opal, and I dig my feet into the ground to keep my legs from shaking.

"Are you all right?" Murdock asks, his brawny arms steadying me.

I give him a weak smile, but he scowls down at me. "It's just nerves."

The trees shake their leaves above me, their branches reaching down to kiss my shoulders in welcome, and moss blooms beneath my feet, grounding me with its gentle cushion. The calming sound of water rushes into the pool at the feet of the Goddess' statue, and she looks no different than she did a year ago. I wonder what would have happened if I had never given her that blood offering. Would I be where I am right now? Or would I have remained a naïve, magic-less human?

Feathers fall above, and I look up.

"Thorne! What on earth are you doing here?"

With a flourish, Thorne flies down, shifting in mid-air. They clear their throat, pull a feather from their mouth, and say, "Well. A little bird, or fish, rather, told me about everyone's plan to rescue Conall and the nymph sisters."

"A fish?" I ask, and Opal turns around. She flashes me her trademark toothy grin. I give her a smile in return. Clever. A question forms on my lips, but Thorne must have known, for they nod and say, "The sword arrived safely, Your Highness, via dwarf mail. But I figured you might also need some Air magic to help."

"Oh, Thorne." I wrap my arms around them and squeeze. The air leaves their lungs in a *whoosh,* but they wrap their arms around me. "I'll take all the help I can get. But please don't do anything heroic."

Thorne nods, and we all turn to the forest before us. Opal and Murdock lead us south to Achill's castle and the tree I mentioned. They hug the shadows, and I watch their receding figures return to a place I once tried to call home.

I must have hesitated to follow, for Thorne takes my hand and squeezes it, giving me a knowing look. "You've been here before, but much has changed since then."

My throat tightens, and I grip their hand. "As long as I get Conall back and free the sisters."

Thorne nods, and I follow in their footsteps toward the Fire King castle. "I have every ounce of faith in you. Just... Remember *who* you are."

They drop their hand and shift into their falcon as Achill's castle grows in the distance, its silhouette looming larger and larger. The trees that once surrounded the castle to the north were burned away. Only patches of the forest survive. Achill created his path through the forest to track me down after I escaped. We stop at the base of the wall, and I take one final look over my shoulder. Behind me, everywhere I step, covering the reminders of his destruction is verdurous new growth.

Twenty-Four
Achill

A self-satisfied smile spreads across Achill's face. He knows that this time, he finally broke the wolf shifter. No cries of agony, no fear registering across Conall's face as the smoke invaded his lungs again. He rolls his shoulders back, not flinching when the dungeon door slams behind him with a clang, and then it's only the sounds of his footsteps as he climbs the stairs.

Let him suffer in silence.

Dried blood coats Achill's hands, staining his nail beds and skin a pinkish hue. Neil pushes the door open at the top of the stairs, and Achill briefly notes the green tinge to the guard's face. He curls his lip up in disgust at the weakness in the lesser fae.

The guard hesitates behind him at the door. Achill looks over his shoulder, a brief warning in the raised eyebrow. Neil apologizes and hurries past his king to open the other door.

Rhys stands on guard in the hallway, holding a wet rag. Achill snatches it and wipes away the dirty shifter blood as best as he can, calling over his shoulder to the guards as he walks down the hallway.

"Any correspondence from the human king?" He spits out the last two words. If he could wipe out every human, he would. Vile, magic-less creatures eager to destroy everything about the fae, spreading their lies with their little folktales and abusing their connection to the Goddess.

"The same as before, Your Highness. A single letter asking to talk to his daughter," Rhys says as he pulls the letter from his breast pocket.

Achill's eyes flicker over the loopy scrawl, noting it was written in the same hand as all the others. He hands it to Neil, who tucks it into his coat pocket.

"Very well," Achill says. "Send him the same thing we always do, but add that there is a possibility she might be with child."

"Y-yes, Your Majesty," Neil nods and breaks off, heading down to the steward's rooms.

Achill smiles to himself again, handing off the rag to Rhys.

"Rhys," the king starts, "I think it's time we pay the front lines a visit."

***

ACHILL WALKS ALONG THE BORDER, testing the weakened warding stones with his magic. Smoke curls before him, playing with the air between the stones, recoiling when the warding magic is too strong. Next, his hands flare with fire. Nothing happens. The loopholes he thought he had found in the treaty must not have been loopholes, after all.

As soon as Achill arrived at the Inn, reports of the human army encampment growing on the other side of the Border circulated. And if the humans were readying for an attack, it could only mean that the human king had finally figured out Achill had been lying.

Only a few warding stones were weak enough last year to send some fae through. The risk wasn't worth the reward when it meant they had to fight with less magic. No, he needed every powerful fae on his side now.

He lost several young fae to the Border crossing. With his numbers already dwindling and his magic not as potent as it used to be, he couldn't afford to lose any more powerful fae. Not until he could be sure that the Border was finally coming down. Too many had abandoned him in the last few days when news of the human princess waking spread beyond the castle walls. Achill could feel his plans slipping through his fingers. He could hear his dead father's admonishments hissing at him from the Forever Night.

If only he could figure out how to break the stones and the enchantments on them, open up the border, and finish what he started a year ago.

"Sir!" Rhys yells, riding his horse down from the eastern camp near the MacSealgair lands. He pulls up short and slides off the saddle effortlessly. Rhys hovers at the edge of the smoke magic, his horse refusing to get closer.

Achill scoffs, remembering when he was still a youthful fae and could maneuver off those large animals. Though his glamour is in place, he stretches his curved, gnarled back, and the bones crack. Immortality wasn't supposed to be this way.

"Speak, Rhys," Achill says, pulling his smoke magic back toward him.

"The MacSealgair stones... are weakening." Rhys flinches with the last words, bracing for Achill's anger. "Some deserters have attacked the Inn."

The Inn where some of his last supporters are stationed.

Fury flares behind Achill's eyes, and the flames on his hands shoot forward, lighting some of the grasses on fire. Shifters are always so predictable. At least it was something he could count on; their baser nature will always win out. The only way the MacSealgair pack would willingly weaken its wards was if it was planning to get to its alpha.

Achill turns from the Border with a flourish. Rhys scurries backward, pushing his horse out of the way of the king and his flames.

With a wave, he opens a portal into the castle courtyard. Before he steps through, he looks over his shoulder at Rhys. "Bring those stones down in whatever manner you can. We are going to end this once and for all."

Twenty-Five
Sorcha

My feet land silently on the other side of the wall, vines gently placing me on the grass in the castle gardens. Murdock perches on the wall above me, signaling that the guards are gone. He climbs down the stones, landing quietly beside me. Murdock shifts his sword from his back to his hip, tightening the belt and withdrawing a dagger. He holds his free hand out to his side, water swirling around the tips.

A year ago, I escaped through a hole in the wall at my back, shimmying my way through to the base of a tree whose roots filled in the gaps and bought me time. Now, Opal and Thorne wait by the same tree, monitoring the surrounding forest for any approaching guards. But, should things get rough, Thorne and Opal have strict orders to meet in a clearing just beyond the Goddess' Grotto, far enough from the castle so we can portal away fast.

Thorne, back in bird form, perches in the tree branches above the garden, watchful and waiting. Should they see something amiss, their sharp shriek will alert us. And though I am familiar with their call, every bird that sings this morning makes me jump, worried it is Thorne.

"One last time, just in case we get separated," Murdock whispers. He points toward the side door near my old balcony. A honeysuckle bush has grown over and around the frame, hiding most of it from view except the handle. Vines have crawled over the baluster of my balcony, curling their way toward the windows. I am relieved that the vines that helped heal my broken body weren't cut down. My eyes scan the rest of the castle. The floors I used to inhabit are dark, and the curtains are pulled tight against the light.

Barely moving my lips, I whisper, "Through my rooms, to the hallway, get Conall out of the castle through the gardens, rescue the nymphs, get the hell out of here. Oh, and save my magic as much as I can."

Easy.

Murdock nods in agreement, his lips pressed into a thin line. The gardens are quiet, and it feels as if the entire castle holds its breath while watching our every move. I palm a dagger, and we run to the door. Murdock turns the handle, but it sticks. He jostles the handle once, and then it creaks open. I cringe, but Murdock's water magic swallows the hinges in water, dimming the noise. With a gentle shove, Murdock slips in effortlessly. I follow closely behind. The vines reach toward me, their leaves a welcome graze as I pass under. At the last minute, I grab a few honeysuckle blossoms for the brownies still trapped in this castle.

The hallway is pitch black and musty. Cobwebs grace almost every corner. I place a honeysuckle blossom near the threshold, hoping the brownies are doing okay, and follow Murdock into the dark. As soon as my foot contacts the bottom step, I run, pushing past Murdock, and shove inside my old rooms. He says something at my back, but I don't hear him. I am too eager to get to my mate.

The door hits the wall with a bang, and I fight against the waves of memories that threaten to take over. My eyes cloud with tears as flashes of Fern and the pixies, the brownies, and Hazel swim in front of me.

"Your Highness?" Murdock asks, coming up the stairs behind me. He places his hand on the door and scans the pristine room. "Are you all right? We have to hurry."

"These were my rooms, Murry," I whisper, still reliving all the moments leading up to my escape from this place. No dust, no cobwebs here. I bend down and leave more blossoms by the doorframe.

Murdock's hand touches my arm and squeezes me gently, "We don't have much time. Conall *needs* you, Sorcha. The mating bond is the only thing keeping him going."

I reach out to Conall with my heart-call and let my presence wash over the empty bond, pouring hope and love down our connection. But, for all I know, the bargain with the Goddess also sealed Conall's fate.

<hr>

IT ISN'T POSSIBLE, but the door looms ten times larger than the last time I was here.

I wait for smoke magic to pour from under the threshold like last time, to feel the pain in my body, to hear the screams of Conall echoing down these halls. But it's so eerily quiet, and I fear the worst. I can't get the image from my dream of Conall lying broken on the ground out of my head—his scream of terror.

My hand shakes so roughly that Murdock clamps his hand over mine to still it. He holds a finger to his lips as he releases some of his water magic, swallowing the handle with water. With a flick of his wrist, it turns, and he pulls it open, quiet as a mouse. I smile and look down at my hands, the blue and green magic pulsing on my fingertips. Opal *has* to teach me how to do that.

The smell of damp earth, death, and mildew wafts into the hallway, filling my chest with fear. We look down a long staircase, torches flickering along the walls. It is too quiet, but I know Conall is down there. He has to be.

Murdock stares into the darkness with me. He swallows and finally meets my gaze. Myriad fears are etched into the frown on his face and his blue eyes. "Sorcha, we don't know..."

I hold my hand out at my side, hoping to comfort him. "He'll be fine," I say.

Right?

We grasp each other's hands and nod at one another, taking our first steps toward the descent. The door closes behind us, Murdock's magic still dampening any sounds, and we are swathed in shadows.

Murdock goes first, letting go of my hand. Each step brings me closer to Conall, and I shake so much that I have to holster my dagger. The stairs are coated in mildew, and I slip, a yelp escaping before I clamp my hand over my mouth.

Murdock stops below me, patiently waiting while I find my footing again. I mouth "thank you" and place my hand on the slimy wall to steady myself. The closer we get to the bottom, the more moss peeks from between the cracks of the stairs. Dampness fills my lungs, and the only light available is the torches flickering in the stairwell. Murdock grabs one off the wall, and the orange light illuminates a long, dark hallway. No cell doors line the walls except for one at the far back.

He turns to me, whispering, "This isn't like the king's other dungeons. There are stronger wards here. I can't see them but can't access my water magic anymore."

I glance down at my hands, and the colors are gone.

Murdock lifts his torch, but I stay rooted to the ground, staring at my human hands, which no longer shimmer with magic. My stomach churns, and a sickening thought crosses my mind.

What if I can't feel the heart-call because Conall no longer lives?

"Sorcha!" Murdock's voice sounds from the far end of the hall, and I snap my head up. "He's here!"

The world comes rushing into focus, and my body shakes with relief.

Murdock leans against the cell door window. "Hold on, mate. We're going to get you out."

I sprint down the hall, splashing through the slick puddles coated with algae and moss. Murdock shines a light through the small cell window, looking for a way to get in. No keys hang on the hook near the door.

My voice cracks. I brace my hands against the door, wishing I was tall enough to see inside. My voice wavers as I ask, "Conall?"

A hushed movement sounds through the tiny window, something shuffling against the stone.

"Conall? My love. I'm here. We're going to get you out," I say, my voice a little louder and more robust.

"Good," Murdock says. "Keep talking to him. Here, hold this. I think I saw something by the base of the stairs."

I take the torch and hold it to the window.

"Conall. I need to know if you're okay. My love? Please?"

Even on my tiptoes, I can barely see beyond the lower lip of the window. I am ready to claw my way up to see inside when I hear the scuffling noise again and a hushed groan.

I can't hold back my tears, and my voice cracks as I say, over and over, through the window, "I'm here."

"I've got something," Murdock says, hefting what looks like a rusted metal spear. He slides it between the bolt and the door. "Step back."

He pulls down on the shaft, and in a quick snap, it breaks in two, the pieces splintering.

"Fuck!" He yells and kicks the tip of the spear out of the way. Murdock tosses the broken shaft down the hall. It lands in a puddle, splashing murky water over the walls and the steps. He has his sword out and wedged between the bolt and the door in seconds.

"Murdock," I warn. "That bolt is too thick. All we have left are daggers..."

He doesn't respond and strains against the metal. Grunting, he puts his foot up against the wall and tugs. Nothing.

"Goddess above," I murmur and place the torch in a holder.

I clasp my hands on top of his sword. He flashes me a look and nods.

"One, two, three!" He counts, and we pull. The metal bolt creaks, and then, with a pop! the bolt comes free, and the door swings open.

Murdock falls backward, landing against the opposite wall as I rush headfirst into the dark room beyond.

Twenty-Six
Sorcha

The first thing that hits me is the stench of blood, urine, and vetiver. Shadows dance along the walls, the torchlight providing minimal illumination. I almost gag, but then I see him.

He is curled up in the corner, his back facing me. His shirt is in shreds, hanging on by a thread at his shoulders. Dried blood coats him like a second skin, and his back has been whipped to the bone. Puss weeps from several of his open wounds.

"Murdock! He isn't moving!" I shout over my shoulder. Murdock grunts. My hands shake, but I take a tentative step closer, whispering, "Conall? I'm here. We're going to get you out, my love."

He says something, but his voice is hoarse.

"What, Conall? I couldn't hear you."

"No," he croaks. He turns his head slightly, and anger flares inside my chest. At the same time, my hopes shatter into a million pieces.

His face is so swollen and battered that I can't even see his eyes.

"Sorcha, let me," Murdock says, putting a hand on my shoulder.

"No," I say, frozen as I tally up the injuries on his body.

Murdock steps in front of me and tries to lean down to get to Conall.

"LEAVE KING!" Conall yells and then groans as he tries to get to his hands and knees. His fingers are bent at odd angles, and a hiss escapes his mouth. I can almost feel the skin on his back tearing open again with the movement.

"Och, Conall. It's Murdock and Sorcha," he says, taking another tentative step forward.

"No," Conall growls. He swipes at Murdock's feet, misses, and then grunts.

Murdock glances at me, his face ashen and his eyes full of tears. He whispers, "I've never... I'm sorry, Sorcha. He looks so..."

But I ignore him and get down on my knees, crawling to my broken mate. Murdock tries to come with me, but I shake my head, pressing into his legs to keep him back.

"Conall? My love?" I whisper, carefully reaching my hand out to his broken ones. "It's Sorcha."

"No," he whispers, and his shoulders shudder.

My hand hovers over his, unsure where to touch that won't cause him pain. Have I lost him forever? "Conall, can you look at me?"

He shakes his head. Conall's body trembles, but he still pushes back to sit on his heels. "I said leave, Achill. Your smoke games won't work this time."

"Games?" Murdock whispers, horrified.

I keep crawling until I am face to face with my wolf shifter. His left eye is swollen shut and covered in dried blood. His right eye is swollen, too, but I can see a sliver of his green eye. I bend down, trying to get him to look at me, but he avoids my gaze.

I sit back on my heels and clench my hands tightly to keep them from shaking. My stomach swirls with the guilt that I sat back and watched him be taken. I broke our bond, and I was the one who left him at the hands of a torturer.

"Do your worst, Achill," he says, his voice scratchy but firm.

"I'm not Achill, my love." I fight tears and bite my lip. "I don't know what he's done to you, but Murry and I are here to bring you home."

There is a flash of recognition at Murdock's nickname as Conall's eye flicks to mine but then away again.

The nickname. I try again to get through to him.

"Conall, Murry is here to help me get you out. But we don't know how much time we have." I lean down to find his green eye again. His eye locks onto mine this time, and I smile. "Oh, what, Conall? See something you like?"

His face falls, and a single tear slips down his cheek. He swallows a few times, and I watch his throat bob with effort. "Sorcha? I thought... I thought..."

"Yes, my mate, it's me." I scoot a little closer and reach for his hands, but he won't give them to me. His fingers are resting at odd angles, and one of his arms looks like it has been broken and healed wrong. His fae body has tried to fix the damage, but it isn't healing fast enough. I vibrate with rage now instead of fear as I whisper, "What did that monster do to you?"

He shakes his head slowly, and more tears run down his cheek. "Please, never ask me that."

"Let's get you out of here." It takes all my effort, but I swallow back all the words I want to say, knowing they won't help. Not now.

Murdock leans down, threading an arm underneath Conall's shoulder, hovering for a moment before he says, "This is going to hurt, mate."

Conall nods and grits his teeth, but it doesn't suppress the guttural moan that echoes down the hall when Murdock hoists him up. Gooseflesh erupts along my skin, and it takes everything I have not to tear this castle to the ground right now.

Murdock cringes as he grabs Conall's side but still jests, "You're in a rough way, Conall. What'd you do, piss off the wrong man?"

Conall wheezes but then goes quiet. Murdock starts up the stairs, but Conall looks over his shoulder at me.

"I'm right behind you. I'm not going anywhere, ever again," I say.

He turns back around, stumbling up the stairs with Murdock,

and my chest tightens. I lift my shoulder and wipe away the stream of tears that fall.

Murdock makes a few jokes on the way up, trying to keep the mood light, but underneath his jovial jabs, there is an undercurrent of genuine terror. I know he wants to get moving so we all don't end up in the same way, but he takes his time for Conall. He shoves the door open, and I rush up behind him so he can get Conall down comfortably.

The door closes behind me with a bang, and I drop to my knees in front of Conall.

I cradle his face in my hands and nudge his nose with mine, the only place that isn't too bloody or broken despite also being broken.

"I'm here," I whisper. His body sags and his forehead touches mine.

"Are you ready, Conall?" Murdock asks but doesn't wait for a response before his water magic coats Conall's body.

Conall grunts, and his whole body tenses despite the gentle caress of the water.

"Hold on, my love. We're so close," I say. My thumbs stroke his cheeks, and he leans into my touch. "Focus on this. Focus on us. Focus on my voice."

"Sorcha." His voice is still scratchy, and a tear slips down his cheek. He heaves with a silent sob but then grabs his ribs and hisses, and all I want to do is take away the pain.

Water magic flows from my hands and mixes with Murdock's.

Murdock gapes down at me, shocked, but shakes his head. "No, save your magic, Sorcha."

I nod, but my magic doesn't stop even though I try to pull it back. The water spills forth, mixing with Murdock's, coating Conall.

Murdock puts his hand on mine, and finally, my magic stops. His voice is firm as he says, "Och, Your Highness, please. We may need your magic later."

"I'm sorry," I say dejectedly. Whenever my fingers get close to Conall's skin, my water magic comes forth, so I drop my hands from Conall's face. I want to touch him so badly, make sure that all of his bones are where they need to be.

"Let me do this," Murdock says. "Please."

All I can do is nod, so I drop my hands and sit back on my heels, feeling utterly helpless. A tiny little shadow catches the corner of my eye. It flutters near the door to the outer hallway, scurrying about like a mouse.

Hush.

"Hello, Hush," I say, kneeling. I hold my hand out, and she scurries up frantically and pulls at my hair. "What's wrong?"

I press my ear against the door. There is nothing outside. Her big brown eyes find mine, and she squeaks a few times.

"It's Puff," Conall says, grunting through the healing magic.

I turn, cradling the distraught brownie.

Finally, Murdock drops his hands, and the magic releases Conall. The water splashes across the floor, leaving bloodied puddles everywhere.

"That's all I've got, mate." Murdock frowns and shakes out his hands. "I couldn't get it all to heal in our short time."

I walk over to Conall, relieved I can finally see his eyes, and the swelling has gone down. "What do you mean it's Puff?" I ask, slightly frustrated that I can't understand Hush's harried squeaking. Is this another ramification for bargaining away my fae blood? I stroke Hush's hair under my fingertips.

An emotion flashes across Conall's face. Can he can tell that I am no longer part fae?

"She's worried about Puff. It seems—" he groans as he shifts forward onto his hands and knees to get up—"that Puff might transform into a boggart."

Murdock raises his shoulder under Conall's arm and helps him stand. They both grunt, Murdock exhausted from using his water magic, and Conall from putting weight on the wrong leg. He almost goes down, his knee wobbling underneath his weight. Murdock catches him, hauling him upright again.

Hush climbs up my shoulder, still squeaking away.

I give Conall my arm so he can lean on me. His fingers are no longer crooked, but he still looks gaunt. I peek around his shoulder to look at his back. The lashing marks remain, but the worst ones have scabbed over. Thankfully, the puss is gone.

"Conall, are you strong enough to walk?" I ask, meeting Murdock's concerned eyes over Conall's shoulder. Worry presses down on me, wondering if we'll be able to make it back to Thorne safely.

Conall clears his throat, releasing my arm. Some of his hair has fallen in his face, and I brush it behind his ear, but he grabs my hand and brings it to his mouth. He gently kisses my palm, and, through gritted teeth, he says, "I can manage."

"Good," Murdock grumbles, hefting Conall over his shoulder some more. "Too bad we can't portal the fuck out of here."

Hush raises her tiny little voice an octave higher.

"Not now, little brownie," Murdock huffs.

"Her name is Hush," I retort. I feel jealous when I see that Conall and Murdock understand her clearly. Both fae look at me.

She squeaks in agreement.

"Sorcha, forgive my tone, but *we don't have time.*" Murdock scowls, sweat beading his brow from holding Conall. "We need to get back to the gardens, and it's faster if—"

I cut off Murdock, "The brownies in this castle don't have a choice. I can run back to my rooms and then meet—"

"No, Sorcha." Murdock shakes his head. "You're the only one with enough magic."

"I'll be all right," Conall says, coughing a few times. "We stick together. Let's just... get the fuck away from this place."

Conall and Murdock wait for my answer, and I consider changing my mind. Rerouting our exit means more time in the castle and less time for me to free the water nymphs. The total weight of this choice sits on my shoulders where Hush sits. "Back to my rooms, then."

After a moment, they nod, and we walk to the door. Conall is still leaning heavily on Murdock when Hush leaps onto Conall's shoulder. Her distress is palpable, and I wish I could understand her so badly. She gingerly strokes his hair, trying to tidy him up even though she's worried about her friend, and I know I made the correct decision.

The nymphs are powerful; the brownies are not. I can't lose the little ones who saved me from Achill that night.

I open the door slowly, hoping it won't creak. The hallway is blessedly empty, so I open the door wide. Murdock and Conall slip through first. Conall favors his right side, and I worry that his more serious injuries haven't had enough time to heal.

We head back the way we came, and the honeysuckles I left along the way are gone.

Guards shout down the hallway, a cascade of footsteps against the stone. My stomach drops, and I turn to Murdock, who is trying to reach for the hilt of his sword while he holds Conall upright. His eyes snap to mine when he realizes his broken sword is still in the dungeons.

"Murry, can you get him back to my old rooms?" I whisper, green magic already tingling in my hands.

Murdock gives me a curt nod and then hefts Conall up, pulling an arm over his shoulders. Hush is already airborne and scurrying along with the shadows. Murdock takes off as fast as he can while hauling my broken mate down the hallway. They disappear behind the corner when a door at the far end opens, and someone shouts, "There!"

I take off at a run, throwing my earth magic behind me. Large spiked bushes sprout in the center of the corridor, their branches curling with thorns that snag the tapestries on the wall. The guards call out again, and their blades sing as they draw them to hack at the thorns.

I CLOSE the door to my old rooms behind me and slide to the floor. Conall lies on the dusty chaise, his breath heavy and sweat on his brow. I hope he has enough strength to get over the wall and beyond the castle grounds, far enough into the woods to portal away. And then he will be safe. He shifts to face me better and groans but meets my eyes. A pained smile graces his bruising face.

"I can't believe you're here." Deep lines crease his brow as he frowns, and he looks like he has aged a few years just from the pain.

I smile at the sound of his voice, even though it is hoarse. But I still can't feel the heart-call. I tug, and I tug, but nothing comes back.

"I'm here," I sigh, walking to where Conall lies. I kneel next to him, and my hand reaches up to brush away some of the hair that has fallen across his face. "I couldn't just leave you here forever, you know."

"Why," he asks. "Do you see something you like, Princess?"

"It's Queen now, you know," Murdock says over his shoulder. He faces the bookshelves on the far side of the room, arms crossed with a frown.

"Holy Goddess, Sor—Your Highness. My Queen," Conall says, struggling to get down on one knee.

"Enough, Conall. There's no need. Just rest for a few minutes." I stop him with a firm hand on his chest, and I have to hide my shock at how weak he feels beneath my touch. Where did all of his fine, chiseled muscles go? Where is the strong fae lord I once knew?

His once-broken hands reach out and cup my cheek. I lean into his touch, hungry for the feel of his skin against mine.

A squeak sounds from the corner of the room. Conall drops his hand and turns to look for the brownie. I squeeze Conall's shoulder and walk to where Hush is frantically trying to get my attention.

I drop to my knees, and Hush peers down behind a tapestry. Crouching, I lift the edge of the woven hanging. Huddled in the dark recesses of the shadows are a pile of honeysuckle blossoms and a brownie trapped underneath a woven basket.

"A boggart," I whisper, realization hitting me square in the chest. "Oh, it's Puff."

I reach forward, and Hush moves my hand out of the way.

Tiny gnashing teeth chew at the confines. I lift the hanging by the corner to see Puff better. He hasn't fully transformed yet, but he is well on his way, and I'll be damned if I let anything happen to him.

Summoning some of my magic, I touch the floor. A tiny trail of sweet white alyssum flowers finds its way underneath the basket. "What happened?"

Conall shifts behind me, saying, "Perhaps Puff was trapped under here a while ago."

Echoes filter through the door from down the hall, and I stand up abruptly. I whip around to meet Murdock's eyes over Conall's head. He grabs the sides of the bookshelves, grunting as he shoves them over to the door. I hurry to help and pull them backward, barricading us inside my old sitting room. My hands glow green, but he clamps a hand over mine and shakes his head.

Murdock says, his voice low and patient, "Wait. Not yet."

His eyes flitter down to his hand on mine. He quickly withdraws it as if my touch burns him. "It took everything I had to—" he looks back at Conall—"help earlier."

"Understood."

The shouts in the hallway go quiet as the guards storm by. I turn back to where Puff lies trapped and know I can't leave him behind. My heart breaks at the sight of his mangy fur and tattered clothing. I thought I had left enough gifts for them, but I never planned on being gone for a year. Hush half-flies and half-climbs up my body, landing in my palm. "Go find Scruff. I'm taking you all with me."

She squeaks and flies off.

Murdock sighs, impatience building. "She better make it quick."

He stacks several chairs in front of the bookshelf. Then his eyes light up when he finds a poker and a shovel by the fireplace. He hands Conall the shovel and then stands guard by the door with the fire-poker.

Meanwhile, I work quickly, pulling up some of my earth magic and weaving a little pouch out of tightly woven vines. I hope it's sturdy enough to keep Puff inside for the journey home. I lean down, place several honeysuckle blossoms inside the pouch, and then nestle the opening against the wicker basket. Puff scoots closer, and I lift the edge of the basket. He smells the tasty blossoms, sniffs carefully, and crawls forward. As soon as most of his half-brownie, half-boggart body is in the new pouch, I tip it up. The vines snap closed, sealing him inside.

At first, he's angry, trying to claw his way out, but soon, he finds the honeysuckle and nibbles away loudly. I touch my shoulder, and vines weave around the straps of my stay, securing the pouch to my upper chest under my shirt. His tiny body shifts as he finally settles down. A tug on my pant leg tells me that Hush and Scruff have arrived. They clamber up the rest of the way and tuck themselves into my hair at the base of my braid.

The door shakes behind the bookshelves.

"Sorcha! We have to go. Now!" Murdock whisper-yells as he strains against the bookshelves. The guards on the other side start hacking away.

My hands glow green, and vines grow, weaving around the bookcase and the door. But why are they hacking with their swords when they could have used their magic all this time?

A bird cries outside - one long, loud shriek.

A warning call.

"Thorne!" I cry out and turn to the balcony. My magic sputters, the vines stalling in their growth.

"Sorcha, stay." Conall grabs my wrist, and I jolt when his hands touch my skin again. Our magic sparks between us, but his green fades as quickly as it began.

Conall and Murdock exchange a glance - an unspoken, centuries-old moment shared between them - and Murdock darts from the door to the balcony. Slick and swift like a river current, he slides onto the balcony. Dagger in hand, he hugs the side of the building and disappears over the baluster.

The guards bang on the door, and creaking metal crawls down my spine. The lock pops open, splintering the doorjamb, and three guards shove their swords in the gap. I stand there, shocked, as I lock eyes with the first guard.

Neil. The guard who escorted me through Fae with the king. A flash of recognition crosses his face, and he fumbles with his sword. It clangs to the floor.

Stalling?

He meets my eyes again and mouths, "*Go!*"

I run to Conall, looping his arm over my shoulders, and try to heave him toward the stairs.

We struggle to make our way the few scant feet - my shorter human figure no match for his larger one. I grit my teeth and half-drag him to the stairs, my hand gripping his side. I hesitate at the top, wondering how to get us down the stairs. Conall grunts and braces himself against the doorjamb.

He turns to me, his bright green eyes calm. "I can make my way down. I don't want us to both fall."

"Okay," I nod, "I—"

The door splinters behind us, and books soar into the room from the impact.

"Go," I whisper, half-shoving him down the stairs. He shuffles his way into the dark, and as he disappears from my view, his back is bleeding again.

The bargain echoes in my head, and I swallow the guilt thickly.

Holding my arms out to my side, the earth pulses through me, beating with the rhythm of my heart. A tree sprouts from the floor, and thick, thorny vines crawl between the stone's cracks—a web of briars growing from nothing. The yew tree grows larger still, blocking the servants' door and sealing off Conall from the guards.

"Sorcha!" Conall calls out from behind the tree.

But I shake my head, standing in the center of the room.

"Go, Conall. I've got this," I grind out, my voice straining as I will my magic to overtake the room.

The guards finally break into the room, only to be met with thick, thorny vines that whip around and snatch at everyone except Neil. Sweat drips from my brow, and I never knew how taxing calling up so much magic in such a short time could wipe my energy. I fight exhaustion as the bookshelf splinters among the mass of vines. One guard screams as vines wrap around his body, encasing him in their roots.

The other guards start hacking away. Neil maintains eye contact with me, and that's when I let my magic falter. He slows his movements and gives me a slight nod. One of his other compatriots palms a dagger and throws it through the gap in the vines. I sidestep, but not fast enough, as it slices the side of my thigh. I hiss and drop my hands, my right hand clamping over the gash. Blood seeps down my leg, and my magic finally sputters.

Neil turns, attacking his compatriot furiously.

"Run, Queen Sorcha!" he yells as he exchanges blows with the other guards. Their clashing swords ring out in the room, metal on metal. I turn, scrambling to get myself to the balcony.

With one last look at the guards fighting their way through the vines, I swing my leg over the baluster and climb down.

Just like I did a year ago.

Twenty-Seven
Sorcha

I jump the last few feet and land on my ankle with a crunch. I crumple onto the ground, crying out in pain as the gash on my leg opens further and my ankle throbs. The brownies clutch my hair tightly, and Puff snarls a few times until the jostling stops. Strewn on the ground around me are tufts of downy white feathers, and I reel back, fear knotting itself in my throat for Thorne's safety.

"Sorcha!" Conall and Murdock both whisper from the shadowy doorway. Murdock has Conall around his shoulders again, and they come running. Conall has healed a little more, but something about his left leg doesn't look quite right.

"Go, I'm fine," I say with a grimace. Conall's eyes fixate on the gash on my leg that refuses to heal. "I'll be fine. Go."

I stand, but my legs wobble beneath me. Conall throws a hand out to steady me. He clenches his jaw, but his grip is firm as he hauls me up to standing.

"Over here!" Guards shout nearby.

My eyes find Conall's. His eyes go dark, and his mouth is a tight line.

We're cornered.

"Go!" I rasp, shoving him away from me and toward where

Murdock and I climbed over. I point to the hedges and tree roots that poke through to the outside of the wall. "You need—,"

"No." Conall cuts me off, standing his ground with a pained face.

"Goddess above, you stubborn wolf!" Murdock curses and twirls the poker in his hand. He turns to face the guards' cries, but we all know they vastly outnumber us. "Both of you, go. Now."

A giant wall of water comes barreling toward us from the back corner of the garden. It parts around our group and rushes past us into the gardens. Opal pops up from behind a hedge, her hands swirling above her head.

"No!" I scream as Opal passes us and stands next to Murdock. "Please go back!"

Sadness and hope swirl in her eyes as she says, "Save all of *us*."

Opal holds her hands up high and turns to face the guards.

Thick ropes of water wrap around their necks, covering their faces. They claw at the magic, unable to peel away the water that suffocates them. The entire garden is quiet for a few moments as the life leaves their bodies. Opal's shoulders sag with exertion, and Murdock quickly takes a blade from a soldier.

"Sorcha, we have to go. I have to get you out of here," Conall says, taking my hand in his.

I yank backward, freeing his hand. "There could be more, Conall. I can't leave them here to fight alone."

Conall frowns, his lips forming a tight line. Whether from disapproval or resignation, I do not know. He clasps a hand over his heart and dips into a slight bow. "At your service, My Queen."

Always the noble warrior, ready to fight despite his injuries, Conall waits for my command. I hand him a tiny dagger, the blade barely bigger than my hand.

"It's all I have?" I shrug.

"It'll have to do," he says. "But first."

He holds up the dagger, takes a handful of my shirt, and slices a long strip off. Despite the sweat that drips from his brow and the pallid color of his face, his fingers make quick work, wrapping the cloth around my thigh to staunch the bleeding. I wince when he ties it off. Can he tell I'm not healing like a fae?

"I'm sorry," he whispers, his fingers lingering on my thigh. "I have to tie it tight or..."

More shouts ring out behind us, and swords ring in the air as the guards withdraw them from their scabbards. Conall takes my hand, squeezing it a few times reassuringly. And we limp back to Murdock and Opal—the brownies titter, burrowing deeper into my hair.

The guards lie sprawled out on the soaking wet grass. Their lifeless eyes stare up at the sky, terror forever frozen on their faces. I stare into the brown eyes of a fae who only looks as if he is only twenty.

Why aren't they using their magic?

Murdock pilfers two more swords and tosses one to Conall, who misses it. It falls to the ground at his feet, cringing when he bends to pick it up. His jaw tenses when he stands, and he leans against the sword momentarily. He readies himself to fight, putting his weight on his right leg. I reach down to pick up another discarded sword and can barely lift the piece of metal. Worried someone will see me struggling, I leave it on the ground and nervously palm my dagger instead.

Opal comes up to my side, dark circles under her eyes, looking more like an ogre now. Sweat lines her brow, but she stands shoulder to shoulder with me on her right and Murdock and Conall on her left.

Conall points to the castle wall, which dips slightly near the honeysuckle vines and the door. "Stay there, Sorcha, and attack the flank from here." He gestures, continuing to give orders as the guards draw closer. "Murdock and I will cut them down until Opal can recover. Our only goal is to get the queen out of here safely."

The guards round the corner.

My hand shakes, and I squeeze my fingers around the dagger tightly.

"We're getting out of here," I say over and over to the brownies but also, in part, to myself, hoping that if I say it enough, it'll come true. They grip my hair and settle in, chittering to themselves.

The guards rush forward, clashing with Murdock and Conall. Immediately, Conall goes down on one knee and roars out as he braces against the impact of the sword above his head. Murdock feigns a thrust and parries, spinning out and then back in toward Conall. Opal, exhausted, takes her water magic and throws what she can at the guards.

My fingers glow green and blue, the magic tingling back to life in my hands. Murdock slips between two guards, knocking one over, and Conall stumbles upward, pushing his attacker back. Then his hand slips, and the guard's sword glances at Conall's side. He sways, and that's when I've had it.

I will not wait in the corner like a cowering field mouse.

Magic flares to life in my hands, and I step out to fight amongst my mate and friends, refusing to believe that, as a mere human, I can't fight alongside them. The vines whip out from all angles. The guards shriek as the plants snatch at them, a gnarled mess of thorns tearing at limbs. One guard lands with a crunch on the other side of the wall, tossed about like a rag doll. The other guard, closest to me, goes wide-eyed and pleading. But I snap my fingers, and the vines snap his neck.

Murdock quickly dispatches his opponent. Conall gets pushed further and further back by an opponent who is much larger and healthier than he is.

"Hey!" I call to the guard. He doesn't hear me and swings wildly at Conall, who struggles to raise his sword. Conall's entire side is slick with blood, and, try as he might, it leaves his right side wide open.

Sweat breaks across my brow, and I push my vines forward. They grab the guard's ankles, yanking him backward. He screams as he's dragged through the mud, the grass, and the blood of his comrades. My body shakes with the stress of pushing my magic too soon, but I hold my hands out and rip the guard asunder with a twist of my fingers.

The voice doesn't sound like mine when I say, "No one hurts my mate. Ever again."

Conall clutches his side, and blood soaks his fingers. He tries to stand but wobbles, falling back down to his knees.

"We need to go," Murdock says, his voice low, urgent. He's covered in blood and has slashes across his arms. A large gash on his head drips blood into his eyes, but he wipes it away with a swipe of his arm.

Opal sags against the wall, utterly spent. She braces herself against the stone, and her breathing is ragged. Still, she smiles at me. "You *save* us."

"Only if we move quickly," Murdock clips. His arm is underneath Conall's, and he hoists my mate to the wall. "We *really* need to go."

I gesture where the root of the tree still sticks out.

"This is where we leave," I say, calling upon my earth magic again. My hands shake, and only a shimmer of green and blue glows around my hands. Then it fades. I kick the wall, cursing. "Fucking Goddess Above!"

I try again. Green and faint blue shimmers at my tips but then sputters out. Sheer exhaustion knocks the wind from my lungs as panic claws at my throat. I need my magic to ask the tree to move its roots, or else how are we supposed to get out of here?

The earth rumbles beneath our feet, the stone wall shakes, and the tree root pulls back, opening the hole in the wall. Murdock's shoulders sag in relief. He walks Conall to the hole and sets him down against the stone wall.

Conall smiles faintly and slurs, "I knew you could do it."

"It-it wasn't me..." I say. Murdock is at Opal's side and helps her up, too.

A strawberry blonde head pokes through the base of the wall, and my father crawls out, muddy and frantic. "Let's go, all of you."

I shove Conall toward my father, who helps Conall get into the hole. I meet my father's worried eyes. "He goes first. He's still bleeding."

At first, Conall fights, but I push him forward, and my father holds onto his hands with a death grip. He gives me a furious look and tries to fight me. I push him down and force him to crawl through the hole. I am close behind but pause, grabbing my father's arm to get him to come with me.

"Murdock! Opal! Come on!" I shout. Opal pushes to her feet, completely exhausted, and Murdock heads our way, a deep frown on his face.

But I hear a shout, and Murdock's eyes flash to mine, laced with fear. He turns.

Everything happens in slow motion.

A guard I had thought was dead grunts, gets to his knees, and pulls his sword up within seconds. It flashes in the sunlight as it slices into Opal's shoulder. She roars and falls to one knee. I lunge forward to get to her, my father right by my side. But no one is faster than Murdock, who snatches a sword from the ground, spins lightning fast, and runs the guard through in one swift motion.

I dash to Opal, who has fallen into the hedges, and wrap my arms around her. The world falls away as I cradle her half-ogre body. Her eyes roll in the back of her head, and I sit there, stroking her hair, tears filling my eyes.

"Shhh, Opal. You're going to be okay," I croak. I press my hand to the gash at her neck, trying to staunch the flow of blood.

She gulps for air, but her blood flows so freely, and soon, we're both soaked in the warmth. Her breathing turns bubbly, and blood trickles from her mouth as she chokes on a few silent words. I try to find my water magic, and it coats my hands, staunching the flow, but only partially.

I don't have enough magic to heal her.

"You are such a dear friend, Opal. My life..." My throat closes, and my eyes fill with so many tears that the world blurs. "My life has been so much brighter with you in it. I need you to hold on a little longer, and then we can swim in the river together. We will have so much fun when we get home—just you and me. And you can teach me all there is to know about water magic. And I'll build you the most beautiful pools with fresh water that empty into a stream that will go directly to the sea. You can come and swim anytime you like."

A warm hand touches my shoulder, shaking me from my trance, and Conall stares down at me, muddy as can be. He shakes his head slowly. "Sorcha, it's time to go now."

"No," I protest, "Opal—she —"

But Opal is gone. Her eyes are closed, and her face is so peaceful that it is as if she is permanently trapped in a gentle dream. I pull my trembling hands away, coated head to toe in a pool of her blood.

I stroke her hair and whisper, "Opal, it's time to go home."

"Sorcha," Conall says as carefully as he can, but an urgency laces his words. "It's time for *us* to go home."

I snap up at the sounds of grunting and swords clashing together. My father and Murdock slice away at several guards, blood splattering their faces and clothes with each blow they land.

When did more guards get here?

They've advanced closer, and I grab onto Opal harder, refusing to part with her body. The brownies chitter in my ear and tug on my hair, trying to get me to move, but my body is leaden, fused to my friend.

"GO!" Murdock yells as his sword pierces another guard. Two more of them lay dead, but three still advance, pressing my father and Murdock back, cornering all of us so our only escape route is through the tunnel. Conall tries to lift me, but I can't let go of Opal. I can't leave her here with the evil king. He'll do unspeakable things to her. He'll torture her endlessly, and what kind of a person would I be if I let her be tortured? She still has to teach me about her visions.

A figure leaps off my old balcony and joins Murdock's flank, pushing the guards back a few more feet. Neil, clothes torn from the brambles but otherwise unscathed, swivels and slashes. He helps push the advancing guards back. Green shimmers in his hands, but again, no magic comes forth. Instead, Neil parries and blocks with ease, his sword wet with blood.

"Murdock!" Conall yells, still trying to get me to stand.

I am fused to my friend, unable and unwilling to let her go. Because if I let her go... "I can't leave her here, Conall."

"You're going to have to, Sorcha. She's gone," Conall says, his voice full of pity. His hands are soft on my shoulders, but the rest of his body is tense at my back.

Murdock grunts, cursing as he lands a final blow with his sword. He pierces through the third guard for good and runs toward us. He limps with a gash of his own above his knee. Slash marks cover his arms, and blood seeps through his shirt.

"Let's go, Queen Sorcha," Murdock says, and the formality in his voice confuses me.

Conall reaches down and peels my fingers free, taking my hand in his and squeezing. "Tunnel. Now."

I hesitate a moment too long, my eyes trying to memorize how she lays and her face's peacefulness. But everything is dark red - her blood seeping out of her body and flowing like a river into the puddle beneath her.

Conall tugs on me again, and I stumble toward the tunnel. He tightens his grip on my hand before he releases it. He goes through first but backward, his eyes lock on me, despite the wounds reopening on his back and the gash along his side. Conall hisses as his injured back grazes the ceiling of the tunnel, and his pain is enough to shake me from my stupor.

"We'll portal back as soon as we meet Thorne in the woods," I tell him, wincing as his back scrapes against the stone again. He gives me a pained smile, but I can tell he's trying to put on a brave face.

Murdock tries to stay behind, but soon, my father is there, pushing him through the tunnel behind me. Father shoves Murdock through with one last heave despite the cries of even more guards at his back.

Finally, Conall makes it to the other side, and then I slide out, followed by Murdock, who drags a sword behind him. But no one else comes through.

"Father?" I ask Murdock, and shock registers on his face when he glances behind him.

"He—he was right behind me," Murdock says. He bends down to go back into the tunnel when the earth rumbles again. Murdock jumps back, and I push him behind me as I peer down into the tunnel. Relief floods my system as my father makes his way toward us.

I reach out a hand. "I can pull you! Come on!"

"Sorcha!" He yells, his fingers glowing green, and his entire body lights up. He finds my eyes and shouts through the tunnel, "You are a *great* queen, and I am *so* proud of you!"

With a thunderous boom, the hole closes on itself, taking my father with it. The rest of the stone barrier wobbles, collapsing on top of the remaining guards. The sound of crashing rubble drowns out their screams.

I stand there, shocked, as the dust clears.

"Papa?" I whisper—the eerie quiet echoes into the forest. My entire body shakes, shock coursing through my bones. I let out a blood-curdling scream. "Papa!"

Conall wraps me in his arms, and I flail, fighting, pushing, thrashing against his chest.

"Let me go!" I scream into him, my eyes shut tight, trying to remember the way my father looked, wanting to keep his face burned into my memory forever. I shove against his hold, and he grimaces. "I said, let me go!"

"I can't, Sorcha. You can't go back there," his voice cracks. He holds me tight despite his injuries and how pallid his face is.

My limbs go numb, and I retreat into my sorrow, carried on the wind by the weightlessness of loss. I tilt my head and look at Conall, shocked to find his dark hair lifting around his face.

A torrent of wind whips around us, tearing at our clothes and pulling at our hair. The brownies cling tight to the base of my neck, and Conall tightens his arms around me, the steady beating of his heart in my ear. Leaves and bracken swirl in the tornado of air around us, and we float higher and higher in a maelstrom of my magic.

Conall squeezes me again, bundling me into his cocoon of safety, and I never want to leave. My mind whirls like the wind swirling around us. I wrap my arms around him, never wanting to let go, but he stifles a groan when I unravel myself slowly. My hands come away wet with blood. The brownies nuzzle under my chin, and their soft fur is a reminder that brings me back to this moment.

I pull back, staring into Conall's pained eyes.

Will everyone I love die because of me and the choices I've made?

Conall, broken and battered, still injured in ways I cannot fathom, smiles sadly down at me. He cups my cheek in his hand, his thumb wiping away my tears. I close my eyes against the loss that wants to pull me further down.

Finally, the air funnel slows, and our feet gently touch the earth. I collapse back into Conall, weak and exhausted. His arms shake, but he holds me against him, kissing the top of my head and stroking my hair. His touch gives me strength where I lack, and for a moment, it anchors me. But melancholy creeps in through the cracks, pulling me into the undertow of desolation from a tidal wave of loss.

"Let's go," I sniff and reach for Conall's hand.

Murdock tries to open a portal for us, but it sputters. We're all too weak, and our magic is too depleted, so the three of us limp northward.

Twenty-Eight
Achill

Achill twirls the sword's hilt in his hand, stalking up the mildewy stairs. He almost leaves the blade down in the dungeons by Conall's empty cell, but he picks it up out of the water, fully intent on returning the blade to its owner soon.

He closes the door at the top of the stairs, and his feet squelch on the wet carpet. It is so unfortunate that the wolf-shifter is free, and Conall can no longer join the hide of his brother in his study. Achill did not know how ill-prepared the young wolf shifter was until he showed up and surprised the entire party. It was almost too easy, killing him in front of his other brother and compatriots.

The rebellious guard kneels in the center of the room. His head hangs as blood drips from his mouth. The tips of his ears have been cut off. Blood drips down his jaw when the tip of Rhys' sword presses into the fae's neck, ensuring the betrayer won't get up.

"So," Achill begins, walking around Neil in circles. "You grew a conscience."

Neil says nothing.

"Speak up!" Rhys says, pushing Neil forward onto his hands.

Achill raises his hand, and Rhys pauses. Achill shakes his head and sighs. "You see, I question why a guard of mine would help a ragtag group of fae, with an impostor Queen, to help a pathetic wolf shifter."

Neil grunts.

"I couldn't hear you," Achill leans down, his smoke unfurling from his hands.

"Cut out my tongue, for I will never speak ill of the earth *queen*."

Achill walks around the two fae, circling them slowly as he considers his next move. Neil shouldn't have rebelled. Achill's smoke magic has been strong enough to prevent this from happening. But now?

Yes, things have shifted. He can feel his power waning, his influence slipping through his fingers with each passing day.

The *queen* has ruined all of his plans.

Rhys stares down at Neil with disdain. But Achill feels nothing toward either of them. He can't remember when he felt anything *real* except for Aerona.

"Oh, but I think you will," Achill whispers into Neil's ear. "Once I'm done with you, you'll tell me everything you know."

Neil cackles, a broken, scattered sound that bounces off the walls. Rhys growls and leans forward, the tip of the sword driving into the back of Neil's neck until a single droplet of blood slides down the collar of his shirt. In one motion, Neil grabs Rhys by the leg, throwing him off balance. Rhys lands on his back, his sword up in the air. Neil lunges, impaling himself on his friend's sword.

"What the fuck?" Rhys screams, looking at Neil in horror.

"Long live the Queen," Neil says, smiling. A thick stream of blood escapes his open mouth, spattering Rhys in the face. Neil's body slides forward with a slump, smothering Rhys.

"I assume," Achill says, walking by Rhys, now pinned to the ground with his dead friend on top of him, "that you will clean all of this up."

He waves his hand dismissively around the room before slamming the door behind him and stalking toward the gardens.

Rubble spills out from the side garden, and an entire section of the wall is destroyed.

Achill knows that Earth Fae magic did this because no other way would a wall twenty feet high and three people wide come down in such a fashion.

A muffled groan comes from the wall's far side near the forest.

Achill pauses, listening.

Achill thought he had found everyone and lit every dead guard on fire. He even found a dead half-ogre, half-nymph, and tossed her unceremoniously into the lake. Did he cackle when the sisters wailed and screamed and cursed his name? Maybe.

The groan sounds once more, and a few rocks tremble as a bloodied and broken hand frees itself.

Achill crosses his arms and watches as the Earth Fae slowly extricates himself from underneath the carnage. A slow smile creeps across his face when he realizes it isn't any of his men, but it must be one of Sorcha's allies. The earth trembles slightly, and more rocks fall away.

A head of strawberry-blonde hair appears, smeared with dried blood. But the ears aren't quite pointed enough.

"Ah, Gareth," Achill says, his voice low and in awe. It's a half-ling. It explains so much. "How lovely to meet you."

"Achill," King Gareth grunts out. He winces, legs still trapped beneath the rubble, and tries shifting to face Achill fully.

"It's unfortunate that our meeting wasn't in better circumstances—like at Sorcha's funeral or as I storm your castle." Flames lick at Achill's fingertips, and Gareth's eyes go wide. "Tell me where she is, half-ling."

Gareth struggles against the weight of the rocks as Achill climbs on top. Bones crunch under Achill's weight, and the human king cries out.

"Did she leave... this way?" Achill asks, gesturing to the gaping hole in his wall. He leans down again, forcing his full weight onto the rubble, and Gareth cries out again.

"I think I should pay her a visit," Achill says, flames dancing in the palm of his hand. He reaches down and wraps his fingers around the half-ling king's wrist, flames encircling the wrist like a bracelet. Gareth screams and writhes under the rocks, shifting the earth with his agony.

The hand falls off, and Achill picks it up, tossing it a few times. He jumps down from the rocks, and Gareth shuffles his body forward, clutching his handless arm to his chest. Achill stalks into the forest and places Gareth's hand in his pocket. Then, he snaps his fingers, and the entire section of the wall erupts in flames.

He walks away, following the tracks into the woods. The only sound he hears is the sweet screams of Gareth as the half-ling burns to death, and he thinks to himself how fun it will be when Sorcha's screams reach his ears.

Twenty-Nine
Sorcha

Conall, weak and disoriented, clings to me and Murdock as we drag him through the woods. I still hear my father's last words as we leave the gardens. I see Opal's peaceful face as I let her go. Her blood coats my hands and dries on my clothing.

With each step, my boots shine with the last of her life source. My throat constricts, and I swallow thickly, fighting down the sobs that threaten to give away our location in the dead of night.

I stumble on a thick root, going down on one knee, pulling Conall with me. My thigh throbs, but the bleeding has stopped, and though I'm not healing like I was when I was a fae, it isn't bleeding as much as it was before.

Murdock grunts, hoisting Conall up as I struggle to untangle my leg from a root. My fingers tingle with green, and the tree shifts slightly, lifting out of my way as soon as it recognizes my earth magic. But even that leaves me weak, and gooseflesh travels up my spine as the last vestiges of my magic sputter.

"Are ye all right?" Murdock asks, his lilt coming in tired and thick.

I shoot Murdock a withering look and throw Conall's arm back over my shoulder.

"Grand," I grind out. Puff chitters in his tiny pouch, and Hush responds with a cooing sound. He settles back down almost instantly, and I hope that at least one of us in this ragtag group is healing.

We half-drag, half-haul Conall through the same forest I ran through last year - the castle retreating further behind us as the twilight wears on. Twice more, I stumble and fall, the weight of Conall pushing me down. My twisted ankle and the gash on my thigh throb with each step.

"You need rest, Sorcha," Murdock hisses through his teeth.

"I'll rest once we get Conall some care. I refuse to lose him, too," I say, panting.

Conall wakes slightly, mumbling "Sorcha."

He promptly passes out again.

We stumble down a small hill and come upon the small stream where the Goddess' grotto is. It takes every ounce of energy I have not to collapse at the water's edge and drink until I pass out. Murdock takes Conall over to a birch tree by the statue, gingerly setting him down, and returns to me. He's already healing, and his fae senses are far sharper than mine, but something isn't right. Though the birds chirp and the wind rustles the leaves, Murdock radiates unease.

"Thorne should've been here by now," I whisper, turning in slow circles. Their piercing cry echoes over and over in my head, and I can't help but think that something terrible has happened to them.

Murdock only nods, his lips a thin line. His braids have long fallen out, and the gash on his forehead is healing, albeit slowly. Dried blood cakes his arms, but instead of cuts, pink scars pepper his skin. "I heard them cry but couldn't find them when I left. Just a bunch of feathers and then some footsteps leading away. This isn't the rendezvous point, but they should have seen us coming."

"And Conall's getting worse," I lift my chin in his direction, fighting the waves of abjection that want to swallow me whole. Murdock's water magic should have healed Conall, but he can't stay awake for more than a few minutes before passing out again.

"I could only heal so much before I wore out. He had so many injuries, Sorcha. I have never-" Murdock's voice cracks. "I've never seen him like this before. I've never had such trouble trying to help heal before."

He looks down at his hands and then back up at me like he wants to ask me something, but I turn away.

"You should go get some water," I say, avoiding his questioning look.

"Sorcha," Conall says. He tries to push himself up to sitting but slips, cupping his side.

"I'm here." I reach out and grab his free hand. The other one, clutching his side, comes away wet with fresh blood. The back of my palm touches his forehead, even though a fever has taken hold. Conall's skin is pallid and sweaty, and he shakes uncontrollably. I look up at Murdock, and he swallows when he sees the fear in my eyes.

"Aye, mate, you've looked worse," Murdock says, trying to make a joke.

Conall's face contorts with pain, but his lips still quirk into a half-smile. Over his head, Murdock is grim. Worry is etched into the lines on his face as his friend fights an internal battle with injuries I can't see. Murdock paces, running his hands through his hair, before he stops suddenly and declares, "I'm going to go look for Thorne."

He takes off into the forest beyond.

"Coward," Conall grunts. His shirt is soaked with blood.

"What?" I look down at him, afraid he's misspoken, and the fever has taken over.

"Murry always runs when he can't fix something," Conall says.

I kneel and cup Conall's cheek but finally understand why Murdock ran from me when I didn't return his affections under the mountain. Hush and Scruff untangle themselves from my braid and scurry down my arm onto Conall. They titter and begin cleaning up his bloodied, matted hair, their delicate hands careful as they separate the knots. A few strands stick to Conall's forehead, and I tuck them delicately behind his ear. My fingers linger near the tips that reach a point, and I stroke his earlobe gently.

Conall shivers and his voice comes out like a guttural, primal growl. He says, "That's not fair, My Queen."

"What isn't?" I ask and continue to tuck some of his matted hair behind his ear, running my thumb along the tip again.

"Teasing me like that when..." he pants. "Our ears are very sensitive - especially wolf shifters."

Oh. Ohhh. "I'm sorry, I didn't mean to—"

"No," he whispers, reaching out to grasp my hand. His voice cracks, "I've missed your touch. I've missed you. I've missed feeling anything *good*." He rests his head against the tree trunk and runs his tongue along the seam of his dry, cracked lips.

"I've missed you, too, my love," I whisper and rub some of the blood from his cheek. He leans against my touch. His green eyes are cloudy from pain and sadness. They used to be so full of life. All I want to do is take it all from him and carry the burden with him. "I should have taken your place—,"

Conall places his bloodied hand on my chest, cutting me off. "No, never, My Queen." I must have looked at him strangely because he sits up straighter, grimacing as he shifts, and in a dark tone, adds, "I would have never lived if it had been you in there instead of me. I was honored—no, I was *relieved* to take your place."

He closes his eyes and wilts against the bark, the last of his strength rushing out of his body. Vengeance courses through my veins, and I fight against a fury I have never known.

"I— You need water," I say, turning before he can hear me cry. My legs wobble as I stand and drift to the grotto, my vision blurry through tears.

While Conall's eyes remain closed, I dip my hands into the stream. The frigid mountain water steals my breath as I scrub my hands with sand, eager to wash away the remnants of death that cling to my skin. The water turns pink, and I exhale as an anchor of grief unravels from the center of my body, traveling downstream with the blood.

With a touch of bitterness, I address the statue of the Goddess, keeping my voice low as I say, "This isn't my blood, but the blood of a dear, sweet friend—" I choke out, my throat tight with emotion—

"and my mate. May you find it within your power to help my mate heal from this. And, I hope that as my father and Opal pass into the Forever Night, they will find everlasting peace."

Peace. Peace after all I put them through. After they fought to save me from the reckless decisions I've made, I was the one who led them to their deaths. Their blood on my hands is all my fault.

The Goddess' statue glares at me; her hands hold the bowl in perpetual acquisition. What else could she want? My bargain wasn't for my father's; it wasn't for Opal's. And it most certainly wasn't for Conall's. It was for *my* fae blood and *my* immortality. I want to smash the Goddess' statue into smithereens, but I don't.

That bitch trickster goddess will have a lot to answer for when I see her again. I touch the top of the statue's head and whisper, "If I ever see you again, I have words for you, Goddess. Our bargain wasn't for his life or anyone else's. Our bargain was for *mine*."

With my hands full of water, I walk back to Conall. He cracks open an eye at the sound of my feet, and his hands reach up and cup mine. His fingers stroke the inside of my wrist as he drinks, sending shivers up my arms and awakening a deep yearning from his rough fingers against my skin. When he's finished, he pulls back and looks me up and down.

"Thank you," he says, his voice still rough and scratchy. "I keep thinking this is some fucked up dream."

"How I wish it were," I whisper, fighting back tears. He doesn't release my wrist but pulls it to his lips, placing the gentlest kiss on the palm of my hand. With the last of the water, he lets me clean the blood from his face. Satisfied with their work, the brownies clamber back up and nest in my hair again. Puff has gone quiet, and I can only hope that he is healing.

Conall tries to get up but groans and clutches his side. I put my hands on his shoulders, forcing him to stay seated. "Don't. Just rest for now. Once Murdock—"

"Sorcha, we need to leave now or..." Murdock cuts me off as he barrels back through the woods. He is ashen-faced, and his eyes are frantic as he searches the woods over my shoulder.

"Or what?" The hair on the back of my neck stands.

"It's Thorne," he says, struggling to find the words. "I found..."

He doesn't have time to finish because I take off the way Murdock came. I follow his footprints toward the rendezvous spot, which leads deeper into the forest. The gash on my thigh throbs, but I hobble as best as I can until I reach the clearing. Feathers float in the air and are strewn about everywhere in the forest. A guard is missing its head, and there is blood everywhere.

Blood and feathers.

Feathers.

"Thorne!" I shout into the trees. Silence greets me, but then I hear shuffling as Murdock hauls Conall through the woods.

"They're gone, Sorcha." Murdock's forehead is caked in sweat from supporting Conall. The infection roars inside his body, and he shivers uncontrollably now, his skin pallid and grey. Murdock continues, "I don't know how many guards were here. But if they took Thorne or even k—"

I hold up a hand, stopping him from saying more. I don't even want to consider that Thorne, too, is dead. But there is so much blood, and there are so many feathers.

"Goddess Damnit!" I scream and kick the guard's feet. Anger pours from me like a sieve. "It wasn't supposed to be Opal. Or my father. Or Thorne. No one was supposed to get hurt. It was supposed to be a simple extraction, and *everything* went to shit!"

"No, Sorcha," Murdock says. "We all knew what we were getting into."

My stomach drops. "What do you mean?"

Murdock gives me a pained look and scratches the underside of his chin. "Aye, well. We all knew what we signed up for. Even your father had agreed to this. He knew it would most likely end this way."

I close my eyes. This was the last thing I wanted.

"How very right you are," a voice says from the darkness.

Gooseflesh erupts down my spine. I turn slowly.

Achill waits in the shadows at the edge of the clearing. His ring glints in the dying light of day, and I have to flinch against the memory of it, slicing my cheek open. My eyes flash to Conall, who stiffens at Achill's voice.

The brownies shiver uncontrollably. Despite the waves of fear pulsing through me, I square my shoulders back, hoping they find comfort in my feigned confidence. A few pulses of magic course through my veins, and my fingers tingle with renewed force.

I look at Murry, who meets my gaze. Does he have enough energy to open a portal?

He gives me a subtle nod, gripping Conall tighter under his arm.

If I can hold off Achill for long enough, I can get them out of here safely.

Smoke curls around the base of the trees, and Achill's eyes flash down to my hands. I curl my fingers into my palms, but it's too late. He's already noticed the sparks of blue and green. Achill's face spreads into an evil smile, and he steps forward. I immediately put myself between him and Conall. Murdock stands stock-still to my right, ready and waiting to fight despite our lack of weapons and magic.

"Relax, *Queen*. I have something of yours," Achill says, reaching into his pocket. He pulls something out and tosses it into the dirt at my feet. "He only screamed a little when I took it."

An object lands at my feet.

Father is alive?

Charred flesh encircles white bones, and I lean down slowly to pick up his severed hand that still has his insignia ring on its finger. I slide the ring off, fighting against the urge to claw out Achill's eyes. Conall growls and tries to stand, his green eyes finding mine, but I shake my head.

I turn my father's bloodied and broken hand in mine and slide the ring into my pocket.

"Thank you, Achill," I say, soft-spoken and meek. I can feel the confusion radiating off of everyone. But I need this to work. "Thank you for returning his insignia to me. Now I can rightfully claim the human throne, too."

Achill's eyes grow wide for a split second, replaced by a frown when I bring my hands up and throw my father's hand back at him.

"Now!" I shout at Murdock. The appendage lands with a thump at the king's feet.

Murdock's hand flies outward, and a portal rips open behind me. I help Murdock haul Conall up, my left hand shimmering with magic. As they slip through the portal, Achill kicks my father's hand out of his way and advances.

I block the portal from his view and watch his hands closely, knowing his smoke magic could pour forth at any moment.

"We're not so different, you and I," Achill says. He tilts his head, and I can only imagine how he looks underneath his glamour with his crooked spine and gnarled fingers.

I scoff. "We're *not* the same."

"Ah, but we are, Sorcha." I gag at my name on his lips, swallowing down a look of disgust. He continues, "You still think you can win like I did a hundred years ago. You think you can have it all: the mate, the power, the responsibility. You want to be the saving grace so badly that you fully believe you can unite the fae and defeat me. Oh, if only it were that simple. The humans will not be so willing to join under your rule. They won't go down without a fight. You're a fae queen now, Sorcha; you're one of *us*. Not one of *them*."

He points to my hand, which still reaches backward toward the portal and Conall. Then he points to the other hand, clenched tight at my side as I try to hide the glimmering sparks of magic that thread around my fingertips.

"How easily do you think they will join you? Do you think a silly little signet ring is enough to convince them? After decades of myths and tall tales about the fae? A century of hatred toward our kind?" He takes a step closer.

"Don't." I hold up my free hand. The brownies have gone quiet, and the only way I know they are there is with their tiny fingers gripping my hair tightly.

"Sorcha, I can't hold this much longer!" Murdock yells at me through the other side of the portal.

I look back, briefly breaking eye contact with Achill. Sweat beads on Murdock's brow. Conall clutches his side, which still seeps blood, but his eyes won't leave Achill's form. If Achill makes the first move, Conall will do anything to stop him.

I flash them a smile and step forward an inch, tempted to end this battle with Achill with my dagger and watch the life bleed from his twisted body.

But Conall lunges and his fingers graze mine.

"Not yet," he grits out.

Achill moves closer.

"You will never be a queen, Sorcha," Achill says, smoke unfurling from his cuffs.

My fingers twitch blue and green. Vines crawl from the undergrowth, their tendrils halting at the edge of the clearing, waiting for my command.

Achill steps forward again, and more smoke billows from his fingers. He says low enough for only my ears to hear, "You are nothing but a peace treaty. He is nothing but a dying wolf shifter."

The familiar scent of vetiver reaches my nostrils. Conall squeezes my hand once more, but I shake him off. With one last burst of energy, I throw my hands out. Gusts of air blast the king backward, knocking him off his feet. Without a glance, I turn and dash through the portal before it closes.

Thirty
Sorcha

Faceless shadows haunt my dreams, preventing me from getting any sleep. I roll over and stare at the vacancy beside me. Conall would have never made it up the stairs once we returned to my castle, but I yearn to be close to him. I wrap myself in a dressing robe and sit on my balcony until sunrise. Despite my best efforts, I keep replaying the countless catastrophes of yesterday. Every time I look down at my hands, all I can see are the nooks and crannies stained pink from blood that refuses to wash away.

My anchor of grief threatens to pull me under the undulating waves of pain, and I am unmoored in the swirling emotions of loss. I run my finger along the fresh pink scar of my healed thigh, the skin knitted together thickly since I am no longer fae.

A rainbow of colors swirls at my fingertips.

I may have Conall back, but at what cost?

Hazel's tiny voice is a hum in the distance as I barely register her talking to me. I move through the motions of getting dressed, letting her choose my clothes and how to fashion my hair. I sit at the vanity, my hands in my lap, twirling my father's insignia ring on my thumb absently. Her tiny hands are soothing, and she works my hair into braids. My other hand drifts to Puff's pouch, its flap torn open and empty. Hush and Scruff have pulled their friend from his hideaway, helping him assimilate with the rest of the castle brownies and boggarts by now.

At least, that is one outcome for which I am thankful.

I scoff inwardly, knowing I should have left the creatures behind as more lives would have been spared. But it was out of the question. Helpless creatures left to fend for themselves? They had no say in their circumstance. I couldn't sit idly by and know what kind of fate they would meet from neglect.

My skin bristles with unspent anger, and the despair shifts to a numbness that settles inside my chest. Hazel deftly wipes away my tears without a word, and when they finally stop, she climbs down from her perch on my shoulder and scurries away into the shadows without saying another word.

As if moved by a subconscious need to be near him, I stand in front of the door in the guest wing.

Guests.

As if he wasn't going to be long for this world when we got here.

I raise my hand to knock but step back, looking down the hall, and wonder if this was a mistake. Since I am no longer fae, he must not feel the connection to me anymore, and if that is the case, will he still want me? Find me attractive?

The door opens, and Dubessa slips through the crack, closing it softly behind her.

She laughs quietly at the shock on my face.

"Calm, Queen." She holds her hands up in surrender. "Water nymphs are some of the most powerful healers in Fae. And this is not a debt to be repaid. I came here willingly."

"Thank you," I say, relief filling my body.

She places a hand on my shoulder. "You should know the water nymphs heard your prayers. Opal was returned to the water, and her soul is now at peace."

I bite my lip and face forward. My throat tightens with the urge to break down, and my jaw quivers with unshed tears. Dubessa squeezes my shoulder once before leaving, her feet barely making a sound down the hall.

My hand trembles as I reach for the doorknob and turn.

The wooden swings open effortlessly, and immediately, I am greeted by a scent my soul has longed for—cedar and mint, fresh rain in the forest.

Conall.

He rests in the large four-poster bed, eyes closed, breathing peacefully for someone who went through as much as he did in the past few days. It takes everything I have not to rush into the room and throw myself onto his prone body. He shifts, and I almost step backward out the door, not ready to tell him what I came here to say.

My hand reaches for the knob.

"Where do you think you're going?"

Caught. "I didn't want to wake you."

"Come here," he commands, calling to something primal inside me. Like a ship to the shore, I am pulled toward his lighthouse. He pats the bed next to him and lifts an arm for me to snuggle against his body.

I sit on the edge of the bed, reluctant to cause him any discomfort. I don't know where to place my hands, so I let them hover over his chest. "Is this—?"

"I'm fine, My Queen. Come *here*," he grunts and scoops my body to snuggle close to his.

The curve of his arm fits perfectly against my back, and I tuck my face into the crook of his neck. His woodsy scent envelops me, and I burrow into him, wrapping an arm over his chest and throwing a leg over his hips.

This is home, I think.

Or maybe not, as he asks, "My Queen?"

His voice is scratchy from disuse and, most likely, screaming.

"I said, '*This is home*'. I can't believe you're here," I sigh. My hands grapple, trying to pull him closer, and his muscles twitch with each pass as I take stock of his healing body. I sigh in relief when there are no bandages, blood, or broken bones.

Underneath his shirt, however, he is gaunt. His hip bones stick out; his stomach has far fewer muscles than before. The color of his skin has a healthier glow but lacks the golden undertones he once had.

Conall nuzzles the top of my head while he fumbles at my clothing, tugging and pulling every layer from my body.

He growls, "I will never leave you again."

"I should hope not," I exhale, relishing his eagerness to touch me. My skin ignites under his touch, the craving to feel him just barely sated. "I don't think I'd survive it."

I gasp when his hand tugs my skirt up, and he grabs my bare backside. He shifts me to ride astride him and pulls me down to meet his lips. This isn't the stone circle, and this isn't the heart-call space. He is here, with me, in the flesh, and I become someone else, a being filled with unadulterated desire.

His tongue dives into my mouth, and he presses me into him, his hard cock pressing against my center through the sheets. I twine my fingers in his hair, tugging at his temples, craving every part of him. Craving to be home, to find shore again.

His vibrant emerald eyes find mine, and our breath mingles together.

"What?" He pants, gripping my backside as I pull away slightly and rest my forehead against his.

"Are you well?" My thighs clench with want, but the last thing I want to do is hurt him.

"Yes." He smiles. "Are you?"

I nod. His finger trails along the pink scar on my thigh, and his eyes find mine.

I swallow a knot of guilt, recalling how tense the air was between Murdock and me last night. After Conall was safely in the hands of another healer, Murdock forced me to sit. The mershifter refused to look me in the eye, but he hovered his hand over my thigh. Through a clenched jaw, he healed my injury quickly, nodded once, and ran from the throne room afterward.

I tug my skirts and try to hide it, suddenly self-conscious and worried he'll ask who healed me. But he says nothing. Instead, Conall reaches up, cupping my cheeks in his hands, and pulls me down for another kiss.

Our mouths collide again as our hands tear away at the fabric that separates us. He rolls us over, and I am bare before him with my soft stomach, and my thick thighs spread wide for him. Will he still love this human body?

I want to cover up the way my breasts deflate while I'm on my back. I want to pull my arms together to make them perky again. I want to look beautiful to him despite the crow's feet in the corner of my eyes and the few grey hairs that now pepper the top of my hair.

And yet, *I* drink him in.

His bushy beard and vibrant green eyes. All the scars that pepper his body create unique constellations on his skin, and I want to waste my days tracing each marking. I also want to destroy those who ever laid a finger on him. His grip tightens on my waist, pulling me from my thoughts.

"Let me look at you," he says reverently. I reluctantly take my arms away from my body and leave them awkwardly at my sides. Conall shakes his head, "Please, never cover up your body in front of me. I thought I told you this before?"

He yanks me closer, gripping my waist, and says, "You're so insanely beautiful."

His hands slide over my hips, up my stomach, and along my ribcage. He palms my breasts, and he tweaks my nipples in his fingertips.

"Ohhh," I whimper, growing less self-conscious the more he touches me.

He pinches my nipples again, and I arch into his touch. My core heats, and I grow wet for him. I reach my hands down to my center, wanting to play, but he snatches my wrists and pins them above my head.

"Let *me* play first," he whispers, nibbling on my earlobe. My breathing turns shallow with anticipation. When I try to wrap my legs around his waist to pull him in, he shifts away with a smirk. I grumble.

He laughs, a bellyful of laughter that shakes throughout his body and travels from my ears to the tips of my toes.

"Patience, My Queen." He breathes into my neck, moving down my collarbone to my breasts, nipping at the hardened peaks. His hand tightens around my wrist. "How I have missed touching you. Do you remember when we sparred in the field by my cabin?"

"Mmhmm," I murmur. I wiggle down on the bed, trying to get his cock inside of me.

"Do you remember how I held you down like this, a knife at your gorgeous throat?" he growls and nips at the sensitive skin on the side of my breast.

"I do," I pant. "Oh, Goddess, Conall. I need you."

"Not yet," he chuckles against my sternum. His mouth continues its worship of my skin. He places kisses between my breasts and up to the base of my throat. I might burst from anticipation. "And do you remember the first time we touched?"

"In the Inn," I whisper. His teeth nibble on my nipples, and then he sucks on them. I buck against him, the tip of his cock barely touching the wetness of my core, and moan loud enough to hear my voice echoing against the walls. Heat floods my body, and he bites the underside of my breast, his teeth searing their mark into my flesh. I close my eyes against the fire that burns underneath my skin.

He murmurs, "You looked at me like you had seen a ghost."

"Yes, I have never felt something like that before." I pant, a knot of desire in my throat. I never want him to take his hands from my body.

"It felt like coming home," he says. He pulls back but doesn't release my hands. "I have never felt that before, either."

I whisper, biting my lip. "That night under the stars, our first night together."

He hangs his head, "I'm sorry. I should've handled that better—"

I cut him off and he meets my gaze. "That night, under the stars, was one of the best nights of my life. I have never felt such bliss before. It was at that moment when I knew something was different."

He leans down then, releasing my hands. I twine my fingers in his hair and pull him the rest of the way in for a kiss. His hand grabs his cock, and he guides himself to my entrance. Conall's eyes are wicked in the lowlight, but he still waits.

"Fuck me, Conall." I shift my hips underneath him.

"Are you sure?" He swirls the tip of his cock against my sex.

"Yes," I purr. "Definitely."

In one solid thrust, he seats himself inside me. I cry his name and arch my back with pleasure. My legs tighten around his waist to take him further. His head pulses against my wall, and he pushes against me a few times without entirely withdrawing. I am so close to him that I never want this feeling to end. A piece of my heart notches into place, and the world around me flares with light.

This. This was what had been missing. I pull him down so we are flush against each other. I tighten my core and roll my hips.

"Come with me," I whisper into his ear, my tongue flicking against his sensitive, pointed ears.

"Oh, Goddess," he shudders.

At first, I think he wants to fight it, but I bite his earlobe and buck my hips.

"There's no Goddess here," I say and squeeze again.

His mouth quirks, and he looks at me devilishly, slowing his movements. But then one of his hands grabs my wrist and pulls it back over my head to the bed frame.

"Hold on," he growls.

Speechless, I do as I'm told, both hands gripping the bed frame tightly. I arch my back, and his hands grab my waist as he fucks me with complete abandon. That dull, aching, irritating feeling lying dormant underneath my skin finally calms. I am overcome with emotion as our sweaty bodies rock together, finally fusing in the flesh. This isn't a dream. My mate is here in the flesh with me. It is so overwhelming that I am peaking, screaming his name as the waves of our release pulse through our bodies. He roars through his orgasm, and my skin erupts with gooseflesh as he collapses, panting heavily.

He plants lazy kisses all over my breasts, and I release my grip from the headboard. My fingers trail over his head, dancing along his ears and down to his back. The scars create little hills and valleys;

I trace them absently, thinking of the dream where he screamed into the void. I don't want to know everything that happened to him; I don't want to know what Achill did to break his spirit.

Conall pulls away, and we look at each other clearly for the first time in a long while.

His hand reaches up to my cheek and wipes something away.

I frown, looking at his finger as it comes away with wetness, and it is only then that I realize I am crying.

"Are you all right?" he asks, his voice hoarse.

"I—." I pull away, sliding out from underneath his body, and sit on the edge of the bed, giving him my back. Shame gnaws away at what could have been the most perfect moment we've ever had.

Thirty-One
Sorcha

"You are incredible, My Queen," he whispers, sitting beside me. He tucks me under his shoulder and kisses the top of my head. "I have never felt more alive than when I am with you, my mate."

"When did you know?" I ask, sobering quickly at the talk of fated mates.

Conall reaches for my hand, weaving his fingers with mine. "It felt like nothing I had ever felt before. It felt like home. Even when we were apart, I could feel everything. It was a comfort knowing you were there with me."

"Why didn't you say anything?" I ask. Did his soul cleave from his body when mine did?

He frowns, confused. "When I felt the bond? It isn't up to me to impede fate."

"Fate," I scoff.

"Sorcha," he says. My name on his lips forces me to pay attention. "There was a lot more at play and, yes, I mean 'fate'. I was ready to sign my life away to ensure you safely made it to the king so you would marry him and finally bring peace to his dark soul. No one realized how bad he was. I didn't realize how far gone he was until I was in that room below the castle."

He walks to the other side of the room, running his hands

through his hair. Conall's vibrant green eyes are glazed with anger when he turns back to me. He growls, "I should have swept you away the second I saw you. I should have never left you in the throne room."

"I looked back for you, but you never looked at me." My voice sounds small.

"I couldn't let the king know we were fated mates. Your life would have been in so much danger. I went willingly with his guards, knowing full well that if I protested, your life would be on the line, too." His voice cracks, and he kneels before me. Conall's hands slide up my thighs and stroke the soft curves of my hips, the calluses on his fingertips leaving goosebumps in their wake. "It was hours upon hours of nothingness. It might have even been days. I was waiting in the darkness for what felt like an eternity. And I was ready to take it, stay there forever in the dark, alone. But then... when he—as soon as he —" He closes his eyes, trying his best to continue. Anger vibrates through me at the thought of him being so hurt. "I could feel you feeling the pain he inflicted on me. That was what almost killed me. It wasn't until he moved me to the dungeons, away from the castle, when he stopped his tortured games, that I finally felt like I could go on. Because I knew that if I wasn't being hurt, you were okay. And then I could feel the pain he inflicted on you. I could feel every time his hands hurt you. I went ballistic and broke almost every bone in my body, trying to wrench the doors from their hinges. I have never known such torment."

My hands reach for him, and I wrap him in my arms, pressing his head to my chest. Why didn't anyone tell me what happened?

"I tried everything I could to get to you, but I will never feel like it was enough," he whispers into my chest, nipping at the top of my breast. His hands stroke my back, and my anger becomes a growing heat in my body. But instead of giving in, I take his face in my hands and pull him away.

"I know you did," I whisper, nuzzling his nose with mine. "Without you, I would have slept forever. I missed you terribly. Every second we were apart, I felt I had left a limb behind. Conall, did you... did you sense anything a few days ago?"

The morning light streams through the window, casting him in a golden glow as he takes a cane that rests against the bed frame. He walks to the far side of the room, the wooden tip clicking on the stone floor, and I wonder if he will ever fully heal from whatever happened in that dungeon. He crosses his arms and leans against the table, regarding me curiously. "No?"

"You didn't feel something like your soul cleaving from your body?"

"No," he says, shaking his head. "Did you?"

I nod, grappling at the clothes on the floor. I tug on my chemise and pace the room. My knotted and frizzy hair has come undone from Hazel's braids. I grab it, twisting and braiding it as I talk. He might as well know precisely what happened with the Goddess before all the secrets eat me alive. "Before you get mad at me, I did it for you."

He watches my fingers closely as I braid my hair and twist the ends around one of my fingers. His eyes drag up to mine, and he shakes his head. "Sorcha, you don't have to—"

"I made a bargain." I cut him off before I lose my nerve. I await his admonishment, but Conall patiently lets me continue. The words rush out before I change my mind. "I forced my rites early and called upon the Goddess." I flinch, waiting for his reaction. It doesn't come, so I keep going. "I couldn't access my magic; something about Achill's magic and me being asleep, and I couldn't call upon the earth. And then I wake up, and you're there, and you trade your freedom for mine. You were captive, *again*, because of me, and I could feel Achill hurting you *again*, and I felt so helpless. I couldn't get you back if I didn't have my magic. And I went into the circle to perform my Rites, and then she showed up, and before I knew it, I was bargaining away my fae blood, and in return, she gave me magic."

Out of breath, I finally stop. I wait for Conall to say something smarmy. But he is quiet, regarding me with those ever-watchful eyes. He pulls on his lip, thinking.

"I know what you're going to say," I say, trying to fill the uneasy silence between us. "I don't deserve to be the Earth Queen now. I have no fae blood in me, so what am I even doing, parading around pretending like I know how to rule."

He tilts his head, frowning. "That's not what I was going to say."

"Well, you're thinking it, at least," I scoff.

"No," he says. "I'm not. I think you're more than queen enough."

I roll my eyes and cross my arms across my chest to hide that I am on pins and needles. "Well, then, what are you thinking?"

"When you made the bargain, did you think the Goddess removed our mating bond?"

"Yes, of course! I couldn't feel you, I didn't dream of you, I couldn't reach you no matter how hard I tried. No matter how badly I needed your heart-call to answer back. I had... nothing." My voice almost breaks, and I hold my hands out in front of me, palms up, and give him a helpless look. I want to tell him about Murdock and how I've questioned, nay, *entertained* the possibility of being with the mershifter, how my thoughts kept circling my loyalty to Conall, and the fear of never getting him back. The desire to be with someone comforting and strong, but I could never really bring myself to see Murdock in the way I see Conall.

"Without your fae blood, you have a choice to make," Conall says, his voice level and unwavering. "You could either mate with me or leave the bond open and choose someone else."

Did I hear him right? "Wait. Are you pushing me away?"

I blink away tears threatening to form, and he steps closer, grabbing my hands and tugging me flush against him. "I'm not pushing you away; I just... want you to know you have a choice. You will always have a choice with me."

He cups my chin, staring into my eyes so intensely that I want to look away. I feel finite and minuscule compared to him, compared to how fast his body has healed and how many terrible things he has survived. What happens when he sees my human body age even more? Will he still love me when my breasts sag, and my stomach is covered in stretch marks from kids?

I shock myself at the thought. Kids?

His voice cuts off my spiraling thoughts. "You should know that I am head over heels in love with you, Sorcha. I have loved you since I saw you running from that horned fae. My first thought when I saw that his flesh was missing from his neck and you were covered in his blood was, 'This woman has *fire*.' From that moment on, I knew that you would fight with your all for the things you believe in. For what's right. You have consumed my soul in a way I never thought possible."

He's loved me this entire time.

"Conall, why would you even suggest us not mating?"

"Because maybe there is someone better suited to you than I," he says. He turns from me, shoulders sagging.

"What...?" I start, but a knock at the door stops me. Murdock's muffled voice filters through.

Conall and I lock eyes. I look away and swallow thickly as I fumble with my clothing, my limbs leaden with overwhelming guilt.

Thirty-Two
Sorcha

Angry energy builds in the room, a tidal wave of emotion threatening to bowl me over. I want to leave the room, but all eyes are on me. Their gazes miss nothing, and I try to call upon the skills my father taught me when he met with his advisors. I let the regal mask filter my true feelings, though inside, I still fight with my worth. I may not have liked the plan of trying to take out the stones, but I still let it happen, and I went to rescue my mate.

I was the one who sent friends and family to die.

The Salonen signet ring sits heavy on my thumb, the gold seal glinting in the light as I turn it over and over.

"My Queen?" Conall's gentle voice cuts through the buzzing in my head. My eyes flash to his, and instantly, I am anchored in his presence.

I shove the waves of emotions aside and nod for Murdock to continue.

"Channe, Opal, King Gareth Salonen, Neil, and Thorne - all either dead or unaccounted for. Fourteen in total." Murdock bows to me and sits back down.

Fourteen. Much more than I expected for a small mission. What will it be like when we declare war? I want to crawl under the table at the thought of losing even more to senseless death.

Murdock continues, and I barely comprehend what he says as I mull over the names. "We have it on good authority that the stones are weaker. At least enough for a distraction and to get a few letters through. Whatever wards hold them in place are strong enough to withstand multiple attacks."

"Thank you, Murdock." My voice sounds far away as my blood rushes in my ears.

Murdock nods at me, a muscle ticking in his jaw. He won't meet my gaze. Instead, he ogles the map in front of him as if it is the most fascinating thing in the library.

Last night, I had asked Murdock to gather everyone here instead of in the throne room. The thought of sitting on the throne, overlooking everyone else who had already sacrificed for me and my mate, didn't seem right. It especially didn't feel right to sit on the throne after I told Conall that I wasn't fae anymore. I couldn't bring myself anywhere near that hallway after we returned.

It is only Murdock, Conall, Hazel, Feothan, and myself. Feothan, despite their jealousy toward Thorne at our first meeting, sits silently. He twirls one of Thorne's feathers in his fingertips. My chest tightens, knowing that Achill is probably holding Thorne at this very moment.

The simple table in the middle of the room is covered in maps and old parchment. The soft light, dust motes, and the smell of leather should be more peaceful, but it only adds to my gnawing anguish and frustration that I am hiding away again.

"Your Majesty," someone's quiet voice says.

Everyone shifts to face the crack in the door.

Conall stands up so fast that his chair tips over, and his cane topples to the ground. He grapples for it, grimacing as he puts weight on his left leg to bend down and grab it. My hand instinctively reaches out to steady him, but he frowns at me and yanks his arm back as if my touch burned him.

I blanch, and everyone averts their eyes.

Conall straightens, turning in time to wrap his arms around the young fae.

I lean over in my chair, trying to see whom Conall embraces

when Hazel materializes out of nowhere and climbs up my shoulder.

"That's Felan," she sighs, a dreamy lilt at the end of his name. I glance at her, perched so delicately on the back of my chair that I did not know she was there. She tucks her chin into her chest, blushing, as she moons over the wolf shifter. She pulls back my braid and whispers, "All the MacSealgair fae are so good-looking."

Hazel jumps down, disappearing to Goddess-knows-where, while Felan disentangles himself from my mate. He steps around Conall and finally faces me. Long black hair, woven into intricate braids, hangs down to his waist. His skin is darker than Conall's, and even Maccon's, a deep amber with a rich golden glow.

He still has dried blood covering his clothes. His grey eyes are puffy and swollen, and he wipes his nose on his sleeve again before he dips into a low bow.

My throat knots, knowing why he is here. I stand up and take his hand. The words leave my lips, but I worry they are hollow to someone still entrenched in grief. "I am so sorry for your loss."

His eyes dart from me to Conall and then back to me again, nodding briefly and wiping his nose on his sleeve. Felan hesitates for a second, but he takes my outstretched hand. Calluses line his palm, and I fold his hands into mine. I pour all of my compassion into the gesture, giving him a brief squeeze and hoping it shows him the depth of my grief. We are companions in mourning.

He swallows thickly and pulls his hand away. He stares up at the ceiling, tears welling in his eyes. The room is quiet enough to hear a feather fall to the ground. Conall puts a hand on Felan's shoulder and squeezes.

"B-b-before Channe passed," Felan stammers, sniffling. "He wanted me to tell everyone he knew what he was signing up for. That he knew — he knew something bad would happen to him."

Tears form in my eyes, too, and I add, "You were close."

He nods, jaw quivering. The rest of his words come out in a rush. "He told me that if it meant we could finally have peace, this was how he was meant to go."

Felan sags.

The weight of the emotions he carries finally lifts from his shoulders. Conall folds him in his arms and lets him cry. Felan howls out his sorrow, and I imagine how they are in their wolf forms—heads leaning into each other, finding comfort in their closeness. The raw emotion coming from Felan and Conall makes my eyes water, too, and I yearn to have final moments with my father and Opal. What would I have said, knowing it had been their final moments? Knowing I wouldn't see them again?

Felan clears his throat and straightens. "Apologies, Your Highness. I just..."

I hold my hand up, choking back my tears. "There's no need to apologize; the doors to this castle are always open. Please call me Sorcha."

Felan gives me a lopsided smile and dips his head in a final bow before he leaves.

I help Conall fix his chair, and he sits with a stifled grunt. His hand finds mine and squeezes, and I give him a tight smile. His pack is one less because of me.

Each unoccupied chair reminds me that I am an imposter trying to claim the crown, and countless creatures rely on my rule. Grindel went back to the Inn to be with his mate to work with the resistance underground. Aodhfin stayed behind in the MacSealgair lands with Maccon to help guard the border. The other Lesser Fae are also absent, and the fire sprites and the pixies are helping Fern down in the kitchens. The emptiness in the room is a paltry display of strength and support. Fourteen dead and unaccounted for. Fourteen too many.

Murdock stands, holding a map, but even his voice seems too quiet, too unsure, as he says, "We need to discuss —"

Something inside me finally snaps. I am suffocating, sitting behind this enormous table. The chair squeals against the floor as I push off the edge. I pace the room, tugging on the back of my dress, wishing to release the strings on my stay so I can breathe better. Tears prick my eyes, and I finally let go, lost in my swirling emotions. The anger building under the surface bubbles up, and my throat goes tight with unspoken words. The earth beneath me tilts, and I'm tossed into a turbulent sea, crashing under wave after wave of all my choices. Each decision has gotten someone I love either injured, tortured, or killed. Whenever I think I'm doing the right thing, I constantly bargain away someone I hold dear, or they lose their loved ones.

What kind of Queen am I when I constantly jeopardize the lives and happiness of those I love?

The tears won't stop, and Murdock stands there, awkwardly holding the map and looking from Conall to me. Conall tries to stand and grunts, which sets me off even more. I can't believe I let him take my place after he had been free.

"Sorcha," Conall starts, but I cut him off.

"You can't tell me *everyone* knew." I fight through tears to form a cohesive thought in front of my advisors and wave my arms around at Conall and the half-empty table. "That they willingly signed up to die for this."

All I see are those missing.

Opal, bleeding out on the ground, flashes before my eyes, and I choke on more tears. My father's last words echo in my head. All eyes turn to me, some filled with grief, some filled with anger, some concerned at seeing me lose my composure in front of them.

"Sorcha," Conall says, trying to reach for me. I take a step backward, out of his grasp. "Sorcha, you are a great queen. You are *my* Queen."

"Oh, yes, I'm a *great* queen, Conall," I mock and wipe away the tears. The grief gives way to more doubt, which seeps into my bones. Did my father ever experience a crushing doubt like this? I never got to ask him, and now I never will. "I just keep sending people to die."

"That's not true, Sorcha. But, where you go, I go," Conall says firmly.

"Aye," Murdock says, dipping his chin.

"And me," Feothan says, standing. He places his hand on his heart.

I give them all a half-hearted smile and sniffle. "Great. A kingdom of three."

Murdock flashes me a bright smile, but it doesn't reach his eyes. "That's enough for some."

Conall adds, "It's enough for me, My Queen."

But is it enough to kill an immortal king?

Thirty-Three
Sorcha

"Conall," I whisper into his pointed ear. We are tangled in sheets, still sweaty and naked from earlier. The only thing that calms my growing guilt and anger is throwing myself at Conall the second we get to my rooms. One touch from him and my worries melt away. I am instantly transported out of my head and into something more primal.

"My Queen," he murmurs into my hair, stroking my back. The way he says my name reverberates down my spine, a tingling that flutters to life low in my belly. In his arms, I am safe in my special place where I can forget the trappings of the world outside. My fingers dance across his skin, memorizing all the new markings Achill left. Each scar adds to the list of things that will make killing that fae much easier.

He shifts, and I nestle into the curve of his sweat-slicked neck. If there is a refuge for me, it is in his earthy scent and arms. He will always be my home.

"Why wouldn't you want me to be your mate?" I ask, wanting to finish our conversation from this morning. I pull my head back, and his green eyes search mine. Without the mate bond, I can't tell if he is sad or puzzled. His face gives nothing away, but his arm tightens around my shoulders.

"It's not that I don't want to; I only want you to be *sure*. You can't break this once you go down this path."

Will he regret being mated to a human with a short lifespan? I can't ask him to sign away his immortality with me since I am no longer fae. But I know that I want only him. Forever. I sit up, pushing off his chest, and his muscles flex beneath my palm. I say, "I think I have known for a long time that we were always meant to be together. But certain moments made me more certain."

"What kinds of moments?" He asks, his voice dropping an octave. His eyes drop down to my lips, and I lick them self-consciously.

"That night in the cabin. The campfire. I always knew something pulled me to you. There was a reason our paths crossed before my magic came in." I rub my thumb along his chin, the scratch of his scruff igniting a fire in my belly at the thought of how it would feel against my thighs. Though he looked wild and untamed with his beard, the scruff he wears now is sexier. "I didn't know something like this was possible between humans and fae."

He growls and leans into my palm. "I didn't either, but it doesn't surprise me."

My eyes find his questioning, but he doesn't elaborate.

Instead, he pulls me down so I am flush on top of him. His muscular arms encircle my body, keeping me pinned to his chest. My left ear rests over his heart; the steady beating blends into mine. I cling to his shoulders, adrift in the ocean of his cedar, rain, and skin. I never knew I could miss how he felt against mine.

But I did. So much.

Conall's hands roam over every curve of my body, stroking my back, my hips, my backside. He coaxes my entire body into deep contentedness. I hum in response, push off his chest, and straddle him. His hands immediately move to my hips and lift me so he can enter. As he does, I move my hands to cover my chest.

He stills, and I whine, the tip of him just resting against my entrance.

Frowning, he orders, "Hands on your head."

"What?"

He lowers me back down, and I pout, wishing he was inside. His arms wrap around my back, and he drags his scruff lightly along my chest.

"Put your hands. On. Your. Head," he whispers into the space between my breasts. His tongue trails across my breasts, and he pulls one of my hardened peaks into his mouth, swirling his tongue around my nipple. While I roll my hips against him, wanting to be full of him again, I raise my hands and interlock my fingers atop my head.

"When I told you I loved every part of you, I meant it. Now, let me look at you."

I swallow thickly, desire pushing away any of my self-consciousness.

He lays back down, stretching out beneath me. One of his hands finds his length, and the other slides between my thighs. I lift my hips instinctively, and his fingers play at my entrance, dipping inside.

"I love how wet you get for me." His green eyes turn hungry, and butterflies swarm my belly. Even though this isn't our first time together, the anticipation of being with him still drives me insane.

A salacious smile pulls at his lips; he knows what he does to me. His eyes alight with yearning as he watches my face when he slides himself inside slowly, inching me down until his thickness fills me. I clench around him, and he growls so low that the vibrations are in my core. I purr, reveling in the feeling of him, and rock my hips back and forth, trying to drive him deeper. He thrusts upward, and I fall forward, my hands brace against his chest. I arch my back and curl my nails into his shoulders. Before he can open his mouth, I push off and raise my hands to the top of my head.

"That's my Queen," he croons and lays back, grabbing my hips. "Keep your hands there."

I ride him, sliding my hands behind my head, and watch him fight his release. A flush creeps across my face, and my nipples pebble at being on display for him. But I don't move my hands. As perplexed as I am about him wanting to look at my human body, I am infinitely more turned on watching his reactions to my subtlest moves.

His piercing green eyes hold my attention, and his fingers trace circles over my soft stomach; they trail a delicate line up and around my bosom, stopping to pinch my nipples and then making their way back down to the softer rolls at my belly. I tighten with each undulation, and he throws his head back, gripping my hips.

Conall grunts through clenched teeth, "There, Sorcha. Yes. Just. Like. That."

I lean back a little, relying on his hands to keep me upright as I keep my hands on my head.

"My mate," I exhale.

"I never felt the pain you spoke of, but I would guess it was the fae part of yourself shearing away. Not our mating bond."

My movements slow as I take in what he said.

"I felt everything you sent me, Sorcha," he says.

"Wait, what?" My hands drop, landing on his chest. "What do you mean?"

"I felt it. All of it. The panic, the pain, the fear, the joy. Every time you tugged on the heart-call, I felt it." His lips quirk into a knowing smile, and he takes a finger, finding my clit. He strokes, but the world comes rushing into focus around me.

I grab his wrist and hold his hand still against me.

"I — How?" I ask. "How did I not know?"

He adds, "I also felt the affection of someone else, but—"

I slide off of him, leaving him in the swinging bed. He doesn't get up to follow me but props himself up on an elbow and watches my every movement as he strokes himself languidly. Suddenly self-conscious, I grab the dressing gown that rests on a chair by the balcony, slipping my arms inside and pulling it tight against my body.

The cold stone of the balcony greets my feet, and instantly, moss appears like a carpet beneath my toes. I lean over the baluster, inhaling the fresh air. Irritation and something akin to shame blooms in the center of my chest again, and I rub a hand over my sternum, wishing I could make it go away.

"Why did you wait to say something?" I turn to him, bracing against the railing. Leaning back on my elbows, I watch him watch me. My palm rubs my aching chest.

He shrugs a shoulder and runs a hand through his hair. His arm ripples with muscles. Muscles that hadn't been there a few days ago. A wave of relief washes over me because he is healing so well. Soon, I hope, he'll go back to his shifter self, and then I can kick his ass for being so ornery.

"I was just so relieved to be with you again,"

"I need to go for a walk," I finally say, pushing off the railing. He moves to get up, and I hold up a hand. "Alone."

The door closes behind me, and my eyes close against the barrage of emotions. My feet take me down winding hallways and twisting stairs that are now silent in the middle of the night. I round a corner and stare at the carved stone chair that glimmers in the dappled moonlight; the tiny flecks of gems glint and gleam in the silvery light like stars in a gray sky.

I drag my feet up the steps of the dais, in no hurry to reach the top, but I am compelled forward by a faint green glow that emanates from its trunk. My hand skims along the surface of the throne, and it is infinitely cooler to the touch than I remember. I face the room, remembering the fae that stared back at me when they woke from their slumber.

A human as the Earth Fae Queen. It seems like a jest of epic proportions because why would the Goddess have chosen me to lead these creatures?

The yew tree leaves reach down to kiss my shoulders, and I lean toward the trunk, lightheaded and dizzy. Bracing my hand against the bark, I rest my forehead against it, but I fall forward, landing on my hands and knees in the center of the stone circle.

"Hello, daughter," the goddess' voice swarms me, pushing around me on all sides.

I sit back on my heels, speechless. Her lilac and mossy scent fills my nose, instantly calming my nerves, but I am not a fool. I don't let myself relax entirely.

Soft footsteps approach from behind. Mist surrounds the outer edges of the circle, and silvery moonlight chases the shadows away as she walks around me.

I bow my head.

"Quite unnecessary," she says, grabbing my chin in her fingers and bringing me up to meet her eyes, but I look away and stare at a spot over her shoulder instead. I don't care if it's disrespectful. I want to pull back from her. My anger simmers like a pot left to boil, and the air is taut like a bowstring. I hold my breath, waiting for her to speak. "You are lost," she says.

I lift my chin in acknowledgment, and though I want to open my mouth and tell her to go to Forever Night, I don't. I won't make any more mistakes around her; I won't fall for her tricks.

She straightens. "You wouldn't have come here otherwise."

Her jet-black skin glistens, and her eyes, which had been a rich, sapphire blue the first time I saw her, now shine silver like the stars above. Her hair was red like flames, but now it is a soft grey. It still smells of lilacs but also something more ancient, like woods steeped in shadow or stones hiding in moss and covered in lichen.

Her eyes are unfocused as she floats around me, searching for something beyond the mist. "You have your mate back. And yet, you've lost those close to you in exchange."

Her insouciant observation makes me roll my eyes and cross my arms over my chest.

"Relax, child," she murmurs. "I do not bring you here to bargain. As with all of my children, I am merely concerned."

"Concerned?" I scoff and then smack a hand over my mouth.

She raises an eyebrow. "Am I not allowed to be concerned? We made a bargain that you have to fulfill."

I sigh. "Fine. Yes, but it's more complicated than I thought."

"You didn't think restoring the balance wouldn't come with death and compromises?"

"It shouldn't have to," I retort, inwardly cringing at my obstinance.

She belts out a mocking laugh. "You have much to learn, Queen, especially when talking to your elders and Goddess."

"Apologies," I say curtly. "You'd have me sacrifice everything I loved to bring a balance back into the world, wouldn't you?"

The Goddess' eyes are full of pity, and her laughter dies in the shadows of the night beyond.

"No." She shakes her head slowly. "I would not wish you more heartache. Sometimes, fate sets in motion a path that cannot be unchanged, no matter how hard we fight against it."

"There were good Fae who didn't deserve to follow me. And they did. And now they're dead." A thick knot in my throat forms as I try to swallow back the anger. A renegade tear slides down my cheek, and I swat it away, displeased with looking weak in front of her again.

"They were choices they made," her voice is sullen.

"They made choices because of me. None of them deserved to die," I whisper, memories choking my throat: Opal's smile and her playfulness, my father and his endless quest for diplomacy, Channe, Thorne, and Neil. I fight back tears, even for the fae that I never got the chance to get to know.

The Goddess sits down, patting the ground next to her. Slowly, I join her, careful not to squish the little flowers that have bloomed where she has touched.

"Are they dead? Or have they just moved beyond the confines of the physical world?" The Goddess' voice cuts into my thoughts.

"I have lost many good fae and good people to the Fire King," I whisper. The goddess waits, her eyes unreadable. So I continue, "I have seen Achill. His misshapen body, how his mood can so quickly change. How he wields his magic. There is power there, but there is madness, too."

"You worry," the goddess remarks.

I almost snap back at her, but I bite my tongue, careful not to offend her with my following words. "Of course, I worry. I do not want to lead my people to certain death. And, I do not want them to leave their mates to die because it is not only one that dies, but two. How is that fair?"

She nods and points a finger to the sky. "I have heard the tales from the land that each of these stars was once aimless, lost lovers, cursed or blessed to stay in the Forever Night sky, waiting for their loved ones to join them. But that is only part of the tale."

I shift, impatience crawling under my skin. Would she cut out my tongue if I told her to get the point?

The goddess moves her hands, and above us, the stars shift, and two outlines appear. The figures come to life in the sky, dancing around the constellations together. Her voice sounds distant, pulled back through time. "When the fae started losing touch with the world around them, and time became too abstract, the mating bond was the only way they could anchor themselves in the world. It gave them purpose."

The two fae embrace each other. One opens their mouth and bites the neck of the other, a thousand stars shimmering and bursting in the sky around them.

"It became the only reason they wanted to finish their rites, connect with me, or find their magic. My lovely little fae had lost their way and assumed that finding your fated mate was the only thing that would bring them joy in their long lives."

As she talks, the stars weave another beautiful story above us. The two figures are lost in a dance, twirling together as cities are built and destroyed, rivers run and dry up, and forests grow and die around them. And as beautiful as the scene before me is, I stare at my mortal hands and the sunspots that are starting to show, the dry, cracked skin, the scar on my palm.

Humans, with our limited lifespans and lack of magic, can choose their pairings whether they want one partner or five, same gender or different, or no partner at all. We value so much more about our lives because our time here is much shorter than a fae's life. Each moment on this earth could very well be our last, and for the first time, I am happy that she took my fae blood.

Perhaps I can rule the fae even though I won't live a longer life.

Perhaps I could even do it *well*.

She nods, watching the realization cross my face. Her lips form a tight line, and she takes my hand. "Finding your fated mate should be a joy, but I did not intend it to be the only reason to find life worth living. Love can help you do so much good." She sighs, and the stars return to their places with a wave of her fingers. They twinkle in the stationary blackness, winking back at me. The goddess takes my hand in hers. "But never did I think it would also bring about such selfishness and evil."

I look at my small human hand resting in her glittering, silver one. Her touch is ethereal, and a transcendental nostalgia floods my body, but not for places I have ever known in the flesh. My eyes flutter closed as she fills my mind, her magic flowing around me. I see countless lives enjoying a well-lived life, but there is also sadness and pain. I see fear and death, broken dreams, and war. Fae after fae trudge on, striving to feel vital again, tired of an endless life, seeking meaning in the wrong places, almost relieved when the end came.

"How can your fae not think that finding their fated mate was their only reason for living when you force their choice?" I ask. My eyes stay closed, but tears wet my cheeks. I am so angry at the injustice of it all, of how she plays with the lives on her earth. "Choose a mate, but when the other dies, you die. Don't choose a mate, and you lose your mind or your magic, and *then* you die. You would have us all dead before we had a say in our lives."

I open my eyes, and she studies my face.

"Within the confines of fate, my child, we are often given choices that can make us feel trapped. It is what we do once we've made those choices that determine who we are inside."

"Fate," I scoff and roll my eyes. "You still talk of fate like we have a choice when *you* have put this on us. What kind of life are we living if, no matter what we choose, we still die?"

She regards me with a head tilt. "Death is inevitable, child. It is always up to them whether the Rites are even necessary for them to find their full potential."

I reel back as if she had slapped me across the face with her words. "You want your fae to be closer to you, so they have to complete their Rites. But they are immortal once they complete their Rites, save for the very thing that can bring about their death —their fated mate."

She smiles, catlike in how her lips curl at being called out. Her body shifts, and I watch her morph into the Trickster Goddess.

"The choice is theirs to make," she says proudly.

I shake my head. "Impossible decisions. You would have them distance themselves from their magic—the very thing that connects them to you—or go through a ritual that makes their death contingent upon finding their fated mate. No matter what they choose, it is wrought with pitfalls. No wonder they don't celebrate the seasons and let your shrines fall into disrepair. I wouldn't want to honor someone who hands out a premature death sentence."

It is my turn to shock her.

Her eyes go wide, and her lips drop the sneaky smile. We sit there, staring at each other. My disbelief in her lack of forethought almost has me cackling in her face with laughter. Can she not see that she has created a self-fulfilling prophecy?

The fae are so listless and devious, warring with each other through the centuries, to feel something beyond the inevitability of an immortal life. They love fiercely, knowing that if their mate dies, they go soon, too. Or they refuse to mate and watch their faculties leave a body that was once powerful and magical.

"What kind of life are you giving the creatures you care about?"

She cowers a little, but then her eyes light up as she says, "You made your choice. Not so long ago."

The goddess points at my heart and the invisible cord that ties me to Conall.

"Not really, no. That was well beyond my choosing."

"Was it? Or did you choose to fall in love and then become fated?"

That sneaky smile is back; it takes everything I have not to reach up and smack it off her face. Instead, I point out the fault in her questioning. "According to the constraints you created, I never really had a choice unless I wanted to go mad. And right now, I cannot afford to do that."

The world shimmers around us, the mist tightening its wall around the stones. She looks over her shoulder, and when she looks back at me, her brow furrows with concern. She holds out her hands, pulling me up with her.

"If I gave you a choice, child, what would you choose? How would you live your life?"

Words escape me; they fall flat on my tongue. All I have ever wanted was the freedom to choose my way, make friends, and love whom I wanted to love. But growing up with such limited freedom, I never thought it would be possible to choose my path forward.

But now?

"You have so much goodness in you," she whispers in my ear. Drawing me close, her arms wrap around me in an embrace that squeezes the air from my lungs. When she pulls back, she cups my cheeks and says, "I would not have given you these gifts if I truly didn't think you are capable. You are much more worthy of the throne than any who have come before you."

Her hair floats behind her on an invisible wind, purple threads of magic swirling around her and weaving around the stones.

"Do you know what your name means, Sorcha?"

I shake my head, unable to take my eyes off the shimmering magic that blooms around us.

"Brightness," she tells me. I finally meet her eyes, which shimmer with a thousand tiny purple stars. Her lips quirk into a joyful, earnest smile. "You are the light to the darkness, the way out of the shadows and the smoke. So shine."

And she pushes me backward.

The ground falls away, and I tumble over and over and over until the world turns white.

Thirty-Four
Achill

Low light cascades around the room. The sconces along the wall flicker with a gentle flame, but the chandelier above his head remains unlit, candles forever frozen in ice crystals. The last time they held any flame, he saw shadows of Aerona everywhere. He refused to light them again should the madness consume him.

"*Aerona,*" he whispers; the sound is sweet on his tongue.

But now, Achill sees her everywhere—out of the corner of his eye when he is getting dressed, every time he walks the gardens, and now out in the Borderlands forest where she died over a hundred years ago.

Her scent of lilac and the salty sea breeze are long gone, though he still smells her dress that hangs in the wardrobe. Achill's hand reaches out and grabs the sleeve, grasping at a faint memory of holding her hand. Did she have long nails or short ones? The lace of the cuff is yellowed and disintegrating, and when he lets go, tiny flakes of fabric float to the ground. His fingers linger in the air, and he sags as if the weight of carrying himself upright is too much for his broken heart.

Aerona had a way with her subjects, earning loyalty from every creature, no matter their station. One thing that irked him about her was that she shirked her royal blood, acting like a commoner and not wearing her crown. He sneered as the memories of Aerona gave way to his recent interactions with Sorcha. He cringed at how similar they really were and still how different.

For a moment, he lets himself entertain being married to her, wondering what it would be like to bed the human, who looks similar to his fated mate. He imagines the human, with her round ears and naivety, crying out beneath him. His gut roils in disgust.

What did that human *do* to earn that kind of loyalty from his fae?

Achill paces, smoke and fire playing on his fingertips the more agitated he becomes.

No answers lie in the library; no answers lie with his servants. They refuse to utter a bad word against her name, but he still hears their whispers behind his back. If he had had enough strength to steal more voices, he would have snapped his fingers and rendered them mute.

He plays with the magic on his fingertips, watching it trail from his hands and crawl down the ground like ghostly creatures of the night. Soon, his room is full of smoke, and he plays with the shapes in the air, forming one that looks similar to his mate. A light evening breeze passes through a small crack in the window, blowing his magic apart.

Furious, he slams the window down with enough force to crack the glass. He storms from the room, determined to meet with the one he vowed never to seek again.

HIS HAND THROBS where the blade of the knife splits his skin. A few drops of blood coat the head of the Goddess' statue, seeping into the cracks and the bowl between her hands. The waves of the lake lap at his feet, and he pulls his cloak tighter around his shoulders. It may not keep the nymphs from watching, but it makes him feel better.

It takes mere seconds, but then the world falls away.

Mist trails around his feet, wrapping him in its cool touch. Achill looks up at the stones looming before him and swallows.

Rarely has he ever felt cautious in his life, but this place... This will always give him pause.

He steps forward, and the mist wraps around his ankles, slowing his progress. Achill struggles to put one foot in front of the other when he glances up and watches a shadowy figure appear between the stones. A flash of light fills the space in the center. He covers his eyes with his elbow but keeps walking. The light fades, and the mist dissolves, releasing his legs. He stumbles forward.

The Goddess calls out between the stones, "I've been waiting for you, Trickster."

Her skin shimmers like the evening sky, her silver hair reflects the light of the moon, and her eyes are so dark it's like looking into the endless night.

If this was meant to intimidate him, she should have known better.

"I need answers," Achill says, feigning disinterest in her games.

"Eternity doesn't look good on you," she waves her hand, and his glamour falls away.

His wrinkled and cracked skin hangs from his form, and he holds his twisted hands up in front of his face. "You think I came here because of my appearance?" he laughs. "You're mistaken."

"Well, then. Out with it," she says, impatience dripping from her lips. Her black eyes find him, narrowing into slits as she watches him walk casually around her circle.

"The human princess," he says, noting the tiny white flowers blooming in the circle's center. "Something has happened to her. She is the Queen of the Earth Fae. She has... magic."

The Goddess looks down at her hand and starts picking at her nails.

He continues, unbothered by her disinterest, "She must have made a powerful bargain to—"

Achill gasps.

Beyond the stones, standing in the mist is Aerona. He shies

away from her gaze. His glamour doesn't work here, and she can't possibly see him in this state. He looks nothing like he did before.

"You were saying?" The Goddess asks.

Achill turns back, stammering despite his best efforts, and says, "Sor-Sorcha must have made a bargain. She must have offered you something in exchange."

"A bargain?" The Goddess asks, leering down at him. A look of mild amusement flashes across The Goddess' face, and he knows she is playing tricks on him when the scent of lilacs and brine wafts through the stones. His nostrils flare at the familiarity, and he fights against his base nature to run after it—to be with Aerona again.

The Goddess steps forward, her entire being filling the night sky, and peers down at him with eyes so black he fears he might drown in their darkness. "You come here asking *me* about a bargain?"

She throws her head back with glee, the sound reverberating off the stones. Gooseflesh crawls up his back to the base of his neck, and his thinning white hair stands on end, scraggly.

"How dare you call upon me," she continues, towering over him. He cowers, his curved spine almost forcing him into a prone position on the ground before her. "When I have given you everything you have asked for, and yet you have given me *nothing* in return. Empty promises do not a happy Goddess make."

A cool breeze blows through the goddess's locks. Streaks of moonlight catch the silver strands as they whip across the sky. The floral fragrance of lilacs, their petals warm from the summer sun, blows around him. He inhales deeply, tears pricking his eyes, and barely hears what she says. He turns in a circle, trying to find Aerona in the mist beyond.

"I..." The words he wants to say die on his lips. Where did Aerona go? Why couldn't she stay? Despair builds in his chest, somewhere inside his hollow heart. When he can't find his mate, when he is sure her scent is gone, he turns back to the goddess, pointing up at her. "You owe me."

"What makes you think I owe you anything, Smoke King?" the goddess hisses. She grabs his hand then, the one that still bleeds, and yanks it to her. "I showed you how to make vessels to prolong her life so you could heal your mate. But you *tricked me*. You never told me your mate had already passed. You *failed* to mention that you held her in your arms, watching as her blood turned the green grass red."

She bends his hand backward, and the cut opens back up, spilling his blood onto the ground below. Where it lands, a sticky, tar-like substance forms. Flames lick at the edges of the black pool. He bites his cheek to keep from crying out as she bends his wrist back even further, bones snapping. She swipes her finger through his cut, scowling at it as she rubs the blood between her fingers.

"You have abused my gifts," she says, flinging his hand toward his chest with disgust. "Go. And never come back here again. You defile my sacred grounds with your darkness."

"Not before you—" He starts, but she vanishes, disappearing into a swirl of mist.

The black pool slowly seeps into the ground, moss growing over what had been there before. The stones shimmer, and he sits down with a huff, landing back on the edge of his bed. Clutching his hand, still bleeding, to his chest, he walks over to the wardrobe. He tears Aerona's dress from where it hangs and flings it into the flames of his fireplace.

Thirty-Five
Sorcha

The stone is cold beneath me, and I shift, unused to sitting in such a stiff seat for so long. Shined to perfection, the formidable weapon rests across my lap. Its blade reflects the yew tree canopy on its surface, snagging the dappled sunlight in its metal edges. Starbursts pepper the shiny black hagstone face, winking at me as I run my thumb over its smooth surface.

A crown of gold and emeralds rests atop my head.

"A simple tiara," Hazel said when she helped me fit it atop my head this morning.

But what's simple about it? I do not know because it is covered in intricate metallic designs, with tiny rows of emeralds that weave around like vines. Slightly larger rubies cluster together like budding roses, all pointing toward the middle peak of the crown, where a large emerald rests. My hair is plaited into an intricate knot, and I sit in a gown of green and red that matches the jewels atop my head. The crown feels heavier with each passing moment, as if it, too, knows a human sits on the throne instead of a fae.

The room yawns before me, a sea of faces that watch my every move, waiting for a few words from their queen. Can they tell? Is that why a few voices murmur in the back?

If I do not have their full support, I cannot ask them to follow my plan in good conscience. I lick my lips, my palms slick with sweat, and meet Conall's eyes from across the room. He bows subtly, and then, like a bolt of lightning, the heart-call pulses between us, bright light a beacon. My eyes go wide at the sensation entering my body again.

The words "My Queen" pulse through our connection, and I fight back tears at the comfort of the heart-call.

Conall straightens and quirks his lips into a knowing smile. I try my best not to gape in his direction, but I can't look away. Conall opens his mouth, his lips forming the words, "My Queen."

I stand, resolving to talk to him about the heart-call later.

The yew tree above me shakes its leaves. A branch kisses my shoulder, and a tremor runs through the crowd. The dryad in the yew tree whispers so low that only I can hear it say, "Queen of Fae."

I take a deep breath and begin.

"Some of you know me from my time with the Fire King. Most of you know me as the Deoir-born heir to the Earth Fae throne. You all now know me as your queen. And as your queen, I will do my best to restore peace and balance to these lands. To right the wrongs done to you and..."

And what?

I look down at my human-sized hands, weaker arms, and shorter stature. Surely, they must all see me for the human I am and not the half-fae I claim to be? How can I rule them when I am not one of them?

Achill's parting words echo in my mind. *"We're not so different, you and I."*

But we are, for his soul is hungry with power. His rule over his subjects is one of terror, and his wrongs are etched upon a body that will not die.

Wishing to protect the fae and the humans from him wouldn't turn me into a dictator, would it? What would it mean to embrace my humanity, my mortality, here before the fae? Between all the lies and betrayals, the half-truths and the hidden secrets, the assault from Achill, the torture Conall endured, and the senseless deaths, I would like to think that it was my compassion that kept me going.

But maybe Achill is right.

We aren't so different because all I want is revenge. My blood boils at everything that has been taken from me. A humming fills my head, and my vision goes fuzzy around the edges, but it is rage instead of fear clouding my sight.

"*How easily do you think they will join you?*" His sneer laughs in the back of my head.

A soothing voice chases it away. "*I would not have given you this gift if I didn't think you were capable. You are much more worthy of the throne of these lands than any who have come before you.*"

"*You are nothing but a peace treaty.*" His slimy voice continues. "*You're one of us, not one of them.*"

Anger rolls through me in waves.

I am not *just* a peace treaty. I never have been. I was and will always be Sorcha Salonen, daughter of Gareth Salonen and granddaughter of Cariad Deoir. Despite lacking fae blood, I am the rightful heir to the Earth Fae throne.

And then, faint as a whisper, as if the wind carries her words to me, "*You are the light to the darkness. So shine.*"

My jaw hurts, and I realize I've been gritting my teeth. The crowd grows restless the longer I stay silent. I will not fit their idea of a Fae Queen because I am not fae. But I am also not just human. I am in-between—a half-halfling who pulled the sword from the tree.

I will never be the queen that they expect, but I will be the queen that they deserve.

Standing a little taller, I take one last look around the room. If this is my last stand before we take Achill down, my people deserve to know my truth, and I plan to fight beside them.

"I promise you; I will right the wrongs done to the fae and the humans. I am the granddaughter of Cariad Deoir, but I am also the late King Gareth Salonen's daughter." I choke on the words '*late king*' but continue, "I am not fae. But I am not wholly human, either."

I rest the sword against the arm of the throne and bring my hands out to my sides. Opal's lessons come through once more, and I surrender, calling out to the elements of air, water, and earth. Blue glitters on my left, and vibrant green shimmers on my right. Swirls of color dance together once I bring my hands before me. I call upon my air magic, and it whips my skirts around my legs. The yew tree shakes in the funnel of wind that swirls around me, and my feet lift off the ground. Earth, water, and air magic all play at my fingertips, and I'd be lying if I didn't say I felt a rush of power watching the entire room dip low into an orchestrated bow. Their heads tilt down, but their eyes strain to see my magic. My feet touch the ground, the wind dies out, as do the water and earth, and I pick the sword back up, clutching to the hilt to hide my trembling hand.

I wait for the shock to finish traveling through the crowd and meet Conall's eyes again. His lips form a tight line, and he crosses his arms, giving me a "we'll talk about this later" look. I lift my chin, challenging him, and he shakes his head subtly.

"We all know that King Achill has lived for too long without his mate, which has turned him into a shell of what he once was. I know because I saw him without his glamour. And then he took from me almost everything and everyone I hold dear. He cut the land into two with his foolish ideas of ultimate power. And he expects us to roll over and take it, to accept that he is the High King and the only ruler of Fae."

The crowd nods, their murmurs of approval rippling through the room. Murdock moves through the crowd and stands next to Conall. He frowns, looks from Conall to me, and then down at the sword.

"But he didn't pull the sword from the tree. I did. And he isn't wearing the Earth Fae crown. I am. He has no idea who he is up against. I haven't come this far and lost so many of my loved ones to call it quits now. As your queen, I plan to bring balance back into the world he has tried to destroy. I have seen how beautiful this land is, how gracious you all are, especially to an outsider like myself."

I try to look at each of the faces in the first few rows, wanting them to know I see them and that I am fighting this fight for them, too. It isn't just for me and my silly revenge scheme to get back at Achill for hurting my mate. Although I won't lie and say it isn't a big part of my reasoning, my eyes meet Conall's again.

"I can't promise there won't be bloodshed in the coming days, but I will need fighters. I will need powerful, magical fae to help me weaken his army."

Hands shoot up, eager volunteers in what I hope is a successful plot to overthrow a tyrant. Conall meets my eyes with clarity, and I know he knows what words will come from my mouth before I even speak them. He bristles, and I raise my chin a little higher, daring him to question me and talk me out of this.

"I promise that, as your queen, King Achill will meet his end."

Thirty-Six
Sorcha

Conall shuts down as the last of my words echo through the room. His entire body goes rigid, and he looks through me to a spot on the wall behind my back. As the crowd disperses, several fae walk up to him. It takes him a second, but he shakes his head and turns to them, listening intently. He leans a little on his cane, the muscles in his arm flexing as he shifts his position.

"Your Highness," Ferns calls out through the crowd. "The brownies..."

But I can't hear the rest of what she says because I can't take my eyes off Conall. The color has returned to his face, the pallid, grey tint long gone. But he could still do with a day in the sun like how he looked when, over a year ago, he stooped to drink water from the stream at the edge of his lands. His ochre skin had a warm golden hue, as if he spent his days in the sun-bright meadows of his home. Does he wish he could be back there instead of here with me?

Despite the tug I give him on the heart-call, he still won't look my way. Is he giving me a cold shoulder?

I huff a sigh of disappointment.

"Your Highness?" Fern asks, snapping me back into the present.

"I'm so sorry, Fern, please continue."

"As I was saying, I just wanted to thank you for bringing the brownies here. It couldn't have been easy to take them from their nest. Typically, brownies will stay no matter how bad the conditions get."

I finally tear my eyes from assessing Conall and meet Fern's grateful stare. "I had no idea."

She nods solemnly, following my gaze back to my mate.

He is entrenched in conversation when Murdock walks up and slaps him on the back. They nod to each other, and Murdock replaces Conall, who slinks back into the shadows with the stealth of a wolf hunting its prey.

Is he coming to get me?

No.

He runs away with his tail tucked between his legs, probably thinking I won't notice. But I do. The heart-call tugs between us, an anchor to my ship. After all we have gone through, this is how he will act. The door closes behind him, and I try to excuse myself from my conversation with Fern politely.

"Fern, I really must—"

She says, "No, dearie. Do what you must. Stubborn, isn't he?"

"Yes," I say, my eyes still on the door he went through. I mumble, "That's one way of putting it."

I finally tear my gaze away and find her smiling at me—beaming. Her cheeks are two ruddy circles high on her face.

"What?" I ask.

"It's just nice to see how you two…" She waves her hands in the air and then flushes a deep red. "Young love, that's all."

I try not to scoff because I am not feeling the love right now. "Yes, well. Now, I really must—"

"Yes, yes, show that wolf who is alpha." She shoos me away and gathers up Hazel from the throne. Fern places the wingless pixie on her shoulder and bows to me before leaving for the kitchens.

Lugging the sword behind me, I twirl my fingers in the air, and a gentle breeze lifts the blade from the floor. It follows dutifully next to me as I push open the door to a dimly lit servants' hallway. I need to find a better way to carry the monstrosity if I'm supposed to have this on me as a symbol forever.

Rounding a corner, Conall leans on his cane while he opens up a nondescript wooden door. I give him a few moments to make it through, and then I dash inside behind him. The door closes with a click, and I blink a few times to adjust my eyes. The smell of dust, moldy old books, aging leather, and his trademark cedar scent greets my nose.

I almost run into Conall's broad back. His shirt is tight across his shoulders. I watch the muscles in his shoulder as he turns to me, and every part of his face screams of exhaustion.

"Sorcha," he says, his voice low but sad.

"Conall," I retort, raising an eyebrow. "Coming to the library to hide, are we?"

He sighs, eyes darting to some spot over my shoulder. "I'm not *hiding*."

"Oh? Then why run from me through a servant's hall and go through a backdoor to the library?" I call his bluff, tugging on the heart-call. I get nothing in return and look at him, confused.

"I just needed some time," he says, shrugging.

A lock of hair falls into his face, and I want to reach up and tuck it behind his pointed ear. But I don't. I cross my arms instead, and the sword falls to the floor. If he's not even going to use the heart-call, I am happy to return the favor of blocking him out.

Conall stoops to pick up the blade, grunting as he puts weight on his bad leg. He lifts it with ease. The sword fades beneath his touch, its usual silvery shimmer turning a muted grey. And the hagstone that usually glints in even the lowest lighting dulls to a rough-hewn stone.

I cross my arms over my chest and refuse to thank him or make a move to take it. "Space? What, so you could devise a good excuse for not agreeing with me?"

"Sorcha, that's not—fine. Why didn't you tell me you were going to ask these fae to join you and fight?"

"I didn't think I needed your permission. But, now that we're talking about it, do you have any other solutions, Conall?" I ask, genuinely wanting to know if he's thought of an alternative. Every angle of this has played out in my head over and over. The only solution I have for finally defeating Achill and returning balance to the lands is a full-fledged war. "I'm not happy with this, either, but this is the only thing I can think of —"

"I don't know," Conall cuts me off, frowning. "I just need some time to process this. You're asking for a lot from your subjects." He looks everywhere but in my eyes.

His body is coiled tight as if sharing this space with me is too much for him. A muscle ticks underneath his eye, and he clenches his jaw.

I wait.

He waits. The silence swells as a chasm of misunderstanding and pent-up anger swirls between us.

"Fine," I say, finally giving in. I hold out my hand for the sword. "Take *all* the time you need."

Conall holds the sword flat on his palms and waits for me to take it. I twirl my fingers and let my air magic lift it from his hands as I head through the stacks of books and out the main doors. They slam behind me, and I let myself sink against their sturdy, ancient wood.

If he is stubborn and refuses to speak to me, then I can do the same.

I think.

• • •

"Ah..." says Murdock, halting as he enters the library. His eyes skim between me and Conall. "Am I interrupting a lover's quarrel?"

Conall leans against the window behind me in the library. He says nothing to Murdock but grunts, crossing his arms over his chest. I turned my back to him when I sat down, but I imagine he is wearing his trademark scowl and worrying his lower lip between his fingers.

"You could say that," I deadpan. Despite my best efforts, I shift in my seat, knowing his glare burns into my back.

If only he could see my side of things, how ill-equipped I am to take on Achill. I may have the power of three elements, but I am still a mortal, and the energy it takes to sustain them drains me quicker than a fae. The only way I can think of defeating Achill is to bring him onto the battlefield and take him on when I have the combined powers of the other High Fae, should I falter. And what better way to lure him out to fight than to put myself in the center?

But Conall won't see my side. He refuses to concede, but he won't offer up another solution. Even my trained warrior mate cannot figure out a way to defeat him. And we haven't had time to patch things up between the chaos of the countless meetings with the volunteers for my arm, countless reports coming in from Fern's secret castle network, and details of the army Achill amasses at the Border.

Each night, we devolve into a screaming match that spirals into passionate, furious sex. Our bodies circle closer, pulled together by an invisible line, until we are pressed together chest to chest. Then, hurried hands and passionate kissing, clothes are torn off, and we curse at the contact of skin on skin.

Each pass of his scruff or callused hands leaves red-hot trails on my skin. And I can't help it, but I needle at his stubbornness, egging him on with barbed words. His anger fuels his desire to claim me with fast thrusts and grunts of contentment. We leave bite marks on each other's necks and chests. I leave claw marks down his back.

My anger fights back until he claims me with a rabid growl. I scream my release, wanting to feel the burn of his love, know that he is with me in the flesh, and know this isn't some twisted dream again.

Then...

A stilted calm fills the room as we climb into bed and face away from each other.

In the morning, we wake to our bodies twined together, legs wrapped around each other, my head nestled on his shoulder.

Three nights and three mornings exactly like this.

And I am bone-tired of him fighting me at every point I bring up. Not only that, I can barely walk, and I am peppered with teeth marks and bruises that I hide with strategically placed collars and hairstyles.

Tiny butterflies flutter low in my belly as my hand strays to the curve of my neck where his teeth leave their mark. Absently, I rub the tender muscles and sigh as the tension slowly unwinds. Conall exhales behind me, and the insatiable pull of desire echoes through the heart-call. My nipples pebble underneath my shirt at the sensation, and I clench my thighs. His eyes never leave my body as he walks around me and sits two chairs down to my right — just out of reach but not too far away.

"I'll take the pithy silence as confirmation," Murdock says, nodding briefly to Conall. "Maybe you two can stop quarreling for long enough to discuss what progress we're making."

He walks past Conall and heads my way, his eyes flicking down my neck. I flush under his gaze and tug my shirt to cover up the marks that peek out behind my collar. Conall emits a subtle growl, and I scowl his way. Too busy handling everything else, I keep pushing Murdock off, which is easy since he seems to be avoiding me. But he deserves to hear how I feel despite the evidence planted on my neck for everyone to see.

"Please, sit," I say, gesturing to the table before me. "Let's discuss."

Conall grumbles to himself.

I glare at him and point at the door. "If you would rather not be involved, Conall, you may leave."

"Oh, I'll stay. Someone has to stay to keep you in line, apparently," Conall grumbles.

"Keep her in line?" Fern parrots, pushing the doors to the library open. She shakes her head at Conall, "Have you met your mate?"

Conall huffs, but his eyes flick to me, and the corner of his mouth gives way to a smile for the briefest moment. I smile at him, a mask to hide the churning emotions underneath. Even though Conall is a seasoned warrior, his taciturn refusal to help with my war plans meant I had to ask Murdock to gather a group of fae advisers. But, with his carefully orchestrated absences, Hazel had to track him down and deliver the message for me.

I smile as I watch familiar faces file into the library. Feothan wears Thorne's feather hanging from a lanyard around his neck. He settles in a chair near Conall. Fern pats Feothan on the back as he settles in his seat, and then she sits a few chairs down on my left.

"Your Highness," Felan says, dipping his chin. He looks much better today than he did before the coronation. His eyes are less puffy, and his skin glows like he spent time in the sun.

Conall immediately brightens, standing to make room for his brother. Felan takes the chair Conall occupied as my mate sits closer to me. His elbow brushes my fingertips, but he doesn't pull away, so I wrap my hand around the back of his arm and stroke it lightly. Immediately, an image of us naked flashes in my mind. Conall shifts in his seat, sitting closer to me, and clears his throat. His eyes flash to the markings on my neck, and I watch as his nostrils flare and his green eyes darken with desire. I smirk and the tips of his pointed ears flush dark red against his olive skin.

"Let me present my youngest brother," Felan says. "The pup of our pack, Rowland."

The moment between Conall and I breaks as the youngest MacSealgair brother enters upon Felan's introduction. Much younger than his older brothers, he couldn't be older than twenty, with his patchy facial hair and less-than-confident stature. Kinky, auburn-red hair stands on end, giving him a frazzled, half-shocked look. Though his face is peppered with freckles, his skin is darker than Conall's, and his bright, curious eyes are hazel. Conall stands, motioning his brother closer. Conall wraps his arms around Rowland. Their embrace is rough but full of earnest love for one another.

I twirl my father's signet ring around my thumb again, wishing I had family left.

"Your Majesty," he says, unsure what to do until Conall tilts his head subtly in a mock bow. The young pup scrambles to bow smoothly, and I bite my cheek to keep from laughing at how uncomfortable he must feel.

"What brings you here, Rowland?" Conall asks, his lilt strong on his brother's name. He glares at me, unamused at the humor coming through his end of the bond. I bite my cheek harder.

"I brought some of Father's things," Rowland says, sheepishly looking down at his feet. He adds, "And Mother's. I figured they would be helpful for the wards."

Rowland sits next to his brothers, and they all visibly relax. Together on one side of the table, their familial traits are unmistakable — their eyes the same almond shape, the shape of their noses and ears. But after that, each one is distinctly their own. Conall, rough around the edges, scarred arms, salt-and-pepper streaks over his ears, and green eyes that miss nothing. Felan, with his rich brown eyes full of warmth and long black braids. Rowland's kinky auburn hair is a perfect nest for brownies, and, sure enough, Huff's head pops up out of the curls. The brownie winks at me once and then disappears into the mass of hair.

"The brownie liked it." Rowland smiles at me sheepishly.

"How many left?" Conall asks Murdock, leaning over the table.

Murdock holds up his fingers. "Six more."

Conall moves a map, scanning all the landmarks and scribbled notes I left in the margins. Having his brothers close is doing wonders already as his eyes find mine. I am shocked at how much clearer his eyes are. For a moment, we forget our anger toward each other as he threads his fingers around my own, and I let myself hope that the worst is behind us.

Thirty-Seven
Sorcha

As much as I hate saying my father had been right, he was right. The only way to create a diversion big enough to call the king forward is to destroy the wards and join forces with the humans. If we're going to do this, then it needs to be done right, and it needs to be done quickly.

The MacSealgair wolves will weaken the stones between the Borderlands. If we let the human armies in, we could ambush Achill's army and draw him out so that I can, hopefully, murder him easily. But there's no telling if the brothers can do it.

Air Fae arrive at the castle in droves, their numbers swelling since word got out about Thorne's possible capture. Dwarves have also taken up residence in the castle. The only fae we don't have are the Water Fae, but Dallis assured me that freeing the nymph sisters would change that. The only problem I now face is how to free the sisters and still be on the front lines to kill Achill.

I stare at the piles of books strewn about the table, the journal from my father on top. Its blank pages are still a mystery.

Someone shifts at the far end, and my head shoots up. Murdock is engrossed in a map. I do not know how long he has been there, but he meets my gaze and scoots his chair back, bracing his hands against the table.

But I don't want him to leave. "Stay, please."

"I — Yes, Your Majesty." He sits back down, shifting uneasily in his seat.

A pit has formed in my stomach each day that passes that I don't give him my answer. The longer I delay, the bigger it grows, and I have had enough of being pulled in too many directions. I feel wicked for having drawn this out longer than necessary, but the simple answer is that I am afraid. What if things don't work between Conall and me? What if our fighting never ends? No matter how many questions I have, it isn't fair of me to keep stringing along Murdock, so I might as well do it now. I close my eyes, guilt coloring my cheeks, trying to form the words in my head so I don't muck things up further. He deserves better.

Finally, I open my eyes.

His sea-blue eyes find mine, and he gives me a lopsided smile.

"You know," I state, a finality in my tone.

Murdock gives me a curt nod. "Aye."

"I wanted to tell you sooner." My hand drifts up to the markings on my neck, and I try not to sag into my chair as relief fills my body. "I didn't mean to string you along."

"Och, no matter." Murdock waves a hand in the air dismissively, but the tips of his ears turn pink, and he won't meet my eyes. He plays with his fingers, tiny droplets of water magic rolling around on his hands. "I knew you had chosen him as soon as I said something back in the dwarf country. It was selfish. I should have never opened my mouth, putting you in the position to choose."

Doubt lingers between us, a million questions on my tongue.

He pushes away from the table and stands. Murdock walks toward me, stopping at my shoulders. His hip is at my eye level, and he brushes away my braid and pulls at my shirt collar. I can't move, or maybe I don't want to, only partially entertaining the idea of what his hands on my body might have felt like. But with the markings so visible, shame washes over me for thinking anything of the sort.

With his easy-going nature, would Murdock and I fight constantly as war looms over our heads? I shake my head. Even though we have been arguing, I *like* being Conall's mate.

I lean back, away from his grasp.

"Murdock," I say, my tone firm.

"I knew you had chosen," Murdock whispers. "I just didn't expect to feel so jealous about it."

He walks around behind me and sits in the chair that Felan vacated moments before.

I shift in my seat, facing him, but I lean back so our conversation is less intimate. "Did you know what had happened to Conall while I was at the castle?"

"Och, aye." Murdock studiously avoids my shocked expression, taking great interest in the grain of the table before him. "I didn't know to what extent until I could get Conall out."

"You... rescued Conall?"

How did I not know this? How often has he put his life on the line for me and my mate?

Murdock's ears flush pink, and he rubs the back of his neck. In a choked whisper, he says, "Aye. He's my brother and your mate."

I cross my arms and let the chair support my back as I stare at him, realizing the weight of the words he just said. "I owe you my life, Murdock. We all do."

And before he continues, I add, "You know that pull you had mentioned?"

He grunts, "Aye. Quite foolish now that I think about it."

"No," I shake my head. "I wonder if perhaps it was the water magic you could sense? If it was something familiar that made you..." I drift off, not wanting to say the words that he might.

"Perhaps," he says wistfully. "I do still find myself inextricably pulled to you. Some would say maybe I—"

The doors to the library slam open. Conall stalks through, jealousy rolling off him in waves.

Murdock flinches and stands up, hands up in surrender, but his water magic swirls around his fingers.

"Take your hands *off of my mate*," Conall growls, punctuating the air with his anger.

My mouth falls open, watching as Conall transforms before my eyes. "Conall, enough."

He growls at Murdock, stalking closer. His teeth elongate, and his hands are half paws with very sharp claws and hands.

"Enough!" I snap.

Conall stops, but the tips of his pointed ears turn furry, and he shivers as his wolf tries to take over.

"I can't take this petty posturing from you anymore. Enough, I said." I touch Conall's forearm, and his head snaps to mine, his green eyes laid with possessive fury.

The black fur of his wolf recedes, and his paws turn back into hands. He pants heavily but in his fully fae form. He folds, then hands rubbing his face as he groans. "Tell me he didn't touch you."

"He touched me," I say. And I don't know why. Maybe I want to see Conall's anger turned on someone else for a change. Maybe I want him to finally commit to feeling something instead of existing in the ambivalence of fighting-during-the-day-but-putting-on-a-front-for-people-and-then-going-to-bed-and-fucking-like-animals-only-to-wake-up-and-do-it-all-over-again.

"Och, thanks, Sorcha," Murdock mumbles under his breath.

"I'll kill him!" Conall lunges again, growling.

Murdock takes a step backward, his hands still up in the air.

"But not in the way you think," I add, grabbing Conall's hand and pulling him back. And then to Murdock, I say, "Well, you did. Even after you knew I had chosen Conall."

"Tell me you don't feel anything for him," Conall says, pointing to Murdock, who shirks away from the attention. But his tone is soft, and his entire body envelops me. Conall's hand wraps around my waist, and the other cups my cheek.

I shrug and say, "I can't say that because I do."

Fear flashes behind Conall's eyes, but he is silent, almost resigned. He looks me in the eye and nods. "I understand."

"What?" I say, shocked. First, he comes roaring through here, claiming I'm his mate, pissed off that Murdock touched me. And then, this? "I'm not—"

Murdock joins in with an exasperated sigh. "You *dobber.*"

"Wait," I say, stepping back a few feet, though the space between us feels like miles. "You think I'm choosing Murdock?"

Conall blinks at me.

"After all the — for heaven's sake! Murdock," I snap, turning to face him. "Some privacy would be most welcome."

With a curt nod, Murdock leaves, shutting the doors securely behind him. When I am confident that he is long gone, I turn to Conall, furious.

"You think I've chosen Murdock?" I almost laugh. Instead, I step backward and cross my arms, waiting for him to see how ridiculous this all sounds. "What was with you storming in here, then?"

He shrugs and runs a hand through his hair. "I—"

"You've been argumentative with me all week, yet you have no problem sharing my bed. I can't feel you through the heart-call, but that's on purpose." The more I talk, the angrier I get. "You think I just want you for a quick lay at the end of a stressful day? That it isn't because I have *chosen* you?"

"I don't know," Conall says, listless. And he almost sounds like a petulant child. I fight every instinct to kick and punch the air at his idiocy.

"Really? After me constantly reaching out to you, you still have to question how I feel about you?" My chest tightens, and suddenly, I am unmoored, tossed about in a giant sea. Maybe he isn't my anchor anymore.

"I just want you to be sure," he offers, trying to step forward and hold my hands.

I snatch them away, stepping from his grasp, and the world spins.

"What more do you need?" I shout, gesturing between me and him. "I am *trying* to make things right. I am building an army, so I can finally get justice for all the shit that Achill has put you, put me, put *everyone* through. You think I wouldn't want you by my side for this? Do you think I don't want you?"

My body shakes, and I am angry, so angry, again. Of all the people Achill hurt, that he was tortured twice in a year makes me blind with rage. He was a calm, capable, confident fae, and now he questions the fine thread holding us together.

Conall swallows a few times, his whole body a question.

"Nothing to say? Really?" I ask my throat tight with unshed tears and fearful of the countless hurtful words just waiting to spill out. "I thought finding your fated mate was supposed to be easy. If you feel this way, then maybe you should go home."

I turn from him then, swiping away the tears that fall against my will.

"I don't want to go, Sorcha," he whispers to my back.

Conall reaches out to me, first grabbing my hand and pulling me closer to him. I fight his pull at first, not wanting to play this game. Then, his hand travels along my back, turning me into his chest. I let myself cry into his chest as his arms hold me.

He kisses the top of my head and squeezes me tighter. "I told you that you had a choice and that I wanted you to be with someone who can give you what you deserve and protect you when you need it. You deserve someone much more capable than a limping, scarred, and damaged wolf shifter. It isn't that I don't love you or that I don't want to be with you. Goddess Above knows that I have tried to stamp down my feelings for you in case..."

"In case, what, Conall? In case I chose someone else?" I ask, muffled against his body. He doesn't answer my question, so I lean back and stare into his eyes. "I may be human with more leniency on this type of thing, but I've chosen *you*, Conall. Can't you see that? Don't you feel it?"

I slide a hand along his chest to the curve of his neck, where some bite marks have bruised his skin. Who is this broken fae standing here? What happened to him when he was with Achill to make him doubt everything between us?

Conall's hand catches mine, bringing my palm to his lips. He plants a kiss in the center of my hand. The light catches in his green eyes, highlighting specks of blue and brown that swirl around his pupils. There is a faint burn scar under his jaw that I never noticed before. I trace it with the tip of my finger and add it to my Reasons-To-Kill-Achill list. "I just wanted you to be sure. I wanted this to be a choice *you* made for yourself. Not something that fate decided, not something you felt you didn't have control over."

The words hit me right in the center of my chest. He let me

choose to cross the border into his homelands. He asked if he could help me off my horse. The night at the campfire, he wanted me to be sure and waited for me to consent. Even when it was time for me to meet the king, Conall has always wanted me to have the final say.

His hands cup my cheeks, his rough thumbs wiping away falling tears.

"I don't know how Sorcha. I don't know why, either, but I knew it from the moment I met you. I knew I would love you until the sun stopped rising. And I will continue to love you until the stars fade into the Forever Night sky, even if that means you are choosing someone else or walking away from me. I knew that no matter where you were, I would try to be happy for the life you *chose*, knowing that you had made that call. The second I saw you, I knew I was ruined. My life was never going to be the same." Conall's voice cracks, but he gathers me up in his arms, holding me close, and all I want is to melt into him.

My arms wrap around his back, and I clutch to him like a lifeline, as if my ship is finally going under. Beneath his shirt, I can make out the misshapenness of his corded scars against his back, and a flash of anger courses through my body.

He must have felt it through our connection because he holds me tight.

"I don't deserve you," he chokes out. "But I promise you that every moment we are together, and even in the moments after, you will never regret the decision you made."

Weightlessness fills my limbs at his words.

Perhaps it is because the possibility of war is right around the corner, or maybe it is because the only time we have had together has been fighting, but our movements turn frantic. One of his hands comes behind my head, weaving into my hair, and he tugs my head back. I gasp. He kisses me enough for me to forget about ever doubting anything between us. I want to tear the clothes from his body and claim him over and over. I want to delight in the vibrancy of his touch and the way his hands play on my human body. My body with the rounder hips and the thicker thighs, and the breasts that are losing their perkiness, and the stomach that is soft and squishy, and the thick thighs that rub together when I walk.

The body that he devours each time I am naked before him.

As if reading my mind, his hands rip my shirt off and fumble their way down to the laces of my pants. My fingers tremble with anticipation, and I miss the knot at the top of his pants a few times. I laugh into his mouth, self-conscious that I can't find the correct string. He smiles back, lips never leaving mine, and pulls my hands to his front. His cock strains the fabric, and I sigh when he finally unties his pants and frees himself. His shirt goes next, and it sails to the floor.

I take him in, naked and panting, as he stands in front of me. His eyes are hazy as they regard me underneath a hooded gaze. I shiver in my half-stay and want to cover up. Conall shakes his head and reaches for my hands, holding them to my sides.

"I *love* your body," he says, a phrase I have yet to become comfortable with. "Goddess Divine, how I love you, too."

He lets go of my hands and reaches around to undo my stay. Each rasp of the tie through the holes grates on my patience, but eventually, he gets them loose enough to slip it off. Cool air skims over my exposed flesh, the hardened peaks of my nipples sensitive already. He dips his head low, kissing his way down my neck and my breasts. His teeth graze my nipple, and I moan, arching my back for more.

"I love knowing when you're ready."

"H-how?" I exhale. "How do you know?"

"Consider it heightened wolf's sense," he says, taking my breast into his mouth. I thread my fingers through his hair, wanting to pull him closer. My body vibrates with need; his touch is never enough.

Conall's free hand traces the line of my hip, and then both hands cup my behind, and he lifts me so that my legs wrap around his waist. I don't even have time to think about how he is holding me up with his hurt leg or if his muscles strain with my weight because his mouth meets mine again, and his tongue teases me open. My tongue plays with his, and I am eager to be full of him in any way I can. He sets me on top of the table and gets down on his knees, spreading my legs, so I am on display before him.

"Goddess Above." He stares up at me with that familiar devilish grin. "You have the most beautiful pussy I have ever seen."

"I'm glad you see something you like," I smirk. He drags his fingers through my slickness, teasing my entrance, and I brace my hands on the edge so I don't tumble forward. He rubs my clit, and a jolt of pleasure travels up my spine.

"No," he says. "Love. I see something I *love*." He dips his head and moans into me as his tongue slips inside. My insides turn liquid as he devours me, his thumb circling my bundle of nerves. I roll my hips forward, shivering as he pushes his tongue further and moans into me. My legs shake, and my breath quickens each time he swirls his tongue.

Conall pulls back, and I whimper at the loss of contact. His voice is raspy with desire as he says, "But you taste even better."

He runs one of his hands around to my backside and pulls me forward so I hang off the edge of the table, resting my feet on his shoulders. I lean backward and spread my legs even farther. He slips a finger inside and dips his head back down to flick my clit with his tongue.

"I love how sensitive you are," he says, his voice rumbling and gravely. My hair stands on end, and I shiver with anticipation. He grips my backside with his free hand and says, "I will never let you go, Sorcha. You realize that, don't you?"

"Uh-huh," I breathe, and he adds another finger. A guttural moan escapes my lips, and I buck my hips against his hand, my core tightening with a climax.

He hums in response and asks, "Want another?"

I nod, eager to take as much of him as possible. His face changes and his warrior's calm demeanor takes over. I shiver, loving how in control he is, wishing he could stay like this, like he used to be.

He slips in a third finger, and I mewl as he stretches me. He slows as I get used to the girth of his fingers. His tongue licks around my entrance and plays with my clit. I relax and undulate my hips, able to take more of him in.

"That's My Queen," he praises, watching his fingers slide inside me.

His eyes are full of adoration, and I wish I could see myself as he sees me. Subconsciously, I move my hands to cover my breasts. He must tell that I am pulling out of the moment because he starts pumping his fingers; each thrust inward, he strokes that spot that makes me see stars. I lose all sense of self, my release winding tighter and tighter the faster he strokes. I cannot focus on anything but the sensation of him filling me, tasting me. And suddenly, I'm floating, adrift in a sea of Conall. No longer unmoored but forever pulled along in his tide, waves of pleasure pulse through me, and I know, deep in my bones, that I will gladly call his ocean my home.

His fingers find that place, and I jerk, crying out his name as I come. My body still shakes when he stands, but he doesn't remove his fingers. He leaves them inside as they tease the last of the orgasm from my body.

Conall watches me with a hunger I have never seen from him before. In his other hand, he grips his shaft, stroking in time as his fingers dive inside me.

"Please," I beg, my hands tweaking my hard nipples. His lips quirk, and he settles himself at my entrance. He slides his fingers out, and I feel so empty until he pushes his shaft in a few inches. I squirm, wanting to wrap my legs around his waist and pull him closer to me. But Conall leans over me, taking one of my legs and placing it on his shoulder.

"Sorcha, you're perfect," he groans, sliding inside a little further. My walls tighten around him, and he shudders. I smile up at him, loving that I can make him senseless with such little movement. He praises me with each push. "You're so tight... and wet... and hot... and... perfect."

His words do me in.

"I choose you," I say, looking him in the eyes.

"It was never a choice for me," he says and plunges inside.

We both gasp. His green eyes blow wide, and he watches my body, my curves, and how it moves with him. He grabs my other leg and places it over his shoulder, angling my hips so he can watch as he sinks into me. His eyes find mine, and he reaches up to cup my face. A gentle wave of emotion plays along the heart-call.

If we only have these moments together, I'd rather they be moments like *this* than moments full of anger and fighting. Our reunion should have been tender and sweet instead of being haunted by the things the king stole from us. What would have happened to him if I had never got him out? Would he have died of a broken heart and gone mad like the Fire King?

"Sorcha," Conall says. He gazes down at me and cups my cheek in his hand. Concerned, he whispers, "Sorcha, my mate. Where did you go?"

"I—I'm here," I shake my head. But the moment is gone, my head spinning with too many possibilities. Conall withdraws and I am too cold, too empty without him. I sit up roughly, grabbing his wrist as he turns from me.

"It's okay," Conall says. "If you're not in the mood, we don't have to continue."

My eyes flick down to his hardness. It glistens, wet from me, and stands erect in its glory, ready to go again. But he's right; I am no longer in the mood.

Thirty-Eight
Sorcha

Eleven pairs of eyes turn to greet me as I enter the library. Feothan, Aodhfin, Fern, Grindel, another female dwarf whom I was told was Grindel's mate, Murdock, Felan, Fia, and Aine, the fire sprites, and Cherry and Lily, the pixies. They all stand around the large table, scattered with papers and open books. The only fae missing are the Water Fae nymphs, but I hope that once I free the sisters of the lake, they will rally behind us.

"My Queen," Conall lilts. His eyes are proud as he turns to me and claps a hand over his chest. He gives a brief bow and then says, "Meet your advisors. Twelve fae are together to represent all four elements in your kingdom: warriors, crafters, and healers, but all masters of their magic."

I wish I had the words to express my gratitude to every one of them, but I am at a loss. The last thing I want to do is ask these fae to fight for me, their human queen. Guilt sits like lead in the pit of my stomach. Asking these fae, again, to commit to something that might not even work makes me so nervous.

Conall's rich timbre shakes me back to the present. "Per your instruction, they have been working nonstop to figure out how to break down the warding stones."

"We think we have some of it figured out," Fern's voice cuts into the noise inside my head, and I meet her amiable smile with one of my own. She knows I love a good puzzle, so she pushes a few papers down the table to where I stand and points to a few strange markings someone roughly sketched.

"See," she says, moving her index finger along the parchment. "Part of the problem was knowing where the stones were and what markings they had carved into their surface. We were able to sketch some of them quickly when Felan was with Maccon back in the MacSealgair lands. But we didn't want to activate the entire Border at the forest's edge for fear of tipping off the king, so our information is limited."

"Well done, all," I say, scanning the various drawings. "Conall, can you grab the books that Felan left? And that one, too?" I point to the leather journal underneath a map at the far end.

"Och, a blank journal?" Murdock drips with sarcasm, and he cocks an eyebrow at me.

"A warded journal," I retort. His ears turn red. Conall hands me the journal and sets the books in front of me. "I'd ask you to watch your tone when questioning me, but, alas, your smarmy remarks are ones I have missed lately. This journal belonged to my grandmother, Cariad. My father gave it to me the day I left to cross the Border into Fae. Fern noticed faint warding marks on the corners of each page, and to this day, I still do not know what they mean or hide. But, they look similar to the markings on the warding stones."

Fern nods empathically as I set the book down on the table and open it up. Sure enough, the faint wards on the pages match the hurried sketching of the wards from the border stones. Conall leans over me to look at the pages, his hand landing on the small of my back. I almost weep at his open display of emotion, the first time he has touched me in front of others since coming home.

He touches an upper corner of the journal, and words flare to life beneath his fingers. I frown at him, and he frowns back at me. Then he lifts his hand off the page, and the words disappear.

"From your grandmother, you say?" Conall asks, pulling on his lower lip in thought.

"Yes, she had several other publications regarding stone circles and their magical properties. She was trying to figure out why fae magic was diminishing and how the stone circles could help." I trail off and grab his hand, placing his finger back on the page, amazed at the words that light up. "But why she warded this particular journal is anyone's guess. Unless..."

Conall's eyes are unfocused as he recalls details from his past. "I don't know if I had ever seen Cariad around, but my father and mother had a few fae help when they raised the stones. Perhaps she was one of them. They talked about the collective strength of the elemental fae."

Felan touches the journal with his finger, but nothing happens.

"Huh." I look between the two brothers.

I take Conall's finger and trail it over the surface, awestruck when the pages unravel their secrets. Several names are vaguely familiar. One, in particular, catches my eye: Dallis. Her likeness appears in a sketch on the page opposite. Around her neck, she wears a stone on a chain, one eerily similar to the hagstone I had worn. Written in the margins, in a scrawl so small I have to squint to read it, are the words hagstone and lake.

My hand reaches for my sword, and I wonder if the hagstone within the hilt matches the one in the image.

"Conall, I'd like you to work with your brothers on the information in this journal," I order. "Then I want to see you and the journal back in my chambers this evening."

I am confident that this discovery will be the key to ending this war before it begins. Relief washes over me through the heart-call. I turn to Grindel and his mate, "Thank you both for your work at the Inn. How many fae does Achill have?"

"Nine High Fae, Your Majesty," Grindel says. "And—,"

But his mate cuts him off, the words leaving her mouth in a rush. "A hoard of ogres is waiting on the westerly side of the forest, tucked away and out of sight. We've had to cull all our livestock to feed them."

The air in the room goes taught at the mention of the ogres, and she stops, suddenly aware that all eyes are on her with this bombshell of new information. Conall shifts slightly closer to me, bristling at the mention of the wild fae. He emits a subtle growl, a

271

rumbling in his chest that sends shivers up my spine. I rest my hand on his forearm, and though his eyes refuse to meet mine, his body twitches at my touch.

"Ogres?" I ask, raising an eyebrow. That's a wrench I didn't consider.

"How many?" Conall clips, barely able to contain his snarl. I slide my hand to his elbow and rub small circles in his crook. He finally relaxes.

Grindel looks at his mate and then to me, "Your Majesty, Lyra didn't mean to offend."

I wave him off, "Far from it, but this changes a few things."

"If he's corralling the ogres..." Conall stops mid-sentence, pulling at his bottom lip. His brow creases, and I know this is a sign that he is slowly returning to himself. The pain and memories may never go away, but I can only hope that they will become duller as time passes.

Lyra worries her lip between her teeth, stepping closer to her mate. Grindel clears his throat and continues, "We had to keep them fed, or the ogres would have gotten destructive. We didn't want them caving in the last of the tunnels in case we needed to use them to evacuate."

"How many more tunnels are there?" I ask, recalling how I escaped the king's conservatory. "Where are they?"

"There are only a few left, but I was worried they'd be discovered, so I hid their entrances well." Grindel points to a few places on the map close to the mountains where the dwarves live. My eyes follow his finger, connecting all of the areas.

"Did you build all of them?" I ask. "Even the ones that went to the castle?"

Grindel proudly nods, puffing his chest, "My brothers and I, yes. Maol and Cloddiwr."

"And how many...?"

"Countless. Hundreds?" Grindel shrugs. He reaches for a much smaller map that hides under a stack of books. He unfurls the parchment, his rough hands scratching against the paper. Lyra jumps in, pointing to several places on the small map. "We used many access points for the resistance through the centuries. We filled most of them in last year. Imminent war and all that. It was against my wishes, but..."

"But, you almost caved in the Inn, Grin!" Lyra tosses her hands up in frustration.

"We did no such thing! Those tunnels were sound, and you know it." Grindel pouts and crosses his arms.

Lyra rolls her eyes skyward and heaves an exasperated sigh. "You'd think he'd grow up after being alive for as long as he has." The admonishment from Lyra turns Grindel's face bright pink, and he pouts even more.

"Any chance some of these tunnels lead back to the Dwarf Mountains?" I trace the route from the Inn to the base of the mountains.

Grindel forgets his tantrum as his eyes light up. His finger taps near mine, and he puffs his chest out proudly again. "Yes, Your Majesty. There are two."

"If we gathered enough of the dwarves, we could launch a surprise attack here and here." I point to the forest to the west of the Inn and a rock section to the north.

My advisers listen closely as I share the plans for strategically ambushing the king's holdouts. If my intuition is correct, this could prevent a war, and I would be able to kill the king without getting anyone else killed.

Thirty-Nine
Sorcha

We savor the early morning quiet of the day before we rise to make choices from which we cannot turn back. Silky flaxen light streams through the tree's canopy, painting our naked bodies in a mottle artwork of golden light. My hips pop as I shift against Conall, another reminder of the mortality of my human body. Conall sits up effortlessly, and I get a full view of his scarred back as his skin pulls taut across his hunched shoulders. I run my hand down his spine, and he flinches, trying to turn away.

"Don't," I say, grabbing his shoulder. "As much as I hate seeing these scars on your body, please don't shy away from me."

I trail my fingers over the pink and white webbing. If I could take back all those scars and memories, I would. I want to hurt anyone who ever hurt him. I want to make it so he never has to hurt again.

Conall swallows, and I watch his throat bob up and down. The lines of his mouth are strained as he says, "It is getting easier, but there are moments where I cannot separate your touch from the memories."

"Then I shall have to make my touch the most blissful you have ever felt." I sit behind him, pressing my bare breasts into his back, and wrap my arms around the front of his chest. He holds onto my forearms and leans his head on my shoulder. He sighs, and I nuzzle his face, nibbling on his ear lobe.

Conall shivers. "I've told you before that my ears are *very* sensitive."

"I know," I giggle, licking my way up to the tip of his ear. I watch over his shoulder as his cock flexes instinctively. I whisper, "I wish I could take those memories away from you forever."

"I don't," he says, dropping his hands. He turns, finding my eyes, and adds, "It reminds me that there are things worth fighting for and that there will be good on the other side of the bad."

He squeezes my knee, using it to push himself off of the bed. It sends the platform swinging. I watch his naked form unabashedly as he rifles through clothes on the floor.

This brilliant fae creature is mine.

He bends forward, grimacing when his weight shifts onto his left leg as he grabs his shirt from the floor. I scurry off the bed to help him, but he shakes me off. I sit awkwardly, watching him shift his weight onto his good leg.

"About your plans to kill Achill..."

"Yes?" I ask, raising an eyebrow, expecting an entire lecture. But I scan his face and see none of his trademark scowl.

"I want you to know that, however this plays out, I will be beside you. The entire time."

My heart skips, knowing he only knows part of my plans. I can't meet his gaze, so I nod and stare at my hands, unsure what to say. He walks over to me and reaches out to help me down from the bed. His grip is steady, warm, and comforting as my feet touch the floor, but I can't tell him what I've planned to do.

"Something else is bothering you, though," he says, refusing to let go of my hand. Instead, he pulls me to him, wrapping his arms around me.

I meet his eyes and brace my hands against his broad chest. "How can I ask them to follow me?"

How can I ask *him*? After he has already given himself over twice to keep me safe, I refuse to ask him to fight for me a third time. That familiar feeling of guilt sticks in my throat, and I bury my face in his chest so he won't see it on my face.

"Hmm," he hums, his voice gravelly. "Do you trust them?"

I nuzzle into the curve of his shoulder. "Yes. And I trust that you and Murdock trust them, too."

But it isn't about trust, not really. It's about asking something monumental from subjects who barely know me. If we defeat Achill, I must spend more time with both the fae and the humans if we are to live under a peaceful banner.

"Then let them make this choice for themselves. I think the amount of people wanting to fight for the promise of a peaceful future will surprise you."

But they shouldn't have to *fight* for peace. No one else should.

"Let's hope you're right," I say, still unconvinced. Underneath his shirt, the jagged scars crisscross his muscles. My hands caress his back, checking him over for the millionth time, and though he is healing quickly, he isn't healing fast enough. If my plan is to work without him figuring anything out ahead of time, I will need to be careful with what I share across the heart-call.

"I have always believed that if you let people choose, most of the time, they will do the right thing. But with you at the helm, your compassion, earnestness, and determination are enough to follow you into battle. It's enough for me."

"But you're supposed to say that. You're my mate." I nudge his chin with my nose, ensuring the deception brewing in my head doesn't transfer over to him.

"I would follow you anywhere," Conall whispers, kissing my temple.

He squeezes me before his hands move up to my hips, and he cups my backside. I tilt my chin, and he gives me a mischievous grin.

"I can't today," I sigh, my nipples pebbling as they rub up against his chest with each breath I take. "I have too much to do."

I tilt my head and nibble at his lobe before pushing off his chest to get ready. He groans but doesn't let me go. My body responds instinctively, heat pooling low in my belly, and I have to clench my thighs to keep away the want.

"Maybe I can convince you," Conall says. He tilts my head back and kisses me; his tongue parts my lips, and I moan, wanting his tongue to part me elsewhere. "Take away your stress."

"You can try," I smirk, loving how confident he has become when it's just us.

"Is that a challenge?" He asks as his thumbs stroke the undersides of my breasts. I lean into his touch, the friction from his calluses driving me mad. Our mouths crash together, our tongues fighting for dominance. He groans into my mouth and presses his length into my belly. I grab onto him, afraid I will drown if he lets me go. I thread my fingers through his hair, but he pulls away.

"But you're right. Better not," he says casually. He steps away, and his eyes scrape up and down my naked body with roguish playfulness.

I am whiplashed with want, short of breath, with swollen lips and a half-melted brain. He picks up my half-stay and helps me slide it on. Carefully, he moves my hair out of the way, and I am so turned on that even the tiniest brush of his fingers against my skin sends a current zipping up my spine. He tugs on the laces, and I am stunned at the command behind his movements. I lean back, his strong hands catch me, and I wonder what it would be like to give into his control. To let myself go. To exist for a minute outside of all the demands, pressures, and countless items on my list.

Tempted, I press my bare backside against his erect shaft.

"My Queen," his voice rumbling low. "You said we didn't have time."

I peer over my shoulder and bite my lip, wiggling against him.

His eyes flick to my lips and then my hips as I push back. One of his hands grabs my waist and places his other between my shoulder blades. With a gentle push, he folds me forward so my hands brace against the edge of the bed. In one swift movement, he spreads my legs with his foot, and he guides his tip through my wet slit, coating his head. I hum and arch my back, giving him better access as one of his hands strokes my backside.

"Quickly," I pant against the tightness of my stays. One of my hands reaches behind me to undo the laces, but he beats me to it, yanking my stay off my body and tossing it behind him.

"Oh, I will be anything but quick," he growls.

I shiver and let myself give in to his primal nature. As if he can sense my submission, he wraps his hand in my hair and pulls my head back as he withdraws.

"And you'll take exactly what I give you, My Queen."

"Yes," I cry out as he plunges inside of me again. His hand runs along the curve of my backside. He withdraws again, and I open my mouth, but before I can say anything, he rams inside me. At the same time, his hand makes contact with my bare skin, and I yelp, tightening around him as he bottoms out inside me.

"That's it, My Queen," he says, driving into me again and smacking me once more. My backside stings, but he rubs his hand over it, smoothing out the tingling. The touch is so gentle but firm, winding me up so tight that I reach my hand between my legs.

He releases my hair but lifts me so my back is flush against his chest. I gulp, shocked at how different he feels inside me from this angle. His fingers wrap around my wrist, and he pulls the hand I'm pleasuring myself with away. He says, "Only I will make you come today."

Lost to the bliss, I close my eyes and lean against him, my head falling back against his shoulder. With a snap of his fingers, green light flickers at his tips, and vines reach down from the tree. They wrap around my wrists and tug tight to hold me aloft, my feet barely touching the ground. Conall slides his hand to the front of my body and spreads me with one hand. His thumb finds my swollen clit, and his fingers play with where we collide. He thrusts and growls when he feels me stretch to accommodate him.

"You're perfect," he whispers. "So perfect."

"I'm going to come," I exhale, barely able to stand it much longer.

"Not until I say." And he licks the curve of my neck.

While his thumb rubs my clit, his other hand tweaks my nipple, tugging it between his thumb and forefinger. Euphoria is dangerously close. He releases my nipple and wraps his hand around my throat, squeezing. Instinctively, I clench around him.

Oh, Goddess.

If this is what giving in to him feels like, I have been doing it wrong this entire time.

"I want you to know that you're *mine*," he growls into my ear. "No one else will make you feel pleasure like this for as long as we live."

And I know he speaks the truth. No one could ever come close.

The vines release my wrists, and he carefully bends me over the bed. The feeling returns to my fingers, and I grip the sheets as his fingers pinch and roll my clit. His tip pulses with each rock of his hips, and he grinds out, "Come with me."

We shatter together, our orgasms rolling through our bodies and down the shared thread of our mating bond, intensifying the connection. His roar fills the room, and I cry his name, stars filling my vision. His sharpened teeth clamp down on my neck while he fills me. Warmth floods my body, and I moan as the last tremor rolls through me.

Spent, he makes to leave, but I reach behind and pull his arm down. He collapses on top of me, his chest pressing me down into the bed. I succumb to his weight, and we breathe together, our heartbeats evening out.

"I wasn't too rough, was I?" His fingers skim over the new markings he left. He pushes up, leaning on an elbow as his other hand trails down my spine. He lightly strokes where he smacked me earlier.

I face him and give him a dreamy smile, more sated than I have ever felt. "Not at all, my love."

Adoration fills Conall's gaze as he looks me over. He walks over to the washbasin and gets a towel wet before he returns to between my legs. "Good. Now, let's get you cleaned up so you look presentable."

His ministrations are gentle and slow, and I know I will never risk losing him again.

THE AFTERNOON PASSED QUICKLY after I convinced Murdock to show me even more water magic. Exhausted and drenched, we emerge from the lower garden by the library. His shoulders slump forward as he walks down the hallway before me. And I almost ask if I asked too much of him, given his confessions earlier, but I know his answer will be no.

So, I turn my thoughts to all the pieces that need to come together. I take a shortcut through the royal gardens, skirting the makeshift encampment of Earth Fae warriors, when I'm stopped by a small group that has gathered on the outskirts of the camp.

A group of young fae face-off with the MacSealgair brothers. Conall stands facing me, his arms crossed over his chest, his cane nowhere to be found. I hover in the shadows, watching.

"All I know is that, for being a halfling, you'd think she'd —" Maccon says.

Maccon.

I thought he was supportive of my crown.

"Easy, Maccon," Conall growls. He narrows his eyes, and his flexed arms twitch with carefully guarded restraint. "That's your Queen you speak of."

"You mean your mate," Maccon scoffs.

"*And* my mate," Conall snarls.

"I'm not allowed to question her?" Maccon rolls his shoulders back, readying for a fight with his brother. "What are you going to do? Put me in my place?"

"No," I say behind him. Maccon's shoulders shirk back with shame. "I will."

He turns, and his brown eyes open in shock.

"Your Highness," he mumbles. His shoulders turn inward with a stiff bow. "I'm sorry, I overstepped."

"Yes, you did," Conall says, his voice low and threatening, at his brother's back.

Shivers erupt across my skin, and my nipples prick with the excitement of his protectiveness, but I shake it off.

"Apology accepted Maccon. I know that your anger is misplaced. I never met your brother, but I know I would miss him, too, if I had the chance to get to know him." Pausing, I wait to make sure my words hit their mark. Maccon looks down at the ground, refusing to meet my gaze. Maybe it's a trick of the lighting, but I think his eyes tear up a little. "And, if you must know, I am not a halfling."

Murmurs echo through the small crowd that has now gathered. I let my eyes finally meet Conall's furious glare, give him a tight smile, and shrug that conveys, *"Might as well,"* because I do not want any fae to go into battle and die under pretenses.

"I know we're all restless, nervous, anxious, and angry—all things I'm feeling, too. I know some of you are scared because I'm scared, too. These are things that we all feel, regardless of whether we share the same features, the same skin, or the same magic. But I am not a halfling. I'm not even a half-halfling anymore. I am a human, through and through."

Gasps resound, and a rumbling of doubt crescendos toward me in a wave. I look around, noticing the entire encampment gathered around our small group.

"How do we trust a queen who isn't fae?" A fae asks from somewhere in the back of the crowd. I try to calm my face despite the fear clogging down my throat.

Several voices pipe up, all speaking over each other, "We've never had a *human* rule!"

"This is simply unheard of!"

"Is she really a Deoir?" A voice asks, and someone else shouts, "Can anyone vouch for her?"

Conall bristles, but to his credit, he mirrors my calm mask and stands behind me. Felan and Rowland shift their position, moving a hair's breadth closer. Soon, they, too, flank me at the crowd's edge. I open my mouth, ready to defend myself, when a scratchy, ancient voice calls from the back of the assembled group.

"I can!"

The crowd parts, and a gnarled, ancient dryad approaches. One look in his eyes tells me I have seen this tree before, that I *know* this tree down to the very fiber of my being. Weathered wooden hands, whose fingers turn into branches, reach out to grab mine. His bark scrapes my skin, but I hold steady even as the roughness bites into my skin. He wraps his gnarled fingers around mine, and I instantly relax; the sensation of being welcomed home washes over me.

The dryad turns to face the crowd.

His voice booms over their heads as he says, "It was I who granted her passage back into her homelands, and it was I who accepted her blood when she first touched the moss at my roots. Do you doubt *my* word?"

He leans down, looming over the crowd, willing anyone to speak up again. Heads all shake in unison, and the ancient dryad dips his stiff head once, satisfied. He turns to me and says, "Go on, Your Majesty."

The dryad releases my hands and plants his feet, sprouting roots to support his unused legs. I hold my hands in front of me, silently willing the assembled fae to quiet. My hands shimmer and swirl with vibrant colors, magic coursing through my veins.

The protestations calm down, and soon, all eyes are back on me.

I let my voice carry far on the current of the wind. "I made a bargain for elemental magic—enough magic to defeat the Fire King, enough magic to ensure that we are no longer under his rule. But in exchange, the Goddess took my fae blood."

Arcing my hands above my head, I let the elements come forth, stronger this time. The earth teems with vines that shoot from the woods. A gust of wind blows the hovering globes of magicked firelight, and they dance about in synchronized movements. The sky is clear, but rain falls. I twirl my fingers and let the magic flow through me, more control over the elements than ever.

I wave my hands in the air, and the orange light overhead goes out with one final gust of wind.

My voice carries in the hushed darkness. "Just because I lack the fae blood does not make me any less worthy of being your queen.

Part of my rule is to ensure that this castle and the Earth Fae lands will forever be a haven to anyone seeking it. I understand if you choose to leave. I, alone, will be the one to bear the weight of my consequences, not you."

I take a moment to steal myself, curious whether I can even call forth the last element. The heart-call between Conall and me roars to life, a vibrant fire that ignites my courage. The bond fades to a light pulsing, but Conall's voice echoes in my head, *"This woman has fire."*

A surge of confidence rocks my entire body, and my fingertips flicker with light. The only time I have ever seen fire dance upon another's fingers was when Achill took me on horseback through the country.

The fire flares bright but doesn't burn the hands that hold it, just like it did with the king. I turn my palms skyward, and orbs of orange light float above my hands. With a flick of my fingers, they leap into the air where the previous ones had been. This time, they flicker with a spectrum of colors instead of a solid orange glow. Dropping my hands, I try to maintain a calm facade, but my hands shake. I vibrate with renewed energy and vengeance.

"Fancy trick," Maccon says, and I swear I can see awe written across his features.

Fancy trick, all right. I hope it's good enough to trick an immortal king.

Forty
Sorcha

"What were you doing with Murdock yesterday afternoon?" Conall asks, his long legs striding down the hallway with barely a limp. He hardly uses his cane but still brings it along if we climb stairs.

I rub my forehead, not wanting another fight before we finally meet with everyone for the final plans.

Conall turns and stops at the library door, and before I can raise my chin to meet his eyes, I am swallowed up in his arms, my face pressed against his chest. His hand cradles the back of my head, and I let myself sink into his firm body.

"I can't help it, Sorcha," Conall says. "I think I may always be jealous of your friendship with Murdock."

I snuggle into his broad chest, inhaling the comforting scent of cedar and leaning into the wall of strength he provides, knowing I will need it in a few hours. "I know, but you have to be okay with it. He's as much your friend as he is mine, and I value his integrity and loyalty."

I reach around him and open the doors to the library.

Conall hums in agreement, and my arms tingle with the sound.

"He has been around for a while," he adds. "And I would trust him with everything I have. It's only..."

"Knowing that he loves me and I questioned our future?" I ask, pulling away to look up at his face.

Conall's brow creases slightly. "Yes."

"Well," I add, leveling him with a stare. I lean back against the edge of the table and cross my arms. "If you hadn't cut off the heart-call, then I daresay I wouldn't have had those crushing feelings of doubt."

Conall sighs, his arms going slack around me. He pulls away, his fingers cupping my chin. "I hated doing it, but it was the only way I could think to protect you."

Tears form in my eyes.

Even when he was being tortured, Conall was looking out for me.

"I know," I whisper, and his lips brush mine. He releases my chin but continues to place kisses on my cheeks. I lean back, putting my hands on his chest, and push back. Staring up at his emerald eyes, I sense his desire pulsing through our shared bond. "But I need you to stop acting like you know what's best for me."

He opens his mouth, but I continue. "I mean it, Conall. We only come out of this alive if you trust me."

"I do," he says after a moment of hesitation. "But I want to know what you're not telling me."

I ignore the last part of his statement and ask, "Did you know Murdock was at the signing of the treaty?"

It was only mere hours ago when Murdock admitted he was present at the signing. He used the illusion of water magic to hide his identity. He also witnessed the penultimate moments of his queen at the hands of the human archers.

Conall closes his eyes, hesitating. "Yes, and he was infatuated with Aerona before they went through their rites. They grew up together. His cave was near this castle, and they spent many days there as children in the sea."

I hide my shock from Conall's admission about Murdock's infatuation toward Aerona. But my mind whirls, a thousand bells sounding the alarm. "What if all of this is connected, Conall?"

He tilts his head and frowns. "All of this?"

"Me, the sword, the arranged marriage, the warding stones—"

"Which we can bring down, thanks to that journal of your grandmothers," Conall interjects.

"The hagstone. Us," I finish. "What if Aerona knew all of this was supposed to happen? Murdock said she was one of the most powerful seers the Water Fae had seen in centuries. Her visions almost always came to pass."

Conall walks around the large table, his hands brushing the solitary map resting in the center.

"If all of this was connected, what is the ending?" he asks. "She married the very man who could do the most harm to the entire land. At the very least, she could have refused his hand and denied the pairing."

"I wonder if she felt she had no choice." The words land between us like leaded weights. I know what it means to not have a choice in the way fate plays out. "Did he tell you that Aerona forced Achill to sign the treaty? In front of all of his advisors?"

Conall shakes his head, staring at the map in front of us. He points to a spot on the map now covered with an ancient forest that lines the Border. Tapping, he asks, "If she forced his hand, why did she sacrifice herself on the field?"

"She had to have known something we don't," I add. "I think freeing the nymph sisters might give us an answer."

Conall huffs out a laugh, watching me closely. "Well, My Queen, please tell me *exactly* what you have in mind."

But I can't, and a part of my heart breaks to deceive him.

***

DARKNESS CREEPS along the corridors like an anxious cat. The daylight is unwilling to let go, but as it does, the energy in the castle shifts when the sun goes down. The hallways are hushed. Though I have told no one outside of my immediate group about our plans, I cannot help but worry that the Earth Fae are readying themselves for a war. One that I will try my hardest to avoid.

Conall and I walk to the library, and my boots, stiff from lack of wear, pinch my ankles. I have forgotten what it is like to wear shoes since most of my days have been barefoot. Two tiny daggers rest in sheaths inside the top part of my boots, fitting snugly against my calves. I kept my hair in a simple braided knot - high on my head and out of my face. The insignia ring from my father rests on the old hagstone chain around my neck. It swings freely against my skin, a constant reminder of my place in this world and my obligations to its inhabitants.

The doors to the library sigh open as if the entire castle was holding its breath. Relief washes over me as the rest of my trusted party is here already.

"We're all accounted for," Conall says, closing the doors to the library.

Gratitude fills my chest as I count the ten of us: Feothan, Felan, Aodhfin, Fern, Aine, Fia, Cherry, Lily, Conall, and myself. Yesterday, I sent Grindel and Lyra to the dwarf lands to gather their army, and I hope things are working out on their end.

"Welcome, let us begin." My skin itches with the thought of retribution and finally being able to set things right and follow through with my promises.

"First, My Queen, a gift." Conall turns to me with a shy smile and produces a chest harness. "This is so you can carry your sword with more ease."

He holds it out for me, and I slide my arms inside, beaming at his thoughtfulness. "When did you come up with this?"

"The second I saw you trying to carry that thing up the dais during your coronation." He tugs on the straps and tightens them, adjusting the buckles slowly. His knuckles graze the peaks of my breasts, and I flush, looking around to see if anyone saw, but his broad chest covers his discreet movements. He kisses my cheek, leaning around me to slide the sword into the scabbard at my back.

I reach behind my shoulder, trying to lift it from its holster. It takes a few tries, but I use air magic to help, and it slides out effortlessly.

"Thank you," I smile earnestly. "This will work nicely."

Murdock asks, "Are you ready, Your Majesty?"

"You know I wouldn't ask this of anyone if I felt like they weren't up to the job," I start. "I don't want a war. I don't think any of us do."

"I do," Murdock and Aodhfin say together. They flash devilish smiles at each other and then at me. I roll my eyes. "As I was saying, I plan to avoid a war, which means us attacking Achill's strongholds tonight. Based on Fern's rumors, he knows the war is coming but doesn't know when."

Fern winks. "Whispers and gossip spread faster than royal messengers."

I nod, splaying my hands out on the map before me. "We know he has made camp by the ogres, since he needs to use so much magic to keep them contained. Aodhfin, Murdock, and Felan will meet Maccon just north of the Inn near the MacSealgair border. Lyra will meet you there with a large group of mining dwarves to help remove the warding stones and provide extra fighting power."

All eyes are on me when I lift my head.

"Any questions?" Conall asks. His calmness presses in on me, and I want to shirk away; the guilt of keeping secrets from him gnaws away at my resolve. He leans against the table, subtly shaking out his bad leg before putting pressure back on his left foot. I force myself to meet his eyes and push my feelings down.

No one protests, so I continue, "Feothan, Conall, and I will meet the rest of the dwarves with Grindel here on the eastern side of the castle, cutting off Achill's supply chain and destroying the roads that would take his soldiers south. Fern's network reports that some have already headed south, and minimal numbers are left in the castle. If we can divide his army here under the cover of night, we can use the tunnels to draw them in and then collapse the earth. Then, we will head south and help remove the warding stones, which should help draw Achill to me."

"And that's where our collective power comes in," Murdock adds, finally understanding why I wanted him to teach me more about my water magic.

"Exactly," I say, glad he caught on. Conall frowns. "I will illusion myself as Aerona and call to him near the place where she died."

"It should be easy enough," Fern says. "Everyone in the castle thinks he has gone mad."

"He is mad," I point out. "Unnatural immortality will do that to you. He has far outlived his time here on earth."

WITH THAT, we leave the library. The evening settles around us, thick with secrets and a thousand worries. Butterflies swarm in my stomach, and dread sits on my shoulders.

Conall's large hand wraps around mine as we head to the forest. He still favors his right side, leaning on the cane once we descend the stairs. His knuckles turn white as he grips the top. I try to shake free of his other hand, worried I'll throw off his balance, but he grips me tighter as if afraid to let me go again.

The few fae that are still awake dip into a bow, their eyes bright with hope as they steal glances at their queen, unaware that I am marching off to kill the king. Conall glances back at me and squeezes my hand. I wonder if he can sense my protectiveness towards the array of creatures in my kingdom.

My kingdom.

The words hit like stones in the center of my chest. I look over my shoulder again, committing the castle and the fae to memory. I left instructions with the yew tree dryad in the throne room should I not return, explicitly stating that the crown of the Earth Fae should rest in the hands of the MacSealgairs as a show of their loyalty and that these lands are henceforth protected. I silently plead to the Goddess, hoping these fae never have to worry about where to rest their heads.

We weave down the stairs and out the door at the bottom of my tower. The repaired walls stand six feet tall, with the thorny shrubs growing artfully up the stone. Impatience crawls along my skin the closer we get to the forest. The sooner we portal into Achill's lands, the sooner I can get to Achill and end all of this—for good.

We meet Feothan underneath a large willow tree at the southern edge of the Deoir Forest. While Feothan opens the portal, I turn to the ancient dryad who guards this forest. His face forms in the bark, and his steady, all-seeing eyes find mine. I dip my chin in reverence and touch his trunk.

I send my earth magic to him, hoping it is enough for this place to remain a haven for fae even if I do not return.

"It is done," his rough voice whispers.

"Thank you," I whisper back.

The Goddess' Grotto shimmers on the other side of the portal, moonlight highlighting her white stone features. Feothan steps through first. Conall wraps his hand around mine, and we step through, the movement less jarring than the last few times. My feet land silently on the grass on the other side, but a wave of nausea has me tilting.

Conall's brawny arms encircle me, and I rest my head against his chest as I wait for the world to stop spinning. I let him wrap me up in his strength, believing, if only for a few moments, that we can win and knowing that as soon as he lets go, nothing will stop my free fall.

Forty-One
Sorcha

Chaos erupts around us, and the fighting overtakes all of my senses.

Grindel screams, slamming his sledgehammer into the side of a soldier's face. Countless dwarves rush at soldiers that are twice their size. Axes and hammers, picks, and chisels, all tools that were supposed to cause the cave-in, are now used as implements of death.

The scent of iron is in the air from maimed or dismembered bodies of fae of all types.

Feothan circles and swoops around the trees, out of sight of the archers atop the castle walls. With one long shriek, he takes off into the night. Thorne's feather floats to the ground in his wake, and I know where the bird shifter is headed.

Soldiers rush toward us, but several dwarves form a tight shield between us. Conall blocks, swings, slices, and kills an attacker in one fluid motion. It is over before I can blink. He lunges and then rolls to a downed soldier, grabbing a shield. He tosses it to me, and I grab it with shaking hands. The dwarves push forward, corralling the soldiers to the middle of the fight.

This wasn't part of the plan, and I am frozen, watching as countless fae lay on the ground, their limbs or eyes missing. I step forward, but my boots squelch. I glance down, and they're stuck in several inches in a mixture of mud and blood. Conall deflects two soldiers, and as more soldiers come through the trees, I shout the only thing I can think of to keep my people from being slaughtered.

"Retreat!" I scream and open my hands for a portal to the Deoir forest.

Conall uses his earth magic, trees reaching down to snatch soldiers mid-step and throw them yards away. Grindel holds the line as the rest of the dwarves come running. I strain under the duress of keeping a portal open, never having done it before. Sweat beads on my brow, and as soon as Grindel and Conall are close enough, I shove them through.

"I love you!" I shout as Conall falls through.

Then I snap the portal closed.

The soldiers rush toward me. I have seconds to throw them off to get into the castle undetected. With my other hand, I open a portal to the western side of the forest to the north of the castle, close to where my father died, and step through.

※

I TUMBLE onto the mossy ground, landing in the crook of some enormous roots, and then I vomit. The world spins tortuously fast, and I wipe my mouth on my sleeve. I sink into the earth to stop the dizziness and then look up.

A large mound of cut rock looms before me; the wall has been left in disrepair since my father collapsed it. I can easily slip into the gardens unnoticed here, especially if the soldiers are all in the woods. I climb the rubble, keeping to the shadows. Burn marks scar the stone on the other side, and I don't let myself think of my father's body trapped underneath as I jump down the last few yards. The earth gives way, cushioning my fall as I land.

Forty-Two
Sorcha

Each step makes my skin crawl, and the crunching gravel sounds like hooves on cobblestones as I head to the garden's center fountain. If I can make it to the lake before anyone notices, I can free the nymphs and bring a formidable power to our cause. A flame of fury ignites the heart-call, and I ignore it. I refuse to feel wrong for pushing him back through the portal.

As I round a hedge, fires flare to life inside the castle. I dart into the shadows of the shrubbery near me as a soft orange glow barely reaches the tips of my toes.

Doors creak open, and a figure steps onto the balcony off the Morning Room. I work quickly with my water magic, wrapping the illusion of Aerona around me. Murdock and I had practiced earlier since he knew her so well. I was going to lure the king into the trap we were setting down at the Land's End Inn, using her likeness to play into his madness. Achill wasn't supposed to be here. But if I can lure him to the lake, perhaps the freed Sisters of the Lake will be strong enough to help me defeat him.

Now is as good of a time as any to put my magic to the test.

Still hidden, I pull my shirt from my pants, letting it hang loosely to my mid-thighs, giving it an ethereal quality. I undo my hair from the braid and shake it out.

"Aerona," he breathes, so much pain in his voice that I almost question whether I want to kill him. The king's shadow creeps along the ground as he paces. Sunlight creeps across the sky, and I hope there is still enough darkness for my illusion to work.

My earth magic softens the ground at my feet. Then, with a wiggle of my fingers, the wind muffles the sounds of my feet and whips my hair and clothes about. I step out from behind the hedge, hoping to look like an apparition from his dreams.

He stops pacing.

"Aerona?" he asks, his voice wavering. He descends the stairs, his mouth open in awe. "I have been looking for you for so long."

I take the path to the lake, meandering around the bushes, glancing over my shoulder enough to grab his attention and keep him on my heels. My magic pulls tight around me as if it wants to shield me from his evilness.

"My mate," Achill croaks, and I am almost positive he is crying. "Wait!"

He follows, babbling about the power of the moonstones and how he knew Aerona would somehow make it back to him. I round the corner, the lake coming into full view just as the sunlight peeks through the turret peaks, and I sag at the effort of keeping the illusion up for so long with little practice.

A shriek from a bird comes from inside the castle. The tension between Achill and my illusion snaps, and he looks over his shoulder, frowning at whatever noise interrupts his delusion. From somewhere inside the castle, two birds call out. Within moments, their figures streak across the sky through the gardens. Guards call out, and arrows pierce the sky from the ramparts. My illusion wavers, and I dip quickly underneath the shade of a tree, hoping the morning shadows will hide me for longer.

But I'm not that lucky.

"You have the sword." Achill's voice is dangerously low, dripping with malice. "How could you betray me, my love?"

His lethal stare bores into my back, and I turn in time to see smoke unfurling around his form, raw anger written across his face. Still, I say nothing. The illusion, or what's left of it, is keeping me safe right now. The sunlight catches the sword's handle, throwing dots of luminescence over the ground.

Fuck.

He lunges forward, and I drop my water magic as a rush of air sweeps behind me, forcing him backward several paces.

"It's you," he says. Is he relieved I wasn't Aerona?

I swipe at the air, panicking, and large thorny bushes sprout to life to keep Achill at bay as I take off at a run. He lights them on fire with a whoosh, quickly striding through the burning foliage.

I reach the edge of the lake, sinking into the soft grass at the edge of the banks.

He corners me like a cat stalking its prey, taking time to play before attacking. I shift on my feet, readying myself with my magic, swirls of colors dancing along my hands. "Give me the sword, Sorcha."

The water laps at the banks, and I step backward, my heels inches from the water. A few guards filter in from the castle with their swords drawn as they watch from the distance.

"You thought I was Aerona," I say, hoping to buy some time while I figure out how to get the hagstone out of the sword and into the water behind me.

His glamour falters, flickering in and out like candlelight. He shakes his head, "The sword."

"What happened, Achill?" I pull my water magic up, weaving a subtle glimpse of her likeness across my features, but I am already reaching the end of my magic as exhaustion pulls at my limbs.

Goddess above, I am a fool. I should have conserved more of my energy.

Achill's piercing blue eyes practically glow, never leaving the sword's handle. His smoke swirls around his shoulders.

"The sword, Sorcha," he rasps.

Fine, if it's the sword he wants, he can come and get it.

With a smirk, I reach up behind me and grab the hilt, lifting it out of the scabbard with the last air magic I can muster. Achill's eyes go wide when I withdraw the large blade. He steps forward, entranced, and fire lights a path straight to me.

"How?" He stutters, "H-how could your human hands hold the sword?"

My magic wanes, and the sword drops to my side.

Achill laughs, sauntering toward me. "Fancy magic tricks, Sorcha. Too bad you don't know how to pace yourself."

His smoke crawls forward, and I scramble backward, dragging the sword through the mud. The water laps at my feet, and I fumble with the hagstone, trying to free it from its locked position in the hilt. I am positive that the hagstone is what the sisters need to be free, but the rock won't budge.

Dallis' words at the river echo in my head. She said I'd need the sword to kill Achill, but I don't need the sword to rule. Realization dawns as I recall all the pieces I've put together: Dallis with a hagstone, the lake full of sisters, the sword in the tree. Dallis muttering about a powerful talisman. Dubessa was shocked when I looked at her through the same hagstone that now sits in the hilt. All this time, I thought it was because I saw her in her true form, but maybe now it is because the hagstone looked familiar.

The Goddess' voice fills my head, *"A sacred symbol can do just as much to unite the land as a confident ruler."*

It takes me a second to decide what to do as I face the lake, winding my air magic up. I chuck the sword as far as I can, pushing the sword along with a gust of wind.

"NO!" Achill screams and rushes me from behind.

It breaks through the glassy surface of the water, giant ripples pulsing outward to the banks. A blast of air follows in its path, cascading over us with a gust. A chorus of shrieks sounds from the depths of the lake. Tails and limbs splash in the water near the temple. The ground rumbles, and parts of the garden walls tumble inward.

Achill's fingers weave into my hair, and he yanks my head back. He drags me from the water by my hair through the mud, and I clutch at his wrist, trying to pull myself from his grasp.

"You stupid bitch," Achill growls.

My hair rips away from my scalp, and I scream as tears stream down my face. My feet struggle to keep up with his long strides. Pain screams through my human body.

I scream as he tears the hair from my head and throws me several feet ahead of him, and I land with a thump, my head smacking the ground. My vision blurs, and a ringing fills my ears. He wraps his hand around my throat, lifting me with ease, and my legs swing freely. My hands clamp to his forearm as I fight to get air.

"You just never learn, do you?" He asks, and then I see something glinting in his free hand.

OVER ACHILL'S SHOULDER, the lake ripples with power, and several water nymphs rise from its depths. I smile, knowing that part of my promise has been fulfilled. The sisters are free.

My vision clouds, going black around the edges as I gasp for air.

Then, a searing pain stabs me between my ribs.

A wolf growls, and then a blur of black fur tackles Achill from the side. The blade slides out from my chest with a sucking sound as the wolf tears into the king. I fall to the ground. Achill flies through the air, tossed about like a rag doll in the giant wolf's maw.

Bright red blood pours from my chest, and I clamp my hand to the wound. Pain radiates through my body as I struggle for air. My lungs work in double time, and I can taste blood in the back of my throat. I can barely distinguish the shapes in the foreground, but I hear guards running down the stairs to attack the wolf.

A sphere of bright orange launches the black wolf into the air. He smacks against the ground with a resounding thud, the stone pathway cracking upon impact. My heart lurches as a searing pain yanks from the center of my chest, and the heart-call slices away.

My arm reaches out in vain for Conall. My boots slide on the ground, trying to find purchase, but the ground is slick with my blood. Why do I have to die scared and alone and in pain?

This can't be how this ends. This wasn't how this was supposed to go.

Shiny black boots enter my fading vision. I blink back tears of frustration and pain but watch as a red, gnarled hand grabs the discarded weapon covered in my blood.

I curl my knees to my chest, my free hand still pressing against my wound when my fingers brush against one of the daggers tucked into the top of my boot.

Gnarled legs kneel before my face.

"Such a pity," Achill says, twisting the knife point into his finger.

I can barely keep my eyes open, but I wrap my fingers around the blade in my boot. Time moves so slowly as my grip on reality slips. I can't focus on his words because it takes too much effort.

Achill grabs a fistful of my hair, yanking my face so close to his that his breath caresses my cheek. He sneers, "Looks like you aren't leaving here after all."

I summon the last of the power I have, my bloody hand reaching up to yank him down. He smirks, and doesn't see the fire magic that coats the blade in my other hand. Achill's jaw drops as I thrust upward and spear the flaming knife into his heart. He meets my eyes, slumping forward on my burning blade.

"My love," he whispers. Then his eyes cloud over as my fire magic burns him from the inside out, and my air magic seals off his lungs.

I fall back, tears flooding my eyes, and groan as the light around me fades.

The scent of lilacs and moss fills the air, and I somehow have the strength to push Achill off my body. I touch my chest, expecting blood to seep between my fingers, but am met with vines and ice instead.

Is this the place after death?

"Whose blood have you used to call upon me, child?" The goddess asks, her voice echoing among the castle grounds.

I shake my head, knowing that I didn't call upon her on purpose.

The stone circles are nowhere to be found, but mist swirls around us. I look around, curious if anyone can see me talking to her or if this is all in my head. Everything outside of the circle of mist is immobile. The guards are mid-fight, swords raised. The water nymphs are anchored in waves that do not move.

Then I look down at my body, covered in Achill's blood. His body lies motionless at my feet. No longer aflame, the blade drips deep red blossoms in water at my feet. And then I realize that somehow I had called all four elements forth, if only by accident. The air magic choked off Achill's lungs, and the fire was present on the blade. I touch my wound, noting the intertwining vines wrapped tightly around my chest as if to stop the bleeding and my shoes that squelch with water.

The goddess's eyes miss nothing, noting the blood coating my skin. She leans forward and touches the vines. They fall away. Through the tear in my shirt, I watch as my skin knits itself back together, and the pain leaves my body.

I take in lungful after lungful of air and fall to my knees in relief.

Her ocean eyes glint in the bright sun as she looks me over.

"You're looking at me like you didn't think I could do it," I quip, surprising myself with my retort. I bite my lip to keep myself from saying too much again.

She smiles and reaches out to touch the tips of my hair soaked in Achill's blood. "You have such fire in your soul. This magic suits you well."

"No, child, I knew you could. I didn't know if he would." She juts her chin toward Achill.

My heart breaks, remembering his last words that sounded like they came from relief instead of fear.

She touches every gash on my body as she walks around me. "You have shone so bright today," she says.

Wait.

Is she... proud of me? I turn to face her, but she won't meet my eyes. Instead, she looks beyond the mist at the world frozen in motion beyond—at Conall's wolf lying prone on the ground. I rub the place in my chest where the heart-call should be.

The Goddess reaches out and takes my hand in hers. "The choices you have made have not been easy. You have lost so much and gained a great burden that you would need a lifetime to set things right. You have one favor you can ask of me as my thank you for returning the balance to this world."

My heart thrums in my chest. I can think of only one thing that I would ask of her. My teeth worry my lower lip as I take a few moments to think about the repercussions of what I am about to ask of her. I can't think of any, not from what I know about the immortality of the fae and the loneliness some of them experience when they go through their Rites. Some have to wait an eternity to find theirs; others would go mad should they be rejected.

"Let it be a choice," I say, raising my chin and meeting her gaze directly. Do not put contingencies on fated mates. Let the fae choose who they want to be with—not out of desperation, retribution, or insanity."

She hums. "And what if they do not choose each other? What if one chooses another? There will still be heartbreak, child."

"Heartbreak shouldn't come with a death sentence." I push back, hoping that I can convince her to free her people from a fate that will never let them win.

"You could choose anything you want," she gestures behind her toward Conall. "An immortal life with your fated mate, peace for centuries, healthy children... But you would ask for this?"

I nod, my heart filling with hope. "Humans don't have fated mates, and some of us choose to live with our partners for decades. We mate, but we don't have the pressure of the knife against our throats forcing us to decide."

I almost add that there are even those who choose to be with multiple partners or none, but I hold my tongue.

"A selfless ask," the Goddess walks around me again.

"It doesn't seem fair to wait an eternity to be happy, and it certainly isn't fair to be driven insane by the rejection of one." My eyes flicker to Achill's gnarled body at my feet.

The goddess squeezes my hand.

"You could choose anything you desire." She gestures once more towards Conall behind her. "This *choice* could wreak havoc on those that are already *mated*."

"But if they truly wish to be together, it should be by choice—a choice that has meaning," I emphasize the last word.

The Goddess nods her head slowly, her eyes swirling with shades of blue that mirror the tides of the ocean. "Done."

I blink, and the waves of the lake come crashing down on the shore.

Two birds of prey dart from the forest, calling to each other as they soar overhead. The white falcon with purple eyes swoops down again, its wings nearly brushing my head. I reach up, letting my fingertips graze its wings. Feothan's bird lets out a screech, and both birds fly back over the castle walls.

The water nymphs walk freely on land they haven't touched in centuries. One carries the sword behind her, the hagstone hanging around her neck. The nymph looks almost identical to Dallis; perhaps this was who my grandmother drew.

I am rooted to the ground, unable to move as I watch the water nymphs go to the guards. As soon as the nymphs touch the guards' throats, plumes of smoke leave their bodies. They stare at their hands and the gardens before them as if seeing everything anew. One after the other put down their swords.

The water nymph with the hagstone around her neck walks over to Conall. I watch in awe as she runs her hands over his wolf form. He shifts into his fae form, lying crumpled on the ground, covered in blood. His breathing is slow and careful, but soon, he stirs. The nymph slides quietly from his side and brushes past me, our eyes meeting for a moment before she disappears without a word.

I walk toward him, his naked form covered in blood. He watches me scan his body for injuries, and he says, "It's not mine. Well, some of it is."

"I know," I say, a slight smile on my lips. I look down at my clothes, covered in Achill's blood. "This isn't mine, either. Well, some of it is."

He exhales a smile. I reach down to help him up. His left leg is a little stiff, but he stands upright. Instantly, he pulls me to him, his arms wrapping around me. I almost collapse into his embrace with relief. He squeezes me firmly; contentedness is the only thought that crosses my mind.

I inhale his scent, despite the iron tang of drying blood, and mumble into his chest.

Conall loosens his grip. He cups my chin and tilts my head back. "What did you say?"

Fresh tears streak down his face, leaving tiny trails through the dirt and blood that splatter his cheeks.

I wipe away a drop, smudging the tears and dirt. "I said I was sorry I pushed you into the portal."

Conall laughs, and then his eyes darken dangerously. "We'll talk about that later."

"Or, we could pretend it never happened," I offer, raising an eyebrow.

He groans and squeezes me tightly against him. I nuzzle into his familiar embrace and inhale his scent of sweat and cedar. As relieved as I am for Achill's death, I can't help but wonder if Conall will stay with me after this. He may have given me the choice, but did I ever ask him?

"What was that?" Conall asks.

"Did I ask that out loud?" I ask, hopeful it wasn't so.

He nods.

"I asked if you would still choose me?" I wave my hand at the lingering destruction behind us. "Despite everything we've gone through and my human lifespan."

"Yes," he says without hesitation. His green eyes bore into mine. "Where you go, I go. Until the Forever Night. And for eternity after that. You're my mate."

My voice cracks, and tears line the edge of my vision as I ask, "Are you sure?"

He leans down and touches his forehead to mine. "Yes, definitely."

Also by Ophelia Wells Langley

Published Works

The Stone Circle Series:

Of Smoke and Shadows

The Borderlands Princess

The Stone Circle Queen

Upcoming Releases

When The Night Swallowed The Moon, early 2025

For more information on works-in-progress, you can follow her socials and keep up with giveaways, signings, and more below:

Content & Trigger Warnings

In an effort to be transparent, this is an adult fantasy romance, intended for audiences eighteen years and older. Please read the trigger warnings carefully.

This book contains scenes that may depict, mention, or discuss:anxiety, assault, blood, bones, death, explicit sexual scenes, fire, grief and loss, murder, physical abuse, torture, violence, war.

This book also contains scenes that embrace body neutrality and acceptance, enthusiastic consent, nonbinary representation (a character with they/them pronouns), found family, healthy family systems, and older protagonists.

Acknowledgments

This series has been through hell and back and would not have been completed without the help of these amazing people: my husband and children (for your constant patience and support), my mom and step-dad (for all of your support and spending time with the kiddos so I could write), and my brother.

To Becks, Alora, and Lacey: Without your support, your friendship, and the countless hours you've listened to me complain, stress, worry, gush, workshop, and freak out over the words in this book, I know I would not have made it. Thank you for beta reading, editing, late-night writing sessions, silly little voice memos, and just being the best friends a girl could ask for.

To Jo, the best developmental editor in the entire world. Seriously. I don't know how you put up with me, but I love working with you and can't wait to collaborate on more stories in the future.

Lastly, to my beta and ARC readers: you all are phenomenal. I am so lucky to have such a fantastic community of readers that I can't thank you enough. You are why I write, and I am so honored that you choose to read my stories.

So much love, so much gratitude,

xo
gwe

About Ophelia Wells Langley

Ophelia Wells Langley is the pen name of a mother to two boys. A mild obsession with Celtic mythology, a strong taste for fantasy, and a penchant for escapism were the basis for her formative years as a writer.

Her goal is simple: create character-driven stories that are inclusive and diverse. She creates lush fantasy worlds that satiate our need for escape from reality.

When she's not writing, plotting, or scheming about her characters, you can find her embracing her theatrical side for her toddlers as a tyrannosaurus rex.